The entertainment screen opposite the bed flickered to life. Like most of the screens in the ship, it could be routed to any readout the computer might display. In this case, Peri routed the external video turret's feed to the screen in Sokolov's room.

Blackness, speckled with stars. Sokolov squinted, trying to make out something, then he caught a glimpse of darkness occulting a star against the night.

"Give me maximum magnification in the upper left quadrant," he told the computer.

The screen blurred and jumped. Now they could see it clearly, although it was still small and faint. It was too far away to tell much about it, but Sokolov and Geille could see two things even from their great distance.

It was a ship, not an asteroid, and it wasn't remotely human in origin.

STAR*DRIVE.

THE HARBINGER TRILOGY
DIANE DUANE

VOLUME ONE:
STARRISE AT CORRIVALE

VOLUME TWO:
STORM AT ELDALA

VOLUME THREE:
NIGHTFALL AT ALGEMRON
(April 2000)

STARFALL
EDITED BY MARTIN H. GREENBERG

ZERO POINT
RICHARD BAKER

STAR*DRIVE

ZERO POINT

Richard Baker

Thanks, Mom and Dad, for teaching me to love books

ZERO POINT
©1999 TSR, Inc.
All Rights Reserved.

Distributed to the toy and hobby trade by regional distributors.

Distributed worldwide by Wizards of the Coast, Inc. and regional distributors.

Cover art by Monte Moore

STAR*DRIVE and the TSR logo are registered trademarks owned by TSR, Inc.
All TSR characters, character names, and the distinctive likenesses thereof are trademarks owned by TSR, Inc.

TSR, Inc. is a subsidiary of Wizards of the Coast, Inc.

First Printing: June 1999
Printed in the United States of America.
Library of Congress Catalog Card Number: 98-88142

9 8 7 6 5 4 3 2 1

T21367-620

ISBN: 0-7869-1367-3

U.S., CANADA, ASIA,
PACIFIC, & LATIN AMERICA
Wizards of the Coast, Inc.
P.O. Box 707
Renton, WA 98057-0707
+1-800-324-6496

EUROPEAN HEADQUARTERS
Wizards of the Coast, Belgium
P.B. 2031
2600 Berchem
Belgium
Tel. +32.70.23.32.77

Visit our web-site at **www.tsr.com**

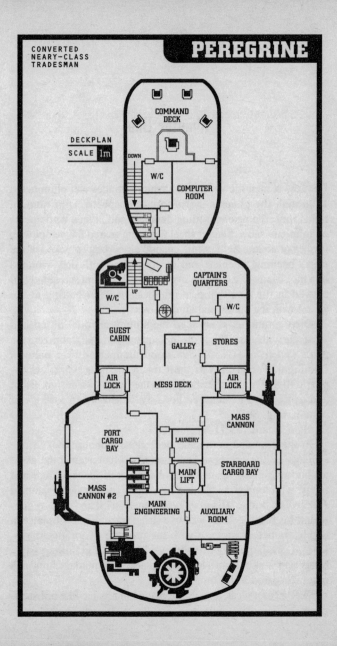

Chapter One

SHRIEKING IN metallic protest, the battered tradesman plummeted through the planet's storm-torn atmosphere. Dim running lights flickered against roiling darkness and jagged battlements of ammonia snow. Scarlet sheet lightning seared the vessel with flashes of actinic light, while chaotic air currents plucked at the ship's beetling antennae and sensor dishes until they vibrated like the strings of a delicate instrument. The wind screamed and clawed at the small ship, a mindless monster batting at the vessel with icy talons and aimless rage.

Dirty ammonia slush iced the stubby airfoils, pitted and streaked with rust. High on the square vertical stabilizer, the name *Peregrine SGL3007898* stood illuminated by a halogen floodlight. *Peregrine* was built for deep-space work; atmospheric flight was an afterthought in the freighter's design. Blunt and awkward, she smashed her way downward in a series of bone-jarring jolts.

"Peri, guard 133.71 megahertz."

In the cramped command deck, Pete Sokolov locked one arm against the overhead and planted his feet against the deck, anchoring himself against the shuddering of the ship. Tall and rangy, with long arms and big hands, his angular body spanned *Peregrine*'s bridge. His gray eyes were as dark and cold as gunmetal; his black goatee, a coarse stripe scarcely a centimeter in depth, framed his mouth with the promise of imminent violence. Dark fatigue trousers bloused into scuffed military-style boots and a skin-tight sleeveless black shirt marked him as a man who cared little for appearances.

"Look for a weak signal," he rasped in a voice like old sandpaper.

Waiting for a reply, a cigarette burning in his mouth, Sokolov relaxed his rigid stance. *Peregrine*'s bridge might have been the only place where he was at ease, but his darting eyes and keen expression betrayed his training as a military pilot. Without moving his head, his attention flickered from the engineering readout to the sensor display and on to the flight station, ignoring the constant jarring of the ship's descent.

"Got the nav beacon yet?"

From the clutter of consoles and electronic modules mounted on the aft bulkhead of the command deck, a female voice answered, warm and alive. "I've got Icewalk, Pete. It's real faint—the EM noise of the storm is playing merry hell with radio reception."

"That's intentional. Icewalk usually doesn't want to be found."

Sokolov adjusted *Peregrine*'s flight path, compensating for the vicious crosswind the ship encountered as she dropped through churning cloudbanks. Dioscuri was a nightmare of a planet, cursed with a creeping rotation that made each of its days nearly two standard years in length. The face exposed to the blinding light of Lucullus's twin suns became broiling hot, while the night hemisphere cooled to intolerably cold temperatures. Since Dioscuri's toxic atmosphere was almost as thick as Earth's, convection carried the super-heated air of the dayside high over the lightless, frozen night side. Bitterly cold, low-level air raced in from the dark hemisphere to replace the hot air rising and moving away, creating a permanent tornado lying on its side across a thousand-kilometer band between the two hemispheres. No one would ever try to settle Dioscuri. It was ludicrous to even consider it.

Sokolov moved over to the comm station, keyed in a set of commands, and said, "Kick the ID transponder over to configuration Sierra-Two. Kill the aft dorsal floodlight and registration display. Illuminate the forward chin light."

"IFF configuration Sierra-Two acknowledged," the computer replied. "Aft dorsal floodlight dark. Forward chin light illuminating." The identification letters, rendered in smart paint controlled from the ship's lighting programs, faded into anonymity.

The white circle of light displaying the ship's name on the vertical stabilizer died, leaving the finlike structure in darkness. Under the vessel's blunt nose, a similar light flickered into life, painting the name *Sabrecat RSV8183587*. In the ship's electronic bay, the identification transponder clicked over to a new setting. "I'll have to report a violation to the appropriate authorities, Pete. It's highly illegal for me to chirp another ship's ID codes."

Sokolov smiled sourly. He'd always had more patience for computers than he did for people. He could have disabled Peri's legal senses long ago, but he'd left the warnings in place. It was one of the rare entertainments he allowed himself, a joke he enjoyed but never shared.

"Don't worry about it, Peri. Icewalk is a highly illegal place. Are we through the high-level turbulence yet?"

"We're dropping past it now." Even as the computer replied, the rough pummeling of wind and hail against the outer hull faded to a dull, distant roar. "I'd estimate eight minutes of clear air before we hit the sunward-moving wind streams near the ground."

"Good girl," Sokolov replied with a trace of affection.

Unlocking his long limbs from their hold on the deck and the overhead, he reached for a black coat and holster draped over one seat. First he strapped the low-slung shoulder holster to his left side, then he drew the long-barreled, heavy sabot pistol and checked its charge and ammo clip. The Wesshaur was a monster, firing a 15mm scramjet slug that housed a 5mm neutronite penetrator. Sokolov would have preferred to carry something even bigger, but the sabot pistol was about the most powerful weapon he could reasonably conceal. He'd tested dozens of handguns before settling on the Wesshaur as his weapon of choice. A craftsman was only as good as his tools, after all.

Sokolov returned the Wesshaur to its place and activated the holster's scrambler field. It didn't make the weapon invisible, of course, but routine weapon checks would show nothing on Sokolov's person. He strapped a second weapon, a small charge pistol, into a normal holster strapped around his left ankle, and a slim carbonate blade into a sheath he wore in the small of his back.

"You know, you haven't registered any of your weapons with recognized law-enforcement agencies," Peri observed, watching him through the command deck video pickups.

"I didn't think Penates *had* any recognized law-enforcement agencies."

"Technically, you should register with the Port Royal Bureau of Weap—"

"Come on. You know I hate paperwork, Peri."

Sokolov straightened and shrugged the heavy black coat over his shoulders. Its carbonate-fiber weave would stop a 9mm charge slug at point-blank range, but it looked like nothing more than a common overcoat. Of course, anyone who took a close look at the CF coat would know what it was, but body armor was not particularly noteworthy in a place like Icewalk.

Once he finished arming himself, Sokolov turned his attention inward. *Nancy,* he subvocalized. *Run a level-one diagnostic on all installed hardware. Stack Speed-Five, Deadeye, and Blade-Three in active memory. Load database Icewalk. I might need to find my way around in a hurry.*

Working on it, Pyotr, the nanocomputer in the base of his skull replied. Its interface recognized Sokolov's native Narislavic and replied in the same language. He could have switched the device to Standard a long time ago, but he found that giving commands and receiving information in a second language helped him to keep the nanocomputer's operation separate from his own thoughts. He'd carried the machine in his head for over five years now, and he'd finally become accustomed to directing commands at the tiny device simply by thinking at it. On the other hand, he never enjoyed the lack of control he felt when he allowed Nancy to co-opt his motor reflexes in order to improve his reactions and fighting skills. Rationally, he knew he was better, faster, stronger with the nanocomputer driving his muscles, but activating an enhance program invited a kind of mechanical possession. *All systems green,* Nancy reported. *We're ready.*

Okay . . . stay loose, he replied.

"Pete? We're being interrogated," Peri said. "Icewalk wants to know who we are."

"Cross your fingers, Peri. *Sabrecat* might not be welcome here."

"How am I supposed to cross my fingers, Pete?" the ship's computer demanded impishly.

"Don't be stupid. It's an expression," he said absently, watching the comm display. Come on, he thought privately. Accept the code. It cost me a small fortune, so you've got to like it, right? The mission could be scrubbed in a hurry if Icewalk didn't want to play. "How long till we're back in the turbulence?"

"Three minutes. Wait . . . I've got an incoming transmission."

"I'll take it at the comm station," Sokolov said at once.

He vaulted over the rail dividing the central command platform from the operator stations and settled into the comm operator's seat. Like everything else on the bridge, it was already adjusted to his preferences, one of the advantages of operating a ship solo. Tapping his fingers together anxiously, he keyed the unit, leaning back to listen.

"*Sabrecat,* this is Icewalk approach control," the bridge speakers crackled. "Hold your position while we run a check on you. Over." Static hissed in conjunction with the flickering lightning outside the ship's hull.

"What's the holdup, Icewalk? I'm getting beat to hell up here. Over," Sokolov replied.

He wasn't in that much of a hurry, but he had to play the part. He wanted Icewalk to think they were dealing with a solitary smuggler looking for a place to lie low. If they guessed what he was really after, they'd never let him get within a hundred kilometers. Or, worse yet, they'd let him in and then make sure he didn't leave.

"We don't know you, *Sabrecat,* and we don't like strangers. Stand by. Out." Icewalk fell silent as they ran the *Sabrecat* through whatever security files they kept on the station.

"Come on, come on," Sokolov muttered, watching the comm panel. After a short time, Icewalk came back on line.

"*Sabrecat,* who's onboard? Over."

"This is Marcus Barrett. Who did you expect?"

"Our sources report that Barrett is currently incarcerated in Port Royal, *Sabrecat*. Who are you, and what are you doing with Barrett's ship?"

Sokolov winced. Icewalk was more up to date than he'd thought. Okay, I'm talking to mercenaries, he thought. These are people who sell their loyalty. They appreciate duplicity, and they won't be especially attached to a small-time smuggler who's never worked with their boss. He scowled and opened the channel again.

"Guess you got me, Icewalk. My name is Andreven. I bought Barrett's ship and routes from the Syndicate when Barrett was caught."

"We don't like the Syndicate either, Andreven. They're the competition. Get lost."

"Icewalk, I didn't part with the Syndicate on the best of terms. They weren't satisfied with the payment plan I came up with for the *Sabrecat*, so I'm looking for some new business partners. Over."

Sokolov leaned over the console, waiting. Outside, the wind rocked the ship. Something was clattering against the outer hull at regular intervals.

The station below remained silent for a long time. That was a bad sign. The watch captain was talking to his superiors about the situation. Sokolov decided to distract himself from the wait.

"Peri, add a blind ownership to the log. Name of Egor Andreven, native to Babel, Alaundril, Citizen Number B55028348. That's the correct number of digits, right?"

The computer seemed to sigh in disappointment. "Yes, Pete. Consider it done."

"What's loose on the hull?"

"Access Panel Number 13-A—hydraulic lines servicing the mass cannon turret. You know, I'm really in need of some basic maintenance, Pete."

"What happens when we go through the next windstorm?"

"The panel cover blows off."

"Okay, screw it."

"Pete! You wouldn't like it if you were shedding pieces of your skin in a class three atmosphere!" Peri said indignantly. "You owe me an overhaul, you know."

"I know, I know," Sokolov replied, rolling his eyes. "Listen, as soon as—"

"*Sabrecat,* this is Icewalk. You're either stupid or crazy to rip off the Syndicate. Either way, that makes you a lousy smuggler, but we can always use a pilot and a ship, so you're cleared to land. Over."

"Acknowledged," Sokolov replied. Smiling to himself, he decided to play Andreven as a little stupid. "Say, you guys won't regret this, over."

"There's a catch, over."

"A catch? What's the catch?"

"If you land, you don't leave until we finish checking you out. Understand?"

"Sure, okay. No problem. Over."

"Just like I said, stupid." The unseen outlaw below laughed humorlessly, a menacing sound over the faint radio link. "Come on down, *Sabrecat.* Icewalk out."

"We've got a landing beacon and approach signal, Pete," Peri reported. "Icewalk is eighty-seven kilometers distant, bearing 033 relative."

Sokolov stubbed out his cigarette in one of the crowded ashtrays that littered the bridge. He stood, stretched, and then took the seat behind the primary flight controls, activating the pilot's console.

"Okay, Peri. Let's get down there."

*   *   *   *   *

The low-level chop was even worse than the first band of turbulence. The cold air near the planet's surface was much denser than the high-altitude clouds, and Dioscuri's broken terrain created vicious local updrafts and eddies. Sokolov strapped himself into his seat. The few people who thought they knew him would have been surprised to learn that Pete Sokolov was basically a cautious man. He had to live with unavoidable risks in his chosen vocation, so he saw no sense in courting routine dangers. Dashing out his brains against the command deck overhead was one of them.

Visibility dropped drastically as *Peregrine* leveled off a few hundred meters above the wind-scoured ground. The ground clutter confused even the best radar, and *Peregrine*'s external sensors couldn't penetrate more than a few hundred meters into the murk. Without the approach vector and glide slope provided by Icewalk's landing beacon, Sokolov would never have attempted the landing. Even with these electronic aids, it was a hair-raising descent that left him bruised and sore from the rattling he received.

Five hundred meters out, creeping along at a few meters per second, Sokolov caught his first glimpse of Icewalk. It appeared as a glowing dome of light in the cold, dark downpour of the storm. Black and forbidding, the station was illuminated by harsh white floodlights that rapidly diffused in the ammonia sleet. Mounted on three massive caterpillar treads, the station crawled through the perpetual storm, rocking softly in the strongest gusts of wind. By equipping his base with a semblance of mobility, Devriele Shanassin had created the perfect hideout. He could roam the depths of Dioscuri's endless storm forever, never staying in the same place and eluding any effort to pinpoint his fortress. Sokolov had paid a small fortune to obtain the beacon frequency of the base.

"They've got some major artillery pointed at me, Pete," Peri said quietly. The vid screen at Sokolov's left flickered, zooming in as the ship directed an external camera at a bulbous weapon emplacement mounted on a sparlike boom. The distinctive jacketed snouts of a quad-mount plasma cannon tracked slowly, pointing right at the camera. "I'm getting some EM noise directly on that bearing. Those guns are charged."

"Don't worry, Peri. They're talking, not shooting," Sokolov reassured the computer. At least for now, he added to himself.

He looked past the weapon boom, studying the station and allowing Nancy to match the exterior appearance to the schematics she held in her databases. The whole thing was several hundred meters long, the size of a container ship or small carrier. It was shaped like a broad arrowhead, with one massive caterpillar tread under its point and two under the trailing corners. The rear edge and upper surface were studded with a dozen flimsy landing platforms; Sokolov counted five ships docked with Icewalk. *Nancy, run the ship IDs. Tell me who's home,* he ordered the nanocomputer.

The ships are the Bad Break, Jerrid, Wolfling, Blackguard, *and* Mon Ami. *The* Blackguard *is Shanassin's ship; the* Jerrid *matches the profile of a* Daring-*class military scout wanted for piracy in Tendril; and the* Bad Break *is Maartens's boat. I have no records on the other two.*

"They don't matter," Sokolov answered aloud. "We know that Geille Monashi hired Maartens. We're after the *Bad Break.*" He filed away the information and steadied on the mobile station's approach indicators.

Icewalk turned slowly into the wind, sheltering the landing platforms at its after end from the screaming gale. Near the center top, halogen lamps flicked on, painting one pad in a circle of yellow light. "*Sabrecat,* you're cleared for spot five. Over."

"Got it, Icewalk. *Sabrecat* out," Sokolov replied.

The ship bucked as he drifted into Icewalk's slipstream, but as the hulking station shielded him from the wind, the air became calm. Sokolov eased into the final approach, concentrating on the job at hand. Carefully he lowered *Peregrine* toward the metal deck, flaring to use the ship's airfoils in conjunction with its gravity induction engines. He bounced once, softly, before he killed the engines and settled into place. Powering down the ship, he stood and leaned over the pilot console to peer out of the narrow plexsteel viewports at the front of the command deck.

In the harsh glare of the floodlights, he could make out a rain-slick metal landing pad and the bulk of the station towering over him. Out of the darkness above, ammonia snow and hail fell constantly, leaving a dirty residue on every exposed surface. Why isn't it accumulating? he wondered. *The exterior is heated to prevent icing,* Nancy stated in response to his unvoiced question.

From the dark structure in front of him, a transit corridor slowly extended, snaking across the wet landing platform. With a metallic boom, the corridor seals mated to *Peregrine*'s air lock.

"I've got normal pressure and O2 content in the airlock," Peri said. "You can disembark, Pete, but be careful, okay?"

"I will."

Sokolov paused to tap in a control lockout on *Peregrine*'s bridge and then made his way down to the ship's air lock. He wasn't giving Peri any blank promises; he intended to bc damned careful. The creation of a captain named Devriele Shanassin, a fraal pirate who had built quite a reputation during his days of active plunder, Icewalk was notorious in a planetary system full of corsairs, marauders, smugglers, and criminals. Six years ago, Shanassin and his *Blackguard* had simply disappeared from Lucullus. The captains and smugglers of Penates assumed that Shanassin had met his end in some ill-fated venture elsewhere in the Verge. Instead, the pirate quietly resurfaced several years later as the master of Icewalk. To Icewalk came the worst raiders, mercenaries, and outlaws of Lucullus, a star system noted for such criminals. Shanassin now portrayed himself as a corsair lord, a force of his own in the chaotic maelstrom of trade and piracy in the Verge.

Taking a deep breath, Sokolov cycled the air lock. The transit corridor was cold and reeked of ammonia. Ducking to avoid the power conduits hanging from the low ceiling, he hurried through to the station air lock. Over the lock, a small turretlike structure housing a vid lens and a laser projector swiveled to follow him. The heavy airtight door hissed open as he approached, then slid shut behind him. Welcome to Icewalk, Sokolov thought grimly. Enjoy your stay.

The station's interior was as battered and utilitarian as its outer surface. He stood in an unfinished corridor floored with metal grating and lined with pipes, vents, conduits, and cables of all kinds. A small alcove to his left contained controls for the transit corridor, the air lock, and its vidcam and laser turret. Before him stood two ursine humans in heavy assault gear. They carried charged pulse batons in their hands, with autoflechette guns hanging at their sides.

From the control alcove, a small but powerfully built sesheyan stalked into view, balancing lightly on the balls of his feet in the typical gait of his kind. Gaunt and gray, the alien might have stepped out of some old human myth. A double row of dark rubylike eyes gleamed in the smooth, rounded wedge of his head; great leathery wings rustled softly as the alien paused, studying Sokolov in silence. Most of the sesheyans Sokolov had met before were indentured to the monolithic consortium known as VoidCorp. Free sesheyans were in breach of contract, rogues and outlaws hunted ruthlessly by the Company. Sokolov returned the creature's gaze as evenly as he could. He had no idea if that was a gesture of strength, respect, deference, or challenge to the sesheyan, but at the moment, he figured that Andreven couldn't be expected to know that either. *Check the personnel database, Nancy. Who am I dealing with here?*

Yeiwei Three-knives, Nancy informed him, instantly retrieving the outlaw's profile and criminal record. *Shanassin's second-in-command and security chief.* The sesheyan wore a light tool harness over a strange wrap-like garment cut to leave his double-folded wings free. In his small forelimbs, he carried a handheld imaging scanner.

"When the Barterer calls at the lodge of the Warrior," the alien stated in the curious staves favored by many sesheyans, "he bears no weapons: but the wise Warrior invites the Barterer to hang his cloak by the door: lest the Barterer later produce a knife in the darkness." Gesturing with the scanner, he shifted to a more human speech pattern. "Raise your arms, Andreven. No guns are permitted on the station."

Sokolov complied. "You guys carry guns," he observed placidly.

The Icewalkers didn't even consider that worthy of reply. They ran the scanner up and down his body. They found the carbonate knife in its holster behind his back, but they let him keep it. They also found the charge pistol strapped to his ankle, and with a sheepish grin, Sokolov handed it to the sesheyan butt-first.

"Couldn't hurt to try, right?" he cracked.

"The Barterer sets his spears by the door: that he might

reclaim them when he departs the Warrior's lodge," the sesheyan told him, dropping the pistol into a pocket of his vest. He returned the scanner to another pocket and nodded at the guards. "He is okay."

Sokolov repressed a smile. They'd missed the Wesshaur in its stealth holster. He could have accomplished the mission without the big gun, but he always felt better armed.

"Great. Say, I'm beat. Where can I find a hot meal and a bunk?"

"Deck Three," Yeiwei said. "What the Barterer requires: in the Warrior's lodge, he shall find: but his promises alone shall not suffice: for he is the Barterer, not the Guest. Nothing here is free, Andreven."

"I understand." Sokolov angled his shoulders and pushed between the two guards, heading down the passageway. He'd only taken three or four steps down the passageway when the sesheyan hissed his name again.

"Not so fast, Andreven. As the Warrior permits the Barterer inside his lodge: so must the Barterer expect the Warrior to visit his wagon: for the Barterer's words are empty and demand proof." Yeiwei seemed to smile. "Open your ship. We want to check your logs, your manifests. Routine security, yes?"

Sokolov wheeled, eyes dark with anger. "It's my ship. You don't go onboard without me."

"It is routine," the sesheyan repeated. "Go up to your meal, your bed. If the Barterer's tales are true: then will the Warrior be well pleased: and gladly invite him to remain in the lodge: until the talk of trade is done. We will not be long. Have no fear for your vessel."

"The ship's empty. No cargo. There's nothing to see."

"Then you will not mind if we look for ourselves." Yeiwei straightened and rearranged his batlike wings, his eight eyes steady on Sokolov as he waited for a response.

They're serious about running the background check, Sokolov realized. He frowned, thinking hard. As far as he knew, no one on the station had seen him before, so he was probably safe using Andreven's identity, but his deception wouldn't stand up to intense scrutiny for long, and it was clear from his earlier conversation that Shanassin had contacts in the right places. The longer Sokolov stayed on Icewalk, the more likely it was that he'd be caught in a lie.

I'd better go along with it, he decided, *but not too gracefully. If I agree to whatever they want, they'll be suspicious.*

"I'll be back to check on you," he said angrily, "and I'll tell you one more thing—the ship's got a tampering alarm. I'll know if you disturb anything you don't need to see."

The sesheyan didn't reply. He turned his back on Sokolov and stepped through the air lock into the corridor leading to *Peregrine.* Sokolov glared after him until one of the guards tapped his coat lightly with a pulse baton.

"Take a walk, spacer. We'll let you know if there're any problems."

"Likewise," Sokolov replied. With one more glance over his shoulder, he followed a garish neon sign toward the station's entertainment district. *Nancy, cue Whisper One.*

Whisper One comm protocol enabled, the nanocomputer replied.

Transmit: Peri, set internal security configuration charlie, he subvocalized. Sokolov's Whisper program instructed the nanocomputer to convert Sokolov's commands into an encrypted data packet. In the biceps of Sokolov's right arm, a cybernetic limb indistinguishable from his original, a small datalink activated, transmitting a signal to the ship's computer. There was a chance that Icewalk might be watching him for a covert radio transmission, but Sokolov wanted to know the instant that Yeiwei triggered any of his ship's safeguards. The program he activated would warn him by silent alarm if Icewalk's security chief broke into any secure files.

Reply from Peregrine, Nancy reported. *Internal security configuration charlie set.*

"Good girl," he said quietly, striding away from the air lock.

* * * * *

Neon signs and smart-paint advertisements led Sokolov through the dim, cluttered passageways toward the so-called hospitality decks, where Shanassin's crew sold food, drink, and entertainment to their guests. A deck above Sokolov, Icewalk's itinerant population of spacers and criminals crowded a handful of seedy bars, gambling pits, drug dens, and high-priced flop-houses, spending small fortunes in exchange for the privilege of a refuge beyond the reach of any law. Sokolov was no prude, since his line of work necessitated spending a great deal of time in red-light districts and other low-class places, but Icewalk's entertainments were legendary in Lucullus.

Sokolov followed the main passageway from the landing platforms to Icewalk's hospitality decks until he reached the last lift shaft along his route. He punched the call button and casu-ally glanced around, studying his surroundings. No one was near. Disarmed and blockaded from his ship by two guards, Andreven was no longer considered a threat by Icewalk's secu-rity. *Which way, Nancy?* he asked.

Take this lift down two decks, then head aft again. The com-puter projected a small blueprint of the station, showing Soko-lov's location as a blinking white dot in a three-dimensional maze of corridors, power lifts, and engineering compartments. The lift car was empty; Sokolov stepped inside and thumbed the button for Deck 6.

"Crew access code?" the car inquired.

Ignoring the security program, he opened the control panel and examined it briefly, pulling a small comptech's probe from a hidden pocket in his coat. *Show me the wiring diagram, Nancy,* he thought. The nanocomputer complied, projecting a detailed illustration of the lift controls. Sokolov had paid a great deal of his client's money in order to obtain the schematics for the station from one of the illegal technicians who'd helped Shanassin to build it. He was gratified to learn that the informa-tion he'd bought was proving accurate.

"The deck you have selected is designated crew access only," the lift car's moronic computer informed him. "Enter your crew access code or select another destination."

Inside the control panel, the security indicator blinked yellow. It allowed a fifteen-second delay before it triggered an alert in the station's security center. Probably a little too generous,

Sokolov reflected. Working quickly, he isolated and rerouted several key circuits in the panel. Maybe they got tired of drunks setting off security alerts when they fumbled their way back to their ships. The probe snapped and sparked softly. Sokolov reached into another pocket, retrieved a small, crudely manufactured circuit chip, and then pressed it into place over the security circuit. He'd practiced this part of the mission dozens of times before approaching Dioscuri.

With four seconds to spare, the security indicator blinked out. "Code acknowledged," the lift car replied. With a small shudder, it dropped down to the station's engineering decks. The car rasped to a stop. Sokolov moved his right hand inside his coat and set it on the grip of the Wesshaur. From this point forward, Icewalk's denizens might shoot first and ask questions later. The door hissed open, revealing a dark service passageway. Sokolov glanced fore and aft, then turned right and trotted down the hall, examining each hatch he came across.

This one, Nancy told him.

With one last look up and down the hallway, Sokolov repeated the security bypass that he'd used to hotwire the lift car and slipped inside the room. Low red lights glowed like embers inside the compartment. Sprawling banks of communications modules, computer data storage arrays, climate control systems, and heavy-duty power supply systems lined the bulkheads. On Nancy's blueprint, this was labeled "CCC Support Equipment Room Number 4," an unmanned electronics room where Icewalk's primary computers, communications, and security systems interlocked at the machine level. One deck above Sokolov, Icewalk's control room ran dozens of computers and radios from the machinery installed in the support compartment. Sokolov allowed himself a satisfied smile.

"Perfect," he said.

He found the station computer's data storage unit and wheeled a battered metal stool over to the unit's dusty keyboard. It wasn't an operator station—there were several of those in the command compartment over his head—but comptechs occasionally needed to retrieve old documents or install new backup procedures at this console. Rolling up his right sleeve, Sokolov triggered a hidden catch and opened a small panel in his arm. With his left hand, he spooled out an interface jack and several feet of comm wire, plugging in to the archive console. *Wire interface protocol, Nancy. Run Ghost Hunter Five.*

Acknowledged. The nanocomputer's lag in responding was actually noticeable, a good indication of the size of the program it was running. Sokolov swiveled the stool around to watch the door while the tiny computer in his head worked stealthily to infiltrate Icewalk's main computer. He checked his watch. Twelve minutes had elapsed since he'd left the guards by the air lock. "Pick it up; pick it up," he muttered to himself. He was beginning to wonder whether he should have made his move immediately or instead waited in order to throw off Yeiwei's suspicions. Doesn't matter now, he decided. I'm committed.

Ghost Hunter completed, Nancy told him. *Full access to Erebus Main.*

"Great," Sokolov replied.

Erebus was the station's main computer. He could reach anywhere in the station now. He toyed with the idea of manufacturing a distraction to get Yeiwei and his thugs away from *Peregrine*, but for the moment he decided to let them look around. The mission came first. He kicked over to the station's security subroutines and searched for a visitor list. He found *Andreven, Egor,* listed as the first file. A monitoring routine based on video surveillance currently listed him as "location unknown." Quickly he kicked the report over to "Deck Three Crash Site." The subroutine now reported to Erebus that its cameras showed Egor Andreven in one of the lounges on the entertainment deck. As long as no one went to look in person, he wouldn't be missed.

"Next step," he said quietly. "Let's find Monashi."

He scrolled down the visitor list, looking for the name. Shanassin's security was unusually thorough. The fraal outlaw provided his bodyguards with top-notch technology. Consequently, every one of the station's crewmen and visitors, over five hundred people in all, were constantly watched, except for Shanassin himself. *Monashi, Geille. Location: Lucky Strike, Deck Three.* The casino . . . that was no good. No way he'd get her out of a crowded place like that.

"So how long has she been there?" he wondered.

Scanning the security records, he determined that Monashi had left her quarters three hours ago after dining alone. By Icewalk time, it was approaching midnight. *Not that anyone here has a curfew*, he reminded himself, but it wasn't unreasonable to guess that Monashi might be close to calling it a night. With a flick of his mental fingertips across the nanocomputer's datalink, he pulled up Icewalk's list of accommodations. *Monashi, Geille. Quarters: Stateroom 533, Deck Two. Occupancy: Single.*

"Okay, we've got a plan," he said aloud.

He buried a command in the system that would show Monashi in her stateroom for the rest of the night, once she left the casino. *Should I try to knock down the weapons grid?* he wondered. It would certainly make his exit route safer if none of Icewalk's weapon systems were working when he decided to leave, but he could tell at a glance that the station's core functions were wrapped in some very tight security. Trying to tamper with Icewalk's guns might set off all kinds of alarms, so Sokolov decided he'd leave it be. If he did his job right, he'd be gone before they knew it.

He was just about to unjack and leave when a high-level security request cut across the screen. Erebus was running a background check of Pyotr Sokolov at the request of security chief Yeiwei.

"Damn!"

Sokolov sat back down and quickly froze the command, thinking fast. Yeiwei had cracked all three levels of blind ownership on the *Peregrine* and was looking for information on him. Erebus intended to interrogate its contacts on Penates and initiate a background search. *If I lose the request, he'll just repeat it*, he thought. *I could wait here for the response and change it when it comes through, but I don't know how long that will take.*

He settled for cueing a fake reply. He fabricated a hasty criminal record—nothing serious, mostly misdemeanors and a few leads to more serious crimes—and built a blind to catch the response from Penates and replace it with his imaginary career. If Yeiwei is really suspicious, he'll start calling around and talking to people in real-time. I'd better not count on holding onto my cover for too much longer.

"Bolzhe moi," he muttered, then built a second blind in case someone else sent out a request for his records.

That done, he yanked the wire jack from the computer, retracted the lead into his artificial arm, and stood up. *Whisper One, Nancy.*

"Peri? Are you all right?"

The ship replied at once through the nanocomputer's datalink. "I'm fine, Sokolov. I've still got integrity on all command lockouts, but the sesheyan cracked the ownership codes. He knows who you are. He just transmitted a request for Icewalk to run your record." The computer paused, then added, "I think you'd better get back onboard. You're in danger."

"Don't worry about me, Peri," he said. "I've got their security system tied in knots." *What did Yeiwei find?* he wondered. *It couldn't have been much, or he would have called out the station's security detail to find me. Is it just routine, or does he really think I'm a threat to Icewalk?* "Don't panic. Hold on to the main directories, and if he shuts down your mechanical systems, I can start them up again. Sit tight."

"I don't have much of a choice," the ship said bitterly. "I hope you know what you're doing, Pete."

"Yeah, me, too." *Nancy, terminate Whisper comm protocol.*

Drawing the sabot pistol from its holster and hiding it in his heavy coat, Sokolov carefully slipped out of the electronics support room and loped back toward the lift. He had a date with Geille Monashi.

Chapter Two

TWO DECKS BELOW Sokolov and almost two hundred meters further forward, Devriele Shanassin meditated, preparing to fight for his life. The fraal drifted in a zero-g room at Icewalk's prow, a spacious gymnasium lined with firm white padding except for one wall of dark plexglass that looked out over Dioscuri's eternal night. A trickle of static electricity kept the wide window free of the endless fall of ammonia slush.

Unusually tall and well-muscled for a fraal, Shanassin was stripped to the waist, revealing a lean torso that rippled with muscle. His skin, gray and smooth, gleamed with perspiration. Dark, soulless eyes mirrored the featureless night beyond the window. Most humans felt that the inscrutable features and studied mannerisms of the fraal conveyed the impression of wisdom and sadness. In Shanassin's case, the small mouth and large, expressive fraal eyes instead revealed an exquisite, ancient cruelty.

Shanassin studied his reflection in the glass, holding himself perfectly motionless. Bare metal glinted in his hands, twin fighting knives as long as his forearm. With a secret smile, he looked up at the other men in the room, breaking the silence.

"Again!" he commanded.

From the ceiling overhead, two men in black fatigues launched themselves at the corsair lord, knives extended. Shanassin waited; adrift in the middle of the room, he had no leverage, no maneuverability. Most experts agreed that zero-g combat required timing, reflexes, and a great deal of training. Shanassin preferred to substitute patience and precision for the first two, followed by tireless practice and study to obtain the third. He met the attack with a snarl.

The first man had leaped a fraction of a second before his fellow. Shanassin kicked his legs hard to induce a lazy spin. Parrying the attacker's slash, he locked his knives around the man's hand to gain leverage and snapped his foot hard into the man's belly. The attacker grunted and sailed clear, knocked off course, while Shanassin soared into the path of the second man.

Blades flashing, he filleted the surprised attacker on momentum alone. Gurgling, the second man crashed into the great dark window, globules of blood trailing him.

"A failure to anticipate and lack of teamwork," Shanassin spat. "You should have considered how I might redirect your companion's attack." He glanced over to the aft bulkhead, where a medic waited quietly. "Go. Repair him if you can. I suppose you need practice, too."

Behind the medic, a panel in the wall slid open revealing a vidscreen. The call light flashed with a soft tone. Shanassin glowered—he hated to be disturbed in his workout, but the call was coded urgent. His subordinates wouldn't interrupt him without a good reason. They knew better.

"What is it?" he snapped.

The screen brightened. Yeiwei Three-knives peered out at him, eight dark eyes glinting. He stood on the command deck of a small ship.

"Following his prey: the Hunter encounters a new trail: and seeks counsel of the Warrior, wise in his years," he said. "Forgive the interruption, but I have discovered that Andreven, the new arrival, is not who he claims to be. His name is Sokolov."

Shanassin frowned. "So? Half of our guests travel under assumed names. Is that your only reason for interrupting my workout?"

The sesheyan flinched. "We have also found evidence of tampering in Lift Seven, recent tampering."

"What kind of tampering?"

"The crew security lockout was bypassed ten to fifteen minutes ago."

Shanassin scowled. "Was Sokolov in the lift during the window?"

The sesheyan consulted some unseen display. "Yes, but so

were five other guests. It is a busy lift. Should we pick him up?"

"Where is he now?"

"The casino."

Shanassin thought quickly. Behind him, the wounded man moaned and thrashed while the medic cut his fatigues away and applied pressure bandages.

"Check up on all six. Keep an eye on each of them. And run Sokolov through our contacts on Penates. Let's see who he really is." The fraal drifted a moment, slowly turning as he studied his reflection in his knife blade. "Go ahead and secure the *Sabrecat*, too. He's not to leave until I decide to let him go."

"As the Warrior speaks: so shall it be done," said Yeiwei. "I am running his name now."

"Keep me posted," Shanassin said. He found himself near one wall and kicked away toward the vast window into night.

* * * * *

Icewalk's hospitality deck was loud and raucous. The confused babble of hundreds of people, shouting to make themselves heard, competed with dozens of different holoscreens and audio systems, all turned up as high as they would go. Garish lights flickered and pulsed, painting the mazelike eating, drinking, and gambling establishments in a confusing display of color. Overhead, wary guards patrolled a network of bare metal catwalks suspended above the crowded floor, scanning the dens and passageways below.

Sokolov sat at a bar, cautiously nursing a deciliter of bad vodka while he studied his quarry.

Geille Monashi was a striking woman. Compact and athletic, she was dressed modestly in a tight-fitting ship's jump suit. Her Asian ancestry was obvious. Her hair was night-black and straight, pulled back in a simple ponytail. Dark, thoughtful eyes and a hint of bronze in her complexion gave her an exotic appearance. She sat at a table alone, gazing absently at a mindless holofilm flashing past at a frenetic pace.

Sokolov found himself wondering why she'd even bothered to leave her quarters. She didn't seem like the kind of person who needed entertainment. *Tell me about Geille Monashi again,* he instructed Nancy.

Female, age twenty-nine Standard years, rated as Grade Five comptech/programmer. High psi-aptitude score, no demonstrable mindwalking abilities. Last employed by HelixTech on Penates. Position, Assistant Director of Research. Employment terminated last month. No criminal record, as Santiago falls in Pict territory and no law enforcement agencies exist there. Highly rated in all employ—

That's enough, Sokolov thought at the nanocomputer. He felt vaguely dissatisfied. A target dossier isn't going to tell me what I want to know, he thought sourly. What was she doing here? She wasn't an outlaw. Monashi was a top-notch computer technician, aggressive, assertive, executive material. She had it made. He worried as he watched her and then pushed it out of his mind. HelixTech is paying me. That's all there is to it. Nothing else is part of the job. Nothing.

"Lonely, spacer?" Sokolov looked up. A tattooed girl, no more than eighteen or nineteen, stood in front of him. Painted bands of blue-green and colorful fish covered her skin in a moving, rippling marine scene, the only thing she wore other than a pair of silver sandals. "You can rent me for two hundred an hour." She smiled and pressed close. "Wouldn't you like to go for a swim?"

Sokolov allowed himself to admire the girl for a moment before reaching up to gently push her away. "Sorry. I want to try my luck at the gaming tables first. Maybe later."

"You might not be able to afford me later," the girl said.

"I plan to win," Sokolov replied seriously.

The tattooed girl gave up with a forced laugh and moved on to the next man at the bar.

Twenty-two minutes and one drink later, Monashi glanced at her watch, finished the drink in front of her, and left. Sokolov watched to see if anyone else marked her departure then followed discreetly. He threaded his way through the crowded corridor, keeping a few meters behind her.

Whisper protocol transmission from Peregrine, Nancy reported.

Go ahead, he thought anxiously. The nanocomputer played *Peregrine*'s radio voice in his head: "Pete! The sesheyan's trying to shut me down!"

I should have expected this, he thought angrily. "Can you keep Yeiwei out of your command directories?"

"I believe so. Your security routines have stopped him cold—oh, damn! He just knocked the stardrive off line."

"What?" Sokolov paused in midstride. "How did he do that?"

"Mechanical shutdown. He's trying to turn me off a system at a time." The ship's computer sounded worried. "You'd better get back here, Pete. He's working on weapon control and astrogation now. If you don't get back here soon, I'm not going to have anything left!" Peri sounded desperate. "He's taking me apart!"

"Five minutes," he answered under his breath. "Five minutes, then we're gone, okay?"

"I'll hold you to it, Pete. Wait—now he's going after comms—" The transmission broke off in midword.

Whisper protocol terminated.

"Damn!" Sokolov winced, but ignored the nanocomp. If Yeiwei seriously damages Peri, I'll kill him, he promised darkly. Assuming that Shanassin's men don't crack my blind file and find out who I am before I leave, that is. This mission is getting more complicated every minute.

At the end of the corridor, Monashi waited for a lift car. He pushed his way past a couple of drunken carousers who staggered past, singing loudly, and surged ahead just as Monashi stepped into an empty car. The woman turned, facing the door.

"Deck Two," she said, quietly stating her destination to the car computer. The doors began to glide shut.

Sokolov forced the doors back open and stepped into the car with her. He offered a bland smile. "Sorry," he said. "I wanted to catch this lift." At close quarters, he towered over her. The top of her head was no higher than his collarbone.

Monashi glanced up at him. "Deck Two," she repeated to the car.

"Deck Four," Sokolov said. "Command override Andreven-

Nine." The car halted, reversed course, and began to descend.

Monashi glanced sharply at him, instantly alarmed. "What do you think you're doing?" she snapped. "You're not one of Shanassin's thugs!"

"You're right."

His face empty of expression, Sokolov reached up and pressed a hypo against the woman's neck. She gasped in surprise, raising her arms to defend herself a moment too late. Monashi recoiled back against the bulkhead, shook her head, and then launched a vicious strike at Sokolov's throat that quickly slowed as if she'd thrust her hand into molasses. Sokolov batted the punch aside and cradled her as her eyes fluttered closed.

"Why?" she mumbled thickly.

"Nothing personal," he said. "It's just a job."

* * * * *

Peregrine waited beneath a thickening blanket of ammonia slush.

The ship watched anxiously through her internal security sensors as the sesheyan worked deliberately on the engineering controls. Step by step, the computer countered Yeiwei's moves to the best of her ability, rerouting commands, cutting out control consoles, invalidating commands the sesheyan entered. Despite her efforts, Yeiwei was slowly shutting the ship down. Peri was a brilliant program, a personality emulator capable of an astonishing range of discretionary actions and leaps of intuition, but she was still a program. She was bound by intractable laws, forced to acknowledge the most basic commands entered through the ship's primary controls.

At the mass reactor control console in the engineering bay, Yeiwei paused to stare into the vid pickup. His eight eyes, dark and small, studied Peri's intangible presence like a spider hunting a ghost.

"This would go much faster if you would cooperate," he hissed. "Relinquish control and your AI will survive. Resist and I will purge your core. Understand?"

"Go to hell," Peri told him.

She found a power distribution panel in the next compartment and used a special damage control routine to cut all power to the control console Yeiwei was working on. The display went dark.

He flared his wings and hammered one taloned fist on the inert console. "Stop that!"

"Stop trying to turn me off!" Peri replied through her speakers. "When Andreven gets back, he's going to peel off your wings and feed them to you."

The sesheyan started to reply then paused, cocking his head to listen. Peri recognized the gesture. He was listening to a subdermal radio. Quickly she scanned all UHF frequencies for any transmissions, finding Icewalk's security net, but with her communications system decoupled from the computer core, the message remained trapped in her comm buffers, where she couldn't read or process it. After a moment, the sesheyan whistled softly, laughed, and then looked up at her.

"I will return later," he said, picking up his tools.

"Where are you going?"

"I must go deal with your master. He has been tampering with our computers, but his deception has now been discovered." The sesheyan drew a mass pistol from his holster and ducked through the hatchway. "We will detain him, and then I will have all the time in the world to deal with you."

Peri switched cameras, following him through the cramped passageways of the ship. Using a special override Pete had installed months ago, she began to pump air into the air lock. It would have been easier and more effective to simply open the air lock to vacuum, but she couldn't do that—her builders had installed a mechanical safety, but no one had thought that somebody might deliberately overpressurize an air lock.

At ninety atmospheres, she stopped and locked the interior hatch. Yeiwei appeared a moment later, hissing again.

"Open the door. I wish to leave."

"I'm sorry. I can't open the interior hatch."

"This is wasting my time! Open the hatch!"

"I can't," Peri replied.

She was telling the truth, of course. She had safety protocols that prevented her from opening the hatch, now that she had overpressurized the air lock.

The sesheyan checked the air lock's gauges and found positive pressure and oxygen on the other side of the door. Angrily he threw down his tool kit.

"Fine. I will open it myself."

He stripped the access panel off the air lock controls, studied the wiring for a moment, and then shorted the door lockout. He picked up his mass pistol and looked over his shoulder at the vid pickup.

"That was pointless," he snapped, then he cycled the air lock.

Air hissed from the parting seal with the force of a jackhammer. To his credit, Yeiwei realized his peril at once. He slapped once at the air lock control, trying to shut the door, but once started, the door would not close until the cycle was complete. The blast of air from the overpressurized chamber caught Yeiwei and smashed him against the bulkhead with bone-breaking force. Throughout the ship, light objects were sent flying, blown by the artificial gale. As the roaring of air died down, Yeiwei groaned and stirred.

"Safety protocols require me to inform you that there is a dangerous overpressurization in the Number One air lock," Peri said truthfully. They just didn't specifically require a *timely* warning.

*　*　*　*　*

Sokolov efficiently handcuffed Monashi then picked up her limp form, holding her upright with his left arm. Dropping to one knee, he hoisted her over his shoulder, shifting his feet to balance her weight. The sedative he'd given her would keep her out for about an hour, and she'd wake with few aftereffects. By that time, he meant to be long gone from Icewalk.

The lift car glided smoothly to a halt at Deck 4. Sokolov set his right hand on the butt of the Wesshaur, waiting for the lift doors to open. It was a good thing that he did.

As the doors hissed open, Sokolov looked up and found himself staring at the two security guards who'd checked him onboard. One stood about six meters from the lift, covering the door with his autoflechette gun, and the other stood only an arm's length away, pulse baton at the ready. Blue energy crackled and danced along the weapon's striking surface.

"Not so fast," the man in front of him said. "You're coming with us. Shanassin wants to ask you some questions."

"I think you got the wrong guy," Sokolov said automatically. "I didn't do anything."

He halted, studying the guards. They've known who I am for ten or fifteen minutes now, he thought. Either Shanassin talked to his sources on Penates and found out why I'm here, or he discovered my computer infiltration. My cover's blown in either event. *Nancy, run security response scenario Foxtrot. Let's see what Icewalk's shooters are doing.* Sokolov had studied the personnel rosters and station plans for days before attempting to locate the station; he'd created a couple of security plans just in case he found himself in such a situation.

Scenario Foxtrot assumed that Icewalk's security experts knew he was onboard, knew roughly what he was capable of, and had some time to plan a counterattack. There were worse possibilities, of course, but Sokolov had figured that if he found himself in a bad situation, he was dead anyway. No point wasting time planning around that contingency.

"Don't waste my time," the guard snarled. "We've been tracking you for a while."

Sokolov closed his eyes, trying to think. The longer he delayed, the more likely it was that he'd never get off the ship. "Why? What's the matter?" he asked the guard.

"You're not who you say who are, for one thing," the guard said, "and we'd like to know what you were doing on Deck Six." He reached forward to thumb the lift's call panel in order to keep the lift car open. "I'm sure Shanassin has a lot to talk to you about."

"Who's the woman?" asked the second guard, keeping his gun aimed at Sokolov over his partner's shoulder.

"An old friend. She doesn't handle her liquor well." Sokolov nodded down the hallway. "Can I put her back on my ship before we go see Shanassin? I don't want to leave a woman in this state lying around."

"Just set her down here. We'll look after her." The guard tapped his pulse baton against the doorframe impatiently. Sparks crackled and snapped. "Now, Andreven, Sokolov, or whoever the hell you are, put her down and place your hands on top of your head. Move slowly and keep your hands where I can see them."

"Sorry. I've got other plans." Sokolov spared the guard a cold smile while he directed a thought at his nanocomputer: *Nancy, execute Speed Five.*

At the base of his brain, the device kicked in a reflex accelerator that co-opted his own neural pathways. Lightning strobed his vision as everything started moving slower; the nanocomputer segmented each fraction of a second so completely that his eyes couldn't follow the picture quickly enough, while his ears caught nothing but silence and thunder in alternation. While the first guard drew back to swing with his pulse baton, Sokolov took one step backward into the car and drew the sabot pistol from its hidden holster.

Slam. The gun was cold and heavy in his hand. The Icewalkers moving like zombies.

Execute Deadeye.

Slam. A laser dot appeared high on the chest of the guard with the flechette gun. Compensating for the inert burden of Monashi on his left shoulder, the speed of his movement, and the imprecision of his eyesight, the nanocomputer expertly corrected his aim.

Slam. Sokolov squeezed off a deliberate shot. The Wesshaur thrummed as its accelerator hurled the slug out of the barrel, then roared as the slug's scramjet motor caught. Sokolov saw the slug leaving the barrel in one lightning flash.

Slam. The scramjet struck the gunman just over the chestpiece of his body armor, snapping his head back and killing him instantly. Sokolov shifted his aim to the closer man just as the pulse baton came down hard on his right wrist. The shock jolted his cybernetic arm without doing him much harm.

Slam. Impact numbed his right shoulder. His gun pointed at the floor. The Icewalker started to recover from his swing. The lift doors slid a few centimeters, beginning to close.

Slam. Sokolov hammered a snap kick to the guard's midsection, driving him straight back. The doors of the lift car were sliding shut. Sokolov retreated into the car.

Slam. The guard sprawled on his back. The pulse baton spun lazily through the air as he let it go. Like a curtain falling over a bizarre slow-motion play, the lift doors hissed shut.

"Deck Five," he told the lift. *Nancy, terminate Speed-Five, terminate Deadeye. Load database Icewalk again.*

Done, Pyotr, the nanocomp replied.

"How do I get back up to *Peregrine* from Deck Five?" he asked aloud.

Abruptly his muscles screamed while a spike of white agony hammered through his skull. Sokolov crumpled to his knees, baring his teeth in a feral snarl as he fought the pain. That was the price of the reflex wiring; a few seconds after it kicked his muscles and nerves into movements they weren't designed for, they protested. He gasped and pressed his forehead against the cool metal bulkhead, sagging under Monashi's weight.

Take the main passageway directly aft for sixty meters, then turn left into service corridor 5-119. There's a service shaft that opens onto Deck Four only fifteen meters from the transit corridor leading to Peregrine.

"Got it," he replied. Shrugging off the twinges and twitches in his limbs, he stood, shouldered Monashi again, and faced the lift door.

This time the corridor was empty. *They must have found me out only moments ago,* he realized. *They're just beginning to set their security protocols. I might be able to stay ahead of the news if I hurry.*

Checking left and right, gun in his hand, Sokolov broke down the passageway at a dead run. Deck 5 was mostly life-support engineering for the rest of the station, a level devoted to atmospheric scrubbers and circulators, water and sewage systems, all the myriad technologies required to sustain life. More importantly, it was deserted for the moment. Sokolov almost ran past the access corridor before Nancy's warning voice got his attention.

He staggered to a halt, then bolted around the corner to the service shaft. Dumping Monashi unceremoniously, he yanked out his tool kit and stripped the access panel open. In a moment, he wrenched the hatch cover away from the shaft and stuck his head inside, taking stock.

The shaft ran the entire height of the station, dropping about twenty-five meters below him to a machinery well of some kind, climbing out of sight in the darkness above. *Another thirty meters,* Nancy informed him. Sokolov shook his head and cursed softly in Narislavic. He hated heights.

Around the corner and down the main passageway behind him, he heard the lift doors open. Company coming. He'd have to move faster. Sokolov uncuffed Monashi, put her arms in front of her, and then cuffed her again. Standing with her behind him, he pulled her arms over his neck so that she was clinging to his back, held by the cuffs. He ducked through the hatch, pulled it shut after him, and worked his way carefully onto a pair of heavy pipes running up the shaft. He hauled himself up toward the next deck.

"You're getting heavier," he told the woman hanging from his shoulders. Monashi didn't reply.

Five meters up, Sokolov found the Deck 4 access hatch recessed into the wall. Balancing on the lip of the recess, he quickly bypassed the controls and forced the hatch. He studiously avoided looking down and clambered out of the service shaft and into a cramped fan room. *Where now?* he asked Nancy.

The door opens directly into the main transit passage to the landing pads. Spot five is ten meters to the right.

Security response? he thought.

Scenario Foxtrot predicts a response team in the vicinity of the air lock. Probably four men.

Maybe I got the response wrong, he told himself. Maybe Icewalk doesn't wake up for another five or six minutes, but I'd better not count on it. Sokolov shrugged Monashi off his back and shifted his hold to her waist, throwing her over his left shoulder again. Moving as quietly as he could, he cracked open the hatch leading to the transit passageway and peered out.

No one was in sight, although he could hear running footsteps approaching. Now or never, he decided. Taking a deep breath, he burst out of the ventilation room into the main corridor and ran for the hatch that led to *Peregrine*.

"There he is!" Thirty meters back down the passage toward the lifts, more guards dashed toward him, raising their weapons. Sokolov wheeled and squeezed off a couple of shots in their general direction, the sabot rounds ripping the air like thunder as the Wesshaur hummed in his hand. The Icewalkers took cover and returned fire. Razor-sharp flechettes rattled and sparked around Sokolov in a rain of flashing death.

Covering his face with his cybernetic arm, he jumped back into the station air lock and slapped the button that closed the hatch. He was surprised to see drops of blood spattering the deck plates; his carbonate fiber coat was shredded to bare wire in several spots, and hot stings burned in his left forearm, on both shins, and across his scalp. He checked Monashi. A bright spot of blood trickled from a wound in her calf, but she'd been shielded by his body. Good—the whole trip would have been pointless if he'd managed to get her killed.

He wrecked the station's air lock control panel with another slug, shorting it out in a spray of sparks. He dashed down the access tube to *Peregrine*. "Peri! Activate 'Getaway' right now!" he hollered as he stepped through the air lock.

"Acknowledged," Peri replied. "I won't be able to run the whole program, Pete. The sesheyan knocked down the stardrive, astrogation, temperature control—"

"I don't care. We need to go right now. Can we fly?"

"Yes, but—"

"Okay, we're flying, then." Sokolov halted just inside the air lock's inner hatch. Yeiwei lay semiconscious on the deck plates, limbs sprawled, wings tattered. "What happened to him?"

"I overpressurized the air lock, but he insisted on opening it," Peri said.

Sokolov barked harsh laughter. "Good girl!" he said.

He shrugged Monashi off his shoulders, leaning her against

the wall, then he seized the sesheyan by his forearm and leg and dragged him clear of the air lock, heaving him into the transit tube. As an afterthought, he punched the controls to seal the station's end of the tunnel so that the sesheyan wouldn't be killed when *Peregrine* broke the seals and pulled away. It's probably better than Yeiwei deserves, Sokolov fumed, then he sealed *Peregrine*'s lock.

"Time to go," he urged himself.

He dragged Monashi to the ship's guest stateroom and strapped her into a bunk, placing an automated trauma pack over the minor injury to her leg. He checked to make sure that she wouldn't wake up anytime soon, then locked her inside. He dashed up to the command deck, powering up the ship's induction drives and flight instruments.

The nav console stayed dark. "Peri! What's the problem here?"

"I told you, the sesheyan cut out astrogation. I can't see where we're going."

"How long until you can bring it back on line?"

"Fifteen to twenty minutes, at a minimum. You could probably do it faster by reinitializing the systems."

"I don't have the time," Sokolov said. He looked out the plexglass windows at the black bulk of the station. Nothing short of an industrial laser would get into *Peregrine* through the air lock, but there were a dozen ways that Shanassin could destroy them.

"I can reset your systems once we're clear of the station, Peri. Are the station's weapons charged?"

The computer hesitated. "Sorry, Pete. We're too close to tell. The bulk of the station is masking us from the weapon systems."

"Call me a pessimist, but I'm guessing those guns are hot," Sokolov muttered. *Show me the main power feeds to the aft batteries, Nancy.*

Complex schematics spooled through his mind while he settled at the controls and absently ran Peri through a very abbreviated form of her preflight procedures. Gleaming threads of light marked the power lines leading out to the weapon booms flanking the landing platforms. Nancy fed information directly into the vision centers of his brain. Luminescent diagrams and phantoms of data imposed their ethereal images over the scene before him. One glance at the schematics confirmed his suspicion: *Peregrine* couldn't hit the quad-mounts while nestled alongside the station, but the station's weapons were similarly masked.

So Icewalk blows me out of the sky the minute I get clear of the station. Sokolov punched through the start-up sequence, lighting up the ship's engines, powering sensors, spinning up the flight controls. *Can't get the station's defense batteries from here, but the capacitor rooms supplying power to the plasma cannons weren't out of reach.* Sokolov checked the schematics; he was right.

He bared his teeth in a predatory grin and said, "Give me the mass cannon, Peri."

"Pete, the minimum safe range for the Krasnya model 6 mass—"

"Give me the gun, Peri!" Sokolov snapped.

He toggled the local control mode on the pilot's console and wrenched at the yoke, slewing *Peregrine*'s mass cannon toward the target, then he cut loose with a blast, hammering at the station with *Peregrine*'s main battery. The mass cannon was a weapon designed for open space. In fact, its manufacturer's specs claimed a maximum effective range of more than fifteen thousand kilometers. It fired a pulse of gravitational energy that could crumple steel. At a range of fifty meters, the effects were drastic and spectacular.

The first blast hammered the base of the station's defense boom like the blow of a titanic, invisible hammer, shattering hull plates and raising a great line of sleet and slush from the boom's upper surface. The second and third pounded into the wreckage, venting great clouds of steam and gas to Dioscuri's cold and toxic atmosphere. The impact of each cannon blast echoed through Icewalk with a dull, thunderous *boom* that Sokolov could feel through the hull of his own ship.

"Pete, Icewalk's calling us," Peri stated.

"I'll bet they are," Sokolov grunted.

A sudden bright shower of sparks flashed in the depths of the crumpled metal and twisted plating, and then the whole station shuddered with an immense secondary explosion that destroyed the base of the tall strut jutting out over the Icewalk's flank. With grotesque dignity, the whole portside boom—a tower maybe eighty or ninety meters long, capped by the quad-mount plasma battery—fell away from Icewalk, streaming white clouds of vented atmosphere and hot blue sparks.

Sokolov squeezed his eyes shut, trying to blink the brilliant explosion from his sight. "Kick power back to the engines, Peri. It's time to go!"

"Pete, I don't have navigation! You'll be flying blind."

"You've got the artificial horizon. That's all I need. Do we have power to the engines?"

The computer sighed. "Yes," she said.

Sokolov tipped the ship sideways, up and away from the landing pad. Metal screamed and crumpled outside the hull as the umbilicals and docking clamps were torn free of their connections. He yanked the control yoke back hard, kicking *Peregrine* straight out at max power as he raced away over the jagged ice and barren rock of the surface. Icewalk was armed to the teeth. He didn't want to accidentally fly into the sights of another weapon emplacement after removing the one that blocked his escape. Dioscuri's incessant gale caught him at once, tumbling the ship wildly, but the artificial glare of the station faded quickly into gloom. In the space of seconds, they were kilometers away and accelerating, battering their way up through the stormclouds.

"Peri, any fire from the station?" he asked anxiously.

The computer hesitated. "They've got us locked in with fire control radars, but I don't detect any weapons fire."

"They'd be shooting if they could," he said aloud, hoping he was right. Dioscuri's winds tore at *Peregrine* as they climbed, battering the rugged tradesman mercilessly. Sokolov clung to the ship's yoke and started to fly the ship instead of powering straight through the atmosphere. Scarlet lightning flashed outside. "What's our altitude?"

"Twenty-eight kilometers. By the way, I'm required to notify you that you haven't filed any flight plan for this trip. That's a Class Three infraction."

"My flight plan is to get the hell away from Icewalk. File it."

The atmosphere thinned rapidly as they climbed. In moments of clear air, Sokolov took stock of the command consoles, gauging the time required to re-initialize the systems knocked off line by Yeiwei's sabotage. Astrogation was out, as well as sensors, half of his engineering controls, and the communication array. I should have just spaced that miserable flapper, he told himself. He could fly the ship by visual flight protocols, but he'd never find his way through the Lucullus system to Penates unless he could plot a course.

In the bridge viewports, the gray haze of Dioscuri's clouds whitened, thinned, and gave way to the blackness of open space. The ship's trembling faded into the smooth, directionless hum of induction drives in the deck plates beneath his feet. Sokolov aimed the ship at a bright dot that might or might not have been Penates and slumped back. I don't believe it. I got away after all.

"Autopilot, Peri," he said. "Just head straight on this bearing as fast as you can go. I'll see if I can bring everything back on line."

Pulling himself up out of the seat, he punched at a storage unit in the bridge overhead and retrieved a computer gauntlet loaded with general troubleshooting and diagnostic software. He pulled it on, rolled his head around his shoulders to battle the tension in his neck, and sighed heavily.

"Okay. Say 'Aaaah.' "

Chapter Three

SHANASSIN STRODE quickly down the access corridor, hurrying with an uncharacteristic purpose. He adjusted his trim black ship suit, an efficient combination of body armor and advanced fabrics that could serve as a space suit in an emergency. As he walked, he drew on the suit's long black gloves. For others, attention to dress at a time like this might have been an affectation, something flippant and callous. For Shanassin, it was part of a very deliberate ritual. He was arming himself for battle.

Behind him, several of his lieutenants jogged to keep pace, jockeying for his attention. Damage reports, casualties, urgent questions from his other guests concerning the unexpected attack . . . none of it mattered. He ignored them, his eyes locked straight ahead on the air lock leading to his personal landing platform.

"Is the *Blackguard* ready to fly?" he asked over his shoulder.

"Five minutes, Captain Shanassin," replied Holse, the ship's chief engineer. The drivetech was an old, scarred human, a veteran of Shanassin's crew since the beginning of his piratical career. "We're bringing the mass reactor up to full power right now."

Shanassin flicked his eyes over at the engineer. "My standing orders required the *Blackguard* to be kept on ready-five status, Mr. Holse. You've had ten minutes already."

"Power surge from the loss of the port boom knocked down the main bus through the station umbilical, Captain, a freak accident. My team's switching out some distribution boards, and Carlisle tells me that we lost several crewmen in the explosion." Holse carefully avoided meeting Shanassin's eyes directly. The old pirate understood the danger he was in.

"It is precisely for circumstances such as these that I created those standing orders, Mr. Holse," Shanassin grated. He considered more direct forms of censure, but decided not to do anything drastic. If there had been any way to anticipate the problems, Holse would have done so. The fraal corsair snapped a glance over at the ranking security man in his immediate presence. "Has anyone found Yeiwei yet?"

The man mumbled into his comm gear then nodded. "Yes, Captain. They just found him in the wreckage of Transit Corridor Five. He's injured but alive."

Shanassin reached the hatch leading to his ship and swept on through without breaking stride. The hangar was a seething caldron of activity; dozens of technicians rushed from place to place, rigging the *Blackguard* for space, while the attack ship's crew boarded. The fraal paused, surveying the scene.

"I want everyone out of here in two minutes," he said to no one in particular. "I intend to launch at that time, regardless of who or what is in my way."

"Sokolov's already off our scopes," the security man said in a low voice. "We might not be able to catch him before he skips the system or gets under cover somewhere."

The fraal raised one hand, interrupting the man. "We will," he said simply. "I will not be denied. We will."

* * * * *

It took almost half an hour, but Sokolov restored the stardrive, flight controls, communications, and the planetary astrogation unit while *Peregrine* climbed away from Dioscuri's roiling clouds. He'd managed to re-initialize everything except the drivespace astrogation program, the software *Peregrine* relied on to plot starfalls across the gap between the stars.

"I'll have to let this wait until we get home," he told Peri. "I don't know what the sesheyan did, but I can't fix it now."

"I can't go into drivespace until you do, Pete."

"We don't need it to get to Penates. At least I got your in-system astrogation up and running."

Sokolov returned to the command deck and leaned wearily

over the chart table, a meter-square holoprojector that showed the triple suns of Lucullus and their threadbare collection of planets and debris in a three-dimensional image. *Peregrine* appeared as a blinking red icon, accelerating away from a fuzzy gray orb—the planet Dioscuri, second of Lucullus's five planets. In the center of the display, two brilliant blue globes showed the twin central suns of the system. A glittering metallic band of tiny asteroids ringed the two stars, the wreckage of unborn worlds that were destroyed in orbits destabilized by the gravitational influences of two large stars. A single red ruby gleamed in the azure glare of the mighty suns—Polyphemus, a molten world that was home to some of the most miserable mining installations in human space. Like the rest of Lucullus's inner system, it was a mineral bonanza for anyone determined enough to harvest it. The third sun of the trinary and its solitary planet, Dione, was several light hours distant, too remote to fit in *Peregrine*'s nav display.

"Give me the most direct course to Penates," he instructed the computer.

A bright green line appeared, linking the ship's icon to a mottled blue and brown planet, the next one out from Dioscuri. Penates, the sole metropolitan planet in the system, was a world of grim domed cities shrouded in nitrogen and ammonia smog. In a system of abundant mineral wealth, it was the planet deemed least inimical to long-term settlement by the original Solar explorers who had founded the colony one hundred and sixty years ago. They'd made it a penal colony, shipping millions of their unemployed and uneducated underclass to the edge of human space. At the moment, Penates happened to be almost directly opposite Dioscuri. The green course line looped high over the blazing pair of stars in the center of the system in a graceful arc.

Sokolov hated the whole system. There was something basically wrong about millions of people living in a place where the most habitable planet required insulated habitats and subterranean farms. In any kind of sane universe, humankind would have charted Lucullus and never come back.

He studied the computer's suggested course. "Any chance of

threading the Arch?" he asked. Tapping in a set of hypothetical course corrections, he tugged the green line down and straightened it until it actually passed between the blue suns—the hundred-million-kilometer gap known as the Arch of Lucullus. *Peregrine* could only stand up to the rigors of the inner system for a few hours, but it would reduce their travel time by half. "The sooner we're back, the better."

"No can do, Pete," Peri replied. The course line changed from green to red. "We don't have a clear shot, which means that you'd roast before you got all the way through. You're not in that much of a hurry, are you?"

"No, I guess not."

Sokolov cancelled his calculations, returning the course projection to its original curve. He'd have preferred to lose himself in the radioactive glare of Lucullus's twin suns; the Arch was generally devoid of commercial traffic, making it a good place to drop out of sight before returning to Penates.

"Remind me to install some heavy-duty refrigeration and rad shielding when we get paid. I'd like to be able to duck in there any time I needed some space." He checked with Nancy and discovered that almost forty-five minutes had elapsed since he encountered Monashi in the lift car. "I'd better check on our guest. Don't hit anything."

"There's nothing around us but starlight," Peri replied.

Sokolov padded back down the passageway to the guest cabin, unlocked it, and stepped inside. Monashi lay curled in the bunk, her breathing slow and deep. He consulted the autodoc clinging to her calf. *Not too much body mass, and I gave her a stiff dose of the sedative,* he reflected, as he examined her blood chemistry readings. *She'll probably be out for another hour or so.*

Sokolov studied her quietly for a long moment, gazing absently at the play of light and shadow on her features. *I'll have to ask you what you did when you wake up,* he thought. Then he left, locking the door behind him again.

"What's our ETA?" he called out to Peri as he stepped into the galley.

"Five hours, if we keep this course and acceleration."

"Great. I'm going to get something to eat, and then I'm going to sleep for a while. Set up internal security protocol 'Prisoner Type Three' and let me know if anything strange happens."

"Acknowledged. When do you—" The computer broke off abruptly. "We're receiving an incoming message, Pete."

"Put it on the speaker." Sokolov turned his attention to his galley's food stores, looking for something to eat.

The room crackled faintly with the random hiss of radio noise before the message became audible: "Sokolov, this is Shanassin." The fraal's enunciation was acrid and precise, as sharp as the blade of a knife. Sokolov looked up at the blank speaker grille, riveted by the voice. "You have grievously erred, my friend. You damaged my station, but you left me alive and unharmed. The woman is nothing to me. The deaths of my guards are unfortunate. Even your invasion of my station computer is a mere annoyance, easily set right, but no one strikes me a blow that I do not return twofold. Do you understand me?"

Sokolov sighed. "Patch this through, Peri," he said. He leaned against the bulkhead and keyed the intercom speaker. "Shanassin, this is Sokolov. Nothing personal, but you got in the way. Your security people were a little too efficient for their own good. Over."

"That does not set right my grievance against you, Sokolov. You will regret the hour you dared to match yourself against me! I am Devriele Shanassin, you ignorant vandal. No one —"

"Don't flatter yourself, Shanassin. I don't give a rat's ass who you are."

The voice on the other side of the radio grew deadly cold. "That much is apparent, but I promise you this, Sokolov: you will very soon learn who I am and how I treat my enemies."

"Whatever," Sokolov stated flatly. "I'm just a freelancer. Someone paid me to do a job, so I did it."

"Do you believe that will absolve you of responsibility?" Shanassin laughed coldly. "I will find your employer and deal with him in my own time, Sokolov, but you personally have wronged me. I will have restitution."

"Fine, Shanassin. Suit yourself. Maybe you can talk Helix-Tech into covering your damages." He resumed his search for food. "I don't ask questions. I just take the money and deliver what I promise. Sokolov out." The cold storage unit was well stocked; he started to build a sandwich.

Shanassin wasn't finished with him. "It seems clear that you do not understand the gravity of the situation," the fraal hissed. "What you do not understand, you detestable mongrel, is that *I built Icewalk with my own hands.* I cannot permit anyone to damage it and walk away.

"You have left me no choice, Sokolov. I must obliterate you. I am coming after you, and I will destroy you. Make your peace with whatever childish deity you revere, for I assure you that you will be dead within the hour."

Empty radio noise hissed in the speakers. Sokolov straightened, the sandwich forgotten in his hands. I don't like the sound of that, he decided. That wasn't an empty threat.

"What was the origin of that signal, Peri?" he asked slowly.

"The *Blackguard,* Pete. I just spotted her. She's on my tail and overtaking me. I don't have the acceleration to outrun her."

"How far back is Shanassin?"

"Based on time lag and Doppler effect, I estimate that we're about two hundred thousand kilometers ahead of *Blackguard.* He came up dead behind us."

"Damn. Right in our blind spot. I didn't think he'd organize pursuit so quickly." Sokolov left the sandwich sitting on the countertop and sprinted up to the command deck. Studying the sensor display, he tapped *Peregrine*'s course a few degrees to the right and was rewarded by the ghostly flicker of a contact almost directly behind them. "Try to raise the *Blackguard,*" he told the computer. "Maybe I can reason with him."

Several seconds passed before Peri responded. "She's not responding to my hails, Pete."

This isn't good, Sokolov decided. He could do the math in his head. *Peregrine* was running straight out at her best acceleration, and the *Blackguard* was behind her and gaining. Even with an engine as powerful as the gravity induction drive, spaceships at high speeds couldn't stop or turn on a dime. He'd have to settle for a long, graceful arc if he wanted to change course now, which Shanassin could easily match, or he'd have to slow down drastically in order to turn more sharply, in which case the *Blackguard* would pounce on them like a hawk.

"Rate of closure?" he asked.

"Approximately eighteen thousand two hundred kilometers per minute."

"He'll be in firing range in about fifteen minutes then."

Sokolov studied the nav display, keying in his database on the stations and outposts of Lucullus. He added the long-range sensor feed to the display, hoping there was something nearby he could use for cover. *Peregrine* blinked alone in the display . . . but now a yellow shadow followed the icon.

The nearest haven noted in his database was Icewalk. Nothing else was even close. Sokolov rubbed his temples.

"Show me what we know about *Blackguard,*" he said. "Maybe we can outfight her if we turn and show our teeth."

"I don't advise it, Pete," Peri said.

She showed him the readouts they'd collected on the approach to the station. The *Blackguard* was a real attack ship, a military hull outfitted with the best hardware Shanassin could buy. She was faster, better protected, and much more heavily armed than Sokolov's ship. The *Peregrine* was a tradesman, a small cargo carrier. He'd armed her as best as he could, but she was no match for Shanassin's vessel.

I can't outrun him, I can't outfight him, and he doesn't want to talk, Sokolov fumed. *What's that leave? I could abandon ship in the escape launch, but he'd see that at once. I could fire the launch empty, maybe set the transponder to draw his attention. . . . No, we're moving fast enough that the escape launch wouldn't get clear before Shanassin overtook us. He'll just blast it and keep coming.*

"What's the tachyon charge on the stardrive? Can we make starfall if we have to?"

"The drive is charged, but drivespace astrogation is still out," Peri reminded him.

"Damn!" Sokolov swore viciously. Leaping into drivespace would mandate a five-day delay in his return to Penates, but it was also a sure escape. Only the most extensive sensor posts could track a ship into drivespace, and Shanassin presumably had no such technology aboard his ship. "Peri, I need more options," he snapped, watching the *Blackguard* creep closer.

"I recommend negotiation, Pete. Escape or combat just aren't realistic choices here."

"I don't think you were paying attention to Shanassin's monologue. He's done all the talking he's going to do." Sokolov abandoned the nav display and stationed himself in the bridge's command chair. One by one, he started slaving the other controls—engineering, piloting, weapons control—to the captain's console. "Batten down the hatches, Peri. We're going to have to fight. Power up the mass cannon and the deflection inducer. Bring the ECM unit on line. Segregate all systems into casualty mode, and seal all interior partitions. I'll take piloting and weapons functions at the command console. You've got everything else."

"Acknowledged," Peri answered. Her speakers carried a note of disapproval in her voice. "Pete, I have to advise you against this course of action. The *Blackguard*—"

"I know, Peri. I'm not going to blow Shanassin out of space, but maybe we'll get in a lucky hit and slow him down. If we can score on his engines, we can turn tail and run."

"We might consider surrender," the computer suggested.

Sokolov glanced up at the bridge's video pickup. "You've got to be kidding." He reached under his seat and retrieved a battered vacuum helmet, connecting its air hoses to the feeds under his console. If the ship were holed, he'd need it close at hand. *Nancy, stash Deadeye and Blade Three. Load Dogfight Eight.* Inside his skull, the tiny nanocomputer readied software designed to boost his reaction time and help his brain sort through the myriad details of a space battle. "Are we ready?"

"I'm locked down. Mass cannon on line, deflection inducers active."

"Showtime," he murmured.

Watching the *Blackguard* on the sensor screen, he abruptly wrenched the yoke to the left, slamming *Peregrine* into a hard turn. Shuddering as the gravity induction drive compensated against the ship's forward momentum, the tradesman dug into the turn. *Execute Dogfight.*

Nancy counted the 1.37 seconds required for the *Blackguard*'s radar signal to paint *Peregrine* in her new maneuver and return, then added another 1.5 seconds as a guess at the reaction time of Shanassin's helmsman. Sokolov slewed the *Peregrine* back to the right as quickly as he could, hoping the *Blackguard* was committing itself to veer left after *Peregrine*'s first abrupt move. The ships were still about half a light second apart. It almost worked.

For a hopeful instant, the *Peregrine* was heading right and slowing down while the *Blackguard* charged left, intent on pouncing on Sokolov's feint. The rate of closure leaped while *Peregrine* bled off speed.

"He went for it, Peri!" Sokolov crowed. "We might get out of this after all!"

Blackguard began to slow and veer right as Sokolov reversed his right turn, slowing more and executing a serpentine turn back to the left. Shanassin's helmsman was good, but he still had too much velocity. Trying to bleed off speed, *Blackguard* looped across *Peregrine*'s bow at a distance of thirteen thousand kilometers. It was a long-range shot, but Sokolov hammered at the corsair with *Peregrine*'s mass cannon. The heavy mount thrummed, battering Shanassin's ship with gravitational energy. The long-range vid cameras showed *Blackguard* staggering under the attack.

"Come right, you bastard," Sokolov hissed.

Blackguard continued to break right, trying to turn toward the *Peregrine* and slow down. Sokolov was already inside the other ship's turn; he kept the control yoke over hard right, continuing to pummel the fraal pirate. Like invisible sledgehammers, the mass bursts dented *Blackguard*'s hull plates and buckled fragile structures on the surface of the attack ship.

While the corsair labored to point her bow back at *Peregrine,* a snub-nosed turret high on the warship's spine slewed to the right and began firing bolts of incandescent plasma at the tradesman. The first missed by several dozen kilometers. The next hit *Peregrine* hard on the flank. Harsh white light flooded the command deck as *Peregrine* shuddered in protest.

"Pete, I'm hit!"

Damage alarms blinked and buzzed, lighting the engineering console like a city at night. Burning insulation from somewhere filled the air with a plastic stink. Sokolov winced and pushed the yoke down, diving fast to get under the *Blackguard* and out of the plasma gun's arc of fire.

"What's the damage?" he called.

"Mostly minor, but the deflection inducer's gone. We've lost the shield."

Above him, *Blackguard* was rolling and turning to follow his move. Despite *Peregrine*'s early success and the damage she'd inflicted to the corsair vessel, Shanassin was still coming. Sokolov punched his acceleration, trying to open the distance again.

A sharp burst of static rippled across the command deck's display screens, setting off another flood of damage alerts. Sokolov's controls darkened and then re-initialized, coming back on line after a split second of unresponsiveness.

"What was that?" he demanded.

"Particle beam. It grazed me," Peri reported. "Pete, we can't take much more of this!"

"Tell me something I don't know!"

This is going nowhere, he decided. He'd known it from the start. *Blackguard* was too much ship for *Peregrine* to defeat. He'd been lucky to land the few hits that he had. Now Shanassin's ship was turning in on *Peregrine*'s right quarter, bringing her heaviest guns to bear.

"Fire control radar locked on to us!" Peri reported. "We've got missiles inbound!"

"Time to impact?"

"Twenty-three seconds!"

Sokolov thought furiously while swinging the ship back around to the right, trying to stay out of *Blackguard*'s gunsights. He could see the missiles on the tactical display, evil green arrowheads easily tracking his move while *Blackguard* continued through her turn.

He made a decision. Keying in an automatic evasion plan, he unstrapped himself from the command chair and vaulted over the railing to the engineer's station. He rapped out a series of commands, powering up an unused portion of the console, and then he moved over to the nav display.

"Fifteen seconds to impact. What are you doing, Pete?"

"I'm going to activate the stardrive."

"We don't have any coordinates!" the computer protested. "We can't jump blind!"

"Oh, yes we can," Sokolov replied. The starplot remained dark, but the stardrive activation display powered up. His fingers flew over the drive controls as he answered the computer.

"So we don't know where we'll wind up. It'll be somewhere within 5.73 light-years. Considering how big and empty space is, the odds of us appearing someplace we don't want to be are millions to one." He glanced at the tac display, where the incoming missiles had assumed final attack profiles. "In ten seconds, I'd rather be *anywhere* than here."

"Pete, engaging a stardrive without coordinates is a Class Two—"

Deliberately, Sokolov flipped up the cover and thumbed the switch.

* * * * *

Devriele Shanassin stood on the bridge of the *Blackguard,* watching a vidscreen with his arms folded across his chest. Around him, his crew of picked men and women, the best he could find in their chosen vocations, worked smoothly and quietly to bring Sokolov and his vessel to a violent end.

"Time?" he demanded.

Behind him, the missile targeting officer hovered over his charges, tapping minute corrections into the final approach of the two deadly weapons. "Impact in ten seconds! Nine . . . eight!"

The fraal corsair leaned forward, staring at the screen. Pinned by invisible lances of radio energy that guided her death toward her, the *Peregrine* twisted and weaved ineffectually. Slender as swords, the twin missiles pursued her, curving gracefully to intercept the lurching path of the battered old tradesman.

At the count of three, each missile snapped open its payload, a dense bundle of tungsten rods hurling forward like a cloud of needles. Traveling thousands of kilometers per hour faster than their target, each would vaporize a couple of cubic meters of anything it happened to strike. The missiles were unlikely to destroy the *Peregrine* outright, but they would certainly cripple her. Shanassin smiled coldly, imagining Sokolov impaled on a tungsten rod.

"Two . . . one!"

Peregrine flared in a burst of iridescent green.

"Impact!"

Suddenly the tradesman vanished, dropping into drivespace as the dazzling cloud of splinters sleeted through the space she had just occupied, slowly dispersing as they drifted farther and farther off into space. Shanassin stared, his fine fraal features blank with surprise.

"He went into drivespace!"

The bridge was absolutely still.

Shanassin snarled, slamming one gloved fist on the command console. "Why now? If his stardrive was charged, why didn't he flee when he first detected us? Did he really think he could defeat me with that simple ruse?" His voice rose to a shout. "Did he turn to fight in order to *mock* me?"

None of his crewmen chose to answer him. Shanassin closed his eyes, seeking composure. A long moment of silence passed on the *Blackguard*'s bridge as the corsairs nervously awaited their captain's next words.

They were surprisingly calm. Shanassin straightened, allowed himself a simple snort of frustration, and wheeled to leave the bridge. "Take us back to Icewalk," he said quietly. The fraal paused in the hatch, glancing again at the now empty vidscreen. "He'll be back. Five days to his destination, a couple of days to recharge his stardrive, then five days back. HelixTech is on Penates. Therefore, Penates is where Sokolov must go. He won't collect his paycheck until he delivers Monashi. She is worthless to him until he does."

Shanassin studied the fading aurora of the *Peregrine*'s starfall. Sokolov would return, he told himself, and I will be ready the next time we meet.

Chapter Four

SIX DAYS BEFORE Pete Sokolov raided Icewalk, he met Karcen Borun for the first time. The first thought that flashed through Sokolov's mind when he met his employer was that Borun was a fake, a fraud. He ushered Sokolov into his luxurious office suite with artificial good cheer. He smiled widely enough to show a mouthful of scrimshawed teeth set with tiny man-made gems, and his tinted eyes glittered blue with the stolen innocence of a child. Despite Sokolov's first impression, Karcen Borun's surgical alterations really weren't obvious. His bronze tan and sun-bleached hair were flawless. Karcen Borun's appearance provoked suspicion only because Penates was a world of domes and cold poison, a world where any natural sunshine that penetrated the murk would kill with its ultraviolet energy. No one on Penates had a tan.

As Sokolov sank into the padded chair opposite Borun's desk, he noticed that the HelixTech exec wore real leather shoes. *Real* leather, on a world where the nearest cow was probably fifteen or twenty light-years away. The shoes probably cost as much as a new skycar or first-class passage back to Old Space. No one would wear shoes like that unless he was trying to make a point. Sokolov read Borun's at once. Ride with me, and you'll have all the gold your saddlebags can hold. I'm the man who can get you what you want.

"I'll bet you're wondering why you're here," Borun began amiably.

"I know why I'm here, Mr. Borun. I'm here because you offered me a two thousand dollar advance to hear you out. With no obligation to sign on, I'll add."

Karcen Borun laughed. "Well, I guess that had something to

do with it. What I meant to say was, I'll bet you're wondering why I contacted you, Pete. I can call you Pete, right?"

Sokolov smiled thinly, lit a cigarette, and gazed out the window behind Borun. The HelixTech compound sat about twenty kilometers outside of Santiago, the Pictish capital. Karcen Borun's office faced the city, and beyond the cold black towers of the corporate fortress he could see the garish lights of the city blazing in the distance. In the revolt of fifty years ago, the Picts—a crude, violent street gang—had seized almost a quarter of the planet, looting and pillaging entire cities. Helix-Tech, located in the middle of their territory, hadn't been touched.

"You're going to tell me in a minute anyway. Otherwise you just wasted two thousand dollars."

"Hah!" Borun slapped one hand on his knee and leaned back in his oversized chair. "Well, you're right, Pete. I am going to tell you." He shook his head as if he were enjoying a particularly good laugh and fixed his warm gaze on Sokolov. "Helix-Tech is the biggest megacorp in this entire system, Pete," Borun began. The scrimshaw designs glinted in his mouth when he spoke. "Our security division outnumbers the enforcement arms of the Syndicate, the mercenary guards of the Free Trade Guild, and the Solar military presence in Lucullus put together. You're a smart guy, Pete. I'm sure you can appreciate that we're in the habit of solving our own problems."

"What can I do for you?" Sokolov returned his gaze to Borun, studying him. Don't forget who you're talking to, he reminded himself.

"Right to the point. Good. I like that." Something in the set of Borun's eyes hinted to Sokolov that Borun didn't particularly like directness, or even Sokolov, for that matter. It was just something to say. Borun leaned back in his vast chair. "I understand that you're a bounty hunter, one of the best."

"So they say."

"Three years ago you showed up in Lucullus after some kind of trouble over in Tendril. You'd worked for StarMech for six months; no one knows where you were before that. Since you've been here, you've collected almost eight hundred thousand dollars by collecting bounties and cashing out contracts of a more direct sort. That's a lot of money you've made by killing or catching people with a price on their head, Mr. Sokolov."

"You've done your homework."

Borun spread his hands. "I wanted the best, Mr. Sokolov."

"You must have one hell of a mess on your hands then." Sokolov found an ashtray in the arm of his chair. It had never been used. "I'll warn you ahead of time that my rates will reflect the severity of your situation. What's the problem?"

"I need you to find a woman named Geille Monashi and bring her back to me alive and unharmed." Borun leaned forward, watching Sokolov's face. "Can you do it?"

Sokolov laughed harshly. "I'll need to know more than that. Who is she? Where was she last seen? What's she look like? Was she one of your employees? A competitor? A romantic interest?" As he stubbed out his cigarette, his smile faded. "Most importantly, why do you want me to get her for you, and why won't you do it yourself?"

"She's a HelixTech employee. You'll have her personnel file." The exec reached into his desk and flipped a holocube across the table to Sokolov. The bounty hunter caught it and held it up, looking inside. The ethereal image of a woman's face floated in the plastic cube: young, probably in her late twenties or early thirties, attractive but not delicate, strong Asian features with a very serious expression. "You don't need to know why we want her. As far as why we won't do it ourselves—" Borun's smile faded—"let's just say that she's someplace where we can't reach her. Our people would never get close, but an independent with skills like yours could pull it off."

Sokolov lowered the cube and stared at Borun, waiting for him to continue. The executive offered a wry grin and shrugged. "We think she's gone to Icewalk."

Sokolov thought for a long moment, then abruptly stood and set the cube on the desk. "Can't do it," he said. "I'll be happy to offer you a couple of suggestions if you want someone else." He started for the door.

Borun stood up, surprised. "Wait a minute! What's the problem?"

The bounty hunter paused, speaking over his shoulder. "Mr. Borun, I'm not going to risk my life on Icewalk without knowing exactly why I'm doing so."

Borun sighed and ran one hand through his platinum hair. "Very well. Monashi's been with HelixTech for almost ten years now. She started in research and development as an assistant comptech, and she's worked her way up. Last year she was promoted to Assistant Director of R and D. She's been involved in a number of very sensitive projects.

"Eighteen days ago she installed a virus in the main R and D computer system, then walked out the front door and disappeared. Six hours after she left, the virus wrecked years of research." The executive picked up a remote on his desk and swiveled his chair to point it at one wall, revealing a wide vidscreen. He clicked on it, replaying a surveillance tape. It showed a dismal lounge or bar, almost empty. Monashi entered and sat down opposite a hulking bear of a man. "We obtained this footage from security over at the Santiago spaceport. This is about two hours after Monashi walked out of HelixTech."

"I know that man. He's Dogger Maartens, small-time smuggler."

"You know your scum," Borun said with a flash of artificial humor. On the screen, Monashi spoke to Maartens briefly. The spacer nodded, paid his tab, and left with her. Karcen Borun watched a moment longer, then shut off the screen. "They went to Maartens's ship, and he lifted off about fifteen minutes later. We've managed to reconstruct the *Bad Break*'s course from traffic control radars. Maartens took Monashi to Dioscuri."

"I don't get it. She's smart, she's successful, she's climbing the corporate ladder, then she destroys your research records and flees to an outlaw station." Despite himself, he was becoming interested. Maybe Borun was more of a salesman than he thought . . . or maybe the dark, introspective expression on the face of the woman in the holocube had already hooked him. Sokolov turned back toward the executive and took a deep drag from a freshly lit cigarette. "What's her motive?"

"We can only guess that she was hired by one of our competitors to sabotage R and D. Icewalk would be a good place to hide after doing something like that. No one can get to her there, except maybe a top-notch independent." Borun reached into the vest pocket of his tailored suit, then flipped a small black credstick toward Sokolov. "She's important to us. That's our offer."

Sokolov caught the credstick with his artificial hand. He glanced down at the display, blinked once, and then looked again more carefully. *More zeroes than I expected, that's for sure.* He studied Karcen Borun for a long moment, thinking. *HelixTech wouldn't part with this kind of money unless he was prepared to take the job on their terms.*

"Why do you want her back alive? You've already lost the research."

"Our comptechs tell us she might be able to undo a lot of the damage she did to our system. We'd like to give her that chance."

You're lying, thought Sokolov. *I don't know what you're lying about, but I know you're lying about something.* He could believe that HelixTech's corporate security team might not be able to get into Icewalk. Borun probably wasn't lying about that, but the story didn't ring true. *If Monashi's sabotage was sponsored by a rival corporation, why was she sitting on an outlaw station? Any traitor with a brain in her head would have made sure that safe exit was part of the deal. If Monashi hadn't been paid by someone to do what Borun said she'd done, why would she have done it at all?*

He looked down at the credstick in his hand. *Do I care if Borun isn't telling me everything I'd like to know?* he asked himself. Icewalk was a veritable outlaw fortress, a sanctuary no lawman—or bounty hunter—had ever managed to breach. HelixTech, with their billions of dollars of assets and thousands of highly trained employees, didn't think they could do it, but the man in front of him seemed to think that Sokolov might pull it off.

Add it up, Sokolov: an extremely dangerous contract paying a damned fortune, the chance to do something that no one thought possible, a beautiful woman with dark eyes and a taut frown, staring out of a holo taken from corporate records, lies, intrigue, deceit.

Sokolov considered a moment longer. "I'll want half in advance, and there are going to be some major expenses I'll want you to cover. I mean *major.*"

"Done," said Borun, smiling his golden smile.

Chapter Five

RIVESPACE, TWO hours after starfall.

Peregrine hung motionless in the black void. Nothing existed for the ship to measure her progress against; no fluctuation or flicker of motion interrupted the silent expanse. Sokolov had already closed all the ship's viewports. He hated the look of drivespace. It made him nauseous, like leaning over to look down the side of a cliff and feeling your center of gravity begin to hover between safe and falling.

He'd never told anyone, but Sokolov had always harbored a secret fear that each trip through drivespace would be his last. He had dreams in which he slowly disintegrated, fraying into nothingness at the atomic level. Sokolov had always felt that when he navigated drivespace, he was cheating the universe of the space between the stars.

He dozed for an hour. After showering and eating a tasteless meal, he decided to visit his prisoner. The door to the guest stateroom was fitted with a narrow vision block. Sokolov opened it and spotted Monashi sitting on the bed, arms crossed, eyes closed. *Nancy, Whisper protocol. Transmit vital signs continuously on 83.3 Megahertz.*

"Can you hear my transmission, Peri?"

"I've got it, Pete. You want Deadman protocol active?"

"Yep. Set Deadman at a five-minute delay, and use your discretion on the definition of hostile action. Don't blow up unless you're really sure I'm dead."

"Understood. Thanks, Pete."

Peri might have been nothing more than a program, but she placed a significant value on her own existence. The Deadman protocol would initiate the destruction of the ship if Sokolov's heart stopped beating. However, Sokolov had left her with the ability to decide that his death might have occurred accidentally, which would abort the program.

"Let me in, then lock the door behind me, Peri," he directed the computer

The hatch's magnetic lock buzzed once. "Be careful."

Sokolov stepped into the room. Monashi looked up at him, eyes blazing with dark fire. "Borun sent you," she grated, "Why? What's in it for you?"

The bounty hunter closed the door behind him, fished a cigarette out of a pack in his coat pocket, and lit it carefully. He kept his eyes on the woman, leaning his tall frame casually against the opposite wall.

"My name's Pete Sokolov. You're onboard my ship, *Peregrine*. You're right. Karcen Borun hired me."

Monashi bit her lip and looked down at her hands. Her dark hair fell around her face like a shroud. "You've killed me," she said. "You know that, don't you?"

"It's just a job. Blame yourself. You made Borun angry enough to retain my services." Sokolov smoked in silence for a moment, watching her. Her face radiated cold fury. "I'm going to go over the ground rules now. Pay attention.

"We're in drivespace, and we'll be in drivespace for the next one hundred and eighteen hours. There's no place to go and no one to call for help. You and I are the only people on this ship, and she's programmed to answer only to me. If something happens to me—" Sokolov flicked ash from the end of the cigarette—"*Peregrine* criticals the mass reactor. Everything within a cubic kilometer goes. Understand?"

Monashi just glared at him. Sokolov sighed and continued. "I've got the control systems tripwired with alarms. If you tamper with anything, I'll know about it. I want you to be perfectly clear on this point: it would be easier and safer for me to keep you heavily sedated for the next two or three weeks to make absolutely sure you don't cause trouble. That's exactly what I will do if you make me.

"On the other hand, if you don't cause me trouble, you can have the run of the ship while I'm awake, and you're welcome to pass the time however you like. Read, watch vids, play computer games—I don't care. I'm not a sadist. You might not like the situation you're in, but I won't make it worse for you unless you force me to."

"I'm overcome by your generosity," Monashi snapped. "Why not just shove me out the air lock and be done with it? Borun's going to kill me when you bring me back to him."

Sokolov shrugged. "He can if he wants to, but it would have been one hell of a lot easier—and cheaper, I'll add—to pay me to kill you on Icewalk. He wants you back alive if possible. Why go to all the trouble if he just wants you dead?"

Monashi snorted and looked at the wall. "There's no point in explaining. Get out of here and leave me alone. I won't break anything."

The bounty hunter waited a moment, but Monashi pulled up her knees and put her head on her arms, refusing to look at him. He grimaced and stubbed out the cigarette.

"I'm locking you in for the night, and then I'm going to sleep. I'll be in to check on you in six or seven hours." He raised his voice. "Peri, let me out."

* * * * *

A day passed. Monashi still hadn't bothered to speak to Sokolov, although she'd left her quarters to explore the ship. In addition to Sokolov's living quarters, there was a guest cabin and storage space that could convert to bunkrooms onboard *Peregrine*. All were small and cramped by any standard. Sokolov invited her to share his meals, but she didn't answer. He learned that she visited the galley and fixed her own meals after he finished his. On occasion, he'd glance over his shoulder to find her watching him. Monashi had exchanged her anger for an attitude of thoughtfulness, of watchfulness. She was thinking of ways to beat him.

Sokolov was fascinated by the determination in her eyes. He would have found Geille Monashi intriguing under most circumstances; she was intelligent, competent, and physically attractive. Sokolov had tracked women, sometimes even beautiful women, on a number of occasions, but he'd never been in a situation like this one, alone with his captive through endless hours of drivespace travel. In fact, he couldn't think of an instance in which he'd had a captive under his control for more than twenty-four hours. Now he was looking at twelve or thirteen days with his prisoner.

Geille Monashi struck him as a survivor, a kindred spirit. Sokolov felt he understood her. He also wondered what her version of Borun's story would be like.

Sokolov spent most of his time making repairs to *Peregrine*, replacing damaged circuitry and reinitializing control software knocked off line by the EMP effects of Shanassin's weapons. The fight had been short but intense. *Peregrine* had sustained a number of grazes and near misses, as well as two or three solid hits. The hits were bad enough—there was substantial hull and system damage that Sokolov would have to repair in a shipyard—but the most serious injury to *Peregrine* came from a couple of the weapons that hadn't hit the ship dead on. Devices such as particle beams and X-ray lasers could damage a ship's most vital systems by inducing electromagnetic pulses in electronics of all kinds. Much of *Peregrine*'s battle damage consisted of ionization in her circuit boards.

On the second day of their trip, Sokolov turned his attention to the drivespace astrogation unit again. Of course, it was too late to affect their current path through the alternate dimension of drivespace. Once an astrogator pushed the button and leaped out of the normal universe, nothing he could do would alter the location of the ship's starrise. That was why most spacefarers routinely spent hours calculating their starfalls before entering drivespace.

When he powered up the unit, the display read out gibberish. "I'm going to kill that sesheyan if I ever see him again," Sokolov swore. Without astrogation, the *Peregrine* was leaping blind. It could take hundreds, perhaps thousands, of starfalls before they'd get lucky and appear close enough to a settled star system to limp the rest of the way home on the induction drive. The ship was only rated for a starfall of 5.73 light-years, but Nancy determined that randomly appearing somewhere within that distance meant that the *Peregrine* could end up at any point within 787.82 cubic light-years. Call that a one-in-a-thousand chance to arrive within a light-year of Lucullus, he thought absently, several hundred starfall cycles, at seven to ten days each . . . and then a year of travel at sub-light speeds to get home. "I hope Borun isn't in much of a hurry to get Monashi back," he muttered to himself.

Sokolov disconnected the astrogation unit from its mounting near the nav display on the bridge and carried it down to what passed for his repair shop, one of the ship's two small cargo holds. He set up the unit on a test bench, opened the casing, and began to examine the components. All of the unit's diagnostics had simply failed. The software seemed okay, but . . . "Son of a bitch!"

The processor that fed nav updates to the unit was missing. Yeiwei had pulled one of the microboards out of the unit entirely. "Peri! Check the repair stores inventory. Do we have a spare microprocessor type NX-77?"

The computer hesitated for a moment. "No, Pete. I've got one on order in Port Royal."

"That won't help now. How about an NX-48 or NX-63?"

"I haven't carried those for years, Pete. We don't have any NX boards on the ship."

"Well, what do we have?" Sokolov demanded.

"Do you really want me to go through the whole list?"

"No, no. Just show me microprocessors. Display them on the screen here." He scrolled through the display. *Peregrine* carried several dozen spare microprocessors, most of them already pre-programmed for specific systems. He rubbed his eyes, trying to think.

"What's the problem?"

Geille Monashi stood in the doorway, arms folded. Sokolov looked up, startled. They were the first words she'd spoken since he'd introduced himself the day before.

He started to snap a sarcastic answer then halted himself. "While I was on Icewalk, Shanassin's security chief locked down my ship."

"Yeiwei Three-knives?"

"That's him. I should have spaced him." Sokolov spun his stool around to face the woman. "I've restarted all systems except for drivespace astrogation. He must have been unable to cut out my nav system from the console, so he yanked the board. I don't have a spare."

Monashi blinked. "What are we doing in drivespace then?"

"Shanassin pursued me after I took off from the station. The *Blackguard* was going to shoot us to pieces. I had no choice but to punch in a blind starfall."

"You have no idea where we're going?"

"It's going to be somewhere within 5.73 light years of Lucullus, since that's what the ship is rated for, other than that, no." He waited a moment for her to absorb the information, then continued. "If I can't rig something to give us navigation again, it might take us years to get back."

Monashi laughed. "Why should that concern me? The longer it takes, the better off I am. I'm in no hurry to be delivered to HelixTech."

Sokolov leaned back. "Two reasons. First of all, you've got to go back anyway, and I really don't think that Borun would go to the trouble of abducting you if he just wanted you dead."

"I've already told you he would." She shook her head. "You have no idea what's going on here, do you?"

"Tell me."

"Is it going to make a difference? No matter what I say, you still have a paycheck waiting at the end of the trip. You're taking Borun's money, so you've already decided that whatever he says must be the truth, if you even care."

Sokolov smiled grimly. "On the contrary, I suspect the man is lying. He told me you'd destroyed years of research with a computer virus. He says he wants you back alive so you can undo the damage you've caused. That doesn't ring entirely true to me."

Monashi snorted. "That's what he told you?" She moved away from the door, pacing absently, subconsciously testing the dimensions of her prison. Sokolov watched, held by her ire and restlessness. She frowned, a curiously innocent expression for a woman of her experience. "You say that you already know

Borun is lying to you," she said abruptly. "Well, I'm going to tell you exactly what he's lying about. It's not what you think.

"I *did* leave a virus in the R and D mainframe to wipe out all traces of the work, and I took the research data, too. Ever since I managed to claw my way out of Santiago, I've worked for HelixTech. I've done everything they asked of me. Almost fourteen percent of the company's revenues last year were based on technologies I developed. I'm the best they've got. I could have had anything I wanted in that corporation.

"Do you know why I did what I did? I did it because Karcen Borun paid me to. *He* approached *me* two months ago. He's a powerful man—executive vice-president, chief of security, chief operating officer—and it's not enough for him. Borun wanted my research for himself. He's going to form a new company ripped from the guts of HelixTech. He bought me, just like he's bought other people in key divisions. After all, the royalties I earned on HelixTech's sale of my technologies weren't anywhere near fourteen percent of the company's overall profit."

This is getting interesting, thought Sokolov. He considered Monashi's story. "So you did his dirty work, then turned on him and ran to Icewalk with the data?"

Monashi shook her head. "After I planted the virus, I left HelixTech and met Borun in Santiago. I handed over the research data. Borun paid me half the fee we'd agreed on, with the other half to be automatically deposited into my accounts when the data checked out. He even arranged my introduction to Maartens to help me get away from HelixTech's security sweeps in the city."

"That makes sense," he admitted. "Borun sent me out to cover his tracks, but that still doesn't explain why he wants you back alive." He ground out his cigarette. "If I were just cleaning up his loose ends, he would have paid me to kill you. There's something you're still not telling me."

Geille ignored his distrust. "I lived up to my end of the bargain. Now I can see how Borun is going to live up to his. If he wants me back, it's because he never had any intention of letting me walk after I'd done his dirty work for him. He's going to keep me on a leash to make technology for him. That's what you're taking me back to, Sokolov." She fell silent for a long moment. Absently she sat down on a molded cargo container and stared at the floor. "You know," she said finally, "you're at risk too. If you'd taken me straight back, you'd probably be okay, but Shanassin forced you to make a starfall to get away. Now Borun's going to worry about what I might be telling you for the next two weeks. He'll probably kill you the minute you bring me to him."

"Not likely. Killing freelancers who work for you is a good way to make sure that no freelancers ever work for you again. Word gets around."

Geille dropped her eyes and tried another gambit. "Okay, here's another way to go. Find a place where we can lie low for a time while you check out my story. I'll give you half the money Borun paid me if you help me walk away from this." Her dark eyes gleamed with a hint of desperation. "There's really no reason for you to take me back."

"You might be right . . . if I knew that your story was true, but I have no way to know. Why should I believe you any more than I do Borun?" Sokolov shrugged. "It's one story against the other, and Borun is paying me a great deal of money. I'll take you back."

She watched him for a moment, then tossed her head angrily and stood. "I should have expected this," she muttered. Without another look at him, she stormed toward the door.

"You forgot to ask about the second reason," Sokolov said.

Monashi paused in the doorway. "What second reason?"

"I told you there were two reasons that you might want to get back to Lucullus. Borun might not kill you—but you don't believe that. Fine, but there's another reason you should care about whether or not we fix the astrogation unit." Monashi simply glared at him, waiting. Sokolov met her angry eyes, unmoved. "I have supplies for maybe three months onboard. Six months, if I don't feed you."

The woman's stern glare faded. "You're kidding."

"I didn't plan on making this into an epic voyage, Geille, and I certainly didn't plan on the possibility of requiring dozens, maybe hundreds of starfalls to stumble back to civilization. I expected to be back on Penates by now." He fished around in his pocket for another cigarette but failed to find one. "We're in the same boat, so to speak."

"I don't believe this." Her hair hid her face. "What are you going to do about it?"

"Well, I was going to replace the processor, but it turns out we don't have any of the right kind onboard. I'll have to try to reprogram another processor to handle the functions of the drivespace astrogation computer." .

"That won't be easy."

"I don't see any alternative, other than executing a few starfalls at five days apiece and hoping we get extremely lucky." Sokolov examined the inventory list on the display screen. "Peri, show me a list of processor boards with power, memory, and speed characteristics equal to or exceeding the NX board."

The computer complied, narrowing the list to four. Sokolov studied the list, thinking. He'd literally be wiping the board clean and trying to generate a couple of million lines of code to perform the drivespace calculations and control the mechanical systems that triggered starfall. Peri could help him write most of the code, of course, but it would still be a job of several days, even if everything worked the first time.

"Use the EC board," Geille said. She'd moved behind him and was looking over his shoulder at the list. "You can probably get away with simply adding new code to do what you want instead of trying to rewrite what's there. It should be easier."

"Are you sure?"

"I'm a computer engineer. This is what I do." Geille returned her attention to him. "Look, I have no interest in starving to death out here. I can help you fix the astrogation unit. I'd go crazy sitting around watching Jack Everstar movies while you worked on this."

Sokolov swiveled the stool around to study her, considering the offer. Monashi leaned over the test bench, refusing to look away.

"I'm going to have to keep a close eye on what you do," the bounty hunter warned.

"I know."

He held her eyes a moment longer, then agreed with a slow nod. "Okay, I'll take you up on it." He hesitated, then added, "I'm still taking you back. But if you help me jury-rig an astrogation processor, I'll see what I can do to help you walk out of HelixTech in one piece."

Monashi flicked her eyes at him and snorted. "I'm not counting on much, Sokolov. I'm doing this because I can, and because it's my neck, too. Come on—let's pull the EC board and get to work."

Chapter Six

MONASHI PROVED TO be better than Sokolov could have imagined. He'd always viewed programming as a strictly logical exercise, a process of figuring out what you needed to do and then doing it. But within an hour of working with Geille, he understood that she had an intuition for the work, a sense of rightness that simply did not let her make mistakes. Processes that would have taken days for him to unravel were as clear as day to her. In fact, he slowed her down considerably by asking her to explain what she was doing at each step.

Sokolov's job was simple. He had to provide the algorithms to perform drivespace calculations so that Monashi could program them into thousands of lines of code. Any pilot rated to fly a ship had to know how to use the navigation equipment onboard, but some academies and schools still taught the exhaustive process of what the computers had to do in order to make a starfall. For the first time in his career, Sokolov was glad that he'd been trained the old-fashioned way.

Geille knew nothing about astrogation and drivespace physics, but she attacked the programming difficulties with a confidence and competence that astounded Sokolov. Her primary tool in writing the code was Peri, of course. Humans couldn't build complicated programs without relying heavily on the computer's own self-programming features. But the conversion of the EC board, a processor loaded with software and hardware connections designed specifically to monitor the ship's mass reactor, to a navigation system would have proved impossible for Sokolov and Peri to handle alone. They started working on generating code for the astrogation calculations and controls thirty-eight hours into their drivespace voyage.

Forty-one hours later, they were done.

"Looks as if I got the right person at the right time," Sokolov said, examining Geille's work. "It's a good thing you weren't the run-of-the-mill thug or criminal I usually go after."

"You'll excuse me if I don't share your sense of good fortune," Geille said blandly. She sat at the main terminal in the cramped computer room behind the bridge. Her eyes fixed on the screen, she flicked her fingers over sections of the program, linking small sections into larger and larger structures. "It's coming together well. How long until starrise?"

Sokolov checked with Nancy. "A little more than forty hours."

"No idea where we're going to show up?"

"There's about a one in a million chance that we'll appear within a tenth of a light-year of Lucullus. Other than that, we could be anywhere by now. Well, anywhere within a few light-years of where we were when I punched the starfall blind."

"Isn't there a chance we might show up inside a star, or on a collision course with a planet or something?"

Sokolov laughed coarsely. "You're a computer engineer. You can do the math. Peri's stardrive is rated for a jump of up to 5.73 light-years, so you can imagine a sphere with a radius of 5.73 light-years, centered on the exact point in the Lucullus system where we made starfall. We'll appear somewhere inside that sphere, not necessarily right at the outer edge either." He sipped at a mug of coffee. "Ninety-nine point nine nine nine percent of that volume consists of interstellar space. We're almost certainly going to make starrise billions of kilometers from anything." He shrugged, then added, "I'll be on the command deck when we hit starrise, just in case."

"That's it." Monashi straightened then leaned back in her chair to stretch languorously. Sokolov admired the smooth curves beneath her jump suit for a moment before she hugged herself tight. Fatigue showed clearly on Geille's face. "We're done."

"Think it will work?"

"We won't know for sure until we let Peri get real sensor data and feed it into the board, but yes, I think it will."

"Good. I'm going to get some sleep." He stepped out into the passageway, holding the hatch open for her. "After you."

She looked up over her shoulder. "I should have said almost done. I've got some housekeeping to do before I can shut everything down."

"All right. Peri?"

"Yes, Pete?"

"Give me a full command function lockdown. Geille can keep working in the applications she now has open, but don't open anything else for her." Sokolov glanced at the comptech, who was watching him with a slightly bored look on her face. "Wake me if Geille does not return to her quarters within thirty minutes—"

"An hour would be better," Monashi interjected.

"Okay, an hour then. Once she's in her room, lock the door behind her."

"Understood, Pete," Peri replied. "Geille, what do you want me to do with the subroutines on your dataslate?"

"Pull them up, Peri," Geille said. "I want to see what I put there, just in case I left out something important."

"Okay," the computer said brightly.

Sokolov watched a moment longer then headed down the passageway to his quarters. He'd slept only once since they started work on the astrogation unit, and he was exhausted. He let himself into his cabin and locked the door behind him. The captain's cabin was the largest stateroom on the ship, but Sokolov had never bothered to provide it with anything more than the most spartan furnishings. He idly rooted through his collection of entertainment crystals then decided there was nothing he wanted to waste sleep watching.

Wincing as various joints creaked in protest, he shrugged off his flight jacket, pulled his shirt over his head and threw it on the deck, then crawled into bed in his trousers.

"Lights, Peri," he muttered. The room dimmed into darkness.

He woke up when the door to his room slid open. Groggy with sleep, he rolled to one side just in time to avoid the blow of a heavy pipefitter's wrench. The bludgeon flashed down on him again, but he parried the attack with his cybernetic arm and was rewarded with a bone-jarring impact. Cursing in Narislavic, he scrambled out of the sheets and found his footing as his attacker, nothing more than a silhouette against the light of the passage outside, came at him again. The long wrench whistled through the air, smashing a lamp into wreckage as Sokolov danced back out of the way.

"Lights!" he called.

Geille Monashi leaped toward him, teeth bared in a fierce snarl. She clutched the wrench in both hands, swinging with all her strength. Sokolov jumped back from one swing and ducked under another, then he caught the bludgeon above her hands, spun toward her, and jerked it away from her with the mechanical strength of his right arm.

"That's enough!" he barked.

Geille slammed her left elbow hard into his jaw, stomped on his right instep, then wheeled to ram her right fist into his breadbasket. The blows rocked him like hammers. He countered with a flurry of strikes designed to drive her away and gained a meter of separation. Blood streaming from a bloody lip, Sokolov panted for breath, still trying to come to grips with the situation.

Geille balanced on the balls of her feet, arms raised. He recognized the stance as a street style common in Santiago. *I don't recall reading anything about martial arts in her dossier,* he thought, shaking off the haze of sleep and pain.

Drawing a deep breath, he circled to get in between Monashi and the open hatch, then he closed slowly, advancing in a wary crouch, ready to parry or strike. He'd studied aikido, tae-kwon-do, and some Aleer kanin. He'd seen enough to know that she was good but not as well trained as he was. He also had the advantages of size and strength.

"I thought you were smarter than this," he rasped angrily. "Don't make me show you what a bad mistake you're making."

His training was the only thing that kept him alive in the next instant. Circling away from him, Geille reached up and yanked the zipper of her jump suit down to her navel, revealing smooth golden skin. Sokolov halted, taken aback. Monashi reached into her clothing and pulled out a small knife. Feinting a low snap kick, she whirled in close, the white blade slashing with blinding speed.

The first cut missed short, misdirection to hide the strike of her left hand to his jaw. Sokolov saw stars but kept his feet, twisting away from the blow. *Damn! Nancy, load Speed Five, execute!*

Acknowledged, Pyotr.

Geille reversed the knife and wheeled inside his reach, spinning to punch the blade at his abdomen, then the world slowed as the reflex-enhancement kicked in, changing her attack into a graceful motion that he anticipated and rolled away from. He slammed his left hand into her knife arm, but she managed to roll with the strike, recovering with surprising speed for an unenhanced human. Her counter would have buried the knife in his neck if he hadn't twisted away, raising his right arm to ward off the blow. He caught the knife blade through the palm of his cybernetic hand and howled as the limb's damage sensors poured pain messages into his neural system.

Automatically he leaned back and kicked her legs out from under her while wrenching the knife away, still lodged in his hand. Geille rolled and darted out the door, dodging down the passageway. In between light-shattered fragments of time superimposed on his consciousness by the nanocomputer and its reflex wiring, he had time to recoil in surprise. *She's better than I expected,* he thought.

Sokolov paused to pull the knife out of his hand, ignoring the sparks and scrape of metal on metal. Tucking the weapon into the waistband of his trousers, he moved out of his quarters carefully, scanning left and right.

"Peri? Where is she?"

"She's on the command deck, Pete," the computer replied. "Pete, Geille cut out my—"

"Not now!" he snapped.

He turned left and padded up the passageway toward the dark command deck. Arms raised to guard his head, he climbed up the short ladder leading up to the bridge. His arms and legs were beginning to ache, twinges of pain rippling through his muscles and joints. He'd have to finish this quickly.

Monashi waited for him by the captain's chair. She'd rearmed herself, this time with a small but sharp probe from the electronics bench. He halted, looking up at her.

"Stop this," he said. *Nancy, load Blade-Three.*

"You can't take me back to Borun," she answered. Deadly determination drove all emotion from her face. "You'll have to kill me first."

"You don't mean that," he replied.

With a sharp cry, she jumped into the air and launched a spinning kick at his head.

Execute. Sokolov stopped the kick with a hard block, then he snapped a twenty-centimeter knife blade of his own out of his cybernetic arm, a gleaming blade normally concealed in the limb's forearm. Moving precisely in the pattern dictated by Nancy's enhancement program, Sokolov slashed the weapon out of Monashi's grasp, laying open her hand. She gasped in shock.

He retracted the blade, then caught her by the leg and arm and threw her to the floor. Geille locked her arm around his and brought him down with her. The nav console went with them, its contents clattering on the deck. Sokolov fell on top of her. She rolled over to straddle him, flailing at his face, but he boxed her ears and wrestled her to the deck again. This time, he pinned her beneath him, trapping both her wrists with his right hand and keeping both her knees safely outside his own.

Geille struggled beneath him, face contorted with anger and effort. "Let me go!"

Sokolov held her fast. Her face was mere centimeters from his, slick with sweat; her hair was plastered to her forehead. "I said *stop this!*" he demanded.

"Go to hell," she grunted. She struggled again, but he held her easily. "Did you think . . . I was going to let you bring me in . . . without even trying to get free?"

"I *trusted* you!" he roared. "I thought we understood each other!"

She glared at him, panting, pinned beneath him. Sweat gleamed on the smooth, golden skin between her breasts as her chest rose and fell. Sokolov closed his eyes, trying to slow his racing heart. *Nancy, stop Speed-Five; stop Blade-Three.* White pain flooded his body, but he gritted his teeth and endured it, refusing to allow his muscles and nerves to distract him from the confrontation at hand.

"Is this how you want to go?" he growled. "Restraints? Sedation?"

Geille's anger faded. "No," she said in a small voice.

Sokolov straightened, searching her face. To his surprise, her features were pale and her eyes were wide with fright. She's scared, he thought. Good. Maybe we won't have to do this again. His stomach ached more than it should have from the punches she'd landed. He checked Nancy and found that he'd been asleep for almost five hours.

"How did you get into my cabin? How did you disarm the curfew Peri was supposed to enforce?"

"I cut into the control panel of your door, disarmed the lock, and cut out Peri's audio in your quarters. She's pretty mad at me." Geille winced and wriggled her hips under him, searching for leverage. "Can you get off me now?"

He fixed his eyes on her. "You tell me," he said softly.

Geille met his gaze for a long moment, then closed her eyes and nodded. "I won't try something like this again. You don't have to knock me out."

"How can I believe that?"

"You're a god-damned cyborg," she snarled. "I guess you don't have to believe me, do you?" She slipped her hand out from under his and glanced at the long cut across her palm before blanching and looking away. Blood streamed down her forearm, spattering the metal deck plates. "Let me up," she said in a weaker voice. "I want to find a first-aid kit."

Sokolov studied her, then abruptly pushed himself up, scrambling to his feet. Geille rolled to her side, staring at the deck. The marks of the struggle showed on her face, on her arms, punches that Sokolov didn't remember landing. He hadn't held back against her; she was good enough, strong and quick enough, that he would have lost if he hadn't fought back hard.

"What would you have done if you'd killed me?" he asked suddenly. "I told you the ship would be destroyed if I died."

Monashi didn't say anything. He sighed and dropped into the

command chair. Across the bridge, lights flickered and played on the engineering displays. It should have been cold and dark in the middle of drivespace. Sokolov watched for a long moment, puzzled, then he tapped the key strokes that echoed the engineer's display on the command console.

The *Peregrine* was returning to normal space.

"Peri! What's happening?" he shouted in alarm. "We're coming out of drivespace!"

The ship's computer delayed a moment before answering. "I don't know, Pete. I agree with your assessment of the sensor data, but it makes no sense. I must have a fault somewhere."

"Open the viewports!"

Around the perimeter of the bridge, the heavy blast shields covering the ship's narrow vision ports began to retract. Instead of the featureless black of drivespace, a black dot hovered at the center of his vision, growing larger moment by the moment. Stars, impossibly distant, flecked its dimensionless surface. Despite himself, Sokolov stared.

"This is impossible!"

In his gut, the familiar wrenching of transition from drive-space to normal space made him queasy. Behind him, Monashi climbed slowly to her feet, clinging to the nearest rail, her bloody hand pressed tightly against her stomach.

"What is it?" she asked.

"We're making starrise."

"It hasn't been five days, has it?"

"No. We're about thirty hours short."

Sokolov swore and began to power up the ship's systems, preparing for their return to the normal universe. Around him, consoles flickered to life. Systems hummed and clicked, initializing themselves under his direction.

"That's impossible! Everything has to spend the same amount of time in drivespace. Everything!" Monashi said. "There must be some mistake."

"You tell me! What did you do to my ship?"

"Pete—" Geille's voice faltered— "I didn't touch engineering or navigation. We've never activated the new board. I *couldn't* have done this."

He looked out the viewport again. From some incredible distance, blackness and stars rushed up on the ship in a phantasmagoric onslaught, as if they were falling bodily into the universe around them. A brilliant aura of shattered photons blazed around the hull, a flash of many-colored light that heralded their return to the tangible cosmos. Radio speakers, dead throughout drivespace, abruptly crackled with the faint hiss of stellar noise. The ship's artificial gravity quietly adjusted, normalizing against the new background.

Sokolov's senses reeled in rebellion.

"How in the hell did this happen?" he roared at the computer. "We cut thirty hours off our submergence!"

"I'm at a loss to explain it, Pete," Peri said. "I have no basis for speculation."

Geille drifted forward, staring at the black starfield beyond the windows. It was dark outside, without a hint of any strong illumination. Faint as the fingers of a ghost, starlight glimmered on the smooth planes of her face.

"Sokolov," she said quietly, "where are we?"

* * * * *

It took Sokolov almost an hour to answer Monashi's question. He had no idea where *Peregrine* was and no immediate references that made sense. He ended up matching constellations by using Peri's navigational database to run projections of where they'd have to be in order for the stars to look as they did. After a dozen tries, he got close enough for Peri's nav program to do the rest.

Monashi stayed clear of him while he worked, keeping to herself in an unspoken truce. After allowing the ship's phymech to dress her hand, she passed the time gazing out the viewport. From time to time, he caught her watching him with reluctant interest, arms clamped tightly around her torso as if to ward off despair. Hostility set her face in a cold scowl; curiosity kept her riveted to the spot, a caged cat measuring its captor. For his part, Sokolov ignored her. He had other things on his mind, although he sensed her attention shifting between the stars outside and the spot between his shoulder blades.

At length he blew out his breath, ran his fingers through his short-cropped hair, and leaned back in his seat. "Got it."

"Well?" she asked.

"We're two and a half light-years from Lucullus, trailward and below the system in relation to rest of the Verge." Sokolov moved over to the viewport, staying a good arm's length from Geille, and pointed at a brilliant blue star. "That's Lucullus. We're far enough away that Alpha and Beta look like one very bright star. We're literally in the middle of nowhere."

"How long will it take us to get back?"

"Three or four days to recharge the stardrive, then a five-day trip through drivespace, assuming that we don't come out early again. If we hadn't come up with a way to jury-rig the astrogation unit . . . well, we're trillions of kilometers from the nearest star system. At her best acceleration, it would take Peri almost five years to get home in normal space." He looked away from the distant blazing stars outside and regarded her for a long moment, his face impassive.

"I guess that means we've got a few days to kill," Geille mused aloud without meeting his eyes.

She continued to gaze out the viewport, eyes dark and wide, a faint apprehension apparent in the parting of her lips, the slight crease in her brow. She'd hardly spoken a word since they arrived. Sokolov studied her, trying to read her expression. Fear? he guessed. Restlessness?

He craned his head to follow her gaze outside, wondering what she saw. The Milky Way was a brilliant band of glory tilting across the sky. No harsh sunlight dimmed the sight of the stars around them. She's awed, he realized. He felt it too, of course, but he'd been out here before. Not in this particular place, but any time he'd jumped into interstellar space instead of making starrise in the warm confines of a planetary system, he'd seen the same thing, felt the same vague terror.

"First starrise?" he asked quietly.

Monashi nodded. "I've been trying to understand it for an hour now. It's beyond words. How can we take something like this for granted?"

"It's easier when you travel from one system to another. You appear, and there's a sun, maybe even a planet in visual range. You've just exchanged one locale for another. Interstellar space is different. It's the absolute lack of location." Watching her reaction, Sokolov was reminded of the awe he'd felt in his first few trips. Something in the human programming demanded a sun in the sky and earth under the feet. Millions of years of evolution had equipped humans with a healthy fear of night, of falling, of solitude, of disconnection and dissociation. "You can't get any further out than this," he added.

"In Santiago they've got an underground reservoir," Geille said slowly, "a straight-sided shaft maybe two hundred meters in diameter and over a kilometer deep. When I was a little girl, we'd creep down there to go swimming. Once, when I was out in the middle, the sector lost power. All the lights went out. There I was, treading water in pitch blackness. I couldn't see the sides or the ceiling, but I could *feel* all that dark, cold water beneath my feet." She shivered and looked up at him. "I knew I could float like that for hours, but I still panicked. I could feel myself sinking without going anywhere.

"This—" she nodded at the dark expanse beyond the viewport— "feels like that."

He understood what she meant. Drifting in the starry darkness an unimaginable distance from light, from life, from the company of others, precipitated a vertigo of the soul. Drivespace made you wonder whether you were real. Open space like this showed you what you were and then rubbed your insignificance in your face. He snorted.

"Enjoy the view while you can. I mean to get out of here as soon as the tachyon collectors recharge."

Geille looked up at him, a wry smile on her face. Their eyes met for a long moment, an abrupt shock of human contact, of companionship, in the face of the cold, dark night. She looked away, turning from the viewport and pacing catlike across the command deck.

"Any idea why we came out of drivespace early?" she asked over her shoulder.

"None at all. I've had Peri running down anything on drivespace anomalies, and I've come up with nothing. No one's ever heard of such a thing. It breaks all the equations."

"There have been drivespace accidents before, right? Things that go wrong?"

"Sure. Peri's databases hold hundreds of accounts of ships disappearing or making course errors of catastrophic proportions, especially back in the early days." Sokolov drifted back to the command console, absently searching his pockets for a cigarette. "If you have something go seriously wrong in drivespace, they just don't see you again."

"That's what happened to us."

Sokolov shrugged. "Don't ask me to explain it. I know how to fly, I know enough astrogation not to get lost, I know a thing or two about tracking people down and getting them to do things they don't want to do. I'm not a drivespace theorist."

"We had an unprecedented, unheard-of drivespace event, and we just were lucky enough to survive it—without knowing what happened or why. I don't know about you, Sokolov, but I don't believe in luck. Is there any way we could have lost track of time? Maybe we came out when we were supposed to but just didn't realize it."

"Peri might have been tampered with. Maybe Yeiwei screwed up her system clock," Sokolov mused. He found a smoke and lit it, thinking.

"He didn't," Peri stated. "I know exactly what Yeiwei tampered with. I can show you the security tapes."

Sokolov smiled to himself—the computer almost sounded defensive. "She's probably right," he observed. Nancy knew to the second how much time had elapsed, and Sokolov was absolutely confident that his nanocomputer could not have somehow been altered without his knowledge. They had been in drivespace for eighty-six hours, nineteen minutes, and forty-seven seconds. He'd recorded it in Nancy's memory banks without even thinking about it. "There has to be some other explanation."

"What are you going to do?"

"Look into it while the drive recharges. We're not going anywhere until it does."

Geille wrapped her arms around her torso, facing him again. She leaned against the rail dividing the command console from the empty operator stations ringing the deck. Ghostly green phosphorescence limned her features in the darkness of the bridge.

"So what about me? This doesn't change anything."

"No, it doesn't."

"You can't trust me. What comes next?"

"That depends on you." He regarded her without answering for a long moment, until the woman lowered her eyes. He reached up to draw the cigarette away from his mouth. His gaze fell on the angry thin-lipped hole that her knife had punched in the pseudo-skin covering the palm of his right hand. She's capable of killing me, he reminded himself. She's probably too smart to try it again, at least not the same way. She'll try to think of some other way to overpower me. "I ought to knock you out and lock you in your quarters for the rest of the trip.

"You're not going to?" Geille frowned.

Again he was struck by the way her confidence melted when she turned her attention to her own thoughts. The hard edge in her expression was a conscious facade, a front she raised against the world. When she wasn't thinking about it, she seemed like another person altogether. The contrast fascinated him.

The edge returned too quickly. When her thoughts ran their unseen course, she looked up sharply, studying him. In a guarded voice, she asked, "Why not?"

"Do we have a truce?"

"You tell me. I've got nothing to promise."

"Do we have a truce?" He stood, unfolding his long limbs and locking his hands in the overhead. The cigarette's acrid smoke gleamed in the dim light. "Don't make me regret this mission any more than I already do, Geille. I'll do what I have to do in order to bring you in. That's what I am. Just this once, I don't want to be an asshole about it."

"You picked the wrong line of work then," she retorted. Her face was taut, tense, but after searching his face in the shadows, she dropped her eyes and nodded. "Okay. Truce. There's no point in trying anything while we're out here."

He didn't believe her. She didn't give up that easily. He could tell by the set of her shoulders and the dull mechanical ache transfixing his right hand. Wondering what she would try next and when she'd make her move, he smiled coldly.

"Truce. We're not going anywhere for a while, and I still need a couple of hours of sleep before I tackle the drivespace problem again. I know you haven't slept for twenty hours or more, so I'm going to lock you inside your quarters for a while. Don't cause trouble. You know the rules."

Geille agreed with an imperceptible nod. "Okay."

*　*　*　*　*

After making sure that Geille was secured in her room, Sokolov went back to bed for a couple of hours. He didn't sleep well. Even though the ship's artificial gravity revealed nothing about their circumstances, he still felt as if he were plummeting unprotected through the endless black void around them. When he finally did fall asleep, he found himself reliving the day when the surgeons had taken off his right arm and replaced it with the cybernetic prosthesis he'd worn for five years now. His new right arm was far stronger and faster than the one he'd been born with, but from time to time he still experienced twinges of phantom pain. The cybernetic limb ached as though it were real.

Nancy assured him that the knife thrust through the machine's palm had not damaged any major systems or structures. The limb's self-repair routines would be sufficient to patch the puncture. The information didn't reassure him. *Can't sleep, Nancy,* he told the nanocomputer. *Run Light Sleep, duration two hours, normal waking conditions.*

Acknowledged. Good night, Pyotr. Blackness descended for a timeless instant as the computer triggered his own sleep centers with gentle precision.

Despite the nanocomputer's clock, it seemed that only a heartbeat had passed before he opened his eyes again. He preferred natural sleep, but allowing his cyberware to mandate rest on an overweary body sometimes worked wonders. He rolled out of bed, feeling physically recovered even if his mind, his will, still ached for rest.

Sokolov showered, dressed in gray trousers and a black turtleneck shirt, and then padded back to the ship's galley to find something to eat. He checked on Geille and found that she was still asleep. Satisfied that she wasn't going anywhere soon, he spent the next two hours performing the most rigorous examination of the stardrive and the computer's sensor data that he could. He wanted to find out how they'd emerged from drive-space early.

He was disappointed. Peri automatically recorded all sensor information she collected, but in drivespace there was nothing to be sensed. Right before they'd begun to starrise, Peri's mass detector had recorded a strange gravitational signature. If they'd passed near a planet in normal space, the signal wouldn't have been unusual, but energy—particularly gravitational energy—didn't propagate in drivespace unless it was enclosed within a drive field such as that projected by a ship in the middle of a starfall. The signal could not have come from outside Peri's hull, but *Peregrine* had nothing aboard that could conceivably create a gravitational signal.

"This doesn't make any sense," he muttered, dropping his note pad to the console.

"I'm sorry, Pete," Peri answered. "I think you're going to have to run a level-one diagnostic on me. I must have a fault somewhere."

"I don't think that's it, Peri. Even if you did record some kind of extraneous signal on the mass detector, the fact remains that we came out of drivespace right after you recorded it. Something made us emerge early. That's not a computer fault." Sokolov stared at the sensor readouts, brow knotted. "I've checked out the stardrive. It says everything's normal, and then the diagnostic on the new board tells me that we're still in drive-space."

"Clearly we're not," the ship replied. "My sensors confirm that we're not in drivespace."

Sokolov glanced out the viewport at the brilliant starfield beyond the glass. "So do mine, Peri. What in hell is going on here? We're not in drivespace, but somehow the stardrive thinks we still are, and no one's ever heard of a mechanical fault that could have brought us out of drivespace early."

"Could the sesheyan have planned this?" Peri asked. "I don't know of any sabotage techniques that would do it. I'm virtually certain that nothing he did would have caused us to starrise before schedule, but I might not be aware of all the possibilities."

"You're smarter than you look, Peri. I know lots of people who couldn't admit to that." He stood and moved over to the nav console, studying the display. In the center, the drivespace astrogation unit blinked and flashed. "Yeiwei pulled the astrogation boards, probably to make sure you couldn't starfall. There are other ways to do it, but you had them locked down. He couldn't kill the power system or the stardrive itself.

"When we jumped, the astrogation unit wasn't even powered. I can't believe that Yeiwei knew some secret way to bring ships out of drivespace and decided to use it for the first time on us." Sokolov thought a moment longer. "In fact, I'm sure of it. If Shanassin's people knew how to do that, they'd be using it all the time. It's perfect for piracy. You get one of your people onto the target, you cause it to drop out of drivespace before it reaches its destination, and you hit it while it's stranded in the middle of nowhere."

He decided to change tactics. "Peri, is anything around here? Any significant mass, anything giving us a radar return?"

The ship hummed to itself for a moment. "Nothing on the mass detector, Pete, but it would have to be close or big to show up. As per your standing orders, I've been remaining on the passive EM sensors. Do you want me to go active?"

"Let's take a few radar sweeps." Sokolov usually preferred not to give away his own location with active radar signals. In general, the ship you were looking for would know you were there before you detected him, and he'd spot you from a lot farther away. Passive systems like computer-enhanced video, the mass detector, and the electromagnetic receiving array made a lot more sense in a system like Lucullus, where you often didn't want to advertise your presence. "See if you can spot anything."

"Okay, we're pinging," Peri announced.

Sokolov moved over to look at the display. The radar screen remained blank. "Nothing yet."

"What did you expect to find?" Peri asked.

"I don't know. I just wanted to see if there was anything in the vicinity." He scratched his head and sat down in the command chair. "I don't know what else to check."

"Pete? Can I ask you a question?"

"What's on your mind, Peri?"

"When you first brought Geille Monashi onboard, you ordered me to set Prisoner Handling Protocol Three, but over the last few days you appear to have relaxed your own security measures. Should I lower mine, too?"

"No. She is not to go into engineering, the armory, or your computer banks unless I am with her. I am clearly not under duress. Also, you will disregard any command she gives you unless I am present and give you my specific consent."

"Understood." The computer paused. "You want me to consider her a threat, but you're not going to restrain her?"

"That's right."

"Can I ask why?"

Sokolov looked over at the small red light marking the video pickup on the bridge. Peri had an uncanny ability to stare at him through her internal cameras.

"She's not that kind of a threat."

"She disabled some of my security hardware so she could make an attempt on your life, Pete. Are you certain?"

"I know what I'm doing, Peri," he snapped. "I— Never mind. You're not going to understand."

The computer fell silent, leaving him to his own thoughts. Sokolov turned his back on the video pickup and threw his attention to a screen full of meaningless numbers, monitoring data that indicated that their stardrive worked perfectly.

"Nothing's easy anymore," he muttered. "We're not supposed to be out here, not supposed to be trying to solve a drive-space anomaly. I should be in Port Royal by now, living off Karcen Borun's money. I didn't ask for this."

Peri waited without speaking.

"Geille Monashi's not supposed to be—"

He bit off the words, angry at himself. *Peregrine* was his ship, nothing more than a computer with some very sophisticated software. He didn't owe her any explanations. He certainly didn't owe it to himself to use the machine as his confessional. He despised vanity and pretentiousness.

"Be what, Pete?" Peri asked quietly. "I don't understand your last remark."

He chose not to answer. He was wondering if he knew what he was doing after all.

Chapter Seven

ABOUT THREE HOURS later, Peri intruded into his dark, silent gloom. "Geille's awake," she reported. "She says she would like to speak to you."

Sokolov stirred, tearing his attention from the displays in front of him. He'd made no significant progress. "Go ahead, Peri. Put her through." The computer opened the ship's intercom. Sokolov thumbed a switch and rasped, "What is it, Geille?"

"I'm awake. Could you let me out so that I can get something to eat?" Monashi's voice was high and distant in the speakers.

"We still have a truce?"

"Yes." She hesitated, and then added, "I need a favor."

He twisted to look at the blank speaker grille. "What?" he asked cautiously.

"Can you bring me something to wear?"

"What's wrong with your clothes?" he asked.

"You didn't exactly give me a chance to pack before we left, Sokolov. I've been wearing this jump suit for a week now, and it's starting to get to me. Just give me something to wear while I clean my own clothes."

He shrugged, even though she couldn't see. "I'll see what I can find. Be there in a minute."

Swinging his feet to the deck, he stood, stretched, and left the command deck. He went to his cabin and checked over his wardrobe. He came up with a couple of ship suits, two T-shirts, and an assortment of socks. He carried them back to her stateroom and checked the door's narrow vision block as a routine precaution.

Geille wasn't lying in wait to attack. She was drying her hair

in the room's tiny shower cubicle, a towel wrapped around her
torso as she leaned forward to tease her black hair beneath the
warm air of the blower. He watched her through the door for a
long moment, caught by the sight of her slender limbs and
smooth features. She almost looked like someone normal, a
beautiful woman getting ready to go to work in some mundane
job for the day, maybe a publicist or sharp young marketing
exec. She didn't look like someone he was planning on taking
back to some black and cheerless fate at Karcen Borun's hands.

She glanced up into the mirror, and her eyes met Sokolov's
through the narrow block in the door. She watched him watching her, her expression unfathomable, and then the hard scowl
slowly returned. Deliberately, she returned to drying her hair,
unconcerned by her state of dress.

"Well?" she asked. "What did you find?"

He keyed the door open and stepped inside, laying out the
clothes he'd brought on the bunk. "Not much, I'm afraid."

Geille glanced at the selection. "You don't get out much, do
you?"

He shrugged. "I don't bother to keep up with the latest look.
. . . Peri?"

"Yes, Pete?"

"Let Geille out when she's ready." He picked up the tidy
bundle of clothes she'd been wearing when he picked her up.
"There's a laundry machine just aft of the galley. It's not much,
but it works. I'll throw these in."

"Don't ruin them," Geille called as he retreated. Sokolov
didn't notice her long, thoughtful gaze following him as he left.

After he started the laundry cycle, he returned to the bridge
and tried to distract himself with a few games of solitaire. He'd
already tackled most of the ship's maintenance during their
drivespace submergence, and according to Peri's engineering
readouts, it was going to take at least another seventy hours for
the ship's tachyon collectors to build up a sufficient charge for
another starfall. The mindless game failed to hold his attention
for long, and he found himself sitting in the bridge, lights
dimmed, gazing out at the stars.

"Do you want some company?"

He wheeled lazily in the chair. Geille stood by the ladder leading to the command deck, dressed in one of his ship suits. It was comically long on her, but she'd cuffed the trousers and sleeves to gain some measure of dignity.

"Sure. Come on up."

Geille clambered up to the deck, circling the bridge to take in the view. "Looks about the same as when I left it."

"It ought to. We're not going anywhere. We're not even drifting."

"How long until we jump again?"

"A little less than three days."

She winced. "I never really realized how much *waiting* is involved in space travel. I'd never even left Penates until a few weeks ago."

"The wait's not bad, compared to the alternative." He put his feet up on the command console. "With a full tachyon charge, the *Peregrine* can travel over five light-years in one hundred and twenty-one hours. A big ship—a heavy freighter or a cruiser, say—might travel two or three times as far in a single starfall. Even if I have to get to someplace twenty or thirty light-years away, I can make it in six or eight weeks of travel, depending on how fast *Peregrine* can recharge after each leap."

"It would still take you something like four years of constant travel to cross human space to the Orion Frontier," she said, eyes distant as she added up the numbers in her head. "Even getting from the Verge to Old Space would be a journey of months."

"Well, if I had to go that far, I'd buy passage on a bigger ship. *Peregrine* can piggyback on almost anything bigger than she is. Just last year, I came from Tendril on *Lighthouse*. I cut three weeks off the trip by paying for a docking ring."

"What were you doing in Tendril?"

"Working."

"Oh." Geille measured him, thinking. "How do you get to be a bounty hunter anyway? Are you from Penates, or did you come here from somewhere else?" She offered a shallow smile. "You seem to know me pretty well, but I know nothing about you."

"You don't need to," he replied. Her face contracted in irritation. She turned away to examine the ship's controls, trailing her hand along the readouts and yokes at the pilot's chair. On a whim, Sokolov decided to indulge her. "Okay, fine. I'll give you three questions."

"That's it? Wait, don't count that as one." Geille stroked her chin. "Okay, first question. Where are you from?"

"Lucullus is as good a place as any."

"If you're going to play the game, play it right. Where are you really from?"

Sokolov frowned, hesitating before he answered. "A planet called Novo Tver. Nariac Domain."

"You're a Nariac?" Geille said. "Don't count that one either. You're a long way from home."

She filed the response away and considered her next question. He could see the wheels turning in her head as she tried to fit the information he'd just given her into the puzzle. The Nariac Domain was a stellar nation on the other side of human space from the Verge; it had never had much of the way in territorial interests in the Verge. That made him an expatriate or a criminal.

When she finished considering the first answer, she scratched her chin and steadied on him again. "Why do you hunt people for a living? You have a ship, and you're a good pilot. There has to be something easier."

Sokolov sighed, mulling over his answer. She'd found one he wasn't comfortable with. "I'm good at it," he said finally, "and most of the time it's a public service. You wouldn't believe some of the things I've seen since I started doing this. The people I go after deserve to get what they have coming to them."

"Even me?" she asked.

He spread his hands. "Not for me to say. It's a little late for me to begin applying some kind of moral code to my life. I do what I'm paid to do. There's a morality in that."

"Not much."

Geille thought about that at some length. He could tell she wasn't happy with that answer—how could she be, given her situation?—and she was seeking some way to apply it against him. Before she asked her next question, Sokolov saw something he didn't expect.

The sensor display flickered and came to life. At the extreme edge of the screen, a single contact flickered, ghostly and faint. "What the hell?" he murmured, sitting up straight. He rapped out a set of commands on the display, checking the scale. "Peri, how far out is that radar hit?"

"I'm checking, Pete." The computer paused. "Okay, I've got a range: one point twenty-six light-hours."

"Light-*hours?* That's more than a billion kilometers away! Your sensors aren't rated for that kind of range."

"Conditions are ideal, Pete. There's nothing out here to interfere with radar. These returns are actually the first sweeps I did when you ordered me to go active."

"That was a couple of hours ago," he said, even though he knew that it made sense.

Radar signals propagated at the speed of light. If something was a light-hour distant, it would take the beam an hour to travel to the contact and then an hour to come back.

"What is it?" Geille asked, moving up to look at the display. "Another ship?"

"There shouldn't be anything out here. Interstellar space is empty. The odds of us showing up in the vicinity of something big enough to give us a radar return are astronomical." Sokolov fiddled with the display readouts. "Could be a ship, although it would be very large if that's the case—a battleship or super-freighter might be big enough. It's more likely that we're looking at an asteroid or comet that was flung out of its own system."

"What are you going to do?"

Sokolov leaned back, studying the display. "It's not maneuvering. Steady course, no acceleration. We're getting radar returns off the contact, so anything there would certainly be able to pick up our radar signal." He rubbed his real hand over his artificial one, thinking. "If it's a ship, it's not paying attention to us. Must be a rock."

"If it is a ship . . ." Monashi paused. "It might not be human, right? Human ships don't jump into the middle of interstellar space, not when they can starrise within a few light-minutes of the planet they're heading for."

He nodded absently. With one hand, he called up the piloting command display and began to key in an intercept course. "How long will it take us to get there, Peri?"

"A little more than nine hours, Pete."

Geille looked at him. "You're going to take a look?"

"We've got time to kill, and I'm curious." Sokolov looked up at her from his seat. "Even if it's nothing but an old comet, it's something to do. We've got days before we can punch the star-drive and head home. You never know . . . it might be something interesting."

The woman fell silent, studying the curving intercept course in the nav display. She moved to face him, leaning over the console. "Could this have anything to do with our early starrise?"

Sokolov scowled. "How in hell would I know that? I guess it could. I'll tell you in a few hours."

Something in her posture, her expression, suddenly clicked in Sokolov's head. He took his eyes from the displays and controls, looking up at her face.

She said softly, "Hours?"

He nodded. His throat was suddenly dry.

"Do you want to know what my third question was?" Geille leaned forward, resting her hands on the arms of Sokolov's chair. "I wanted to know if there's anything I can do to convince you not to take me back to Borun. There's got to be some kind of arrangement we can reach."

"I can't promise—"

"I wouldn't believe you if you did," she replied.

As if he were watching someone else, Sokolov saw his hands rise to reach for the seal of her jump suit. He deliberately pulled the zipper down from the golden skin of her throat to the base of her smooth, hard belly. She stood bared to him, daring him to touch her.

It's another ploy, he realized, a different tactic. She knows what she's doing to me.

He decided he didn't care. He reached up to circle her small, perfect breasts in his hands. She sighed and closed her eyes, leaning into his caress, and gasped softly when his mouth found her skin. Her arms twined behind his neck, pulling him close.

"Geille—" he started to say.

Her mouth came down hungrily on his. Surrendering to the fierce drives burning in him, he pulled her down and returned her kiss forcefully, peeling the battered suit from her shoulders. They didn't have anything else to say for a long time.

* * * * *

Several hours later, they dozed in Sokolov's bed, limbs tangled in the sheets. Peri watched them for a time, the single red light of the video pickup focused on the two. Eventually she decided that Pete would want to know what she'd found out.

"Pete?" she said quietly.

Sokolov raised himself on one elbow, looking at the lens. "What is it, Peri?"

"I have some video of the contact we're moving to intercept. You'll want to see it."

"Put it on the screen in here," he said sleepily.

He swung his feet to the cold deck plates and leaned over with his head in his hands. Geille sat up, brushing her hair out of her face.

Blackness, speckled with stars. Sokolov squinted, trying to make out something on the vidscreen, then he caught a glimpse of darkness occulting a star against the night.

"Give me maximum magnification in the upper left quadrant," he told the computer.

The screen blurred and jumped. Now they could see it clearly, although it was still small and faint. It was too far away to tell much about it, but Sokolov and Geille could see two things even from their great distance.

It was a ship, not an asteroid.

And it wasn't remotely human in origin.

Its fluted surface hinted at convolutions and secrets. Spires and buttresses soared from the cylindrical hull, black as pitch against the darkness. Its makers had despised straight lines;

everything curved across rounded surfaces and asymmetrical wells. Not a single light showed.

Geille leaned against his shoulder, staring at the screen. "Who are they?"

"I don't know," Sokolov answered. "It's not fraal, mechalus, or t'sa. Their ships don't look anything like that. I'd guess it's a race we haven't seen before."

"Should we get any closer? That ship is a lot bigger than *Peregrine*."

He concentrated, thinking hard. "They haven't changed course or applied any acceleration. They're not radiating any EM energy." He reached up to catch her hand in his. "I think it's a derelict, dead or abandoned. They're not reacting to us in any way."

"Appearances can be deceiving."

"Look at it," Sokolov said quietly. "It *feels* dead. It's traveling at only one-half of one percent lightspeed in the middle of interstellar space. They're not trying to get anywhere."

"I don't know, Pete. Why take chances?"

He stared up at the screen on the wall, trying to pierce the millions of kilometers that separated him from the alien ship. Why take chances? He mulled over Geille's question, working it through, chewing on it. Sokolov rarely listened to his intuition. He preferred to work things out in a logical order, hammering away at a problem or puzzle one step at a time, but something about this tugged at his mind, teasing him with possibilities.

He could feel the weight of Geille's gaze on him as she tried to fathom what he was thinking. He ignored her.

"Peri, repeat the main engineering displays on this screen. Show me the readouts on the stardrive."

The computer complied; the ship could display any control station at any reasonably sized screen. The starfield and its monstrous vessel vanished, replaced by a screen full of dense information and overlapping tables. Sokolov studied it for a moment until he found what he was looking for.

"I don't believe it," he said. He rubbed his eyes and looked again to make sure.

The stardrive hadn't started to recharge. It simply wasn't working, and the anomalous gravitational signal still showed up on the engineering boards.

Geille pulled up the sheets to cover her bare body. "Something's wrong?" she said.

"I think the alien ship pulled us out of drivespace," Sokolov said. "Do you see that mass reading? It's wrong. It's a signal like we saw when we made starrise, and now it looks like the drive isn't recharging the way it should be. We ought to be reading some kind of slight progress toward the one hundred percent recharge mark, but we're still at zero."

"That could be a mechanical fault," Geille said.

"Yeah, but look at these readings. They're directional and that alien ship is on the exact same bearing as the signal we're receiving. It's generating some kind of field that's preventing the operation of the stardrive." Sokolov twisted to look at her. "In fact, it's the same signal or energy field that precipitated our starrise. Somehow that ship is creating a signal that's covering light-hours of space and reaching into drivespace, too."

"Is that possible?"

"I don't know of any way to do it," Sokolov said. He climbed out of the bed and padded over to the screen. Quickly he ran through some calculations, trying to guess how fast the signal produced by the derelict might attenuate. *"Mertye!* The field might extend for a thousand light-hours or more from the ship."

"So we can't recharge the stardrive while we're within a thousand light-hours of that vessel?" Geille asked. She squinted at the screen, thinking. "What's the top speed of your ship?"

"Acceleration is more relevant," Sokolov replied. "We could build up to close to lightspeed, but it would take weeks and weeks."

"So it might take—what?—two or three or four thousand hours to travel a thousand light hours?" Geille asked. "That could be a hundred days or more! Are you sure about that, Sokolov?"

He scowled. "No, but the signal had this strength here, when we first made starrise." He pointed, highlighting the first reading on the screen. "Now it's this strong *here*, after three hours of travel. Assuming that the signal degrades at a predictable rate, I'm guessing that we'd still be able to measure it as far as a thousand light-hours away. Of course, it just might stop ten meters from where we are right now, or maybe it goes on forever. There's nothing in the books about this, Geille. I'm just guessing."

She fell silent for a long time, watching him in the dim luminescence of the video screen. He studied the display a few moments longer, then changed it, bringing back the feed from the exterior cameras. He faced her.

Quietly she asked, "What do we do now?"

"I think we've got to take a closer look at that ship."

"I don't like this, Sokolov."

"Me neither…but do you know how much a find like this could be worth?" he asked. "Even if I do nothing but shoot video and mark the location, I can sell this for millions. And if this is actually a first contact situation . . ." He drifted back to the bed, slipping back under the covers. "I don't take chances without a good reason, and you don't have much to lose. You're kidding me if you expect me to believe that you don't want to take a closer look."

Eyes riveted on the faint image glimmering on the screen, she simply nodded. "You're right. I want a closer look, but let's be careful, Pete. I don't like the looks of that thing."

Sokolov looked up at Peri's video pickup. "Run the course backward, Peri. Tell me where she came from." He studied the shape a moment longer, then asked, "How long until we intercept?"

"Five hours more, Pete."

"Make sure I'm up on the bridge an hour before that, Peri. Let me know the instant anything changes with that contact. Understand?"

"Yes, Pete." The computer's video pickup blinked out, and the exterior screen went dark.

Sokolov lay back down beside Geille, searching her face in the dim light of the cabin. She met his eyes with a strange expression he could not decipher. Silently he brushed the sheets back from her body, tracing the curve of her hip with his fingers.

She trembled at his touch. "I'm scared."

He turned her face toward his and touched her again, watching her. "I know," he said.

* * * * *

Two and a half light-years distant, Devriele Shanassin sat in his magnificent office in Icewalk's prow, gazing out at the endless storm around the station. The room was richly appointed, decorated with archaic weapons of a dozen worlds. He preferred more spartan quarters, but Shanassin understood the value of the trappings of power. People who stood before him in this room recognized his strength and respected him for it. As such, the palatial suite was a useful tool.

On the rich mahogany of the desktop before him, Shanassin studied the dossier of Pyotr Sokolov. A dozen holoshots showed pictures snapped throughout the Lucullus system. A security camera had caught his picture at a casino in Port Royal, just before an influential city councilman had been discovered dead with a briefcase full of illicit drugs. Another taken by a reporter showed Sokolov standing behind a local gang lord, the subject of a news article. Apparently Sokolov was just one more passerby in the frame, but the gang lord had been killed the next day. The tracker appeared in a number of court records, routinely collecting bounties leveled against various criminals. The list of his accomplishments was long and sordid.

Real information about the man himself was next to impossible to find. Shanassin steepled his long fingers. No address. No known family. Few associates, no friends or lovers. No financial records.

Sokolov might as well have been a figment of his imagination. Shanassin leaned back in his chair, studying the last holoshot. It was a surveillance record from a grimy subrail station buried in the bowels of Santiago, the Pict capital. Dozens of people crowded the image, engaged in nameless errands. Shanassin had obtained the picture by having his hackers search every security database in the system, seeking matches on Icewalk's records of Sokolov's features.

The human bounty hunter was stooping to board an automated train on a track that ran from the Pictish capital out to the
corporate headquarters of HelixTech. Dressed in his long black
coat, he wore a massive pistol low on one hip—a wise precaution in Pictish territory—and the security cam had caught him
raising a cigarette to his mouth. The date on the picture was
only four weeks before Sokolov had come to Icewalk. Four
weeks before Sokolov had come for Geille Monashi, he'd been
at HelixTech. Monashi had worked for HelixTech.

Shanassin snorted. He should have seen the connection
immediately. He dropped the flat images to his desktop and
spoke at the ceiling. "Yeiwei."

Hidden speakers relayed his commands instantly. The
sesheyan replied at once. "I hear you, Shanassin."

"Sokolov was hired by HelixTech to recover Monashi. Find
out exactly who hired him and when they expect him back. I
want to know everything HelixTech knows about this man."

The sesheyan paused. "Few of our hunters walk under those
shadows: and fewer still will aid us without reward. We have
few assets in HelixTech. What you ask will cost us."

"Cost is no object. Find out everything. He'll have to deliver
his captive. That means we'll have a chance to spot him."
Shanassin picked up a knife at the side of his desk and absently
admired it. "Do what you can to get some assets in place within
the next twenty-four hours. Once we make contact on Sokolov,
we are never going to let him out of our sight again. Am I
clear?"

"Yes. I go to do your bidding."

Shanassin cut the contact with a curt gesture of his hand.
Time was on his side.

Chapter Eight

THE DERELICT DRIFTED, silent and dark, against the stars.

Only one thousand kilometers distant, *Peregrine* paralleled the alien vessel, course and speed perfectly matched. If nothing else happened, the two ships would continue in company until the end of time, two black ghosts in the limitless void. The derelict dwarfed the tradesman. A dozen *Peregrine*s might have fit comfortably in the keen, barbed spire that jutted from the ridged mass of the ship; hundreds could have been lost within the precipices and hollows of its twisted hull. Still the leviathan showed no sign of acknowledging *Peregrine*'s presence, no hint of life or light.

"How long do you think it's been out here?" Geille asked quietly.

Without recognizing it, they had fallen into the habit of speaking in hushed tones in the command deck, as if a careless word might carry across the intervening void and wake the dragon they watched.

"Peri backtracked its course. Even taking stellar drift into account, it doesn't seem to have passed through any of the systems near Lucullus. Assuming that it's had the same course and speed long enough, it came from somewhere out past Hammer's Star." Sokolov performed some quick calculations on Nancy. "About three hundred years, if it entered human space on this trajectory. Maybe a few days if it made starrise out here and just happened to set off in this direction. Or thousands of years— maybe millions—if it's just been coasting through interstellar space long enough. There's no way to tell."

"It *feels* old," Geille said quietly. She straightened from the video displays, looking up at Sokolov in the command chair.

Her face was impassive, unreadable. She'd donned her own snug jump suit again. "I've shot all the video we can get from this range. What do we do now?"

An electric challenge hung in the air between them; their confrontation, lulled on some fronts, continued unabated in other ways. Sokolov sensed a deadly serious weight to Geille's words, her gestures. If the derelict they paralleled hadn't presented them with questions that demanded answers, a mystery far more significant than human sexual tension and control, he had no idea what the next move would have been.

The tension in her face and posture made the bounty hunter want to hit something. She was waiting to see whether giving herself to him had worked.

I knew I shouldn't have slept with her, Sokolov told himself. He shook his head angrily, clearing her scent from his nostrils, the sight and the feel of her from his mind, then concentrated on her question.

"The more we get, the more it's all worth," he rasped. "If there was anybody alive on that monster, we'd have seen some sign of it by now. I want to see if we can board it."

Geille's eyes snapped up, locking his. "Are you insane? We have no idea what might or might not be on that ship. Maybe there are thousands of them, and they've just been watching us to see what we would do, or if they haven't been paying attention to us, maybe there's a reason." She gripped the rail in front of him. "If that was a human ship, I'd agree with you, but how do we know that they have the technology to send us a signal we'd recognize? They may be incapable of indicating that they object to our presence. For that matter, it might not occur to them to send such a signal. Nothing in the human makeup would let us sit onboard that ship and just watch an unknown alien craft surveying us without giving some sign that we wanted to communicate.

"But that's not a human ship. How do you know that they don't have a first contact protocol that says, 'Don't do anything if someone looks you over, but incinerate them if they come within a hundred kilometers'? What if that ship's carrying something we don't want to meet? Maybe it's out in interstellar space because the creatures who launched it wanted it under quarantine." Geille crossed her arms, glaring defiantly at him. "How can you justify the risk?"

"Don't you see the opportunity we have?" he replied. "The video you just shot is going to be worth hundreds of thousands of credits to the right people, but video can be faked. We're going to need some tangible hard evidence to sell this story. It's nothing but science fiction until we can lay something real on the table."

"Money? Is that all?" Monashi snorted in disgust. "That makes me feel much better. I've spent the last two hours taking the pictures that will make you a millionaire—if you don't get us both killed, that is."

"The money's attractive," Sokolov admitted, "but I'm also concerned about our ability to recharge the stardrive. That ship is generating some kind of drivespace anomaly—you saw the readings. I'm thinking we may not have a choice of whether or not we try to board the alien ship. It might be the only way we can ever get out of here." He activated the pilot station and dropped down into the seat, tapping the control yoke to check the ship's response.

"You don't know that."

"I know my stardrive's dead when it should be recharging for the next jump out of here. I know that we didn't do anything with the new nav board that could account for what we've seen in the last twelve hours. I want some answers, Geille. I think we'll find them over there." He paused to light a cigarette, then took control of the ship. Peri could have done it herself, of course, but Sokolov wanted his own hand on the stick just in case. "Besides, we're here now. Do you expect me to believe that you don't want to have a look?"

Geille remained silent. He glanced over at her. Her face was set in a grimace, but circles of thought turned behind her eyes.

"I guess I don't have anything to lose," she said bitterly. "Just be careful."

"Okay." Moving slowly, he began to close the distance between the two ships, bringing *Peregrine* spiraling in on an oblique course. Sokolov steered his tradesman closer, watching his displays. "Keep an eye on the ship. Let me know if it does anything."

The alien vessel was a very large ship, almost two kilometers in length and nearly a kilometer in diameter. Exact measurements were difficult, since its weirdly gothic design sent spurs and pinnacles soaring hundreds of meters from the main mass of the hull, while vast areas of its structure were nothing but empty space spanned by solitary spiked buttresses. Every square meter of the derelict's hull was different, ridged or etched in complicated designs that might have been some kind of machinery, cooling structures, or nothing more than decoration. The entire thing was jarringly asymmetrical, with no universal pattern or form that Sokolov could discern—it was like nothing he'd ever seen.

"How close are we now?" Geille asked over her shoulder.

"About ten kilometers. We're still getting no signs of electromagnetic activity, radioactivity, or anything of that sort." Sokolov checked his displays again. "The only sensors it shows up on are the mass detector and the active radar scans."

"And visuals," Geille added. "God, that thing is big. It's the size of a small city."

"A fortress ship is even bigger than that—not by much, though." Sokolov scratched at his goatee and took a drag of his smoke. "I wonder if they have any kind of faster-than-light travel. If they don't, we might be looking at some kind of generation ship."

"Like the old fraal city-ships?" Geille frowned. "I don't know how anyone could stand it. A lifetime, and you never get to where you're going."

"Humans are shortsighted," Sokolov replied. "The fraal spent thousands of years wandering around the Orion Arm before they came to Sol. They didn't care if they didn't live long enough to see their destination, as long as their children or grandchildren got there. After all—"

"Hold on. I think I spotted an air lock." Geille reached for a control knob to steer the ship's sensor turret manually, scanning the image across the black hull. "Look there. See that big circle? Doesn't it look like some kind of hatch?"

Sokolov nodded. "I think you're right. Look, there's another one."

"Are you still going to board the ship?"

The bounty hunter didn't reply. Instead, he leaned back and looked at Peri's lens. "You're still transmitting the contact message?"

"I've been transmitting continuously for the last hour, Pete," the computer replied. Sokolov had keyed up a standard first contact message when they'd first approached, a simple radio signal that ran through various universal constants—prime numbers, pi to one hundred digits, properties of hydrogen and helium atoms. Peri was transmitting on several radio bands at once, as well as flashing her signal laser at the derelict. "I have detected no response."

What do we know about this ship? he asked himself. One: It's clearly an artifact manufactured by intelligence. Somebody made it. Two: It hasn't maneuvered since we've seen it. Three: It hasn't replied to our presence or any of our communications efforts. Four: Just a few hours before we encountered it, we were pulled out of drivespace early, something that's supposed to be physically impossible, and now we're experiencing some kind of suppression of our stardrive.

Pete Sokolov was a man who thought carefully when he was about to put his life on the line, but he was not afraid to do so when he thought the rewards were worth the risk. He viewed curiosity as a survival instinct, a voice of warning that told the primal creature buried deep in any human brain that there was something it needed to figure out. Geille Monashi had engaged his curiosity from the moment he began to read her dossier in Karcen Borun's office.

Now the derelict had engaged his curiosity just as fully, if in a different way.

"Sokolov?" Monashi turned away from the viewport. "What next?"

"Let's see if anyone's home," he said.

*　*　*　*　*

Tethered to the maze of hull structures by four magnetic grapples, a battered beetle of dull metal clinging to the flank of some reptilian monstrosity armored in scales and spines, the *Peregrine* glided alongside the titanic vessel. Beneath the ship's belly hatch, Sokolov and Monashi stood on one of the oddly smooth, regular portals that they'd discovered in their visual inspection of the ship. Both were dressed in full environment gear, light, tough space suits not much bulkier than their own clothes.

"Got my voice, Peri?" asked Sokolov.

The ship's reply hissed in the speakers of his helmet. "Five by five, Pete, and you, too, Geille. I can't promise that we'll be able to stay in touch once you enter the hull, though."

Sokolov slapped a light reel of fine cord hanging at his side. "That's why we brought the tether."

He twisted in his helmet to face Monashi. She was wearing one of his spare suits, and it was big and awkward on her. She also hadn't had any training in suit work before, a lack of experience that gave him cause for concern. He'd debated leaving her on *Peregrine* but decided that he was better off keeping her close at hand. Geille stood by a rounded nodule that was inset in the hull plating, the only feature in their immediate vicinity that seemed as if it might have anything to do with the portal.

"Any luck yet?" he asked her.

Floundering as she tried to shift her footing, Geille went to all fours on the hull. She looked up at him, glaring through her steamed faceplate.

"Where am I supposed to start?" she snapped. "It's not as if they left directions in Galactic Standard."

"If we don't find any way to open this from the outside, I'll have Peri blast it open with her mass cannon. That should get us in."

"I don't think that's advisable, Pete," the computer replied. Her personality emulation was good enough to convey a real sense of worry and unease.

"Your ship's right," Geille added. "So far we haven't done anything that could be construed as hostile. Firing weapons seems like a bad idea."

"Maybe it won't be necessary."

Sokolov finished surveying the area and joined Monashi by the recessed module. It was blank except for three odd, raised circles with small indentations in them, each about the size of his palm. He reached out with one gloved hand and pushed at the first; it rotated and sank in at the same time, but returned to its original height when he let go.

"I hope you're not pushing what passes for the burglar alarm," Monashi observed, "or the self-destruct switch, for that matter."

"It's the only thing near this hatch that looks like it's supposed to be manipulated. What else should we try?"

"Maybe going back to the *Peregrine*?" Geille looked up into his face across a meter of vacuum. The lights of her helmet made her features pale and indistinct. He could hear the sounds of her breathing over the radio link. "I'm having second thoughts about this whole idea, Pete."

"I know." He sat back, trying to imagine how an alien astronaut might approach the hatch. The hatch was perfectly circular, about two meters in diameter. The panel they were looking at was probably two meters from the edge. "The portal isn't all that large. They're probably not too much bigger than we are, but why would these controls be set so far from the entrance?"

"Maybe they've got long arms, or maybe there's something dangerous about the way the hatch opens, so you don't want to stand right in front of it while you operate it." Monashi snorted. "Maybe this panel has nothing to do with the door at all." She tried the other two circular pads one at a time, to no effect.

Sokolov watched, thinking. "Let's try pushing all three at once. I'll get these two, and you get that one." Geille agreed with a curt nod. Together, they depressed and twisted all three pads.

Beside, them, a thin mist of gas puffed silently into space as the portal's surface shimmered and vanished. Sokolov stood at once and peered inside. He saw was a long, narrow passageway about ten meters in length, virtually the same diameter as the portal. Another three-pad panel waited at the far end.

"It's an air lock," he decided. "Come on."

The derelict was large enough to possess a faint hint of effective gravity, a subtle influence that made Sokolov's inner ear decide that he now stood on top of the ship and was dropping into it. He helped Geille to negotiate the edge of the alien hatch and stepped off into space, sinking gracefully into the chamber below. He trailed the thin tether behind him; the narrow comm line linked them to *Peregrine*.

Like the exterior of the ship, the inner surfaces were sculpted in an irregular fashion. "Your aliens must like going in single file," Geille commented. "This is the longest, skinniest air lock I've ever seen."

"I'm beginning to wonder if they're remotely humanoid," he replied. "Maybe they're built more like snakes or weasels, long and narrow."

"That's not reassuring." Geille looked up at him, frowning, then her eyes traveled up, over his head, and grew wide. "Pete! The hatch is closing behind us!"

He looked up as well; the portal was shimmering, like a projection from an old holoplayer just beginning to warm up. "Peri, you know what to do if you lose contact with us," he stated.

"Yes, Pete." the computer replied. "I'll wait—"

Abruptly the radio contact died as the hatch returned to place. The severed end of the comm tether drifted in the air lock with them. The chamber was completely lightless except for their suit lights, shining pure yellow circles of light against the walls. No atmosphere caught the sweep of their beams. Geille gasped in panic and seized his arm in a surprisingly strong grip.

"We're trapped!" she said.

"It's an air lock, it's just doing what it's supposed to do . . . I hope." Sokolov drifted to the wall nearest them and anchored himself with his magnetic boots. A control panel waited by the inner surface of the hatch. Together, he and Geille triggered it, causing the outer door to flash and disappear again. "See? Here are the controls that let us get out."

Peregrine still hovered overhead, a warm and friendly sight. "Pete? Are you okay? The hatch closed and severed the comm wire," the computer said.

"No problems, Peri. We were just making sure we knew how to let ourselves out. We're going exploring now. Don't panic if you don't hear from us for a while."

"Do you want to modify your standing orders?" Peri asked.

"No, leave them as they are. If you don't hear from us in four hours, use the mass cannon to open a breach in the hull." Sokolov detached Geille from the wall and released his own magnetic clamps; they began to drift back down into the darkness as the hatch overhead shimmered again. "Mind the store, Peri. We're losing contact again."

At the bottom of the air lock, they worked the three-pad control panel in the same way they'd operated the previous two, then waited together as the interior hatch vanished. Beyond lay a curving corridor that ran out of sight both left and right. Moving quickly, they hurried through the open portal before the smooth surface of the hatch reappeared.

"That seems damned dangerous," Sokolov remarked. "Weren't they worried about losing an arm or leg in one of these things?"

Geille shrugged. "Maybe it's got a safety factor built in to prevent it from closing while there's someone in the door. The comm tether might not have been big enough to trip it. Try it again, but stick your arm through and leave it there."

"No, thanks. I'll think of some other way to see how these things work." Sokolov checked his suit vidcam and made sure the tiny device was taking footage, then he quickly used a laser ranger to feed the dimensions of the new passageway into his dataslate, creating a basic map of their immediate vicinity.

"My instruments tell me that there's air pressure and oxygen in here," Geille commented. "Think we can take the suits off?"

"Check your temperature."

"I—oh, damn! It's eighty below zero in here!"

"You can actually tolerate that for a brief exposure, but you don't want to do it for long," Sokolov remarked. "Besides, who knows what kind of toxins or bugs might be in the air? I'm going to keep my helmet on until we get a chance to analyze the air in detail." He shone his suit light down both directions of the corridor. "Which way from here?"

"Which way to what? Are we looking for something in particular?"

"I'll know when I find it," Sokolov said.

"Then there's no difference." Geille gestured with her light. "Left for now."

Clanking awkwardly along in their magnetic boots, they rooted themselves to the deck and started down the passageway. Sokolov had worked in zero-g enough to learn the knack of rolling, slow steps that gave the electromagnets in his soles time to sense his pace and click on and off as needed. Monashi made several starts and stops before she began to get the hang of it.

"This is hard work," she observed.

"Faster and safer than floating." Sokolov stayed behind her to match her pace. "What do you make of the temperature?"

"Eighty below?" Geille fell silent, grunting with each step while she thought. "The ship's cold because no one's turned on the heat. If it's been abandoned, that would fit."

"Not true," Sokolov broke in. "We're in interstellar space with nothing but starlight to warm the hull. The temperature in here should be close to absolute zero. Either the ship's life support systems occasionally cycle to preserve this temperature, or they cycle continuously to keep it here because that's what the owners prefer."

Geille halted in her tracks. "Are you saying you think someone's home?"

"Probably not. The climate control could be automated."

They walked on in silence for a time before they came to a pair of round metal hatches on either side of the corridor. They seemed to be controlled by the same kind of three-part console they'd seen in the air lock, but these were smaller. Repeating their procedure at the air lock, they opened the door on the right-hand side.

They found themselves staring at a small, low-ceilinged room that resembled nothing so much as the inside of some monster's stomach. Weird, veined ribs framed the walls and ceiling; a loose powdery substance covered the floor to the depth of several centimeters. Several tubelike tunnels led out of the room. In silence, Sokolov and Monashi ventured into the smaller passageways and discovered a tangled nest of still smaller passages and rooms, twisting through a three-dimensional maze. They explored all of the convolutions but found nothing of interest other than several large pools of water, frozen solid.

"A waterslide?" Geille remarked.

"A shrine? A running track? Hell, maybe this is how they arrange living space. Who knows?" Sokolov checked with Nancy; they'd been inside for almost thirty minutes already. "Let's check out the room across the hall."

They let themselves out and opened the next hatch. This portal led to a room full of machinery; Sokolov guessed that it was some kind of life support equipment. He shot some video and was about to abandon the room as generally uninteresting when Geille called his attention to a long, soft bundle lying on the deck.

"What do you think this is?" she asked.

"I don't know. Does it open?"

Monashi knelt by the bundle and prodded it with her flashlight. Sokolov had a sudden paranoid flash, a dead certainty that the thing would not only prove to be alive, but supernaturally fast and strong. I've been watching too many movies, he thought. He blinked to clear the offending thoughts from his skull.

Geille poked it again, then reached out with one hand to tug it open. It was a square of black cloth or fiber about a meter square. It had been wrapped around a half-dozen implements or tools of some kind.

"I think we found someone's tool kit," she muttered. She held up a curving piece of metal with a strange shepherd's-crook shape at the end. "What do you make of this?"

Sokolov took the implement from her hand. It was about seventy centimeters long, and quite heavy. There was no single grip, but three widely spaced indentations along the handle. The whole thing appeared to be shaped from a single piece of dense black metal.

"It's a keeper," he said, dropping it into a heavy-duty pouch at his belt.

"It's just a wrench, Sokolov."

"Do you realize how much this tells us about these creatures?" Sokolov reversed his motion and held the alien tool up. "What's it made of, and how did they make it? It's not vanadium steel, and it's not tungsten carbide. Maybe it's just plain old iron under some kind of coating. People make tools out of the toughest, cheapest stuff that will do the job. We've just learned something about their metallurgy.

"Also, do you see any seams? This isn't a casting. It's more likely rolled or forged in some way." He examined it for a long moment, trying to figure out how he was supposed to hold it. "Look at the grip. Either these are really small guys with three arms, or they're so big that they hold this wrench with only three fingers."

Geille held up a smaller device of the same type. "Their hands must be huge. I bet those three-pad control panels we've been seeing are their notion of a palm key. If you were the right size and shape, you stand in front of the round hatch and push all three buttons at once." She looked up at him through her faceplate. "I don't think I want to meet one of these guys, Sokolov."

He searched the machinery nearby until he found something that looked like a fitting. It was distinctly oval. The curved hook he held in his hand didn't fit.

"This is crazy. If this is a wrench, how the hell is it supposed to work?"

Geille watched him for a moment then took the device out of his hand. She slipped it over the fitting so it fit loosely, then she pulled it to the right. The interior curvature of the tool caught the curve of the oval fitting.

"It works. When you pull it tight, the fitting's got to turn, but you're right, it's not the way we would do it." She returned the implement to him. "Come to think of it, I don't know that I've seen a straight line anywhere on this ship."

"So they're bigger than we are, probably long and thin. They use hand tools. They hate straight lines." Sokolov shook his head. "All that from a couple of doors and a wrench."

"Do we keep going?"

He looked up at her through the faceplate of his helmet. Geille seemed almost comical in the oversized suit, but her face had a keen expression, a drive and alertness that he could sense across the icy cold between them. Despite her misgivings, she was stimulated by the mystery around them.

"Listen, we could take forever checking each door we come to. We're going to be here several days. Maybe we ought to try to cover a lot of territory now, try to get an idea of the general layout. We can go back and check areas that look interesting later."

"Agreed," said Geille.

They left the odd mazelike passages and resumed their exploration of the main corridor. As each intersection revealed nothing but more lifeless passages, they moved with more confidence. Sokolov carefully mapped their route, while Geille concentrated on recording their findings. From time to time, they opened random portals to see if they'd discovered anything interesting, but the ship was long abandoned.

They found no stairways or elevators, but instead asymmetric decks connected by curving ramps. Internal partitioning was haphazard; sometimes they walked for hundreds of meters without passing through a portal, while other times they had to pass three or four in a few meters of passageway. Some chambers were crowded with massive banks of cold, dead machinery. Sokolov couldn't begin to guess at the function of many of the devices, although he suspected that they had something to do with the ship's power plant. They'd found no nozzles or reaction drive apertures during their survey of the ship's outer hull, which led Sokolov to believe that the derelict's builders had relied on some kind of gravity induction drive or space-warping device.

They didn't find anything in the way of a central control chamber, although Sokolov's map revealed a great hollow sphere in the center of the ship that they couldn't reach. No passageways or portals seemed to open into the very center of the ship.

"I'll bet that's the main power system," Sokolov speculated, showing Monashi the map projection he'd fashioned in their rough survey. "Some kind of machinery space that you don't want to go inside."

"Either that or it's a citadel. A secure place in the middle of the ship where they're all lurking right now, watching us."

"Well, they picked up after themselves, that's for sure. Other than your tool kit, I haven't seen anything small or portable left lying about." Sokolov returned the dataslate to his belt clip and found himself patting his pockets in search of a smoke, despite the fact that he was still sealed inside his e-suit. He cursed silently and settled for a sip of cold water from his suit's reservoir. "They knew they were leaving, and they took everything that wasn't tied down."

Geille leaned against the wall, facing him. When they looked at each other, their searchlights showed as one bright circle in a sea of darkness. Nothing stirred or moved except the rasping sounds of their own breathing.

"So where did they go?"

Sokolov had no answer. "We've been at this for almost three and a half hours. We'd better get back outside before Peri starts shooting."

Hours of walking in magnetic boots had left Sokolov's calves stiff and his knees sore, and considering her inexperience in space, Geille must have been even more tired than he was.

She straightened with a wince and nodded her assent. "Okay."

They returned to *Peregrine,* retracing their steps by the most direct route they could find. Nothing had changed outside. Their ship still rode on her magnetic tethers, pinned to the derelict's side. The two ate a bland meal from Peri's stores then made love with a strange sense of desperation and dislocation. Sokolov knew that Geille was contesting him with the best weapon at her disposal, but he didn't care.

Eventually he drifted off into a restless sleep in which the leviathan beside them dominated his dreams, a vast black shadow looming over him like a mountain about to fall.

Chapter Nine

ON THEIR SECOND expedition, they found a picture of the derelict's vanished masters. They'd been exploring another of the strange tunnel-and-water chambers when they encountered a few spartan furnishings. One was a flat screen that showed a highly stylized series of drawings or etchings. If the images were at all accurate, the aliens were sinuous, vaguely reptilian creatures. Sokolov thought they looked like something between a weasel and a snake; Monashi compared them to the dragons of her family's Old Earth homeland. Sokolov tried to remove the screen to take it with them, but the device shattered when he pulled it from the wall.

They gave themselves eight hours this time and explored dozens of smaller chambers off the main passageways. The builders of the ship had constructed it so that no more than a handful of crewmen ever had to work side by side, eat together, or share a duty station. The two explorers shot hours of detailed holo footage and found a number of perfectly preserved small tools and artifacts. The prize of the day was a cache of eleven strangely marked cylinders that might have been data storage devices and a bulky egg-shaped machine that might have been a computer. Sokolov and Monashi were only guessing, of course. Nothing was actually powered, and they wouldn't have had a clue how to operate the device even if it was.

They returned to *Peregrine,* ate and rested, and then boarded the derelict again as soon as they'd caught a couple of hours of sleep.

Sokolov wasn't sure, but he was beginning to think that the mammoth vessel had been crewed by no more than a few dozen of the builders. They'd found about forty of the convoluted tunnel rooms, some with simple furnishings and indecipherable decorations. It seemed to him that the chambers were denlike, possibly the lairs of creatures who fiercely valued the sanctity of their own quarters.

"The ship's too big for such a small crew," he said quietly as they studied another of the strange chambers.

"One person could fly it with enough automation," Geille replied. "We have superfreighters as big as this ship, and they only carry a few dozen crewmen."

"True, but if this is a freighter, where are the cargo holds? You wouldn't build a ship this large for so few crewmen. It's a waste of resources. They don't need thousands of square meters of living space for each member of the crew."

"Maybe they do, Sokolov. They've got claws; they've got fangs. They're carnivores, and there aren't many big carnivores that assemble in large social groups. It's not a life pattern unique to Earth. It's true in most ecosystems. A big carnivore near the top of the food chain can't socialize like other animals, because any large grouping of them would kill all the game off. They'd be forced by evolution to favor competition over cooperation."

"They've got to socialize at least a little bit. We're standing in a starship, and forty or fifty of them were onboard."

"I didn't say they were feral killers, Sokolov. I'm just speculating that there might not be a great number of them, or even if there are, they just can't stand to be confined in close quarters with their own kind."

"I thought you were a comptech, not a xenologist."

Geille shrugged inside her bulky suit. "HelixTech gives people like me a first-rate education, and if you don't pass, you're dropped off the payroll. That's a good incentive to learn how to use your brain."

They continued with their search. Later that same day, their explorations brought them to the ship's slave pens. Three of the leviathan's spires held cramped penlike holds in which large numbers of small humanoid creatures had been carried in dismal warrens. At first Sokolov had thought that the leviathan might be a troopship or personnel transport, but as he examined the rows of man-sized sleeping niches, he realized that the creatures who built artificial caves for themselves could never tolerate the kind of living conditions that must have been the norm in the pens.

"Prisoners?" Geille asked, examining the cavernous room.

"Possibly, or a race of slaves."

Sokolov had seen such places on his home world, the camps of the wretched and dispossessed who were wrung dry of the meanest labor the authorities could find for them. Despite the alien construction and materials, the empty warren had familiar echoes of hopelessness, of squalor, lying dormant in the metal walls and bare decks.

He knelt beside an oval niche, wondering what kind of creature had filled it. They would have been a lot smaller than the masters of the vessel. The dragons were maybe two or three times the size of humans; these creatures would have been substantially smaller. Did they serve willingly? he wondered. Were they made by the shipbuilders, a race engineered to perform menial tasks? Or were they a sentient race that had had the misfortune of meeting the builders when the situation favored the dragons? Or were the pens nothing more than the ship's provisions for a long voyage?

Sokolov studied the structure blackly. He decided that he didn't want to meet the builders after all. Wherever they were, he hoped they didn't like it. That night, Geille and he returned to the ship wrapped in their own thoughts, their eagerness to unravel the mystery of the derelict tempered by what they'd seen. They slept restlessly, rising early to continue their explorations, now proceeding in a mechanical routine that called for little thought or speculation.

Sokolov dreamed of dragons.

* * * * *

The next day, on their fourth expedition into the derelict, they discovered the bridge.

It took almost an hour of examination before they were certain what they had. They'd seen that the dragons had valued privacy and space to an astonishing degree. The bridge was a central chamber where three of them could gather, but a dozen ancillary stations—weapon control, sensors, navigation, and several other Sokolov and Monashi couldn't positively identify—weren't actually in the same room. They were in isolated chambers nearby, safely out of sight of their neighbors. Each member of the command crew had functioned largely in isolation, linked to his fellows by a simple intercom system.

Sokolov crowed in delight when he found the navigation niche. "This is what we've been looking for! We can see where these things came from, how long they've been out here, maybe where they were going."

"I'd still like to know where they *went*," Geille observed. "We've been all over this ship and haven't even found a single body. I don't get it."

Sokolov didn't reply. He was busy scrutinizing the star charts, delicate screens that slid in arabesque frames to show the same region from any perspective. He keyed a panel by the chart, illuminating it with a field of unintelligible characters—names of worlds, course plots, bulletins about various hazards?—he couldn't tell.

"I'd give my eye teeth to be able to understand this stuff."

"We've filmed enough examples of writing for the linguistic experts to figure something out," Geille said. She came over to watch him manipulate the chart. "See anything familiar?"

"No. I don't know what direction I'm looking in, so I can't even begin to match constellations. It might be the Verge. It might be something else. There's no way to tell."

"What about this one?" Geille activated another screen. This one displayed a galactic disk. A few tiny markings were clustered in one small corner. "Is this the Milky Way?"

"Looks like it," he grunted. He moved over to study the map beside her. "This corner," he said, pointing to the end of one spiral arm, "could be the Orion. . . . Hey!"

The projection blurred and jumped drastically in response to the motion of his hand. Now he was looking at the Orion Arm in some detail. Carefully he repeated the gesture and slowly drove the projection down to the trailing edge of the arm, in the vicinity of the Verge. Now several dozen white markings circled a small number of stars in the uncharted space beyond the edge of human knowledge.

"I think we've found them," he said quietly.

"Those are their worlds?"

"They're not ours." He looked over at her. "Get this on video. We need this information."

Geille reached up to activate her shoulder-mounted camera, circling slowly to film the projection from all sides. "We have no way of knowing how accurate this information is now," she said. "It might be a couple of thousand years old, a couple of million, for that matter. The derelict could have been out here for a very long time."

"You're wrong. We do have a way to know." Sokolov grinned fiercely. "All we have to do is compare the stellar positions in this view of the Orion Arm against our own current charts. We'll be able to deduce the age of these charts precisely by tracking known stellar drift."

Geille glanced at him. "Can you do it?"

"I'll need to find a couple of stars I can identify precisely, and I'll need Peri's navigational databases to put it together."

Deliberately he moved his hand into the projection again, selecting a white-circled star at random. The display blurred again, narrowing to a field depicting a half-dozen stars. The marked one still lay at the center, so Sokolov continued to zoom in. The image shifted again. Now he gazed, godlike, at an entire star system from some omniscient point of view above and outside the orbit of the outermost planet. White markings circled several of the planets.

"Are you getting this?" he whispered.

"It's some kind of system map or diagram," Geille said quietly. He heard her shifting behind him, carefully recording the screen's contents. "What do you think the markings mean?"

"Writing, I suppose." Sokolov leaned closer, examining the diagram more closely.

The white circles around the system's planets weren't solid lines; they were composed of fine characters or lettering of some kind. Complex pictographs or hieroglyphs—all composed

of compact curls and graceful sweeping lines—formed a legend
to the planet's image on the screen. With another motion of his
hand, he zoomed in on the planet in the center. The screen now
showed nothing but the flat disk of a planet as seen from high
orbit. Numerous features were highlighted by more white markings, but Sokolov couldn't seem to make the display show any
more detail. Still, the gray smudges of cities and glint of large
structures in lower orbits were visible.

Holding his breath, Sokolov withdrew his hand and checked
another planet then other star systems. Planets by the dozen
flicked before his eyes, blue, gray, and green orbs wreathed in
feathery clouds. Around some, he saw gigantic orbital structures, dark spires and needles that bore a distinct resemblance to
the gothic complexity of the ship itself.

"This is a damned atlas to all their settlements. It's priceless," he said. The bounty hunter straightened, searching the
console for more displays.

"Why did they leave this behind?" Geille wondered aloud.
"They were so thorough in removing other materials and tools
from the ship. If you were going to abandon a ship in interstellar
space, you'd never leave your starcharts behind. You couldn't
take the chance that someone else might find them and collect
the kind of information we've found here."

"You're right. It's almost too good to be true. Maybe they
overlooked it."

"I don't buy that for a minute," Geille said. "Okay, I haven't
spent any time in space, but I've read enough science fiction to
know that you would *never* want to leave a map to your home
worlds lying around someplace where another species might
find it. Aren't most of the navigational databases in commercial
and military spacecraft rigged to destroy themselves under the
right circumstances?"

Sokolov nodded in confirmation. "I've seen some that have
been disabled, but yes, most of them will self-destruct. It's part
of the first contact protocols incorporated in most ship registra-
tions and licensing materials. If you want to fly a legal ship,
you've got to abide by the protocols." He laughed softly. "All
that's gone to hell in the Verge, though: too many systems with-

out any central government. No one enforces the basics out here."

"How we enforce it doesn't matter, Sokolov. What I'm trying to say is that we would try to prevent our charts from falling into someone else's hands, but no one seems to have taken that basic precaution onboard this vessel." Geille lowered the camera. "Did they want to be found? Didn't they care? Is all this information a hoax, a misdirection of some kind?"

He didn't have an answer. For the thirtieth or fortieth time in the last couple of days, he fumbled in his e-suit's pockets for a pack of smokes. Angrily he stilled his hands and paced away.

"It doesn't make sense," he admitted. He turned away from the nav display, surveying the rest of the bridge. "Let's try a couple more panels. Maybe we'll find a log or something."

Geille nodded. They examined several other stations in the bridge decks. Most were completely incomprehensible, glassy dark screens that glowed briefly with white script at their touch and then faded away. Gauges, displays, controls . . . nothing matched what Sokolov would have expected. Information was presented in forms that he couldn't relate to any tangible ship function.

Abruptly the lights came on. Sokolov leaped meters into the air, so startled that he jumped before his magnetic boots could sense his hesitation. The Wesshaur was in his hand, a comfortable black weight. The vast, shadowy bridge stood revealed as a labyrinthine complex of chambers and tunnels, stretching for almost sixty meters in front of him. Overhead, harsh green-white lamps glared angrily in open panels. He spied Geille in a nearby niche, floundering to her feet.

"What did you do?" he demanded.

"I activated this console," she answered, her voice strained. She stood in front of the station, arms hugged tight across her chest. Her voice seemed curiously distant and detached. Her attention was riveted to the machinery in front of her. "I'd been trying a few of them. I didn't think I'd found anything different here."

"Well, turn it off again!"

"I don't know how," she answered. "Besides, what's the

harm? I'm tired of walking around in the dark anyway."

Sokolov found himself sinking quickly back down toward the deck. "You've turned the gravity on, too," he growled. When his weight settled back to his feet, he deactivated his magnetic boots and stalked over to the console Geille stood beside. The light in the bridge was painfully bright; his face shield was already darkening to compensate. "Thank God these guys weren't built for three or four Gs. We might have been pinned here like beetles on our backs if the gravity had kicked on too high for humans."

"That's a cheerful thought."

Sokolov looked at the console. It seemed much like the others. The control surfaces—flat, dark screens in the other consoles on the bridge—were now glowing with complex symbology, dancing and flickering to display some kind of information.

"Damn. What did you push?"

She simply stared at the flickering displays, eyes locked on the screen. "I don't know," she mumbled.

The screens seemed to flicker and jump. Data cascaded across the screen, halted, started again. Menus or symbols seemed to select themselves, opening new fields of unintelligible information. The bounty hunter watched the luminescent display, trying to make sense out of it. Systems status? A program activating? The captain's log? He shook his head and glanced at Geille to ask her what was going on.

Even through the darkened visor, he could see that she was locked on the screen in rapt attention. Her eyes flickered back and forth across the datastream; she licked her lips absently, completely engaged by the information.

"Geille? Are you actually getting something out of all this?"

Reluctantly she tore her attention away from the screens. "What? . . . No, I don't think so."

"Are you okay?"

"Sure," she said. She shook her head. The screens slowed and steadied on a string of symbols. "I was just trying to figure out what that computer was showing us. Guess I didn't get much."

Sokolov glared at her, but she ignored him, glancing around the bridge. Beneath his feet, he could feel deep stirrings, rumblings, vibrations somewhere deep in the belly of the derelict. The cold, still air in the bridge seemed to whisper in the audio pickups of his suit, moving after unknown years of frigid solitude. What did she really do? he wondered.

"It feels like the whole ship's waking up."

"Lights, power, gravity—that's not bad," Geille observed. "It would make our work a lot easier."

"That depends entirely on what else we might have activated," Sokolov mused. "Security systems? Powered alarms or locks? Hidden cryo-chambers where the owners are now waking up?" He thought a moment longer, then cursed. "*Nasmertnyi!* What if the ship's collision or intrusion alarms are active now? *Peregrine*'s less than one hundred meters from the hull."

Geille winced. "So what do we do?"

"Back to the *Peregrine*. We'd better see what this has done to the derelict. If we need to get out of here fast, I'd rather be onboard Peri and ready to go."

"Good idea," Monashi said. She gathered her tools and recording devices, hurriedly stashing them in her shoulder satchel. "I feel like I've been caught burglarizing someone's house."

"It's probably nothing to be worried about, but let's leave things alone for a while and see what happens." Sokolov finished stowing his own gear and led Monashi back into the main passageway. The tubelike corridor seemed harsh, acrid, under the unforgiving lights. Their sun must be brighter than Sol, he thought distantly, still piecing together information, maybe a G1, or even a low F, hotter and more energetic. That wouldn't fit with the cold temperatures, not unless their home world was a long way out . . . or the ship's temperature wasn't actually the climate the dragons had preferred.

They rapidly traversed the length of the spire in which they'd found the bridge, returning to the main mass of the hull. There they turned into a ringlike passage that girdled the derelict's inner hull, circumnavigating the great empty space in the heart of the ship. They'd used the corridor a number of times in their previous explorations. It was the closest the derelict had to a central passageway, except now it was blocked.

Two great curtains of black metal had materialized at either end of the curving corridor, blocking their route back to *Peregrine*. Sokolov dropped his tool kit and stood staring.

"Son of a bitch," he muttered. "Geille, what did you do?"

"It might be an automated response," she shot back. "Maybe I triggered a general close-doors switch, something like that. We'll just go another way."

They retraced their steps and found a connecting passageway that promised to circumvent the barriers in the main corridor, only to find that the secondary passageways were also blocked by solid black walls. Monashi let her hand rest against the smooth, dark surface.

"I'd love to know how these things work," she murmured. "The dragons seem to know how to make solid matter appear and disappear. You'd think there would be something more useful for that technology than making doors and hatchways out of it." She turned to Sokolov, not trying to hide her growing alarm. "Whatever it is, it's doing a good job of keeping us in this part of the hull."

"What a crazy way to partition a ship," Sokolov snarled. "When the power's on, you've got more compartmentalization? What's the point of that? I'd want it to be the other way around, so that if my main power system was knocked out by enemy fire the ship would revert to the highest condition of hull integrity."

"You're assuming that these passageways are being sealed for damage control."

"We're in a spaceship, Geille. It's a dangerous environment. No matter how advanced your technology is, you've got to make sure that you can keep air in and space out. It's the absolute minimum for a spacefaring vessel. What else would you want to seal the ship for?"

Geille snorted. "Come on, Sokolov. You're the breaking-and-entering expert. You'd seal the passageways to limit the movements of an intruder, wouldn't you?"

Sokolov stood staring at her for a long moment. "Oh, shit."

"No kidding. So what do we do?"

"Hold on. I'm thinking." He paced anxiously, watching the stark shadow his body threw against the wall in the glare of the powerful lights overhead. "Okay, we've been trying passages that would lead us toward the outer hull. Let's try moving deeper into the ship. We've mapped a couple of chambers that might have been generators or power distribution centers of some kind. Maybe we can find a way to kill the derelict's power again. If these barriers are maintained by a continuous power feed, that should take them down."

Monashi frowned, her eyes distant as she considered his plan. "I guess it's better than sitting here and waiting for things to change," she said. "Let's give it a try."

Moving faster in the comfortable gravity and bright light of the ship's passageways, the two explorers retraced their steps and chose a different branch of the main passage, one that led toward the center of the ship. Unlike a human ship, which would have designated one side of the ship as the bottom and applied gravity straight down toward the lower decks, the derelict's artificial gravity was oriented toward the exact center of the vessel. It was like a miniature planet in which the outer hull was the surface; descending into the interior of the vessel was like burrowing into a mine. Sokolov carefully noted the arrangement, appending his observations to the extensive map he'd created on his dataslate. Knowing which way gravity was supposed to work onboard the derelict made sense of many other details of the interior arrangement.

They dropped down six or seven decks, winding back and forth between intersecting corridors and black, seamless dead ends. Several times they were forced to double back on their tracks, but at least they were able to keep moving. After an hour of exploration, they decided to stop for a short rest. Sokolov set up a portable heater from his equipment sling and warmed one corner of an immense hallway; then they removed their helmets to eat a quick lunch, shivering in the intense cold. The space heater made the bitterly cold air of the derelict tolerable for a short time, if not comfortable.

Sokolov finally located his cigarettes and indulged himself

in a smoke. He thought hard about their predicament.

"I think we're near the center," he told Geille. "I've been tracking our progress on the map. We don't have many more options to explore."

"You mean we're trapped?" Her breath clouded the air before her face and glittered on the chest of her e-suit. Swallowed in the bulky protective garb, she looked like a child trying to wear a grown-up's clothes. "I should have seen this coming."

"Maybe. I don't intend to give up until I've examined every possible alternative path. For all we know, the lights could go out again on their own. Maybe the derelict doesn't have much capacity left in its power systems, or maybe the auto-start you triggered has a finite duration, and it'll cut off by itself after a certain amount of time."

"I never would have considered you an optimist, Sokolov," Geille said. She offered a wan smile. "You don't seem like the kind of man who leaves anything to chance."

"Not when I can help it, I don't." He shrugged and stood, dropping his smoke to the deck as he screwed his helmet back on. "Come on. Let's finish running down the obvious alternatives before we start worrying about what to do next."

* * * * *

Two hours later they found the heart of the vessel. They'd had to switch their magnetic boots back on. As they neared the center of the ship, the gravity lessened, just as it would in a naturally occurring mass, although at a much greater rate of decline.

In an otherwise unremarkable chamber, a straight-sided shaft dropped down even lower yet, beckoning from the mysterious territory in the ship's center that they had not been able to reach yet. The face of the well was covered by a smooth, dark circle of a metallic hatch, but unlike the others that they'd encountered in the ship's corridors, this one was equipped with a familiar three-pad control unit.

"It's an air lock," Geille said. "What's it doing in the middle of the ship?"

"Whatever's on the other side must be in vacuum?" Sokolov guessed. "Who knows? It's about the only direction we haven't tried to go yet."

He moved over to the panel and waited for Geille to join him. Together they operated the device as they had opened the other airtight hatches, standing back to let the hatch shimmer into nothingness for a brief time. Sokolov leaned over and looked inside. The air lock was about ten meters long, a deep and threatening pit.

"It's an air lock all right. It's the exact same dimensions as the ones in the outer hull."

He attached a small tether to the inner surface of the lock and rappelled into the shaft; Monashi followed a few meters above him. At the bottom, standing on the hatch leading to the chamber beyond, he recovered his line and fixed it to secure them in place.

"Ready to see what's on the other side?"

Monashi nodded in her helmet. They set their hands on the control unit and cycled the inner hatch. Below them was nothing but vast, empty space.

The inaccessible region in the center of the vessel was a monstrous spherical space, easily two hundred meters in diameter. While the gravity at this level was very weak, there was enough of it to fool Sokolov's brain into believing that he clung to the side of a sheer wall above a horrifying drop. The jolt of terror brought sweat to his brow and left his heart thundering in his chest. Geille flailed in sudden panic, screaming over her suit radio as she dangled over the edge.

"Pete!"

Sokolov tightened his grip on the tether and caught Geille with his cybernetic arm. "It's okay," he told her, reassuring himself at the same time. "There's almost no gravity here. Your magnetic boots are enough to stick you to the wall. Go ahead, try it."

Gasping for breath, Geille followed his instructions. Together they worked their way out of the lock until they hung from the inner surface of the globe, studying the structure. At uneven intervals around the globe's perimeter, other hatches

offered the possibility of escape. Strange metal girders, wide
and flat, honeycombed the inner surface like a series of raised
walkways, connecting the air lock ports to each other. The walls
themselves were constructed of some strange material Sokolov
hadn't seen elsewhere on the ship, a ribbed greenish metal that
seemed *grown* rather than made.

In the center of the chamber, a green-black sphere about ten
or fifteen meters in diameter floated motionlessly. Convoluted
grooves and whorls marked its surface. The entire chamber was
starkly illuminated by great white arc lights blazing like suns
around the outer walls. Sokolov's head reeled with the conflict-
ing perceptions. His inner ear told him that he was hanging
upside down from the ceiling of this chamber, while his eyes
told him that he stood at the bottom of a great bowl, looking up
at walls that curved to meet overhead.

"I think I'm going to be sick," Geille said weakly. She hadn't
released his arm yet.

"Push the red button on your suit's control panel and make
sure you get everything into the yellow bag in front of your
mouth," he warned.

He cut out his suit speakers and looked the other way while
she hunched over. He wasn't feeling very good himself and
didn't want to think about what she was doing. He spent the
time examining the strange catwalk structure immediately overhead. Off to one side, he noticed that it led to the only thing that
interfered with the symmetry of the room, a rounded nodule
protruding into the chamber about fifty meters to his left.

After a short time, Geille tapped him on the shoulder. He
turned his radio back on. "You okay?"

"Better, I guess. I didn't know suits came with sick bags."

"If we'd been somewhere else on the ship, I would've told
you to open your faceplate instead, but we're in vacuum here."
He pointed toward the metal tracking. "Let's turn over to put
our feet on this catwalk here, and then go see if there's another
way out. Do what I do."

Securing himself to one of the track supports, Sokolov
released his boots and lazily turned himself over so that his feet
were pointing toward the middle of the dome. He then relaxed

his grip enough to drift down along the strut until his feet touched surface of the black metal walkway. Now he stood right side up at the very apex of a curving room, walking along a narrow catwalk with two hundred meters of space beneath him.

"I guess the dragons didn't mind heights," he muttered. He steadied Geille as she repeated his maneuver.

She knelt on the walk, crouching to study the room below. "What is this place? What's it do?"

"How should I know? Maybe they love zero-g acrobatics and spend all their free time plummeting from one side of this room to the other."

"It's got to be something important. The stardrive? Their main power plant?"

Sokolov laughed harshly. "It's nothing like any power system I've ever seen."

He chose the direction that led toward the module on the sphere's inner surface and started walking. The dragons hadn't bothered to provide any kind of handrails. Sokolov concentrated on putting one foot in front of the other and ignored the view.

The catwalk ran right into the round structure, a hemisphere about ten meters in diameter clinging to the wall. A narrow black metal hatch marked the meeting of the structures. Sokolov and Monashi carefully opened it and peered inside.

This was a control room with a floor of glass. From this chamber, the miniature sphere hanging in the center of the room seemed to be directly below, but some kind of magnification effect made it seem much larger and closer than it was. Dozens of displays, gauges, and indecipherable panels lined the walls and the ceiling, many now flickering with red and yellow lights.

In their godlike view of the chamber below, they could clearly see fine webs of green-white energy wreathing the orb, crackling fiercely in some spectrum beyond the acuity of the human eye. Meters on the walls danced and flickered with each pulse of the device beneath them.

"What is that thing?" Sokolov asked softly, eyes fixed on the sight.

Geille didn't answer at first; she was too busy considering the ramifications. When Sokolov tore his eyes from the eldritch play of energy to wring a reply from her, she was lost in thought.

"Geille?" he asked. "What do you see?"

"I think," she said slowly, "that the dragons have learned how to get something for nothing."

"What's that supposed to mean?"

"Zero-point energy. Vacuum fluctuations. It's an idea that's been around for a long, long time. They demonstrated the phenomenon as far back as the twentieth century, but no one's ever figured out how to make it work on a commercial or military scale."

"I don't know what you're talking about," he rasped.

"At the quantum level, particles spontaneously come into existence in vacuum," she explained. "There's a universal balance sheet at work here, since the particles pop in with an antiparticle of the exact right kind in close proximity. Almost always, the particle and anti-particle annihilate each other, and the books are clear again. No energy was added, no mass was added, since for all intents and purposes the two particles that fluxed into existence weren't here long enough to matter."

"Okay, I've heard some of this before, but what's the point? If they both just annihilate each other, they might as well have never existed."

"That's the trick," Monashi explained. "Sometimes, they *don't* annihilate each other. If you find a way to separate them before they can, you've just created something that didn't exist before. Tthat means that you've broken the old laws of thermodynamics. You've gotten energy out of a process without spending more energy than you harvested to make it happen."

Sokolov gestured at the structure under his feet. "So? They've got to be paying the energy bill somewhere, right? We have to use energy to run the devices, the processes, that let us demonstrate vacuum energy, so we're not really getting anything for free."

Geille shrugged. "You're right. A number of computing technologies make use of this effect. We have to put energy into very specialized devices to get the effect we want, but look at this thing, Sokolov. It's making the energy that powers this colossal shipwreck. I don't know how the dragons are paying the bill, but it seems clear that they've found a way with this technology to get more for their money than we have."

Sokolov remained silent for a long moment. "This is what caused the Big Bang, isn't it? Given enough time, nothing will sooner or later flux into something. So here we stand."

Geille shrugged. "You'd have to ask God about that, but yes, some physicists think that the Big Bang started as a vacuum fluctuation before anything else existed."

"So all we have to do now is find a way to shut it down again in order to get those damned hatches to open," he muttered. He looked up, searching the walls around them for some kind of controls. "The dragons did a lot of things differently than we do, but I'd bet my ship that this is an engineering control station: someplace where a crewman could monitor the operation of the main power plant, keep it running at the optimal level, maybe choose different distribution strategies in case of an emergency. Somewhere there's got to be a way to shut it down."

"Pushing buttons at random might be dangerous," Geille warned.

"As far as I can tell, we'll starve to death onboard this hulk if we don't try something. How did you activate the console up on the bridge?" Sokolov moved to the nearest console, closely scrutinizing it. Two flat, dark panels seemed to mark the location of the control surfaces, but nothing he did seemed to bring the unit to life.

Geille grimaced, watching him, then she fell to studying the controls more closely, ignoring Sokolov's mindless efforts. After a moment's study, she drifted over to the console opposite the hatch and passed her hand over the dark surface.

Green and blue characters came to life under her fingers, dancing on the screen. She smiled faintly and then fixed her concentration on the display, streaming data past her eyes. Behind her, Sokolov straightened as he caught sight of the illuminated panel.

"Geille? What have you got there?"

She spared him a single glance but didn't answer. The streaming displays glimmered against her visor, concealing her features. Abruptly the room plunged into darkness, and the eerie green glow coming from the orb in the power room's central vacuum began to fade.

"Check the mass reading on your sensor gauntlet," she said remotely.

Sokolov blinked. "What?"

"I think I killed the ship's power. That ought to bring down the security curtains," Geille said. "I need to know if that strange mass reading you were picking up went away, too."

The bounty hunter raised his left arm, studying the sensor unit he wore over his suit glove. The gauntlet's mass detector was so weak as to be virtually useless, but Sokolov knew exactly what he was looking for by now. He quickly tuned the device and scanned the vicinity. After a moment, he lowered his arm and stared at Geille.

"It's gone. You shut it down somehow."

"I was pretty sure it was going to work," she admitted. Her face was unreadable beneath the dark visor. "So there's no reason we can't get out of here now?"

"I don't think so," Sokolov said. A chill of caution seemed to cut through his chest. She's up to something, he realized. She's figured something out. Slowly and deliberately, he let his right hand fall to the butt of his sabot pistol. "Geille, what—"

"That's what I wanted to know," she said absently.

She glanced up at a strange spiral apparatus suspended from the ceiling. Sokolov followed her eyes; to his surprise, the device began to glow, crackling with a nimbus of green energy.

He had the gun only halfway out of the holster when the spiral flared into emerald brilliance and speared him with a bolt of living energy. Verdant light filled his faceplate; static squealed in his suit radio. She made that happen, he thought in stunned silence, then darkness swirled up to drown him, dragging him down.

Slowly, in the light gravity, Sokolov collapsed like a puppet with its strings cut. Carbon charred the faceplate of his suit. Anchored by the magnetic grip of his boots, he came to rest in a strange, slumped posture, arms drifting aimlessly at his sides. His light drifted soundlessly to the deck and went out.

Geille studied him for a moment before turning back to the console. "Don't go anywhere," she said coldly. Information streamed by her faster and faster, a manic rush of indecipherable symbols and strange characters. She leaned over the alien machine, drinking it all in.

Chapter Ten

PYOTR DREAMED. The war had been over for nine years. He was fifteen, a child of the war. He'd spent his youth in the internment camps, gray and hopeless places of razorwire and prefab huts. Since a few days before his eleventh birthday, he'd called Byelokus home. It was like the others, a place where food was scarce and people seemed to appear and disappear as if conjured by the whim of some monstrous, blind entity. He'd never known exactly why he was being detained, what he might have done to earn freedom from his confinement, or even what conditions must come to pass in the torn and tattered society beyond the wires of Byelokus for the internment camp's purpose to be accomplished. It was a place of waiting, of indecision, where the planetary authorities of Novo Tver saved for later the problems they didn't wish to be troubled with today.

Pyotr was one of those unpleasant problems. They'd separated him from his mother when they sent him to Byelokus. He'd never found out where they had sent her, or even if she'd lived. At Byelokus, he was alone, a stranger among strangers, each concerned with his own survival.

For Pyotr, survival demanded that he become a thief. He wasn't big enough to take what he needed by intimidation, nor did he have any friends or relations to offer him safety from the camp's predators. He learned to be smarter, faster, more ruthless than everyone around him.

The most important lesson of his childhood, far more important than the drab instruction the camp administrators offered by rote to all of Byelokus's younger denizens, was simple: don't get caught. Nothing else approached the significance of that lesson.

Interminable days, months, years passed. He learned to steal from the guards, the administrators, his fellow prisoners, and—when he had a means of egress—from the dispirited populace of the grim factory town outside the gates of Byelokus. Despite his efforts, he was caught and caught again, always for minor larcenies. The typical result was a beating administered by his fellow internees, a miserable work assignment posted by the guards, or least odious of all punishments, a few weeks of droning reeducation at the hands of the administrators. Pyotr accepted these penalties as the price he paid for the many times he was not caught.

In August of 2481, he was caught in a much more serious crime. He'd killed a man. Unlike the other times when he'd been brought before the camp administrator for evaluation and assignment to reeducation, Pyotr had been picked up by the town police and delivered to the camp guards. He spent long, hot weeks in the sweltering guardhouse, caged in a plastic cell while the dull wheels of due process at Byelokus slowly turned. In his guts, Pyotr understood that The System was now, for the first time, considering whether it would be better off without him. There would be no extra work assignments or reeducation classes. Something new and unprecedented was going to happen to him, at the very least reassignment to another camp for a different sort of internee. The possible consequences of his actions went downhill rapidly from there.

In his dream, Pyotr recalled one of an endless series of days spent waiting in his windowless cubicle, considering his fate while he gazed aimlessly at the propaganda scrolling across the info display. The plastic walls were made of some blue, pebbled material that tended to become sticky when the air was too warm. A plastic-frame cot with a hard mattress and a small commode completed the furnishings. By the end of his third week of confinement, Pyotr would have cheerfully slit his own throat if he'd only had a knife.

The government man came to see him on the last day of the month. He was a short, round-faced bulldog of a man, thick and direct. Old-fashioned spectacles offered the only feature of note on one of the blandest faces Pyotr had ever seen. Without warning, the government man simply opened the door to his cell and stepped inside, placing a plastic stool by the door and seating himself on it. He regarded Pyotr in silence for a long time.

"You are Sokolov," he stated at last.

"Yes?"

"I am Durenkovic. I will ask you some questions about last month." The government man reached into his coat pocket and pulled out a battered metal dataslate. He activated the device and scanned its screen for a long moment. "You are quite a troublemaker, I see. You have been reeducated five times, if my records are correct."

"Six now."

"Six? Ah. I will note it." The man recorded something on the dataslate and looked up again. "One wonders if you are making any valuable contribution to the Domain, young Sokolov. We do not expect someone of your years to be a productive citizen yet, of course, but we do expect that you should not require the constant supervision of the guards and administrators of this camp. More to the point—" he lowered the dataslate to his lap and fixed his watery eyes on Pyotr— "we do not expect to consider the issue of a capital crime before you have reached the age of majority."

Pyotr could think of no good response. Durenkovic studied him as if he were some kind of caged specimen, finally adjusting his glasses and continuing.

"The camp administrator recommends termination," he said simply. "That would certainly save us the trouble of keeping an eye on you, eh, Sokolov?" Durenkovic snorted sour laughter at his own humor.

"Before I can forward his recommendation, I must interview you, so here I am. Now, why don't you tell me what happened last month?"

Pyotr shrugged. "The police report is accurate."

"That I do not doubt. I wish to hear the story from you, though."

At fifteen, Pyotr had already attained much of his full height, although it seemed to be all legs and arms. He found himself standing awkwardly, pacing back and forth with jerky motions. "There isn't much to say. I was in the town. I broke into a store to steal cigarettes, since I can sell them to the other internees for money and food. When I was leaving, two bullies found me in the alley behind the store. They attacked me."

"Why did they do that?"

"No one in town likes the internees. If we're outside the wire, we're fair game to anyone. Most of the townspeople just ignore us or call the camp guards. Some of the men beat us if we're caught. They want to make sure we know where we belong."

"Obviously this lesson has been lost on you. Continue— what happened next?"

"I ran. One could not keep up with me, but the other chased me for a long way. I turned into a blind alley, trying to escape him. He cornered me and pulled out a knife. I think the long chase angered him." Despite years of experience in confessing his misdeeds to the face of authority, Pyotr began to tremble. He'd seen many things during his time in the camps, but the gleam of the metal in the ruffian's hand still burned like a dark brand in his mind's eye. "We fought. He cut me here and here, but I took the knife away from him and stabbed him. The city police picked me up when I was trying to retrace my steps back to the camp."

Durenkovic tapped one finger slowly against the dull metal of the dataslate in his hand, measuring the story. "The details of your encounter interest me," he said finally. "You've demonstrated the ability to leave and reenter this camp at will, despite the fact that all quarters are electronically monitored and the guards are under orders to specifically watch for you. You broke into a store by hot-wiring a sophisticated electronic alarm, and when cornered, you killed not just a common ruffian, but a gang captain who was a cyber-enhanced veteran of the Talisoi campaign." He paused then added, "In fact, if not for some bad luck, you would have gotten away with your exploit."

Pyotr simply stared at the floor. He could not see where Durenkovic was going and feared that he would not like it when the government man finally came around to his point.

"No response, I see. I will take that as a confirmation of the details in my briefing. So young Sokolov, what do you expect will happen now?"

"I don't know."

"I shall inform you, then." Durenkovic stood up, dropping the recorder to the seat. Pyotr looked up in time to spy a gleam of metal inside the man's jacket, an ugly sidearm. "I have ordered your termination. However, for the moment, I choose to stay my sentence. You will not die today, young Sokolov, if you agree to certain conditions."

Pyotr's heart hammered in his chest. "What . . . conditions?"

"The Domain has need of certain men who do not contribute to society in the usual ways," Durenkovic said with a humorless smile, "men whose skills have no place in any civilized society, who can do those things which are demanded of a nation in the name of survival. The Domain is founded on rational, scientific principles designed to inculcate productivity, compliance, conformity. Yet in order to meet the threats that face our Domain in the hostile universe around us, we must have operatives who can set these principles aside. Do you understand me?"

Pyotr nodded weakly, although he did not really comprehend what the government man was telling him. "I am leaving Byelokus?"

Durenkovic smiled again, a bland and soulless expression. "Consider yourself dead. No one who knows you shall ever see you again or even suspect that you still live. You have much work ahead of you." The man's sour grin faded into deadly seriousness. "But understand me, Sokolov. You are dead. I simply have not pulled the trigger yet. I may carry out the Domain's sentence against you at any time for any reason. You will have to work very hard to persuade the Domain that you may still be of service."

Durenkovic picked up his data recorder from the stool and rapped sharply on door. He seemed tired, disinterested, bored with the entire interview, but Pyotr knew the man was watching him closely.

Over his shoulder, the government man said simply, "Are you coming?"

Pyotr glanced around at the blue plastic walls of the cell. They would be the last thing he'd see if he refused Durenkovic. He stood, trying to quell the trembling in his bony frame.

"Yes, Comrade Durenkovic. I am coming."

INTERRUPT Emergency status override active START Reinitialization program Sokolov 15/A6/3300:3950// k STATUS Main cybernetic interface inoperative reflex/enhancement program stack unusable ACTION Seek technical support immediately REPEAT INTERRUPT Emergency status override active START Reinitialization program . . . .

In one merciless instant, Sokolov's consciousness balanced on some razor-thin barrier between the past and the present. Images twenty years old cluttered his mind—the pebbly blue plastic of the cell, the sour smell of his own unwashed body, the shabby overcoat Durenkovic wore over his drab suit—but Nancy poured information into his brain, ruthlessly jolting him awake, shocking him into consciousness through the neural connections that linked his mind to the nanocomputer.

He came awake with an agonized gasp, hammers of white pain piercing his skull. He started to sit up, only to be checked by several tight straps across his chest. He struggled fiercely for a moment before he realized that he was in the guest stateroom of *Peregrine,* strapped into place with the bunk's nylon restraints.

His cybernetic arm hung unresponsive at his side, refusing to acknowledge the motor impulses his brain fired at muscles and tendons that had been replaced by duraplas-covered steel. *Nancy!* he thought anxiously. *What the hell's going on? What time is it? Why can't I move?*

You are currently aboard Peregrine, *the computer replied. System records show an interruption of seventeen hours in consciousness. It is now 2322:15 hours on May 9th, 2502, Galactic Standard Time. All installed systems were affected by EMP effect of unknown origin at 0631:44 hours. Approximately eighty-seven percent of device operations are currently unavailable due to system damage and dropped software configurations.*

"Eighty-seven percent?" Sokolov muttered aloud.

He twisted his head—about the only motion permitted him in his confinement—and searched the cabin for something that would jar his memory. *I haven't thought about Durenkovic in years,* he thought absently. *Byelokus was something he deliberately tried not to recall. Why would I be dreaming about that?*

Insufficient data, Nancy told him.

"I wasn't talking to you." Sokolov hadn't even realized he was still thinking in Narislavic. Seventeen hours. He was back aboard *Peregrine.* Clearly he hadn't gotten here under his own power. His head ached abominably. His left arm and shoulder itched and throbbed, the familiar aftereffect of autodoc treatments. "How badly am I hurt?"

Second-degree electrical burns and radiation injuries to the left arm and torso. Inoperative cybernetic systems. Some minor neurotrauma caused by energy feedback in main neural interface devices, Nancy reported.

"Minor, hell. You don't have this headache." Sokolov closed his eyes and let his head fall back to the pillow. "Okay, Nancy. Show me the schematics on the damage. Let's see how badly you're hurt."

I cannot comply.

His eyes flew open in surprise. "What? What do you mean, you can't comply?"

Security protocols installed at 1933:58 hours prohibit me from taking action to reinitialize systems and subroutines that are currently off line. I cannot comply with your request. Nancy had a certain level of subdued personality emulation; it could express basic emotions when necessary. The nanocomputer punctuated its report with a vague unease and disappointment.

"New security protocols? What the hell?"

Sokolov strained again at his bindings, as if he could wring an answer from the computer inside his skull with brute force. Something was drastically wrong, and he was beginning to have his suspicions. When he gave up struggling against the tireless straps, he collapsed back into the bunk, fuming. *I need a smoke,* he thought. He closed his eyes and started to consider his options. Nothing occurred to him.

Forty-seven minutes later—Nancy's clock worked just

fine—Geille Monashi opened the cabin door and advanced into the room, Sokolov's Wesshaur in her hand. She stood silent, watching him with a complete lack of expression.

"Good. You're awake. I didn't know how badly the energy discharge had injured you."

"I think I'll pull through. What happened?"

She'd donned her own jump suit, newly washed and pressed, and her hair gleamed as if she'd just gotten out of the shower. Keeping the gun trained on him, she leaned against the door, measuring him.

"I killed the ship's power and security systems. The internal partitions vanished. I followed the map you'd been making on your dataslate and towed you out. It's not that hard in zero g."

"How did you shut down the power?"

She studied him for a long moment. "Do you remember the engineering control chamber?" she asked suddenly.

"I—yes, I do. You were looking at a console or something." Sokolov groped for the memory. A flash of green light, and before that . . . "You triggered that weapon. You got the derelict to shoot me!"

"You didn't leave me too many alternatives, did you?"

"Damn it, Geille! What if that thing had killed me—or both of us, for that matter? How in the hell did you know what was going to happen when you started up the machine?"

"You'll be okay. The energy discharge knocked you out, but I don't think there's any permanent damage."

Sokolov closed his eyes. A green flash of light, Geille standing by the control panel, arms crossed, simply watching the symbols and characters flicker past, studying them. Focusing on them. *Nancy, display authentication for commands entered while I was unconscious,* Sokolov thought at his nanocomputer.

1731:58. Monashi 010.

1754:09. Monashi 010-A.

1757:30. Monashi 020.

Okay, that's enough, Sokolov snarled silently. Somehow Geille had gotten inside his head. She must have found the concealed wire jack in his arm and hacked his nanocomputer. How did she know it was there? he thought. Seething in anger, he opened his eyes again and fixed a black, murderous look on the woman.

"What did you do to me?" he growled. "How did you do it?"

"I've taken away some of your cybernetic programming," she said. She allowed herself a small, satisfied smile, but her eyes were flat and hard. "You've already shown me just how dangerous you really are. I figured I had to level the playing field. You don't need to know how I did it."

Geille hadn't even lifted a finger to activate those consoles. She'd simply stared at them, concentrating. Something clicked in Sokolov's head. *High psi-aptitude scores, no demonstrable mindwalking talents.*

"You've got a psionic talent. Some kind of empathic link with computers. That's how you operated the controls onboard the derelict." He narrowed his eyes, virtually snarling. "That's how you compromised my nanocomputer."

Some of the self-assurance fell away from her face. She started to shake her head in denial, shifting her weight uncomfortably. Sensing that he was close to the truth, he pressed on.

"You've been hiding that little secret for years, haven't you? One little edge to help you climb the corporate ladder. They'd burn you at the stake for that anywhere on Penates, so you just kept it to yourself." He laughed bitterly. "No wonder Borun wants you back. You're priceless. The Picts would have gutted you if they'd ever figured out that you had a little something extra going for you."

Geille flinched. She shoved herself away from the door and stalked over to the bunk. Dark resolve crystallized in her face; her mouth settled into a firm, hard line.

"You want to talk about secrets, Sokolov? You have some good ones. You're only half a man. You're a damned *cyborg,* fitted out with machinery that would make a mechalus proud. Nariac military intelligence, if I read it right. No wonder you work as a bounty hunter—you have to see who will pay you to tell right from wrong. It's pathetic."

Sokolov surged against the restraints, but without the mechanical strength of his cybernetic arm, he was pinned in place. "Let me out of here!" he barked. "I mean *now!* "

"I wonder how many times you've stood right where I'm standing, looking at someone else saying the same thing," Geille replied. "Enjoy your own hospitality for a while, Pete. It might build character."

"Is this why you dragged me off that alien ship? So you could get even with me?" he snapped.

Geille simply watched him. "You're just a hunting dog. Why bother? I might as well try to teach a fly not to eat shit."

Sokolov stopped thrashing. He fixed his eyes on her, cold and deadly. Geille met his fierce gaze with chilly contempt, tapping the gun in one hand, then deliberately, she paced away, holstering the weapon.

Speaking at the bulkhead, she said, "Getting even isn't important. I carried you off that ship for two reasons. First, I was afraid that Peri might blow her mass reactor if I didn't bring you back alive. You went out of your way to explain to me what would happen if the ship decided that you'd died.

"Second, I can't fly this wreck. I don't know anything about astrogation. I have no intention of staying out here with that alien derelict until the air and water runs out, so that means I'll need you to pilot me out of this mess."

He kept his eyes on her. "Take the tutorial. You'll be ready to plot starfalls in two, maybe three months. I'm not flying you anywhere."

She wheeled on him. "I can do this the hard way, Sokolov. Is that what you want?"

He clenched his jaw but said nothing for a long moment. Maybe she was capable of that and maybe not, but it was becoming clear that Geille Monashi was a lot more than he expected. She'd found a way to reverse their positions; he'd have tried to do the same. In fact, now that the situation was reversed, he wouldn't rest until he'd gained control again.

"So how do you want to work this?" he rasped.

"I'm going to release you long enough to plot our starfall, then I'm going to lock you in here and keep you sedated for the rest of the trip. When we get where we're going, I'll walk away from this whole thing, and so will you. You get your ship, your life, whatever you can do with that alien hulk outside. I get to vanish. Do we have a deal?"

Sokolov bared his teeth, fighting back a snarl. He'd never been good at losing. "Where do you want to go?" he grated, trying to keep his temper.

"Not Lucullus," Geille said. "Aegis seems like a good place. I'll think of some way to pen you up for a couple of days after we land. I'll buy passage on a ship going somewhere. By the time you get out, I'll be long gone."

"What if I refuse to cooperate?"

"You know I can't kill you because I need you alive, but I'll start by blowing holes in your legs until you begin to see things my way. You've probably noticed that I've disabled your cybernetics, and you can believe me when I say that I'll be watching you like a hawk. I can be as ruthless as I have to be." She moved close, reaching out to seize his face and force him to meet her eyes. She leaned forward and hissed, "What I want right now, Sokolov, is my *freedom,* freedom from you, freedom from Karcen Borun and HelixTech, freedom from that stinking cesspool of a city that I grew up in, freedom to be my own person and do what I want with my life. Do you understand me?"

He narrowed his eyes. "I think I get it."

"Good." She reached for something in her suit pocket—a black, gleaming hypo pistol. "Peri tells me that we'll be ready to starfall in about two more hours. I'll wake you up to plot our course. Until then, you're going to get some sleep." She leaned forward, pressing the device against his exposed neck.

"Geille, don't you—*zachyestu!*"

Something pinched the skin over his jugular. He glared at her, but his eyes couldn't focus on her face, and before he could find anything more to concern himself with, the room sank away into darkness.

*   *   *   *   *

Another pinch, this time in his arm, brought him back to wakefulness. The first thing he did, even before he opened his eyes, was to check with Nancy. *Time and status report,* he ordered. *0137:28,* the computer replied. *Seventy-three percent of all installed systems remain locked out by new security over-rides.*

"Get up, Sokolov. You have a course to set for me."

Geille waited across the room from him, still menacing him with the pistol. He looked down his torso and saw that the restraining straps had been released. Cautiously he swung his feet to the deck and stood up. His hands had been chained in front of him with a simple plastic binder, and his ankles were cuffed together as well. She kept the gun on him, staying out of reach—not that he could have overpowered her easily with the binders on his limbs and his right arm dead and unresponsive. With his cybernetics operational, he might have tried it, but Nancy reported that he was still locked out of his muscle drivers and reflex enhancement.

So this is what it's like to be on the other side of the gun. She must have missed something, he told himself. *I'll find it sooner or later.* Grimacing, he stood carefully and faced her.

"It would be easier with two hands."

"I'm patient. I'll wait while you do it with one."

"Can I get something to eat first? I'm starving."

Geille smiled coldly. "I know that you've seen every ruse in the book, Sokolov. Every prisoner you've ever had under your control must try something new. I'm going to assume that any request you make is designed to distract me or trick me into giving you just what you need to get loose. The answer is no."

"You don't intend to feed me until we reach Aegis?"

"No. You'll be sedated. You won't care." She gestured at the cabin door with the pistol's barrel. "Go on. Lay in the course so we can make the jump."

He scowled and shuffled past her. The thing that really annoyed him was that he *was* hungry. He hadn't eaten in close to twenty-four hours now. Fine, he thought angrily. Let's see what I can do to reverse this development. *Nancy, is the sub-dermal transceiver operational?*

Yes, Pyotr. However, the primary communication protocol is locked out by security directives.

"I expected that," he mumbled under his breath.

He turned toward the bridge, taking his time as he moved forward. He glanced behind him. Geille followed several meters back, gun leveled at the small of his back. She might claim that she wouldn't kill him if he tried anything, but he didn't trust her instincts. If he surprised her too much, she might just fire on pure reaction. That could be the last mistake he'd ever make.

On the other hand, if he didn't surprise her enough, she'd have time to do exactly what she promised. The Wesshaur's 15mm slug would put him down on the deck, regardless of whether she just shot him in the leg.

As if reading his thoughts, Geille fixed her eyes on his. "Keep moving. Don't even think about it."

"Don't worry," he told her, then he raised his voice and said, "Peri? Flashpoint Seventeen."

Geille covered the distance between them in one swift bound, sweeping his legs out from underneath him with a skill-ful kick. He hit the deck hard, unable to break his fall. She whipped him across the face once with the heavy-barreled pistol. Stars danced in his eyes.

"Peri! Override Geille-Atlas," she snapped.

The computer was slow in answering. Her voice seemed slurred and emotionless. "I'm sorry, Pete. I can't comply with your order. Geille has installed new security protocols that prevent me from accepting any commands from you."

The woman held the gun in his face, kneeling astride him. A faint sheen of sweat covered her face. Sokolov found himself recalling the hours they'd spent engaged in a competition of a different sort. All an act, he realized. He was surprised by how much it hurt, even though he'd seen it coming the whole time.

Something dark and violent twisted in his soul, the arrogant pride that refused to allow him to accept defeat, refused to let him treat anyone around him as anything but an adversary. Thinking of Geille as an enemy was comfortable for him. When you expected the worst from people, you were seldom disappointed. Sokolov had survived as long as he had by cultivating a thoughtful and cautious brand of hatred.

Geille had saved his life because she needed him, then she had taken every step she could to ensure that he would not defeat her. He could give that back to her in spades.

"You're going to be sorry for that," he said through the pain.

Hovering over him, Geille searched his face and found something that unsettled her. The resolve in her eyes weakened; her mouth tightened. She stood slowly, poised to strike or shoot as necessary.

Ignoring his threat, she asked, "So what's 'Flashpoint'?"

"Command override. It tells Peri that I'm under duress."

"That's it?" she demanded.

"There are some things she won't do if she knows I'm in trouble." Geille didn't need to know he had instructions that could inform Peri that she was under duress, too. A warm, wet trickle edged down the line of his scalp—blood. "Of course, I don't know what effect your instructions may have on all that."

"Don't try to issue any more commands to the computer. They probably won't work, but just to make sure, I'll fire. Do you understand?"

He met her eyes. "Yeah, I understand." Moving deliberately, he struggled to his feet, ignoring the ache in his skull and the unsteadiness in his legs.

Nancy, activate subdermal transceiver in Test Mode Zulu, he thought at his nanocomputer.

Acknowledged, the computer replied. Sokolov resumed his slow progress toward the command deck so that Geille wouldn't see his smile. She'd locked out all direct commands to his cyberware. She'd made sure that none of the drivers or interfaces could respond to his orders, but long ago he'd programmed a handful of extra codes into his nanocomp. Test Mode Zulu was one of them. It circumvented Geille's security lockouts by masquerading as a simple system test, a routine interrogation to verify that the nanocomputer and the transceiver could pass instructions back and forth.

It also gave Sokolov the ability to transmit in Whisper protocol. Now we're getting somewhere, he thought. *Nancy, Whisper transmission: Peri, execute Duress Nine. Show me what alarm conditions Geille has set to warn her if I communicate with you.*

Acknowledged, Pete, came Peri's reply. The computer

responded by means of her radio, transmitting silently to the subdermal transceiver hidden in Sokolov's inoperative arm. While Sokolov hauled himself up the short ladder to the flight deck, thousands of lines of code flooded into his mind, the summary of Geille's efforts to transfer Peri's loyalty from Sokolov to herself. As he'd expected, almost any direct command he gave to the computer would be halted by Monashi's security buffers and held inactive until she confirmed the instructions.

Naturally Peri couldn't tell him how to disable Geille's security structure. Monashi was too good to leave anything that obvious open to his tampering. Sokolov was astounded by the depth and detail of the defenses she'd already installed in the ship's computer. *I have to remember that she's better at this than I am,* he reminded himself. The only advantage he had was time and preparation. She'd had his ship for nineteen hours; he'd had it for years. Sokolov was not a man who was going to be beaten by lack of preparation. *Comply with anything Geille tells you to do, Peri,* he directed the computer. *I'll be back in touch.*

Sokolov dropped himself into the seat in front of the nav display and activated it. A globe of blue space appeared in the holoprojector, showing *Peregrine* and the stars nearby. An icon for the derelict drifted a few million kilometers distant, faint and small.

"You moved us away from the dragon ship?" he asked in surprise.

"I decided we were too close for comfort. I had Peri give us some open space, just for my peace of mind."

"Good idea, I guess." He reached up and switched on the jury-rigged astrogation unit; Geille watched his every move. He called up the nav database, examining his charts of the Verge. "We can't reach Aegis in one jump. Looks like four starfalls to get there. Call it about thirty-two, maybe thirty-three days altogether."

"That's okay. I want you to program each one now."

"So you can keep me knocked out the whole time? Sorry, it doesn't work that way. There's a fair amount of uncertainty in each jump. I don't know exactly where we're going to wind up at the end of the first jump, so there's no way I can calculate the next one now. I'll have to plot each one we make when it's time to jump." *Don't make it look too easy. She'll get suspicious if she thinks I'm going along with her.*

"Peri, is that right?" Geille asked the computer.

"Yes. The actual amount of uncertainty is infinitesimal, but drivespace navigation calculations don't have any room for guesswork. We have to replot each new starfall using current navigational data." The computer offered a forced laugh. "That's how we ended up out here, Geille."

She frowned then nodded. "Okay. I can see how that might be true. Go ahead and plot the first starfall."

"Give me a couple of minutes."

Sokolov began to manipulate the display, taking his time. The local display faded, and a view of the inner quadrant of the Verge appeared. He deliberately began to plot a starfall leading back toward Lucullus, creating glowing red probability circles on the projection and narrowing them as he ran the calculations. *Nancy, Whisper protocol. Peri, Duress Nine. Disable voice response relays. Disable fault/alarm readouts on all system displays. Place the nav console in practice mode. Set true destination at Waypoint Eleven.*

Pete, Geille's security directives have been tripped, the computer replied.

I know, but you can't use your vocal interface, right? Your display screens aren't going to show any alarms while the repeater mode is disabled, correct?

The computer paused. *Vocal interface is disabled. Screen repeat mode disabled. She's bound to figure it out, Pete! I can't talk to her!*

"Wait and see," he said quietly.

He issued Peri a stream of instructions and commands, each setting off dozens of Geille's provisional security alarms. He glanced up at her; she watched him from the command chair, keeping the gun level at him.

She was frowning, uncertainty clear in the pensive set of her eyes. Ignoring his gaze, she stirred and leaned forward. "Hold on a minute. That course doesn't lead toward Aegis."

"It's the shortest way," he said. "I don't want this trip to take one day more than it has to, Geille."

"Peri, what's the name of the star Sokolov currently has marked as his first waypoint?"

You can answer, Peri, Sokolov told the computer.

"The first waypoint in the plan Pete is preparing is Lucullus," Peri said.

Geille sneered. "How stupid do you think I am? Do it right, or I'll find some way to make sure you don't screw around."

Sokolov gave up and replaced the display with one that showed the course she wanted. "This one is Reyjaa. It's the first starfall toward Aegis." He stood up and moved over to the engineering console, circling closer to her while powering up the stardrive controls. He only needed a small number of monitors and settings, but he turned on everything he could. "We're almost ready," he told her, nodding toward the nav console. "Go ahead and verify the destination if you want."

Geille stood and walked over to the nav display, keeping one eye on Sokolov while studying the holographic projection. She moved around so that she was facing him.

Peri, switch to infrared mode on all security cameras. Prepare to stream video on command deck camera Number One.

Acknowledged, Pete.

He moved slightly, so that he was standing underneath the overhead bin where he kept his tool chest. Geille looked up at him then went back to looking at the display.

Peri, execute Sokolov Alpha, he thought deliberately.

The lights went out, plunging the bridge into darkness.

The gravity went out at the same time.

Sokolov leaped up to the overhead and locked his unresponsive arm around one of the I-beams that crossed the ceiling, reaching for his tool kit on memory alone.

"Peri, lights and gravity *now!*" screamed Geille.

Ignore vocal interface, Sokolov reminded Peri. He closed his eyes, groping past the tools for the other device he kept in the same compartment. A smooth plastic grip met his fingers. *Stream the bridge video in infrared.*

Through Nancy's optical interface, Sokolov saw the bridge as Peri saw it in the darkness, cool blue shapes and outlines flecked with red where machines hummed smoothly, generating heat. One figure flailed in midair, spinning helplessly. Another figure clung to one wall. Sokolov moved his arm slightly, measuring the angle at which the computer's lens viewed him, then towed himself along the ceiling toward Geille.

He could hear her panting and cursing as she tried to ground herself and find him. "Sokolov! Don't make me shoot you! Turn the damned lights back on!"

Only two meters from Monashi's twisting form, Sokolov aimed the stutter pistol and fired. Compressed air coughed in a curious mechanical bark, slamming into Geille with the force of a hammer. She grunted once before the impact slammed her into the bulkhead. The sabot pistol in her hand fired with an ear-rending scream, throwing a shower of sparks from a damaged console across the command deck. Sokolov aimed and fired again, then once more to be sure.

The red image he saw in his mind floated motionless, drifting slowly away from the wall. *Lights, Peri,* he thought through the nanocomputer.

Battered into unconsciousness, Geille floated in the air, the Wesshaur drifting away from her loose fingers. Sokolov moved over to catch her and lower her to the deck before ordering Peri to restore the gravity. As an afterthought, he reactivated the computer's vocal interface.

"Pete, is she okay?" the computer asked at once.

"Stunned hard, but I don't think she's seriously injured," he replied.

Stutter pistols had been known to kill from time to time, but the spare that Sokolov kept hidden on the bridge—one of many weapons he had concealed around *Peregrine*—was a light model, unlikely to do real damage. Blood streamed from the woman's nose and ears. When he checked her pupils, the whites of her eyes were already begin to show an ugly web of broken vessels, but she was breathing evenly and her pulse was strong.

"I'm going to take her back to her room and secure her, then we'll have a look at what kind of instructions she added to your command directories," he told the computer. "Is there any reason why we can't starfall in the next thirty minutes or so?"

"No, Pete. We're green for Lucullus."

"Fine. I'm ready to get out of here." Carrying Geille with his one good arm, he left the bridge and limped back down to her cabin. His victory seemed cold and cheerless, like ashes in his mouth.

I need a new line of work, he decided.

Chapter Eleven

DRIVESPACE again.

As far as Sokolov could tell, Geille had succeeded in shutting down the anomalous influence that had dragged *Peregrine* out of drivespace thirty hours early on their last jump. He watched the stardrive closely for any signs of unusual fluctuations, but nothing came up. He attacked the layers of new instructions and reprogramming Geille Monashi had stacked both on *Peregrine*'s mainframe and his own internal nanocomputer.

While Geille slept in a sedated haze, Sokolov began to unravel her work. She'd had only a few hours against the hundreds he'd spent in preparation for defense against just this kind of attack, but she was good—very good. He realized that if she'd had a few more hours, or if he hadn't spent so much time and money in setting up system defenses for Peri and Nancy, Geille Monashi would still be the master of *Peregrine*.

Sokolov hated to lose. With each command he reprogrammed and each lockout he released, he understood exactly how close he'd come to doing exactly what Geille wanted him to do. He reminded himself that he was Pete Sokolov, and that *no one* beat him, *no one* coerced him into doing anything that he didn't want to do.

He would rather have cut off his remaining arm than capitulate to anyone. When the Domain had abandoned him five years ago, he decided that he'd taken his last order. That was the only principle he honored.

While Sokolov ghosted alone through drivespace, he carefully studied the directives that crippled his cybernetic enhancements. Geille had knocked his cybergear off line by installing a security buffer that prevented any active commands or motor messages; the test mode bypass he'd used was about the only way he could have brought his subdermal communicator on-line. She'd also set up a number of encryptions and lockouts on hundreds of files stored in the nanocomp's memory.

Sokolov worried at the problem for half a day before resorting to his dataslate. He loaded one of his break-in programs into the hand-held computer, mated the notepad to the interface jack in his arm, and spent hours hacking his own nanocomp in order to decrypt files and dump Monashi's security programs. Bleary with fatigue, he finally recovered the use of his cybernetics thirty hours into the drivespace trip. He checked on Geille and then crawled into bed for a few hours' rest.

When he woke up, he tackled the job of expunging Geille's commands from *Peregrine*. It took most of the day, but he was slowly getting the knack of how she'd worked, so he made better progress than he did in debugging Nancy. Geille had made an understandable mistake in setting up her priority controls in Peri's main processors. She hadn't known about the duress instructions. The duress codes were invisible, files that didn't show up on the mainframe until they were activated. The Flashpoint command had restored Sokolov's access to Peri, and from that point forward, all Sokolov had to worry about was Monashi's gun.

By the time they were halfway through starfall, he'd regained control over his computers with the exception of one set of encrypted files. They defeated every one of Sokolov's attempts to decode them, and even Peri couldn't say what was in them.

"I'm sorry, Pete, but I don't have the software to peek into a secure file of this type. I know exactly where it is in my hardware, but I just can't read it."

He scratched his sparse beard. "When was the file created?"

"About six hours before we jumped."

"So Geille did it. I'd be surprised to learn that you'd been carrying anything like that from your previous owners." Sokolov thought for a long moment. "Can you tell if any crucial information has been removed from other locations in your memory? Maybe she shuffled data out of an open file and into one she could encrypt."

"I'll check, Pete. That could take a while."

"Sort your operation record by time of operation and look for file transfers around the time the encrypted file was created," he suggested.

Peri sighed indulgently. "I know, Pete. What did you think I would do, a random search?" She fell silent for a few minutes while Sokolov leaned back and smoked a cigarette. "Wait, here's something. I'm missing some navigational records."

"What exactly are you missing?"

"Our nav records for the last six days have been removed from the navigational database and encrypted, Pete."

He dropped the cigarette to the deck and crushed it out. "Damn. So we have no record of exactly where the derelict is located?"

"I'm sorry, Pete. That is correct."

"Continue to look for sleeper commands and hidden files," he told her. "I think it's time I woke up Geille."

He stood and stretched, then dropped down from the command deck to the living spaces below and behind *Peregrine*'s control center. At Geille's door, he paused to check the vision block. She was still asleep, which wasn't surprising considering the level of sedation she was under.

He consulted the tiny medcomp in the ship's galley and drew a hypo with the right mix of stimulants to bring her out of the drug-induced haze that he'd kept her in for three days, then he went back to her cabin, let himself in, and gave her the shot. He locked the door and settled back to wait, watching her. The bruises inflicted by the stutter pistol were mostly gone now, and she seemed much better, if somewhat thinner, more angular, in her face and figure. *It's as if she's being hammered into shape somehow,* he reflected, *tempered to something harder than she was.*

About five minutes later, she stirred and opened her eyes. "Thirsty," she gasped.

He gave her water and waited for her to come around. At length, she sat up slowly, focusing on him.

"What time is it? Where are we?" she rasped.

"About 0100 on the thirteenth. We're in drivespace. We've been in transit for about three days now."

She stared dully at him until a light of understanding began to gleam in her face. With it came resentment. "You got the ship back. The lights went out. Something hit me—"

"I stunned you with a stutter pistol."

"How did you do it? How did you get into the computer?" she demanded. "You should have been locked out altogether. I watched you the whole time. You were never near a command console."

"You don't need to know how I did it," he replied. "All you need to know is that I did it, and I've got my cybernetics restored. You're not going to get another chance."

She winced and slumped back. "So why'd you wake me up?" she muttered.

"You encrypted our navigational data. I want you to decode it."

"Go to hell," she said. She rolled over and faced the wall.

Command access interface Monashi-04 activated, Nancy reported. Sokolov tensed, easing his left hand down to the stutter pistol in his pocket. He'd expected this. *Attempting core memory wipe. . . . Interface access denied, as per protocol Sokolov-Last Laugh.*

"Don't bother trying that again," he grated. "Your psi-talent caught me off guard once, but I learn fast. Forget about trying to manipulate Peri, too. She's now under strict security routines that only allow her to accept my authenticated commands. If I even suspect that you're trying to circumvent them, I'll knock you out for the rest of the trip."

She remained silent, staring at the wall. He could read the despair in the set of her shoulders. She really thinks Borun is going to kill her, he realized. She's been fighting for her life from the moment I brought her onboard.

Sympathy wasn't part of Sokolov's emotional makeup, but understanding was. There was no point in getting angry. She was doing what she thought she needed to do, and that meant he had to keep that from happening. It's like a game of chess, he thought, played with physical confrontation, dirty tricks, and distrust. Geille chose this for herself when she tried to kill him in his sleep, when she gave herself to him to gain his trust, and when she tried to take his ship away from him.

It all comes down to who wants to win more, he thought. That's going to be me. "Listen, Geille. I'm going to get those files open one way or another. Work with me."

"What's it worth to you?" she said over her shoulder. "If I decode them so you can go back and capture your derelict, would you let me go?"

"Is that why you locked them? So that you could trade the key for your freedom?"

"I knew I'd have to have something to keep you off my trail when we got to Aegis," she said in a tired voice, "some reason I could give you to just walk away from the whole thing. I figured that you might let me go if I gave you your files back."

"That's not going to happen," he said flatly. "Give me the key to the files."

She rolled back and found her feet, standing to confront him. He'd undressed her before putting her to bed; she crossed her arms fiercely across her breasts and glared at him, defying him with her nakedness.

"Why do you have to bring me back? You could tell Borun anything you wanted. What the hell do you owe to him that you don't owe me?"

"He's paying me," Sokolov answered.

"I spared your life!" she shouted. "I could have let you die on that ship, Sokolov! It wouldn't make any difference to me if I died out there, too! I don't have anything to lose—Borun is going to kill me the moment you deliver me to him."

Something in him snapped. He found himself gripping her arms, shouting back at her. "No, he's not! Why would he send me to kidnap you from Icewalk instead of killing you? He needs you alive, Geille."

"You keep saying that," she retorted. "Who are you trying to convince? Me or yourself?" Her voice broke; she tried to restrain a sob, but it grew to a rasping wail in the back of her throat. "Is that how you live with what you do?"

"Borun told me—"

"Karcen Borun is lying to you, damn it!" she cried. Hot tears coursed down her cheeks. "He wants that research destroyed! I don't have any magic potion that's going to fix the damage I did before I left. I *know* what I did, Sokolov. I permanently wrecked the machines I sabotaged. There's no hope of recovering the data on them." She met his eyes, trying to match his resolve with her passion. "Don't you get it? Karcen Borun isn't working for HelixTech anymore. He's working for himself. He didn't want HelixTech to ever be able to recover the data. That's why he paid me to steal it for him."

"Then why am I supposed to bring you back alive?" he roared.

Suddenly her nerve failed her. She seemed to slump in front of his eyes. Quietly she said, "Because I double-crossed him, Sokolov. I corrupted the data I gave him. He paid me to give him the research and destroy the records, but I didn't do that. I wrecked the machines, like he wanted, but I kept the research for myself."

"What did you do that for?" he said.

"It was my work. If I'd given it to Karcen Borun, he would have made a fortune off of what I'd developed. And—"

"What else?"

"I was his lover. He set me up for the whole thing, Sokolov. He seduced me more than a year ago, made me part of his plan. I never would have gone along with it if I'd thought I wasn't doing it for him." She looked up at him again, finding new strength. "If all I'd done was run out on the deal, Borun might be satisfied just to get the research I promised him, but I don't think he's going to be satisfied with anything short of killing me, not after what I did to him. His pride won't let him rest until he's evened the score."

He stood silent, staring at her face, his heart pounding and blood rushing in his ears. She's lied to me before, he reminded himself. She tried to kill me when she thought that might win her freedom. She was perfectly willing to threaten him with death, injury, weeks of sedation when the circumstances were reversed. It's all an act, all calculated, every last word of it. But something in her frightened eyes, her trembling frame, told him otherwise.

"Do you have the real data?" he rasped. If she did, if she could prove to him that what she was saying was true, he would do it. He would go along with her. He'd break his deal with Karcen Borun. He didn't care anymore. "I need proof, Geille. Do you?"

She stared up at him with a stricken expression. "No," she said. "I hid it on Icewalk."

Emotions he couldn't control exploded in him. He picked her up by her arms and pinned her against the wall. *"How in hell am I supposed to recover anything from Icewalk now?"* he shouted.

She winced at the touch of cold metal on her bare skin, as surprised as he was by the violence of his motion. "I know the decryption key," she panted. "I can decode the data for Borun. He doesn't need the data crystals. All you have to do is give him the key. You don't have to bring me in."

He wanted to yell at her, to demand answers, the truth, anything. Instead Sokolov dropped her to the deck. He had nothing more to say to her. If she'd said something then, tried to convince him one more time of Borun's duplicity, he might have done something crazy. Wheeling away from her, he stormed out the door and slammed it behind him. He thought he understood why Karcen Borun might want to kill her.

* * * * *

The derelict drifted silently in the endless night, watching and waiting. A small distance away, the tiny alien vessel that had matched its course for four days generated a huge momentary mass signature and disappeared from normal space, falling out of view as swiftly and as certainly as if it had ceased to exist. The derelict's sensors recorded the event carefully. It was important data, indicating as it did that the aliens had mastered a form of faster than light travel that eluded its own builders. This was now the second major species known to make use of this particular technology. Clearly it had its advantages over the technologies employed by the derelict's masters.

The ship attempted to apply the mass interference device again in order to prevent the alien craft's departure, but the field generator was off line. The aliens had somehow managed to infiltrate several levels of the ship's engineering control systems, and the derelict was still trying to restart the systems they'd shut down. That might have been the most surprising and distressing development of the entire examination period. The derelict couldn't have established communications or command protocols against an alien computer even with thousands of hours of trial and error. The bipedal aliens had managed to analyze and shut down critical systems in a few hours of concentrated effort.

That, in turn, led directly to the second most distressing aspect of the encounter: namely, the derelict's failure to capture the alien ship and her crew intact. The whole reason the derelict was in this vicinity of space was to take a sample of this particular species, whose radio signals and travels through short-lived wormhole constructs had attracted the attention of the derelict's makers. They'd very carefully crafted the derelict as a trap designed to draw a small alien ship from its wormhole travel and study it at great length. Based on the glimmer of information they already had about the alien species, they'd built the derelict as the lure of a very elaborate trap. The builders were fond of such things.

Failing to capture the aliens after they'd actually boarded the derelict was less than satisfactory. The prey had been allowed to seize the lure and escape before capture, a total waste of materials and effort. Hidden in a subdeck that the two small bipeds had never explored, and would never have been allowed to leave had they somehow discovered it, the derelict's brain came to terms with its failure to execute its plan. It settled for examining the information it had gathered about the unknown species.

Fantastically sensitive chemical sniffers scrutinized the derelict's atmosphere for traces of any foreign elements the visitors had introduced. It concluded that they were carbon-based oxygen breathers, with a sophisticated and differentiated cell structure. Tiny particles of skin carelessly flaked from their bodies revealed a great deal about their organic chemistry and their genetic plan. Dozens of microbes were found in the samples and analyzed as well.

Sound-based imaging devices that had scanned the two intruders without attracting their attention revealed that one possessed a significant amount of mechanical augmentation and replacement, a fact that provoked some curiosity in the derelict's brain. Had the organism been badly damaged at some point in the past? If it had, why had it not been destroyed? That would have been much more expedient than fitting it with mechanical systems. Other sonar images showed their internal arrangements in great detail. The derelict identified respiratory, vascular, and digestive organs with considerable accuracy.

It knew a good deal about their technology. They communicated with radio waves that functioned as carrier waves for some kind of audio signal. They were capable of protecting themselves against vacuum and bitter cold. They relied extensively on artificial intelligences. Their ship was powered by some kind of gravity induction drive. Their suits and tools showed a high level of accomplishment in material science, although nothing that indicated that the aliens knew about virtual matter or zero-point power. The ship they'd brought alongside the derelict had been scanned from stem to stern, every detail recorded carefully.

Their minds proved much more difficult to analyze. They showed curiosity, boldness, patience, and great perseverance. The ability to interface with the derelict's own systems control computers was astonishing, yet the first thing the interfacing alien had chosen to do after disabling the security functions and shutting down the interference device was to employ an internal weapon against its companion. Instead of killing its helpless victim, it had apparently chosen to carry its companion back out to the alien craft rather than leave it behind. Why strike down an enemy and then go to great effort to save its life? The derelict could make no sense of the alien behavior.

Carefully the hidden brain considered its options. It would be questioned for its failure to prevent the aliens from leaving unmolested, but it calculated that their obvious curiosity and interest would bring them back. It ran through dozens of different variables and eventually arrived at a decision.

On the mottled exterior of the ship, a large structure quivered and changed shape. Something like a strange, exotic flower rose from its hull, pointing toward the place the derelict had been instructed to remember, then the derelict beamed out the sum total of everything it had seen and recorded over the last four days, barking static into the great void. Its masters would be pleased.

* * * * *

Three days later *Peregrine* returned to normal space in a burst of violet light.

Sokolov manned the command station on the bridge. As the ship emerged from drivespace, contact with the outside world resumed in a chaotic burst of radio signals, sensor information, and starlight. It took him only a moment to confirm that they'd returned to the Lucullus system.

"Looks like we're home," he observed.

Strapped into the copilot's seat against the slim possibility of a collision or impact following starrise, Geille ignored him. She had nothing left to fight with; she simply sat quietly on the bridge, avoiding Sokolov's eye. Shoulders slumped, arms folded under her breasts, she stared out the viewports.

She'd spent most of the last two days ignoring him. He hated her resignation. It would have been easier if she continued to fight back, to struggle, to hurt him somehow.

Sokolov triangulated on the nav beacons orbiting Penates and punched in a course toward the mottled brown crescent visible through the bridge viewports. He was carrying her to a situation in which she'd be lucky to stay alive for twenty-four hours. She'd fought him with every weapon at her disposal, but still he'd won. She'd also helped to save his life by repairing the damage Yeiwei had inflicted on the astrogation computer. She'd shared in his discovery of the derelict, and she'd probably saved him again by disarming the security stations and the device that prevented them from entering drivespace. Even if she had turned against him at the first chance, she'd made efforts to preserve his life. He also knew that Karcen Borun had lied to him about who she was and why he wanted her.

Don't forget that it was all part of the game, Sokolov reminded himself. Nothing personal, right?

She'd saved her own life by fixing the astrogation computer. She'd lied to him, tried to kill him, sabotaged his ship's computer and internal nanocomputer with her psi-talent. She'd intended to keep him prisoner on his own ship. She'd even seduced and used him without remorse.

Karcen Borun had lied, but he'd also paid him to do a job. Sokolov had accepted the contract; he was going to do what he'd promised. Geille might not have done anything to merit the fate Sokolov had been paid to bring down on her, but any pity he might have felt had been extinguished by her cold contempt when she had him in her power. When all the arguments were over, when there was nothing more to be said, it all came down to one thing: He didn't trust her enough to sway from his course. He wanted to believe her story, to believe her passion, but he didn't have that kind of trust in his soul, not after what she'd done to him.

Sokolov sat in the command seat, jaw clamped shut, eyes darting from instrument to instrument in the mindless performance of his duties. For the first time in a long time, Sokolov hated himself for playing the game to the best of his ability.

Ahead of them, visible as a dark circle blotting out the stars, loomed Penates. The jury-rigged astrogation unit had worked perfectly. They'd made starrise less than ten light-minutes from Penates, right on time. Sokolov drove *Peregrine* toward the planet on a long, looping course, watching carefully for any other traffic in their area. He hadn't forgotten the way he'd been driven out of Lucullus before, and Geille had sowed enough seeds of doubt in his mind to make him suspicious of anything that flew.

"Peri, see if you can raise Santiago traffic control," he said wearily. "Let's get this over with."

"Okay, Pete," the computer said.

In a moment, the bridge speakers crackled to life. "*Peregrine,* this is Santiago Control. Be advised that you have been cleared all the way to HelixTech. Follow the blue glide slope. Over."

"Who cleared me for that?"

"HelixTech local control keeps an eye on our traffic," the Santiago tech replied in a bored voice. "They called us up and told us to kick you over to them. You are going to HelixTech, right?"

Sokolov felt Monashi's eyes on him. He tried to ignore her. "Roger, we're bound for HelixTech. *Peregrine* out."

"They've been waiting for you," Geille said, breaking her silence.

"I'm surprised. I thought they would have given up on me by now. We're two weeks overdue, after all."

"Borun must have had his men on the lookout for you."

"Guess so." He looked up from his instruments long enough to meet her gaze. She sat wrapped in her own misery like a shawl, eyes ringed by dark circles, defeated. He forced his shoulders to relax, leaning back in his seat to study her. "Listen, Geille. Do you have anyone you want me to contact when we get down there? Someone who can keep Borun honest? Maybe you can walk away from this after you give him what he wants."

"My best chance to walk was to talk you into not bringing me back," she snapped. Scowling, she rubbed at her temples. "There's no one who will look out for me. Don't you get it? I sold out everything when I agreed to do what Borun wanted me to do. If I had any patrons who could check Karcen Borun, they'd want me dead now, too."

"You grew up in Santiago. Don't you have any family or friends? A good attorney?"

Geille swiveled in her seat to look at him. "It's Pict territory. I left it ten years ago when I scratched and clawed my way into HelixTech. I grew up as *chattel,* Sokolov. Anyone who isn't a blooded member of the gang is property. That's the way the Picts work. You have three choices: You can bow and scrape to those thugs for the rest of your life, praying that you never run across one in a malicious mood. You can join the club by killing a Pict in a fair fight. Or you can get the hell out, finding a way to make yourself so valuable to somebody that they'll buy you from the city lord.

"In Santiago, HelixTech is the way out. They rented me from King Steel for a couple of years until they decided I had enough skill and wits for them, and then they bought me. I spent the first three years of my employment paying back my purchase price."

She literally snarled in distaste. Sokolov was struck by how similar their situations must have been. Both had to fight their way out of childhood merely to survive.

Geille's anger slowly failed her. In a small voice, she continued. "HelixTech answers to no one, Sokolov. The Picts sure as hell don't care what the corporation does inside its own compound. Karcen Borun could have me drawn and quartered on prime time holovision, and the Picts would just think it was family programming."

"Okay, so you don't have any friends in the company," he replied, "but I'll bet you can find allies. If Karcen Borun is that powerful, he must have enemies, people who would just love to hear what you have to say about him, Geille. I can try to get them involved on your behalf."

"Like I told you, Pete, I've burned my bridges. As far as the rest of HelixTech cares, I'm a saboteur caught by Borun's bloodhound. I might be expected to say or do anything in order to get free." She laughed bitterly. "If anyone's my patron, it's Borun, and I double-crossed him. No, my prospects don't look very bright at HelixTech."

He tried to think of some kind of reply and failed. He returned his attention to his flying. They were close enough now that the dark mass of Penates hung over them. Patches of harsh light glowed here and there underneath the thin, toxic smog of the planet's atmosphere. Sokolov had always thought that from space, Penates looked something like thin fog over black swamp water with some kind of phosphorescent light glimmering near the surface. It wasn't an image that cheered him at all.

Geille surprised him by speaking again. "Don't take me back, Pete."

"What? Why?"

"Maybe you owe me something, maybe you don't. It's clear that's not going to reach you." She looked up at him, gaining force and resolve as she spoke. "You've got your reasons not to turn me over to Borun. I can tell you don't want to do it. Here's your chance to change your mind."

"The hell I'm not going through with this," he muttered automatically, but the weight of Geille's gaze demanded more from him. He glanced up and was caught at once by the fire, the iron, now surfacing as she readied herself for one last fight. He simply stared at her as if she could read minds. "I can't," he told her.

"Why?" she demanded. "Do you have a disorder that drives you to do things you don't want to do? Are you deriving some kind of sick pleasure out of punishing yourself by punishing me? I know you don't want to turn me in. Well, don't do it!"

He looked away from her and didn't say anything. What could he tell her? He was doing it for the money? That was ridiculous. It was a lot of money, but he didn't need it that badly, not with the derelict to sell. He was doing it to preserve his professional reputation, to adhere to some kind of honor code? The Mounties always get their man, he thought with a snarl, or woman.

Just maybe, the dark vitriolic part of his conscience said, you're doing it because you can't handle her. Once she's off the ship, you can go back to being your same old abrasive self, walling the world away behind a bastion of contempt. You never have to make any hard choices when you're looking out for number one.

Monashi didn't need to know that. He kept his mouth shut, refusing to answer her.

She surged up out of her seat and confronted him across the command console, forcing him to look at her. "Listen, Sokolov. This is the only time I'm going to say this. Don't turn me over to Karcen Borun. I swear you'll regret it. For one thing, you'll never decode the nav files without my help. The derelict is gone."

"Sit down," he replied. Geille had put him on familiar ground again. "I've got the stutter pistol in a holster under my seat. I'll stun you if I have to." He showed her the weapon and returned it to its holster. "Besides, I know some people. I'll get those files open."

Livid, she wheeled and threw herself back into the seat she'd been. "Spend your money fast," she said in a low voice. "I don't think you'll have a lot of time to enjoy it."

Sokolov ignored her threats and followed the glide slope down to HelixTech. The viewports misted over as they began to descend through the atmosphere. The display in front of Sokolov's controls showed a computer-generated terrain view marked with several flight paths. As he'd been advised, he chose the blue one. This descended at a shallower slope than the others, crossing all the way over the city of Santiago instead of descending to the wretched spaceport at the city's edge. Yellow domes and black towers rushed past beneath him, illuminated by the cacophonous glare of thousands of advertisements and decorations. They were over the city and gliding toward the black, monolithic towers of the complex beyond Santiago's ragged perimeter. One floodlight illuminated a gigantic logo in the center of the largest building: *HelixTech—One Step Ahead*.

"*Peregrine,* this is HelixTech local control," his radio said. "Follow the green lights to Port Two, over."

"This is *Peregrine.* Port Two, roger. Out."

Sokolov slanted the ship into the gentle curve indicated by the approach lights. He was heading for the north tower. Borun's office was there, if he remembered the layout correctly. Keeping a wary eye on Geille just in case she decided to make a move while he was busy landing the ship, he flared in for the final approach and touched down in the center of the pad.

Chapter Twelve

HELIXTECH'S BLACK walls, cold and pristine, towered over *Peregrine*. The landing platform was clean and well maintained, a far cry from the dilapidated facilities that served the other spaceports of Penates. He looked around for a transit corridor or jetway and was surprised when he didn't see one. Abruptly the platform beneath him jarred into motion, slowly sinking down into the rock and metal by the tower's flank.

"Power down, *Peregrine*. We're bringing you inside," the radio said.

Power and money to burn, Sokolov thought idly. Retractable landing platforms? He began to cut Peri's drives and power systems while dark gunmetal walls rose up, encircling the ship. Directly overhead, a heavy circular door shut, cutting off the view of the surface. He tried not to think that he and Geille were being swallowed alive. When the ship stopped moving, the radio spoke again, much clearer and closer this time.

"Okay, *Peregrine*. Give us about fifteen seconds to cycle the lock, then you can disembark. We've got a couple of escorts waiting for you by the door. Over."

"Roger," Sokolov answered. "*Peregrine* out." He cut the consoles and patted the bulkhead. "Okay, Peri. You're in charge. Finish the down checklist. Standard dock security posture."

"Can do, Pete." The computer began to lock down various minor systems around the ship, searching for components that demanded maintenance and running through the long list of minor details associated with making port.

Sokolov stood, picked up the stutter pistol in his right hand, and waved Geille toward the ladder leading down. "Come on. Let's go."

She thrust herself to her feet and stormed off the bridge as if her anger could defend her from what waited at the end of her walk. Sokolov followed her down to the air lock, checked to make sure HelixTech had provided an atmosphere to the other side, and opened both hatches at once. His ears popped with the subtle difference in pressure.

"After you."

Together they walked down the ship's steep access ramp into HelixTech's hangar. It was a huge cylindrical room, easily sixty or seventy meters tall, painfully illuminated by brilliant arc lights. The chamber was almost empty, as a room that might be opened to Penates's toxic atmosphere should be. Sokolov glanced around and spied several small access hatches and a set of windows leading to a control station about two decks up. One large double hatch was emblazoned with the corporate logo. While he watched, it slid open, revealing a pair of black-clad security guards and between them, Karcen Borun himself.

As soon as the hatch had parted enough to let him pass, the executive broke into a long, vigorous stride. "Sokolov!" he said, beaming. "I was beginning to think I'd never see or hear from you again! Geille . . . we've missed you around here. In fact, you might say we've been very anxious for your return."

Monashi stiffened. Sokolov looked down at her; her face was set in an iron scowl. Slowly she began to walk toward Borun and his guards. He followed a step behind her. They met Borun halfway between *Peregrine*'s lock and the entrance to the complex. Borun's predatory grin stretched wider, and his scrimshawed teeth gleamed in the harsh lights of the hangar. Trim and tan, he was dressed immaculately. While the two guards fitted a set of binders to Geille's wrists, he enthusiastically shook Sokolov's hand.

"You were supposed to be back two weeks ago! What happened? I mean, I'm glad you got her back, but I've got to tell you, Sokolov, I've had quite a few sleepless nights lately!"

Geille's dark eyes transfixed Sokolov where he stood. Arms bound behind her back, she stood watching him. With a conscious effort, he tore his eyes from hers and concentrated on Borun. Remember who you're dealing with, he told himself.

"Sorry for the delay. Shanassin pursued me when I left Icewalk, and I had to punch a starfall to get away. Five days to the middle of nowhere, four days recharging the stardrive, then five days back again. It was unavoidable."

Borun's gleaming facade flickered for just an instant, but the exec shrugged it off and clapped Sokolov on the shoulder. "Well, the job got done, even if it didn't work out quite like we thought it would. I want to hear about the whole thing—a blow-by-blow account of the last two weeks, but right now, I want to speak to our wayward Ms. Monashi here. We have a lot of things to talk to her about."

Borun nodded sharply at the two guards. They took Geille by the arms and marched her toward the hatch. Another guard, an attractive young woman in a tight-fitting black outfit, appeared in the doorway and approached Borun and Sokolov.

"I have to attend to Monashi first," Borun said. "It might take a couple of hours. In the meantime, I'd like to offer HelixTech's hospitality, Mr. Sokolov. You must be tired from your trip. Relax, take a bath, get something to eat, whatever. We have a guest room ready for you."

"You're paying for my time, Mr. Borun. I'm at your disposal."

Borun grinned. "Good! I'll debrief you in a little while, and then we'll take care of your payment." He trotted after Geille and her guards.

Sokolov watched him for a moment, then stepped forward before he knew what he was doing. "Just a moment, Borun." The man paused, turning at the sound of his voice. Forcing nonchalance into his manner, Sokolov said, "I have a question for you. Was I supposed to recover some data Monashi had in her possession?"

The executive's smile froze. His eyes glittered like glacier ice. "Why? Did you find anything like that?"

There it is, Sokolov thought. He knows what I'm talking about. Geille was telling the truth. He winced and forced a noncommittal shrug.

"No, it was just something Monashi talked about. It sounded important." Despite the guarded look in Borun's eyes, he decided to press on quickly. "One more thing, then. If you have no more use for her, I'd be interested in buying her from you."

"Buying her?" Now Borun was definitely alarmed. "What did she say to you, Sokolov?"

"Mr. Borun, in my line of work, you hear a lot of stories. People say just about anything to give you a reason not to take them back to where they're going." At that moment, Sokolov wanted nothing more than to shoot Borun on the spot. "She's a very attractive woman. If you have no further use for her, I know people who are interested in acquiring merchandise of that sort. There are techniques for making awkward knowledge and personalities go away, so you wouldn't have to worry about that. It's certainly more profitable than just shoving her out the air lock without a suit, hey?"

Karcen Borun stared at him. Finally his suspicion faded and his winning smile returned. He laughed out loud. "You kill me, Sokolov. I was thinking you'd gone soft on her. You're the most ruthless son of a bitch I've ever met!" He laughed again, shaking his head. "Sure, why the hell not? We'll talk about the details when I finish up with her."

He gestured at the woman standing nearby, politely out of earshot. "Come on over here, Trai. This is Mr. Sokolov. He'll be staying with us for a short time. Take good care of him."

Trai smiled in an unmistakable fashion and attached herself to Sokolov's arm. She might have been dressed in one of the corporate security outfits, but Sokolov was fairly certain that she was no guard.

"This way, Mr. Sokolov," she said. "I've heard a great deal about you." She led him toward the main hatch.

Sokolov looked back just long enough to see Karcen Borun sauntering off after Monashi and her guards. He was still laughing.

* * * * *

Sokolov spent more than three hours waiting for Borun. The guest quarters were extravagant, but he found he had little appetite for Karcen Borun's hospitality. Trai didn't interest him at all. Eventually he sent her away and simply stretched out on the sumptuous bed, idly channel surfing in the hope that he'd find something to engage his thoughts. The one thing he was determined not to allow himself to think about was, of course, the very subject his mind refused to relinquish.

Are they torturing her? he wondered. Ripping her memories, her soul, from her with neural probes? Coercing her with psychoactive drugs, or maybe a corporate mindwalker? He hoped Geille was smart enough to cooperate with anything they asked of her. In this day and age, there were far too many instruments of coercion available. Refusing Borun would bring her nothing but needless pain.

What really worried him was the possibility that Karcen Borun would apply those techniques even if Geille did cooperate. She might not resist at all, but that didn't mean that he wouldn't inflict pain on her. She'd betrayed him; now Sokolov had put her back in Borun's power.

To distract himself, he started to consider what he might do with his knowledge of the derelict. Any of the major factions of the Lucullus system would be interested. The derelict's technology was potentially worth millions. Billions, if we can figure out that zero-point power system, he thought. He ruled out the Picts immediately. If he led them to the treasure, they'd probably kill him the moment they had the prize in their hands. Helix-Tech he struck from his list simply because he was sick of dealing with Karcen Borun. Of the other major factions of Lucullus, the Syndicate and Union Penates were likely to honor any deal he struck with them, although there were certainly risks to minimize. The Technospiders would certainly deal with him honorably, but they were the weakest of Penates's factions, and whatever he gave them someone else would take away.

"I hate this whole system," he muttered.

Lucullus was as close to institutionalized anarchy as you could get. Founded by the Solar Union in the years before the Verge was cut off from the rest of human space, it was a penal colony and population dump for the Solars. When the Solars lost contact during the Long Silence, the inmates of Penates overthrew the supervisors the Solars had left behind. Those revolutionary factions still ruled the system, despite the fact that the Verge had been reunited with the rest of human space for four years now. In fact, the Solar Union had been working on reestablishing ties with their wayward colony since the Return. Their warships and merchantmen frequently called at Penates's battered spaceports. The crime lords and gang kings of Penates secretly feared the day when a Solar armada might descend on the system, ending their illusion of freedom.

The Solars . . . now, there was an idea. A stellar nation would have resources far exceeding those of even the most powerful local faction, and they were least likely to balk at paying him a suitable finder's fee for delivering the derelict to them. In fact, just about any of the stellar nations would be reasonable, and other Verge powers—Aegis, Oberon, or maybe Tendril—might be willing to meet his price and deal honorably.

With a grim smile, Pete Sokolov realized just how far he'd left behind his life in the Nariac Domain. A few years ago, the notion that he might turn over a militarily significant find to any government besides the Domain would have left him aghast. He laughed out loud in the silence of his sumptuous surroundings, imagining the indignant outrage of his younger self.

"Walk a mile in my shoes, Pyotr," he told the past. "You'll learn to give the Domain its due."

The call tone of his door chimed. "Mr. Sokolov? Mr. Borun is ready to see you, sir."

"Right. Give me a minute."

He rose and stalked over to the bathroom, rinsing his face with cold water. Trai had administered a shave and a haircut; he looked almost respectable. His hip felt naked without the weight of a gun, but he shoved his misgivings to the back of his mind. He was Borun's guest.

At the door, he found two uniformed security guards waiting. They inclined their heads politely. "Please follow us, Mr. Sokolov."

He assented with a nod, and they set off. The guest quarters proved to be surprisingly close to Borun's offices. Clearly these levels of the tower were reserved for HelixTech's executives and those visitors they wished to impress. They rode a lift up two or three floors, walked down a short corridor that struck Sokolov as familiar, and then ushered him into the same suite where he'd first met the HelixTech vice-president.

Karcen Borun reclined behind his desk, feet propped on its gleaming surface. Two armed guards, both plainclothes security types, stood behind him. They held guns, pointed past Sokolov.

He knew that something had gone terribly awry. He ignored the two guards at his back and took the seat opposite Borun. A single glance at the two men behind Borun was the only sign of concern he allowed himself.

"Mr. Borun," he said. "I assume Monashi was able to correct the problems you told me about?"

The exec offered a cool smile. "We've regained access to the data she sabotaged," he said carefully. "In fact, we're pretty much done with her."

"Glad to have been of service, then." Sokolov reached slowly into the chest pocket of his jacket and withdrew a slim black credstick. He pushed it across the table to Borun. "I'll accept the balance of my fee on this account, unless you've decided to accept my offer to dispose of her for you, in which case we'll want to set a fair price."

"Actually, we've decided that we're going to retain Ms. Monashi's services," Borun remarked. "She's very good at what she does, and she's made me a very interesting proposition." He swung his feet from his desk and leaned forward. "That's another issue. First I want to hear about the mission. Tell me how it went."

An interesting proposition? Sokolov wondered. What rabbit had Geille pulled out of her hat? Reluctantly he pushed Geille to the back of his mind and began to relate the events of the last two weeks. He told Borun about his infiltration of Icewalk, his pursuit of Monashi, and his flight from the station. He told Borun about the crippling sabotage inflicted by Yeiwei Three-knives. He described the brief battle with the *Blackguard* and how he'd elected to try a random jump in order to get away. He even explained how Geille had helped him to repair Yeiwei's handiwork by rigging a new astrogation processor, and the attempt she'd made on his life.

He specifically did *not* mention the drivespace anomaly. Nor did he see fit to tell Borun about the alien derelict they'd encountered, and he very carefully avoided any mention of the fact that he and Geille had become lovers.

When he finished, he lit a cigarette, seemingly unmindful of the armed guards who'd kept him under their guns for the entire time. "Other than the unplanned drivespace trip, I think it went well," he said. "If you don't have anything else for me, I'd like to go spend your money."

Karcen Borun bared his dragon-marked teeth in a ruthless smile. "On the whole, I have to say I'm quite satisfied with your work, Mr. Sokolov. I don't know of anyone else who could have pulled it off. I have just two questions for you.

"First of all, would you care to tell me why your ship transmitted a message encrypted in a Syndicate code about an hour after you landed?

"Secondly, I'd like to hear about the alien vessel you encountered in interstellar space. I'm a little surprised that you didn't deem that significant enough to include in your report."

Sokolov hid his surprise with a long drag of the smoke. "What message are you talking about? I sent no message." He knows about the derelict! Damn it!

Borun picked up a remote and cued one of his display screens. "This one, Mr. Sokolov. I don't know much about astrogation, but that certainly looks like a set of coordinates that have been encrypted. My cryptography experts tell me that's an old Jamaican Syndicate code. We know you weren't onboard, of course, but it's a simple matter to have your ship's computer cue a message for later delivery."

"Mr. Borun, I couldn't tell you what's in that message. I've never seen it before."

"Geille told us you would probably say that." Borun flicked off the display and swiveled to regard Sokolov again. "Fine. We'll check your computer's communication log in a little bit and find out what you sent and why. Let's get back to the really interesting omission in your report. Tell me about this alien vessel you encountered."

Sokolov stubbed the cigarette out in annoyance. "There's no

such thing, Mr. Borun. I expect Geille's looking for some way to extend her usefulness to you. I would be, if I were in her shoes."

"No such thing?" Borun pointed his remote at another screen and punched a command. He chuckled to himself. "That's funny. Geille predicted you'd say that, too. Are you sure this isn't the ship you encountered after you emerged from drive-space?"

The screen flickered, then darkened into a familiar image. The black hull of the derelict glided by in one of their survey recordings, probably shot during their initial approach. Sokolov said nothing.

"Geille smuggled one of your recordings off your ship in her sleeve," Borun said. "She told me you'd spent several days exploring this ship. Is that true, Sokolov?"

The bounty hunter looked back at Karcen Borun. Clearly there was no use in pretending that Geille was lying. This is what I pushed her into, he thought. She sold news of the derelict to Borun in order to stay alive a little longer. He spat a curse and fixed his eyes on the HelixTech executive.

"All right, Borun. Let's talk. I'll sell you the location of the derelict, the footage I've taken of its interior and exterior, even the notes and maps I made while exploring it. In return, I'll want ten million credits and a ten percent royalty on any technologies you develop from what's on that ship."

Borun rocked idly in his comfortable chair, studying him. "Mr. Sokolov," he said quietly, "I don't know that you have anything to *sell* me. What do I have to purchase from you that I can't just take?"

Sokolov stood so suddenly that the guards almost panicked in response, yanking back the slides of their weapons in readiness to fire. He ignored them, leaning forward over the executive's desk.

"That's *my* find, Borun. I'm offering you the first chance at buying my rights to it. You might be able to take it, but you'd always have to worry about whether or not your criminal action would come back to haunt you. Deal with me, and you'll have the wreck legally."

" 'Legally'? That's a strange argument to use on Penates, Mr. Sokolov. Beside, how can I know that I have any kind of exclusivity now? Your message to the Jamaicans puts me in a very difficult position." He looked at one of the guards. "Would you ask Monashi to join us, please?"

The man spoke into a hidden communication link, never taking his eyes from Sokolov. A moment later one of the panels in Borun's office slid aside. Geille walked in, dressed in a high-collared black blouse and pants. Obviously she'd been waiting in the other room. She didn't bother to meet Sokolov's glare.

"Karcen," she said, by way of greeting.

"I've decided to invoke corporate privilege in our dealings with Mr. Sokolov. We're going to confiscate the information in his ship's computer banks and take this matter into our own hands." He smiled broadly. "If this ship has half the promise you claim it does, I'd be inclined to overlook our past differences, Geille. I'll admit that nothing like this was in my plans, but I've learned to jump when opportunity knocks. I want that ship."

"So we're settled?" Geille asked.

"Soon, Geille, soon. I have to verify that it's really out there, see what we can make of it. You'll have your freedom after I've seen the ship."

"That's not the deal we worked out," Geille said slowly.

"You'll forgive me if I don't trust you," Borun replied. "You're lucky we didn't settle your account the minute Sokolov brought you in. You can wait a couple of weeks to prove that you're selling me something worthwhile in exchange for your freedom."

Studying her from the side, Sokolov could distinctly see the muscles along her jaw bunching. She thought this would get her out the door, he realized. He almost laughed out loud. Borun's going to keep her on a very short leash until he sees the derelict for himself, and then what does she have that he needs anymore? He'll just kill her later instead of killing her now, and she knows it.

Borun turned back to Sokolov. "Here's my counteroffer. You're going to help us get to the wreck. When I'm satisfied that it's worth as much as you think it is, we'll negotiate for your rights."

"If you want my cooperation, we'll deal up front, Borun."

"I don't need your help, Sokolov. Either you help me, or you can sit here until I return. You're a lot more likely to be happy with the final arrangements if you volunteer your assistance." Borun offered a warm smile. "After all, you've done a lot of good work for HelixTech of late."

Sokolov asked. "So what the hell am I going to get out of this? What if I just walk?"

"You don't understand, do you? You're now a security risk, Mr. Sokolov. You happen to possess extensive knowledge of HelixTech's newest and most important secret project. You're going to help us transfer all the data in your ship's computer to our own systems, then you're going to disappear. You help me out, and you get to disappear with a tidy bonus and some incentives to never mention your role in finding this derelict to anyone. If you don't help me out, you just disappear."

"I understand perfectly." Sokolov scowled at Monashi. "You weren't kidding when you said I'd be sorry."

Cool and composed, she met his eyes. "What else was I supposed to do? You didn't give me any other options." She turned back to Borun and smoothed her clothes, ignoring his agitation. "You'll find almost everything you need on Sokolov's ship, Karcen. I can break his files for you."

*   *   *   *   *

Bound securely, Sokolov was marched down to *Peregrine* at gunpoint by Borun and his security forces. He fumed every step of the way, seeking some kind of escape. Unfortunately the binders on his wrists were heavy enough to resist the strength of his cybernetic arm, and the HelixTech security men knew their job. They watched him closely.

If I ever get out of this, he resolved, I'll kill Karcen Borun. I won't even find someone who wants it done. I'll just kill him for free.

He wasn't as sure about what he would do with Monashi.

Although she was not restrained, Geille was strictly escorted by another of Borun's men, as much a prisoner as he. Sokolov knew that he should have planned on her using the derelict as a safety net, a last effort to persuade Karcen Borun that she had something he needed. Tthe moment she opened the files and gave him the coordinates, she'd be dead. For that matter, so would he. The only question was whether Borun would wait until his men had confirmed their find.

They entered the lift leading down to the hangar. The executive, his face alive and alert in an artificial good humor, studied Sokolov as they rode down. "Who built this thing, Sokolov? You must have found something about the aliens who put your ship together."

He looked away, refusing to answer. Borun waited a moment, then gave the nearest guard a sharp nod. The fellow pulled a black baton from his belt with one gloved hand and activated the device. An abrasive vibration hummed in the car, then the thug stepped forward and rammed the end of the pulse baton into Sokolov's belly. Sokolov grunted and fell, surprised by the sharp *crack* of the weapon's discharge. Everyone watched as he groveled on the floor of the lift, contorted by the fiery pain in his gut.

"Bastard," he coughed. "Someday I'm going to feed you your balls."

Borun squatted next to him and seized Sokolov by his hair, twisting his face up to meet his fake blue eyes. "The minute I believe you don't have something I need," he said warmly, "you stop breathing. When I ask for your opinion, you're going to give it to me. For now, you have experience that I need to tap, but when you decide to play the strong, silent type, your usefulness quotient goes way down. It's nothing personal, Sokolov. I just need you to understand the rules."

"The hell it's not personal," Sokolov growled between gasps. "I would have sold you the derelict, Borun. You just heard about it three hours ago. Now you'd kill me for it. What's the rush?"

The exec shrugged. "I've hit the ceiling here, Sokolov. There's nowhere else to go. I've spent years thinking about where I could go from here. Your mystery ship might be exactly what I'm looking for to make a big move."

"You're not saying 'HelixTech' when you're talking about your plans, Borun." Sokolov managed a pallid scowl. "What would the board of directors have to say about paying Monashi to steal company research for you? Or taking my claim at gunpoint?"

"Results are all that count, Sokolov. As long as I provide them, the board's not going to question my methods." Borun slowly rubbed his hands together. "There are two kinds of people in the world, Sokolov: lords and serfs. It's been that way since humans first stumbled out of caves. Lords are the shakers and movers, the people who make things happen. Serfs are the people things happen to. And when you're one of the lords, well, you find out that the people you have to worry about aren't the serfs—they're the other lords, so you find ways to fight for a bigger domain, because if you don't, some other lord is going to make his bigger at your expense.

"You know, the Picts might be violent, crude, and ultimately self-destructive, but at least they're honest. A man might learn some important lessons from watching them. I have three, maybe four, other lords I have to contend with here at Helix-Tech. If I don't grow my domain, they'll grow theirs. I'm going to make your derelict part of my domain, and like the barons and dukes of old, I'll reward my serfs when they help me, and I'll punish them when they don't.

"Be a good serf, Sokolov. I can be generous when it suits me."

"Go screw a sesheyan," Sokolov replied. The remark earned him another shot with the pulse baton.

When he woke up after that, two of the guards were dragging him up the ramp to *Peregrine.* The ship seemed small and crowded with so many people onboard at the same time; he almost didn't have space to find his feet beneath him.

"Pete! What's going on?" Peri asked at once. He could hear the concern in her voice.

"Duress, Peri," he croaked. The computer fell silent; it would refuse all further communication and commands until he released it. It might slow Borun down for a couple of hours, until HelixTech's comptechs cracked Peri's brain open and forced electronic compliance from her. "You know what to do."

Borun looked back over his shoulder. "Break his jaw if he speaks another word to the ship's computer," he told the guards holding Sokolov, then he climbed up to the command deck.

The guards pushed Sokolov up the short ladder and threw him into the spartan harness seat by the engineer's station. They spread out, keeping a close eye on him. Sokolov settled for glaring at each in turn, although he didn't seem to make much of an impression.

Geille went straight to the computer operator's station and sat down. She started typing at the terminal, using the keypad.

"I had a chance to bury some hidden files while you were unconscious a few days ago, Pete. I figured I might need something to buy you off when I made my move. You didn't give me a chance to use them before you turned me over to Borun." She finished entering the set of commands and leaned back. "Peri, disable all duress conditions," she said.

"Acknowledged, Geille. Sorry, Pete."

Sokolov closed his eyes. His gut ached from the pulse baton strikes. *They want to play hardball. Fine. I'll show them what hardball is all about. Whisper protocol, Nancy.*

Whisper protocol enabled, Pyotr, the nanocomputer replied.

Peri, can you hear me? Sokolov thought, carefully subvocalizing his words. *Reply via transmission at this frequency.*

I hear you, Pete, the ship said. *I'm sorry. You no longer have exclusive access to my command directories. I have to accept Geille's commands for now.*

Don't worry about it, he told her. *Deadman protocol, time delay fifteen seconds, no conditions. Do you understand?*

He could almost sense the trepidation in the AI's response. *Acknowledged,* she said.

He hesitated, unwilling to take the final step he had in mind. He looked around the bridge. Karcen Borun stood at the back of the command deck, grinning. Geille worked at the other console, getting ready to implement the commands that would make his next action impossible. She glanced over her shoulder at Borun, trying to gauge whether she'd bought her freedom yet. The guards watched Sokolov closely, waiting for a sign of resistance.

Sokolov ignored Borun and the HelixTech thugs, focusing on Geille. Their game was about to come to an end. She'd forced him into stalemate. *Peri, load Sanction. Parameters 'Preserve' Deadman protocol. Execute.*

That program requires a confirmation, Pete, the computer replied. *Are you sure you want to do that?*

Confirmation vol'nye. Despite his resolve, his heart ached. He turned his head toward the red vid pickup that covered the bridge. *Good-bye, Peri.*

Sanction confirmed. The computer hesitated, then added, *I'm scared, Pete.*

"I know," he breathed aloud.

Good-bye, the ship whispered, then the connection inside his head went dead. He looked up just as every screen on the bridge went blank at the same time. The lights flickered; then the engineering plant died away into silence.

Geille flinched then tapped the reset button. When that didn't work, she slowly twisted to look at Sokolov. "Tell me you didn't do that," she said quietly.

He met her horror with stony silence. His heart ached as if he'd taken a knife between his ribs, but he refused to show any emotion. He'd let them know how the game was played.

Karcen Borun took a step forward, staring at Geille. "What's going on here, Geille? What's wrong with the computer?"

"Sokolov killed it," she said in disgust. "It's wiped."

The exec didn't say anything at first. He sighed and raised one hand to knead at his face. In a deceptively mild voice, he asked, "Are you sure that's what happened, Geille? Because a core dump of this computer would mean that I don't have any coordinates for the derelict you promised me, which would mean that you didn't give me anything. If you didn't give me anything, then we're back at square one, aren't we? So make sure you're telling me what you really want to tell me. Is the computer wiped?"

She turned back to the station, attempting to restart the system. She worked anxiously for a long minute, then two, while everyone on the bridge watched her. "It's dead, Karcen. He wiped it clean. There's nothing here but one program called Deadman."

Borun stalked over to where Sokolov sat. "Is she right?" he asked.

"Yes. I ordered a total purge of the computer core. There's nothing left but the Deadman program."

"And what's that?"

"A deadman switch, Borun. Kill me and the ship criticals the mass reactor. It probably wouldn't destroy the HelixTech compound, but I think the damage would be pretty bad."

"That's supposed to impress me?" Borun laughed without humor. "Come off it, Sokolov. I'm starting to run out of patience with you. Tell you what I'll do—you don't blow up my corporate headquarters, and I'll let you walk away. And you'll count yourself lucky." He straightened, looking over at Geille. "As for you, Geille, it seems to me you failed to deliver on your promise. I think we'll have to terminate your employment."

The two guards at the back of the bridge trained their charge rifles on the comptech. She stood awkwardly, raising her hands. "Wait a minute, Karcen. I didn't have any control over this! Sokolov killed the files, not me!"

"Doesn't matter," the exec said. "You promised me the derelict's coordinates; I don't see them. We don't have a deal, do we?" He nodded at the guards, who worked the slides of their guns and took aim.

"What if I told you that you still have the coordinates?" Geille said quickly.

Borun raised a hand, staying her execution a moment. "I probably wouldn't believe you. Better make it good."

"Sokolov knows where the derelict is," she stated. She threw a desperate look in his direction. While he grappled with his astonishment, Geille continued. "Sokolov isn't as human as he appears," she told Borun. "He's carrying a great deal of cybernetic enhancements, top-grade Nariac military intelligence gear. That includes a model NA518-00 nanocomputer. The only place in the world where you'll find the coordinates leading you to the derelict is inside Sokolov's skull."

The exec looked back at Sokolov. "Is that true?"

Connection report Monashi-01, Nancy suddenly said. *Accessing file Ghostship. Verifying—*

She's doing it again, he realized. She's accessing Nancy without any physical connection whatsoever, transmitting data with nothing but the power of her mind. While he watched in amazement, Geille casually pulled up a file he didn't even know he had in his head and made it available to him. Sometime while he was unconscious, she'd stashed the nav coordinates in a hidden file in his nanocomputer.

Nancy, run Riposte, he thought angrily. *Get Geille out of my head!*

Acknowledged, Pyotr. Riposte active. Riposte was a counter-intrusion program, one of several similar programs he had at his disposal. Sokolov had no idea if it would prove effective against Geille's psi link, but he was determined to make sure she didn't pull any more surprises like that if he could help it.

While the program ran against Geille's mental link, Sokolov deliberately pulled his attention away from Monashi and focused on Borun. He had one last chance to keep the derelict for himself.

"It's half true," he said wearily. "I have several cybernetic systems, and it's Nariac hardware, but I don't have the nav files. That's what the ship's computer is for."

Riposte complete, Nancy reported. *All unauthorized command access channels have been deleted.*

Fine. Stash Riposte. Run Linebacker, parameters Red Dog Seven. Riposte was a good program for dumping unwanted intruders. Linebacker would allocate a portion of Nancy's attention to scanning for new intrusion attempts. Now that Sokolov knew what to look for, he was determined to make sure that Geille didn't try anything else.

Borun literally growled. "Do we have the location of the derelict or not?"

"They're in Sokolov's head," Geille snapped. "I should know. I put them there myself."

Linebacker active, Pyotr, Nancy instructed.

Good. If any external system interfaces with you, kill file Ghostship. I'll be damned if I'm going to let this bastard take anything else away from me.

Sokolov glanced over at Geille and smiled. Sell me out to Borun, will you? he thought. Make me pull the plug on Peri? "I have no such files stored in my nanocomputer."

Geille paled. "He's lying! I gave him full access to those coordinates! Karcen, you've got everything—"

"How in the hell am I supposed to believe either of you at this point?" Borun snapped. He glared at Monashi, the first time Sokolov had seen him show any kind of real anger on his face.

"You don't have to believe me," Geille said. "You can pull the file out of Sokolov's computer. Verify it for yourself. He has the coordinates."

"If any of this doesn't check out, you won't live ten minutes past the moment I confirm Sokolov's claim, Geille." The executive lowered his hand. Behind him, the gunman dropped his rifle, taking his hand from the trigger. Borun smiled magnanimously at Geille and Sokolov. "Somebody else on Penates has those coordinates already, thanks to the coded transmission one or the other of you sent from this ship. I'm behind the eight ball here, and I don't like it. So I'm going to dig the truth out of the two of you.

"Take them to the security center. I want them both interrogated. Extreme measures are authorized."

Chapter Thirteen

FOUR THOUSAND kilometers to the east, Marius Grayes stood in a dark room of glass and watched money pour into his pockets. The glamorous main floor of the Silver Comet, the largest casino in the Lucullus system, sprawled in all directions beneath him. His office hung above the floor, suspended by gossamer cables. None of the hundreds of gamblers below had any idea of who he was. He could have ridden the lift down from his luxurious suite and walked among them in complete anonymity. That was one of the advantages of holding a powerful position in the Jamaican Syndicate; no one except your immediate superiors and your favored subordinates knew who you were.

Like most other members of the Syndicate, Grayes was not Jamaican in any sense of the word. The Syndicate's name came from the three major cities under its control—Port Royal, Kingstown, and Ocho Rios. Back when the Solars had colonized the poisonous and cheerless planet of Penates, they'd brought the names of Old Earth with them, clinging to the nostalgic words despite the bitter irony of naming the sites on a world like Penates after cities of the ancient Caribbean. Grayes was no historian, but he'd been laughing at that joke all of his life.

Grayes was a startlingly short and stocky man, a solid cube of muscle and bone not even a meter and a half in height. He was descended from a stock engineered for the conquest of high-gravity worlds, even though his family was now three generations removed from the crushing, arid hell of a planet they'd been bred to tame. Despite the fact that he'd never seen natural sunlight, Grayes was as dark as a block of mahogany, one more adaptation wasted on a life in Penates's habitat domes. His hairless scalp gleamed in the soft light.

"So?" he said to the tall woman standing behind him. "Is this for real?"

The woman, a lean, athletic security specialist who wore a pair of laser pistols on her hips, shrugged. "I wish I knew, Marius. It could be a hoax, but our communications people say our codes are pretty tight. It's a *professional* hoax, if it is a hoax."

"Let me see the message, Nona."

The woman glided forward. She towered over him, a thin and willowy figure compared to Grayes's compact solidity. She passed over a slim dataslate into Grayes's massive hands. Each of his fingers was as thick as a flashlight and nearly as long; Nona had seen Marius break a man's arm simply by crushing the fellow's biceps in his grip.

" 'Zero point energy'? What's that supposed to mean?"

"Our techs say it could mean a lot, Marius. If it's real, it's a major find."

"I'll take their word for it, but who sent this message, and why? Did somebody at HelixTech just decide he was having a bad day and wanted to screw the boss?" Marius Grayes frowned and dropped the dataslate on the desk, pacing heavily toward the window. "I assume the numbers are some kind of location?"

"Drivespace coordinates. Our techs say it's in the middle of interstellar space, as close to nowhere as you can get."

"We're supposed to drop everything and rush out there to take possession of this derelict?"

Nona shrugged. "It's your call, Marius. You can move, you can stand pat, or you can kick it upstairs and see what they say."

Marius turned ponderously and eyed her. "Why would I want to do that? My techs intercepted this message. It's my territory. I'll make the call myself." He looked out over the casino floor again then shook his head. "If the codes check out, we'll hire a ship to see if there's a goose at the end of this chase. We're not going to say a word to anyone about where we're going or what we're doing. If it's a fraud, it'll be our little secret, and if it's real—" Grayes offered a wide, predatory smile—"I don't see any reason to share."

* * * * *

Sokolov drifted in a realm of nightmare and memory, powerless. In his lucid moments, he knew he was dreaming again, dissociated from his body by the drugs and probes of Borun's technicians. They'd taken him straight from the *Peregrine* to the security center. There, alone in a chamber of gleaming metal and spotless plexiglass, he strained against his shackles while the HelixTech doctors prepared to extract the derelict's coordinates from his internal computer. They couldn't risk establishing any kind of communication protocol with the nanocomputer; his threat held them in check, but his gamble left him no protection from other kinds of duress.

When his lucidity failed an hour or two into the program, Sokolov's mind wandered off into a gray, misty realm of shapeless memories and vague menaces. His limbs seemed heavy and slow, as if he were mired in molasses. The simplest questions—his location, the reason for his capture and torment, even his name—began to dance fleetingly away from his mind. A droning voice in his ear patiently exhorted him to *cooperate,* to *help,* to *find the way out.* Somewhere in his dim consciousness, Sokolov began to think of the voice as a thin, gray raven that clung to his shoulder.

The misty landscape started to take on a familiar and terrible appearance. He moaned in protest when he realized where he was being taken by the vile thing on his shoulder.

Night descended over him, a fierce, hellish glare of yellow sodium lights in acrid fog. A steel jungle of great round tanks, meter-wide pipes, and contorted pump stations stretched as far as he could see. He lay on his belly, clutching a long-barreled rail rifle, across the asphalt-shingle roof of a two-story building, the complex gatehouse. Black body armor didn't shield him from the stink and humidity of the refinery.

Not this again, he whispered in his dream. I buried this years ago.

Voices he hadn't heard in years crackled in his headset radio. "Damn! There goes another one!" That was Jaanik, the team leader.

"They're all around us!" Stolypin. Silent and usually unshakable, but now breaking under the strain. Two of the point team were down already.

"What the hell *are* these things?" Chegeyana, fierce and quick. She was the veteran, a survivor of dozens of black ops.

The dream-Sokolov concentrated on his job. He was the perimeter man, the safety. It was his job to make sure that none of the things that had infected the refinery escaped to breed and pollute the nameless industrial colony he and his teammates were trying to sterilize. His vantage gave him a good line of fire down the main avenue of the complex, although the machinery and structures on either side quickly obscured his vision. He cued his mike.

"Jaanik, do you want me to move closer? You're out of my line of sight. I can't see where you are."

"No, Sokolov! Stay where you are. These things are hiding in everything. They'd take a lone man before you were a hundred meters into the buildings." Jaanik paused, muttering something. Sokolov heard the rattle of automatic fire and the godless screeching of the creatures over the leader's open mike. Jaanik's voice came back a moment later. "I think we'll need your gun to cover our exit."

Sokolov wiped sweat from his eyes and blinked, trying to steady his aim. "Get back on the main boulevard, Jaanik. I can help you when you're clear of the machinery."

"We're working on it, Sokolov." Jaanik clicked off, busy with the task of staying alive.

Sokolov waited. He considered praying to a god he didn't know, but instead began a catechism of sorts, speaking the names of his teammates under his breath, over and over again. "Come on, come on," he whispered. "Get out of there!"

In the tangled shadows of the big centrifuge fifty meters to his left, something stirred. Sokolov spotted the glint of metal and wire wrapped around something feral. It crept out of the shadows, scuttling toward him—a chukka, the local equivalent of a rat or small rabbit. It was infected with the metal virus they'd come here to destroy. Bands of steel covered its back, and gleaming copper wires wreathed its legs.

Sokolov watched it approach, sickened. He wasn't sure, but he thought that the animal trapped in the metal jacket still lived. Insanity rolled in its surviving eye as it increased its speed, desperate to sink its metal into his body and spread its infectious madness.

He blew it in two with one shot of the rail rifle. Some of the pieces lamely twitched and continued to move toward him for a few heartbeats before they stopped moving.

Thirty-seven engineers and workmen had been inside the complex when the weapons lab hidden beneath the administration building had disgorged its latest invention. He prayed that they were dead, but the first team to respond hadn't reported finding any bodies before they had disappeared. That made forty-three men and women.

"Stolypin, behind you!" It was Chegeyana's voice. More gunfire, and an agonized scream that went on for an obscene amount of time.

"Another one!"

"Another!"

The radio fell silent. Sokolov waited for an eternity. Nothing moved in the complex. He swallowed and cued his mike. "Jaanik?" he said softly.

The answer was a long time coming. "Sokolov, you've got to detonate the bomb." It was Chegeyana. Her voice came in hissing gasps. "They got Stolypin and Jaanik. One of those things is in my legs now. God! Get back to the van and . . . use the radio detonator. Damn the Domain for . . . hiding something like this." She screamed again and didn't stop until Sokolov ripped the headset from his ears.

He climbed unsteadily to his feet, staring out at the sprawling acres of metal and concrete in front of him. Why didn't they call in the army? he thought angrily. Jaanik, Stolypin, and now Chegeyana, all dead to bury a secret the Domain wanted to keep quiet. What kind of horror had his government been developing in the weapons lab?

He saw movement now, several hundred meters down the boulevard. Sokolov froze, squinting through the acrid haze. Two human figures limped away from the metal alleyways.

"Jaanik! Stolypin!" Sokolov called. He almost forgot to replace the headset and use the radio. "Hurry up!"

The two figures made no response, lurching toward him in awkward, injured steps. A grim horror gripped Sokolov. Moving like a marionette, he slowly raised the rail rifle and activated the high-magnification sights. The two men approaching were indeed Jaanik and Stolypin, or at least they once had been. Bright metal spears impaled their bodies. He almost lost his stomach at the sight.

Gagging, he sagged to his knees and raised his rifle again, then deliberately, he shot them both through the head, dropping the metal monstrosities in their tracks. As more of the things emerged from the refinery, he slung his rifle over his back, climbed down from the gatehouse rooftop, and loped back to the transport van a couple of hundred meters away.

Metal-wrapped figures gathered at the refinery gates, watching him with the eyes of the damned. He ignored them, clambering through the transport's command compartment until he found the black box with the green keypad. Hands shaking, he punched in the sequence of numbers each team member had memorized, then he triggered the bomb.

A kilometer away, in the lift shaft leading to the concealed lab, the fusion warhead Jaanik and Stolypin had carried into the complex exploded. In one brilliant flash of light, it seared the heart of the refinery to vapor and extirpated anything on the grounds. Metal obscenities in the shapes of men screamed as their steel frames crumpled under the blast.

Sokolov watched in awe through the filtered screens of the transport van. If there'd had been any hope for Chegeyana and the others, it was gone now. He closed his eyes, dropping onto a spartan gray bench in the team's compartment.

He never saw the shock wave until it picked up the transport and flung it like a child's toy. He was thrown against the ceiling, then the floor, by some invisible demon of force battering him inside the vehicle. Sparks exploded around him, and then there was darkness as the interior lights failed. The last things he heard were the screech of tortured metal and his own screams.

Darkness claimed him.

* * * * *

When Sokolov woke again, Karcen Borun was waiting for him. He was still in the security center, although now he was strapped to a reinforced armchair. Swimming back up through the murk and haze that had clouded his mind, he dimly noticed two technicians in white coats packing up an array of sinister instruments and wheeling carts and monitors out of the room. They were interrogating me, he realized. Drugs. Psych programming of some kind. *Nancy, what time is it?*

It is now 0644:18, May 17th, the nanocomputer replied.

Twenty hours? Sokolov winced and shook his head. Everything between his ears ached as if his brain had been poured into a taffy puller. They worked on me for a whole day?

Borun spoke briefly with the technicians before they carried the last of their gear from the room. With a comic grimace, he slowly approached the bounty hunter.

"Good morning, Sokolov. I understand you didn't sleep very well."

Sokolov made an effort to focus on the executive. It was becoming easier to think; the techs must have injected him with a counteragent before they'd left.

"Get what you want?" he asked thickly.

"You have a much more colorful past than we'd guessed, Mr. Sokolov," Borun said, ignoring his question. He settled on a desktop near Sokolov, crossing his arms over his chest. Sokolov noted dully that Borun had changed his clothes. Instead of the tailored shimmerweave suits he's seen before, the exec wore khaki pants and a rugged equipment vest over an olive turtleneck. "Nariac Intelligence Directorate, Special Operations Division—quite impressive—and a defector as well. The Domain would love to get its hands on you again, my friend."

"They don't know I'm alive," Sokolov muttered. "I died with the rest of my team."

"The Canis Epsilon Two incident." Borun laughed. "You picked the right time to run. No one else survived, and the detonation obliterated any evidence. So how does a highly trained and conditioned Nariac operative become a bounty hunter in the

Verge, anyway? Most defectors have a motivation, after all."

"I didn't like taking orders, and it's not the kind of job you can just quit. That's it. No ideals, no great cause. I just wanted out."

"I can't believe you just lost your nerve, Pete. After all, your conditioning is mostly intact, and your hardware is top-notch. My interrogation experts had one hell of a time getting anywhere with you." Karcen Borun's easy smile faded. "My computer techs, on the other hand, tell me that your nanocomputer is set to kill a file called Ghostship if we make any attempt to read or extract it. You want to tell me about that?"

They found it, Sokolov thought blackly. They couldn't dig the file out, but they know I can. So much for the possibility of walking out of HelixTech with the derelict in my pocket. Of course, Geille took care of that for me the minute I turned her over.

The only thing left for him to do was to make the best deal he could for the alien wreck . . . and for his life. "It's the location of the derelict," Sokolov said. "Geille must have stashed a copy in my nanocomputer while I was unconscious and she had control of the ship. I set the system to kill the coordinates to make sure you wouldn't be tempted by the notion of offing me without risking your prize."

"Well, that puts us in an awkward spot, doesn't it?" Borun said. His cold blue eyes gleamed with artificial sympathy. Sokolov could read this message. Got a problem here, pal, but we can work around it, right? "Maybe we could get the file, maybe not. Some of my people think they could get around your programming, but I'm not going to take that chance. I think I know you well enough to know that you'd pull the pin and damn the consequences."

"I'll sell you the derelict. Sign over all the rights, everything. You go get your prize, I take a long vacation, and we never bother each other again," Sokolov said. He started to sit up but discovered that he was still restrained. "Make me an offer."

"It's not quite that easy," Borun said. "You see, I won't know that the coordinates you give me are the real ones until I check. You might give me a set of fake coordinates, while the Jamaican

Syndicate investigates the real ones, so I have to take you along with me, just in case."

"I'll need some kind of guarantees, Borun, some kind of good-faith gesture to show me that you'll still be willing to talk after I give you the derelict."

The exec shrugged. "We'll work something out once I see the brass ring on this little merry-go-round, Sokolov. In case you hadn't noticed, you're not in a position to negotiate."

"I could kill the files right now," Sokolov warned.

"Why would you do that, other than to spite me?" Karcen Borun laughed deeply. "It's not as if you'd be causing me any real losses, Sokolov. I'd be back at square one, less a little time and effort I spent dealing with you. On the other hand, you wouldn't like the way things turned out if you made sure that a technology potentially worth billions fell into the hands of whoever blunders across it next, Pete. Don't threaten me again."

Do I give it to them or not? Sokolov wondered. He couldn't see any alternatives, so he elected to stall for time.

"What about Geille?" he asked.

Borun straightened and fixed Sokolov with a dark look. "What about her?" he answered in a tone that hinted of aggravation, old anger. He knows what happened out there, Sokolov realized. "She offered me the derelict for her chance to disappear. She doesn't go anywhere until I've got the ship in my hands. I think I want her where I can keep an eye on her. She's doing what she can to come through on her end of the bargain, but I don't believe that her change of heart is very sincere, do you?"

Sokolov rasped laughter. Borun halted, angry. "What's so funny?"

"I think she outsmarted herself," he said. "The last thing in the world she'd want to do is help you take the alien wreck, especially with me as her ace in the hole. She has nothing left once you get what you want. She's screwed if she helps you, and just as screwed if she doesn't."

"So are you," Borun snapped. "Until I get the derelict, you're going to be on a very short leash."

"Tell me what's in it for me, Borun. As far as I can see, I'm nothing to you once I lead you to the wreck. Why should I help you at all?"

The executive shrugged and spread his hands. "You give me what I want, Sokolov, and I'll let you go. I really don't have anything against you. Hell, I owe you a debt of gratitude. You're going to make me the most powerful man in this system."

Sokolov met Borun's bright eyes. "I don't believe you, but I'll take you to the ship."

"Believe what you want." The exec stood and muttered something into a comm unit. A pair of guards entered the room and began to unstrap Sokolov from the chair. "You're coming with me no matter what you think." He chuckled and walked out with a strong stride. "Bring him down to the *Adroit*, gentlemen."

Nancy, system status, Sokolov ordered.

Reflex wiring disabled by software lockouts, the machine replied. *Muscular systems in right arm inoperative due to removal of power supply. Sorry, Pyotr.*

Not your fault, Nancy. Sokolov twisted around to look down at his right arm, pinned behind his back by the manacles at his wrists. Sure enough, his sleeve had been stripped up to his shoulder, and the plastic synthskin that covered the artificial limb had been opened at the biceps, elbow, and forearm. Bare metal musculature and framework glinted in the damaged regions. His arm was as dead as an aircar with its engine removed.

The guards took him by the shoulders and steered him to the door then out into the passage. A hundred meters of smooth, gleaming hallway led them to a lift overlooking HelixTech's main landing platforms. A half-dozen ships were scattered across the noxious plains below, gleaming wetly in the ammonia haze.

Sokolov ignored the view, concentrating on a series of programs and keywords that might unlock the HelixTech codes or restore his neural interfaces with his cybernetic gear. He had a dozen restart programs and decryption routines. In the space of the ten-minute walk, he ran them all, looking for some kind of weakness in the invisible fetters that restrained him.

Nancy reported failure after failure. "I'm never taking another job for Karcen Borun again," he growled aloud.

The guards ignored his remark and dragged him out of the lift and into a wide transit corridor leading to a ship's air lock. The corridor bustled with all the signs of a ship preparing for departure—technicians coming and going with last-minute maintenance, supply cases stacked up against the bulkheads, heavy umbilical cables feeding power, air, and water to the ship.

Wide viewports lined the corridor just before the air lock. Through them, Sokolov got his first look at the *Adroit*. She was sleek and deadly, a military hull three or four times the size of *Peregrine*. Paired mass cannons jutted from her hull in wedge-shaped turrets; a spotlight illuminated the HelixTech logo on her smooth flank. In the distance, a kilometer or so across the landing field, he caught a glimpse of *Peregrine*'s familiar lines. They'd moved his ship to a maintenance bay and seemed to be overhauling the battered old tradesman.

They're not refitting her for me, he realized. A driveship is worth hundreds of thousands of Concord dollars—no sense throwing it away. The next conclusion was obvious. If Helix-Tech expected to let Sokolov go once he delivered the derelict, they wouldn't be rebuilding his ship. As far as Borun's concerned, I'm dead already. Sokolov narrowed his eyes.

"Come on, Sokolov," one of his escorts said. He took Pete by the arm and pulled him from the viewport and into the ship. "The ship leaves within the hour, and we're supposed to make sure you're secure for travel. We'll catch hell if you cause a delay."

"Fine. Let's go," Sokolov replied.

They led him into the ship. The *Adroit* was divided into two full-length decks, plus a third half-deck on her upper hull—the bridge and electronics rooms. Sokolov kept a careful count of the people they passed in the passageways. He eventually guessed there was a crew of about fifteen to twenty. At least five or six of them were security, hard-looking men and women who wore black body armor and carried charge guns in tidy shoulder slings. Makes sense, he figured. Borun's supposed to be the

head of HelixTech's security division. He must have a private
army at his disposal.

Under normal circumstances, the *Adroit* would have been
roomy and comfortable for a small warship. However, the
corvette was jammed with extra personnel and equipment, a
dozen scientists and technicians who fussed over the stowage of
delicate sensors, computers, recording devices, and rescue and
salvage gear. Even though he didn't think he'd get much of a
chance to make use of the knowledge, Sokolov committed the
details of the layout to Nancy's memory. Planning an impossible escape was better than doing nothing at all.

On the third deck, the guards escorted him into a cabin that
had been converted into something like a small brig. A cramped
cell about three meters square had been fashioned from clear
durasteel. The guards removed his restraints; Sokolov sat down
on his bunk and offered no resistance. The guards left after
checking to make sure he'd been locked securely. He needed
time to think.

Chapter Fourteen

AN HOUR AFTER liftoff, the *Adroit*'s security team came down to the brig to bring Sokolov to the bridge. Sokolov had already examined his quarters for a means of escape without much luck. The perforated sheet durasteel had been welded into place at the deck and the overhead, leaving a door of reinforced mesh secured by a scan-recognition bar lock. If Sokolov's right arm had its power units, he might have been able to do something, but as matters stood, his improvised cell performed its task well.

His escorts were wary and vigilant. Borun's security chief was a veteran named Harmon, a body-builder with massive arms and legs like tree trunks. Sokolov counted several new security personnel on the trip, bringing the total to eight plus the chief. At first he was flattered to command such attention, but he quickly realized that Borun was bringing the extra gunmen along for security at the derelict. Just like the technicians and scientists, the security team was preparing for first contact scenarios, too . . . although their scenarios were probably much less friendly than the scientists' drills. Harmon's team seemed fairly competent, so Sokolov decided he'd give them a couple of days to get a little complacent in their duties before he tried anything. He accompanied them without resistance, saving his strength for later.

The lift doors opened, and their escorts led them out into the *Adroit*'s bridge. It was a spacious room, maybe ten meters across, with a dozen crewmen and technicians consumed in as many different tasks. Sokolov was impressed despite himself. He recognized some of the equipment and hardware installed on the HelixTech corvette, and he could tell at a glance that the *Adroit* was top of the line.

A generous set of viewports roofed the compartment, providing a breathtaking view of space outside the windows. High and to the right, the brownish-gray crescent of Penates lingered in view, a couple of hundred thousand kilometers distant by Sokolov's guess. No other ships or installations seemed to be nearby. In the center of the *Adroit*'s bridge, Karcen Borun stood next to a gaunt, lantern-jawed man. The executive beamed when Sokolov appeared.

"Our guest is here, Captain Mills," he said to the man next to him.

Mills stood slowly, studying the two of them. He wore a gray jump suit emblazoned with the HelixTech insignia, just like the other crewmen and technicians, but a cap marked with gold braid set him apart from the rest of the crew. A trim laser pistol in a thigh-strap holster and a bulky flight jacket zipped to the middle of his chest completed the officer's attire. Mills was almost as tall as Sokolov but far leaner, a colorless scarecrow in the bland uniform of the HelixTech corporate fleet. Gray stubble was all the beard he permitted himself. His face was long and dour by nature, so that his habitual expression was one of grudging resignation.

"Did he give you any trouble, Mr. Harmon?" he asked the security chief in a voice as dry and raspy as gravel.

"No, sir," Harmon replied. His flat gaze implied that it would take more than one prisoner like Sokolov to qualify as trouble.

"Don't relax your vigilance." The captain descended from his raised command chair, moving up to study Sokolov face-to-face. "Mr. Borun informs me that you are a dangerous and capable individual. Regardless of Mr. Borun's mission, my primary responsibility to HelixTech is the safety of this ship and its crew. Be assured that I will take whatever steps are necessary to make sure that nothing jeopardizes the *Adroit*."

Sokolov merely returned his gaze until the captain sat down again. He glanced up at Borun. "We're ready to starfall whenever we have coordinates, Mr. Borun. How do you want to work this?"

"Mr. Sokolov here will provide you with the drivespace solution you need to get under way," the exec said.

Sokolov hesitated, examining the bridge. The *Adroit*'s command deck was manned by seven or eight techs and officers. There were empty stations where additional crewmen probably sat when the ship went to battle stations. At one side, he saw Geille Monashi at the main computer station, speaking softly into a headset and running through warm-up procedures for the ship's computers. She was dressed in a black, tight-fitting jump suit, with a golden HelixTech logo emblazoned over one breast.

Karcen Borun trusts her enough to give her a post on the crew. That's interesting, Sokolov thought. This ship's big enough that he could fly with another comptech at that station, and keep her locked in her quarters. She's still trying to show him what a change of heart she's had.

Sokolov allowed himself a smile of appreciation; Geille was more duplicitous than he'd given her credit for. Despite betrayal and counter-betrayal, she was probably his only chance for an ally against Karcen Borun. He'd need an ally if he had any hope of surviving the discovery of the derelict. Of course, she'd need a little push to see that she needed an ally, too.

"The coordinates, Pete?" Karcen Borun prompted.

Geille must have felt his eyes on her from across the compartment. She set down the headset and swiveled in her seat, meeting his eyes defiance in her face. Seeing her like that—beautiful, treacherous, angry—he found that he almost didn't care about the losses he'd suffered since she crossed his path. Adversity transformed Geille into something magnificent. Even if Borun shoots me tomorrow, I don't know if I would have passed this up, he thought.

For no reason he could name, he returned her glare with a bitter smile. "Sorry. I've got the files, but Geille's encrypted them. I can't unscramble them until Geille tells me the key."

Geille frowned, her eyes like dark, icy daggers. "He's lying," she said flatly. "He can give you the coordinates anytime he chooses."

"Somebody tell Captain Mills where we're going," Borun said affably. He leaned against an unused console, master of his surroundings. "I'm anxious to get underway."

Sokolov shrugged when Karcen Borun looked his way, then turned his eyes back to Geille. He didn't want to overplay this.

Geille wasn't so secure. "He's got the coordinates," Geille repeated. "There is no encryption."

Borun pivoted to face her. His smile froze into something cold and dangerous. "I wasn't asking for explanations, Geille. Make it happen."

"Damn it, Karcen, how many times do I have to say this? *There is no password!*" Geille's voice cracked with strain. She surged up out of her seat in agitation. "Sokolov has full and unrestricted access to those files, and you've bought into his bluff! There is nothing more that I can do!"

"Geille, there are going to be some serious repercussions if I don't get what I want very soon," Karcen Borun said. He reached into his coat pocket and drew out a charge pistol. Without looking directly at her, he worked the slide and checked the clip.

Monashi recoiled. She wheeled on Sokolov. "Give him what he wants," she hissed. "Whatever stupid little game you're playing, it's time to stop it."

Sokolov snorted. "You painted yourself into this corner, Geille. Sooner or later people stop trusting you after you've betrayed them enough."

Her eyes narrowed. "Fine. You want to play this game? Let's play it. Command authorization Monashi-zero five." She offered a predatory smile and looked at Karcen Borun. "There. The lockout's gone. Sokolov can give you the coordinates now."

Not bad, he mused. What better way to get rid of imaginary encryption routines than by coming up with imaginary authorizations? She's learning. He crossed his arms—difficult, with the right one nothing more than dead weight at his side—and gave Borun the most pained look he could manage.

"She's just unlocked my files, Borun, but there's a timer running on them. They're going to be dumped in ninety seconds if she doesn't follow with another code word."

"Well, what's the code word?" Borun snapped. "It's in your own damned nanocomputer, Sokolov. Stop the count if you want to keep breathing!"

"I don't know what it is," Sokolov replied. "Geille set this up. Ask her!"

"Don't play this game with me, Geille," Borun drawled in a low voice. "You know what happens if you let Sokolov's computer wipe the coordinates."

Geille's eyes smoldered. "It's all part of the—" she began, then she abruptly realized that by coming up with the imaginary password, she'd admitted to Borun that there was a lockout in Sokolov's files. She stopped short and turned a look of pure incendiary hate on Sokolov. "You miserable bastard," she whispered.

Now you're starting to understand, Sokolov thought. He jumped in to help out. "I can probably guess for her, Borun," he said quietly. "You'll lose any chance of ever finding the alien ship. We end up dead." Geille took a half-step toward him. Sokolov continued. "You're a smart guy. Think about it. You don't care whether we live or die, but Geille's gambling that you *do* care about finding that derelict. I guess she figures that if you kill us now, we win." He paused, then added, "Sixty-five seconds left."

"He's playing with you, Karcen," Geille said. "It's another bluff."

In a single bound, Borun leaped over the console and caught Geille by her collar. His hand flew back almost of its own accord, and then he slapped her so hard that she spun in a complete circle before she fell to the deck.

"Stop the count!" he screamed. Geille's head lolled from her shoulders. Sokolov could see blood on the deck plates.

Forcing all emotion from his voice, Sokolov stated, "Fifty-five seconds. I wouldn't hit her again, Borun. If you knock her out, we're all screwed."

Karcen Borun knotted his fist in Geille's collar and dragged her up, slamming her against the bulkhead. He rammed the barrel of his charge pistol against her forehead. "Stop the count, Geille. I'll kill you if you don't."

Eyes glazed with pain, blood running freely from her mouth, Geille spat in his face. "You're pointing the gun at the wrong person," she gasped.

"For the love of God, Borun," Captain Mills said. Approbation stretched his dour face taut.

"This is not your concern, Captain," Borun snapped over his shoulder. He cocked the gun's hammer.

Geille threw a look of pure desperation at Sokolov. *"Pete!"*

Wry amusement soured in Sokolov's mouth. He'd pushed this as far as he wanted to. Where does it end? he wondered. Do I let him blow her head off? Does that even the score? The derelict was the only card she had left to play, and he was preventing her from doing so. Geille might have betrayed him, but behind each of her actions stood Karcen Borun. Geille Monashi wasn't an angel, not by any stretch of the imagination, but Karcen Borun was the real villain.

Carefully Sokolov said, "The count stopped at thirty seconds. I think Geille programmed in a positive confirmation step to make sure the files didn't get killed unless she wanted them to. She didn't confirm the file destruction command."

Borun looked up. "Are you sure?"

Sokolov made a show of absent concentration, as if he were communing with his internal computer. "Yes. There are no other triggered instructions concerning the nav coordinates."

The exec stood slowly, holstering the gun. He glanced back at Geille, who was trying valiantly to restrain sobs of terror. "Good choice, Geille," he said quietly. "Don't ever try anything like that again." He paced over to the bounty hunter and nodded at the ship's control console. "Enter the course, and if you enjoy being alive, don't find any more hidden files. I can find a way to do this without you if I need to."

* * * * *

Seven hours later and a few thousand kilometers distant, the *Blackguard* drifted in the hideous glare of Lucullus's fierce twin suns. On the corsair vessel's bridge, Devriele Shanassin watched a recording of the *Adroit*'s departure from Penates. The image was grainy; in order to avoid detection, the three-man crew of the spy ship had trailed the *Adroit* at a considerable distance. Shanassin had posted several pickets in space over Santiago, small launches and tugs doing their best to look as if they belonged in the vicinity. While he watched the video, he absently considered whether he should punish the crews who failed to note the *Adroit*'s departure or reward those who did.

Hands pressed together before his chin, Shanassin watched the entire recording without saying a word. When it was finished, he deliberately keyed it to replay and watched it again. Like a praying mantis readying its strike, he absorbed the information presented to him while restraining his instinct to action.

"We are certain," he asked of the crew around him, "that Karcen Borun's prisoners were onboard when this recording was made?"

Yeiwei Three-knives stirred behind him, eyes masked behind the dark visors most sesheyans favored in normal light. "Our contacts in HelixTech's security division are reliable," he hissed. "Sokolov was guarded too well to be reached, but they could follow his movements. He was taken aboard the *Adroit* an hour before launch."

"Why did they stop here? They spent hours drifting in open space," Shanassin demanded.

"I cannot say. My contacts reported that the *Adroit* was outfitted quickly for a long voyage. Many scientists and technicians were added to her crew."

"Scientists? What kind of scientists?"

"I will check." The sesheyan turned his blunt snout aside and hissed into a comm device pinned to his shoulder. "Two physicists. A structural engineer. A hull systems specialist. Two xenobiologists. Two xenoarcheologists. Several other technicians."

Shanassin smiled. "What does that tell you, Yeiwei?"

"First contact or the discovery of an artifact of some kind." The sesheyan's talons clicked on the deck plates as he pranced anxiously. "Why bring Sokolov and Monashi then? This is a hunt of a different kind."

"Indeed. I came out here to find Sokolov, but I suspect that other opportunities may be emerging." The fraal corsair lost himself in his thoughts for a long moment. At the end of the tape, the grainy image of the *Adroit* abruptly ringed itself in a brilliant spray of colors, then vanished. "There. They entered drivespace."

"Where does Curuyfi the Father of Stars carry them?" Yeiwei said quietly. "Could Sokolov have found something of interest when he fled from us?"

"That seems the most likely conclusion," Shanassin said. His gaze fell on his sensor operator, a young human woman who was noted for her expertise with the attack ship's sensor suite. "Sherena, do you see any sign of ibn Beighur?"

For months now, the corsair king had been pursued by Solar forces in the system. The *Birmingham*—a heavy cruiser under the command of the skilled and aggressive Captain ibn Beighur—was the only one that concerned him. It infuriated Shanassin to demean himself by skulking about like a field mouse fearing the appearance of the hawk's shadow, but sooner or later he intended to teach ibn Beighur that command of the largest warship in Lucullus didn't insulate him from the criminals he hunted.

"No, Captain. No Solar military craft are in the vicinity of Penates," Sherena replied.

"Excellent," Shanassin breathed. "Eh'tel!"

At the side of the *Blackguard*'s bridge, another fraal, old and wizened, turned to face him. She was dressed in a simple white shift, belted at the waist.

"You wish to follow the vessel, my lord?" she asked in stilted High Fraal.

"At once," Shanassin replied.

Eh'tel closed her eyes, adopting a posture of contemplation. Shanassin watched the mystic at her work. In her silent meditation, she probed the very fabric of reality, seeking the intangible wake of the HelixTech vessel. Shanassin had never developed his own psionic talents to any great extent. It was a gift most fraal took for granted, but he'd never had enough patience for the study of the mind. He was born with an inclination toward physical action instead of mental contemplation.

The old woman stretched out her hand to the *Blackguard*'s nav computer. Without even touching the keypad, somehow she made numbers begin to flash and flicker across the unit.

"I have the ship," she intoned. "Energize the stardrive now! I will guide you."

Shanassin motioned with his hand. The woman sitting at the engineering console stabbed the button that launched the ship into drivespace, guided by nothing more than Eh'tel's astrocognitive talents. Space around the *Blackguard* flared with the colors of the rainbow, then faded into darkness as the stars whirled away.

* * * * *

The *Adroit* silently waited out the hours of the jump in the stillness of nonexistence. The deck plates quietly hummed, mechanical systems sighed and mumbled, the computers and sensors chirped and clicked to one another. Outside, nothing but endless black void surrounded the ship. Sokolov marked the time considering and discarding various plans for extricating himself from his situation. He would have given his eye teeth to know what was happening outside the small compartment that served as the ship's brig.

He had an idea or two about how he could escape his quarters. The problem was: what would he do if he succeeded? The odds of physically controlling the entire ship were slim; he couldn't run the *Adroit* by himself. That would imply killing or confining most of the crew so they couldn't interfere with his activities, and there were just too many people aboard. Someone would sneak up on him and take him down while he was trying to keep an eye on everything.

He might be able to sabotage the ship, perhaps rigging the main reactor for catastrophic failure if Borun didn't comply with his wishes and set him free. Unfortunately Sokolov's security training reminded him that very few people who take a hostage or deploy a bomb threat actually escape once they've played their trump card. Sooner or later you had to either walk away from the threat or push the button, and at that moment your opponents would splatter your brains all over the nearest wall.

As a measure of true desperation, he could try to get to the ship's lifeboat and jettison himself into drivespace. That had the virtue of assured success; once he blew the explosive bolts and separated from the *Adroit,* the lifeboat would be instantly lost in the random energies of drivespace, and the *Adroit* wouldn't be able to track or recapture him. The downside to that plan was stark and simple. No one who'd ever left a ship in the middle of drivespace had ever been heard from again. In a sci-fi holo, Sokolov would find that benevolent aliens of great power and wisdom policed drivespace, rescuing stranded travelers. He decided he'd rather not bet his life on it.

Most of Sokolov's escape plans fetched up hard against one unanswerable question: if he managed to get out, where was he going to go?

Late in the third day of the trip, Karcen Borun came to visit him. Dressed in a white turtleneck and olive trousers, he wore a HelixTech cap and an affable expression. The exec must have watched public holovision to see how famous deep-space explorers dressed, Sokolov reflected. He almost expected Borun to set up a display screen and lecture his prisoner about the new planet they were going to survey.

Sokolov watched while Borun shooed Harmon, his jail-keeper, out of the cabin, then Borun spun a metal stool from a desk and faced the cramped cell, sitting down as if he were chatting with an old friend.

"Mr. Sokolov, I'd like to have a word with you." The executive reached into a pocket and tossed Sokolov a pack of cigarettes and a lighter. "Go ahead," he said magnanimously. "I understand you haven't had a smoke for several days."

"I've been meaning to run down to the corner store," Sokolov said, guarding his expression. He fished out a smoke and lit it, watching Borun the whole time. *Borun's trying to be friendly. That means he wants something.* He dropped the cigarettes and the lighter into his front pocket. "Thanks."

"Are you comfortable here? Harmon's not treating you too badly?"

Sokolov studied the ceiling. "A cell's a cell, Borun. Your security chief treats me like I'm the guy who molested his baby sister. Other than that, well, I'm doing great."

"Harmon is just trying to do his job," Borun said. "I'll tell him to lighten up. We're all grown-ups here."

"What brings you down here, Borun? Drivespace getting to you?"

Borun ran his hand through his hair. "I'd hoped I could reach some kind of understanding with you, Sokolov. The present situation really isn't profitable for either one of us. You think I'll kill you once I get what I want. I'm afraid that you might screw all of us because you think you don't have anything to lose." The exec leaned forward. "You said you wanted to cut a deal before we found the derelict. I'm ready to put something on the table."

Sokolov tried to keep the skepticism off his face but failed. "Go ahead, Borun," he said. "This ought to be good for a laugh, if nothing else."

He smiled and spread his hands. "Just hear me out. Sokolov, what if I told you that I'd be willing to pay you a million Concord dollars and let you walk away scot-free if you simply agreed to sell me all your rights to the derelict? You were going to sell it to someone anyway. It might not be the best deal you could have put together, but considering the circumstances—" Borun nodded at the cell— "you'd be coming out clean."

Sokolov took a drag from the cigarette and studied Borun. What was it that Borun had told him about lords and serfs a few days ago? Why would a man who thought that way look to strike a bargain now?

He shook his head and said, "You wouldn't pay me before. Why are you willing to buy me out now? You laughed in my face when I told you what it would take." He leaned back against the bulkhead and blew smoke in the executive's direction. "You told me to be a good serf, remember?"

Borun straightened in his seat. "Two reasons, Pete. I can call you Pete, right? First, everything has a price. If I were to shoot you and take your jacket, well, it wasn't really free. I spent a bullet to get it. If we weren't in a system like Lucullus, then that jacket might have one hell of a high price. I'd be risking arrest, incarceration, maybe even capital punishment any time I killed someone to take his goods. That risk is the cost of the purchase. Nothing is free.

"Five days ago, I didn't have very much of a risk to pay in order to take the derelict from you, Sokolov. After all, Geille just gave it to me! Now I'm looking at some of the points you raised about the legalities of the situation. It's become worth my while to take a look at different ways to pay for what I want." The executive flashed an insincere smile. "The lords plunder the serfs, Sokolov. That's the way of things, but a lord who knows what's good for him doesn't plunder his serfs all the time. Sooner or later a peasant with a spear is going to call in the debt."

He's good, Sokolov thought. Borun can charm the paint off the walls when he puts his mind to it. I don't buy it for a second, though.

"What's the second reason?"

"I need something from you, Sokolov," Borun said amiably. "I need you to let me get a look at what's in your nanocomputer. I want the file with the coordinates in it, so that I don't have to renegotiate this deal if we make starrise in the middle of nowhere and you decide to up the ante. I also need to know if you were just pulling my leg about Monashi's file erasure. I think you can see why I don't want to play out that scene again."

Now his reasoning was clear. He's trying to decide just how badly he needs Geille Monashi, Sokolov thought. Everything else is a diversion. He leaned back in his bunk, savoring the acrid scent of smoke. Was Borun concerned that Geille might have more tricks up her sleeve, or was Borun determined to make sure that Geille couldn't pull a trick like that again? In either case, a wrong answer might make Geille very expendable.

"If you let me out of this cell, fixed my arm, and allowed me to get a couple of guns out of your armory, I'd start to believe that you meant what you said," he said, stalling.

Borun laughed. "Sorry, Pete. I don't see that I need to provide you with the means to hijack the ship. Let's make sure we avoid any misunderstandings and say that you'll stay here until I see the derelict."

Sokolov climbed to his feet, moving awkwardly against the dead weight of his right arm. He paced back and forth across his cell. He tried to assume an air of indifference.

"I can't sign over the rights until I have some kind of insurance, Borun, and I can't give you unrestricted access to my nanocomputer. I've got more to protect than the location of the derelict." He paused and finished his smoke, dropping the cigarette to the deck. "I will tell you that I wasn't kidding about Geille's kill command. She encrypted the coordinates, probably to guard against the possibility that I'd ever get a chance to use them after I dragged her back to you. I think she started the countdown to remind you that you can't be sure what you might need her for."

The exec glared at him. "It seems like a stupid stunt. Geille knows better than to play hardball with me."

"The point's pretty clear. She's warned you that you need to think twice before getting rid of her, not just for the derelict, but for the research she stole, too." Sokolov crossed his fingers, hoping he wasn't condemning Geille by choosing the wrong tactic. "What if you decide to make her disappear, and then six months from now, all of your R and D files—you know, the ones she supposedly stole and restored—suddenly tell you, 'Hey, we're going to vanish if you don't ask Geille Monashi to make sure it doesn't happen?' "

"If she wanted to threaten me, she would have come right out and threatened me," Borun replied, "but she denied that she had anything to do with that countdown, Sokolov. As far as I know, you're making this up. That's why I want to examine your computer."

"You were pointing a gun at her head," Sokolov said. "Sometimes that impedes clear thinking."

Borun stood and scratched at his chin, weighing Sokolov's words. "If you let me get a look at your system, Pete, I'd know for sure. I'll even throw in a significant bonus when we talk numbers on the alien wreck. We'll call it a consulting fee."

Sokolov snorted. That promise cost Borun exactly nothing. "I'll keep it in mind. Let me think it over," he said.

The exec made a show of inspecting Sokolov's cell. "Feel free to take all the time you want," he said with a predatory smile, "but remember this, Pete: all bets are off if we get to where we're going and there's no alien vessel waiting for me.

Understand?" He rolled the stool back across the deck to the desk and strode out of the room, whistling tunelessly.

Sokolov watched him leave, then waited a good ten minutes to make sure Borun wasn't coming back. Whether he'd meant to or not, Karcen Borun had addressed one of the questions nagging Sokolov over the last three days. Instead of asking himself where he could go if he escaped from his cell, Borun had changed that question to, what would he do? For the first time since starfall, Sokolov had an idea of how to answer it.

Ironically enough, Karcen Borun had also provided him with exactly what he needed to get out of his cell. From his coat pocket, Sokolov fished out the lighter Borun had given him. It was a decent pocket igniter, a small casing for a lanthanide cell with a heating element at one end. Sokolov opened the skin on his cybernetic arm and manually pushed the knife blade out, locking it in position, then he pried open the lighter case, exposing the power cell. Studying the mechanical innards of his arm, he pulled up the design schematics from his nanocomputer. *I need about four or five centimeters of superconducting wire, Nancy. What can I pull out of the arm that won't matter much?*

Pain sensor 119-A-3 carries damage signals from your right little finger, the nanocomputer replied. *Its removal will not cause a significant degradation in safety or performance, although I advise against any such action.*

Desperate times demand desperate measures, he told the nanocomputer. He reached into his right wrist cavity and yanked out the indicated wire. Fashioning the wire into a small loop, he knelt by the door to his cell and wedged one end into the interior of the scanning lock that secured the door. The other end he threaded into the lighter's power cell output terminal. Carefully folding the unresponsive fingers of his right hand around the power cell, he flipped the on switch and held the power cell against the door lock.

Instantly the cell started to grow warm. If his arm had been operative, pain signals would have been sounding like little klaxons in his head. With no power, the heat sensors didn't work. His fingertips scorched black, but the lighter cell dumped even more heat into the lock.

After a minute and a half, the lock's fuse blew with a distinct *pop!*

The cell door swung open. Sokolov grinned and stepped out into the rest of the compartment. He had at least two things to do before he could afford to be caught. He quickly crossed to the hatch leading out to the rest of the ship and cracked it open, peering into the passageway beyond.

It was empty. The office was located on the *Adroit*'s lowest deck, and there was little traffic in this part of the ship. Sokolov turned right. About ten meters down the passage, he found the room he was looking for: Compartment 3-8, Hull Workshop. Please let there be no one here, he mouthed, then he opened the door a crack to look inside.

The room was empty. Two long workbenches lined the bulkheads, fitted with a variety of heavy-duty machine tools for working on major structural repairs. Sokolov slipped inside and closed the hatch behind him. Quickly he moved over to the intercom unit and checked the directory display. Then he punched in the designator and pinged the room he wanted. He left the vid pickup blank.

"Monashi here."

"Miss Monashi, this is the hull workshop. Ah, we have a problem we need your help on. Can you come down here?" Sokolov said, trying to mumble. He wished there were an easy way to find out if she could talk openly, but he couldn't think of any discreet way to ask.

"It's after midnight," Geille replied. "Can it wait a few hours?"

"Sorry. We need you to double-check something for us before we finish a job. It should take only minute."

There was a long silence on the other end. Finally Geille keyed the intercom again. "All right. I'll be right there."

Sokolov keyed off the intercom and surveyed the shop. *Nancy, I need a shopping list. What kind of standard power cells will fit my arm? What about motor-drivers? Any chance that I can adapt standard units for use in my cybernetic systems?*

Two type CXY lanthanide cells and two type CGT lanthanide cells would restore normal operating power, the nanocomputer replied. *With work, you could modify the power-assist units from an armored e-suit, exoskeletal walker, or suit of powered armor to fit in your arm. A Marsstat Motors 2.3 K-amp power-assist unit for the IPK Rough Terrain Walker would be ideal.*

"Let's see what's here," he muttered.

He moved over to the spare parts storage unit and rifled through it. The power cells were easy; he was able to install what he needed in a matter of minutes. The tougher part of the job consisted of replacing the mechanized muscle units that provided his arm with mobility and strength. They were specialized pieces of equipment, and nothing in the hull shop was going to come close to fitting in his arm. Sokolov decided he might have better luck in the ship's cargo bay or suit lockers.

While he searched for materials, the door buzzed. Sokolov quickly moved over to stand behind the hatch, then keyed it to open. "Is anyone here?" Geille called.

She stepped through the hatch, on the opposite side of the door from him. When he judged that she was clear, he quickly shut the hatch and stepped into the light.

Geille whirled in alarm, raising her arms to defend herself. She wore the standard black HelixTech jump suit, and her hair was pulled back in a simple ponytail.

"Sokolov! You scared the hell out of me!"

He deliberately held still, trying not to alarm her. "This was the only way I could think of to contact you."

"Aren't you supposed to be in the brig?"

He didn't consider that question worth answering. "I probably don't have much time, Geille. I called you down here because I need your help."

"You want me to help you?" She stared at him for three, maybe four heartbeats, her face blank with amazement. Cold fury began to gather behind her eyes, settling over her features like an iron mask. "You have to be kidding me. You almost got me killed with that little game you played on the bridge. You can rot in hell, for all I care."

Sokolov leaned against one of the workbenches and grimaced. "Sorry about that. I was pretty angry about the loss of my ship, and I guess I wanted to get even."

Geille tossed her head. "So what's changed?"

"I've had three solid days to think about what happens at the end of this ride, and I don't like the answers I'm coming up with," Sokolov said. "I need an ally. I think you do, too."

She snorted and crossed her arms, but her eyes betrayed a hint of uncertainty. She's done some thinking, too, Sokolov decided.

"Do you have a plan?" she asked.

"Not yet. Whatever we do, our chances are pretty slim. We're both in deep trouble here, Geille." Sokolov stood up and paced away, circling the workshop.

"We wouldn't be if you hadn't insisted on dragging me back to HelixTech."

Sokolov resisted the impulse to go down the whole long road of who'd done what to whom and why. Instead he focused on her face, refusing to let his anger show, refusing to let her look away.

"That doesn't matter now," he said. "You know what Borun has to do in order to make sure that we don't ever trip him up again. I don't care what you think about me"—that was not quite true, but she didn't need to know that—"but we have a common cause."

"I disagree. I'm doing just fine, thank you. I did what I had to do in order to save myself. When I give Karcen the derelict, I'm off the hook." She looked at him, her resolve firm. "The last thing I want to do is give Borun any reason to associate you with me. In fact, I ought to leave before someone catches me in here with you."

"Geille, figure the odds. What do you think the chance is that Karcen Borun is going to let you have your resignation and let you walk away from HelixTech, considering what you know about him? Fifty-fifty? Forty-sixty?" He paused, timing his words for maximum effect. "Personally, I'd give you maybe one in ten. I'm even worse off than that."

He managed to hold her with his urgency. She tried to look away, but he wouldn't let her. "Listen, here's what I need you to do. Sometime before we make starfall, I need you to reinitialize my cybernetics and get me a set of motor units that I can adapt to my arm." He rattled off the specs for her. "That'll at least give me a chance to surprise Borun when he decides he's done with me."

"So how does that help me?" Geille asked.

"It's something you know that he doesn't," Sokolov said, "and I'll promise you this, Geille: whatever happens, I'm going to do my damnedest to get *both* of us out of this mess. I can't do it alone, and I don't think you can either."

"Sokolov, I don't know if I can promise you anything. Why should I believe anything you say? And why do you think I won't run right to Borun and report this conversation?" Geille hugged herself tighter, agitated. "What you're asking is likely to cost me my life. What if Borun catches me helping you?"

"First, you can believe me because I don't have anything left to lose. Second, do you seriously believe that you would be any worse off than you are right now if you helped me?" Sokolov asked. "Think it over, Geille, but don't take too long. You know what I need and where I am." With that, he cracked the door open and glanced out into the hallway.

"Wait a minute," Geille snapped. "Where are you going?"

"Ship's armory," Sokolov replied. "Borun's going to learn that I got out of the brig—I can't hide the damage to the lock. I need to go someplace in order to get caught. If I don't do something logical like trying to arm myself, he's going to wonder what I was doing when I got out of my cell."

Geille frowned. "You're covering for me?"

Sokolov looked back with a grimace. "I need you, Geille. It was stupid of me to turn Borun against you. Do me a favor, and don't let anyone see you going back to your quarters. I'll try to give you ten minutes before Harmon and his thugs catch me."

He left her in the hull workshop, hoping that the seeds of distrust he'd planted would grow and bear fruit sooner rather than later. She was the only person on the *Adroit* who might actually have more at stake than he did, and he knew what it was like to have her for an enemy. He wanted that determination, that duplicity, on his side for a change. As it turned out, Harmon caught him before he even got within ten meters of the gun locker.

Chapter Fifteen

CAPTAIN RAMIL IBN Beighur of the Solar Union heavy cruiser *Birmingham* climbed up to the *Sirocco*'s command deck, staring at the blank black void visible through the generous viewports. Somewhere in the timeless, dimensionless space beyond his ship's hull, Devriele Shanassin and his *Blackguard* ghosted through nonexistence a dozen hours ahead of him, engaged in some unfathomable mission. Ibn Beighur had hunted the fraal corsair lord for almost a year now, scouring the maelstrom of Dioscuri and chasing the pirate's trail across the Lucullus system.

He'd missed Shanassin on two previous occasions. This time he meant to catch the outlaw. To that end, he'd left the *Birmingham*—the largest and most powerful warship in Lucullus—in orbit around Penates. With a handpicked crew of only a dozen of the *Birmingham*'s most experienced officers and technicians, he'd refitted a captured pirate vessel and named it the *Sirocco*. The *Sirocco* was only a tenth the *Birmingham*'s size, a small gunboat that could skulk through Lucullus without attracting the attention that a capital warship commanded. Of course, corsairs who would flee the approach of the *Birmingham* might turn and fight against the *Sirocco,* but ibn Beighur trusted his skills, experience, and his veteran officers enough to take that chance.

Ibn Beighur was a handsome man of fifty years, narrow-waisted and slim, an officer who carefully fostered an air of dash and gallantry. Like most Solars, he believed in preserving the past by modeling his life, his mannerisms, his cultural identity after one of Earth's ancient lands. Beighur considered himself a student of the Ottomans and tried to conduct his life and command with the wisdom, the subtlety, the refinement, and the scholarship of a noble-born Turkish officer of the sixteenth or seventeenth century. Three-quarters of the *Birmingham*'s thousand-man crew shared similar cultural models, embracing vanished times and places from all of Earth's convoluted history.

Lucullus was an assignment that required all of ibn Beighur's patience and cunning. A Solar colony only a century ago, it had rebelled during the Long Silence that isolated all of the Verge from the nations of Old Space. Now with the resumption of contact, the Solar Union's allies and rivals—VoidCorp, StarMech, the Rigunmors, the Orions, all of the great nations— maneuvered to reestablish their presence in the Verge. The Union's return was largely in Captain Beighur's hands. With courtesy and discretion, he bided his time and studied the feuding crime lords and strongmen of Penates, carefully formulating his plans for the day when he would intercede directly to bring the former colony's chaos and strife to an end. Eliminating powerful crime lords like Devriele Shanassin was only the first step in bringing some semblance of law and order to the former Solar colony.

The *Sirocco*'s bridge was small and cramped, even though in its original design it had been spacious and open. Every cubic meter onboard the ship had been jammed with extra weaponry, sensors, and suites of defensive jammers. No one would mistake it for the light freighter it had once been . . . but they could easily mistake it for a pirate vessel. Most illegals had to make use of whatever weapon systems and materials they could lay their hands on, giving their ships a distinct patched-together look. The *Sirocco* followed that model perfectly. Ibn Beighur had even gone to the trouble of constructing a fake career for the small ship, posting a record of hijackings and raids in nearby systems and attributing them to a ship fitting the *Sirocco*'s description.

To catch a jackal, you must become a jackal, he reflected. He settled into the command chair and enjoyed the view of drive-space. The *Sirocco*'s hemispherical command deck was roofed with great panes of transplas, permitting a generous view despite the bulky equipment and cramped quarters. Reclining in the couch to gaze up through the viewports, ibn Beighur felt as if he clung to the edge of existence. Usually the slow drift of imagined patterns and shapes in the blankness of drivespace intrigued him, externalizing the things he wished to examine in his own mind, but today it seemed to be nothing more than a pattern of unpredictable and destructive change.

Ibn Beighur stared into the darkness and tried to fathom the mind of Devriele Shanassin. Where was the corsair going? Why had he pursued the HelixTech ship? The *Sirocco*'s mass detectors were sensitive enough to project the course of the corsair and the ship he shadowed. The *Adroit* had, with great care, made a jump into the middle of interstellar space, billions—no, trillions—of kilometers from anything of interest. The Solar captain considered it extremely unlikely that the HelixTech ship had made that starfall by mistake. What errand could they possibly have out there?

What did Shanassin hope to gain by following them? The *Blackguard* was certainly no match for the *Adroit*. If ibn Beighur knew it, Shanassin must know it as well. With a sigh, he leaned back in his antique chair and keyed the intercom.

"Mr. Moreno, would you join me on the bridge?"

"At once, Captain."

The *Birmingham*'s chief engineer served as his second-in-command onboard *Sirocco,* while ibn Beighur left command of the heavy cruiser in the hands of his executive officer. True to his word, Moreno clattered up the ladder only a few moments later. The *Sirocco* was small enough that you couldn't be too far away from the bridge no matter where you were. Raul Moreno was young, a handsome fellow who studiously preserved the grace and passion of old Spain. He'd had spent most of his career on the tension-filled border between the Union and the Thuldan Empire.

Moreno was an efficient, courageous, and tactically skillful officer who viewed the Verge as something of a sideshow, a terrible misallocation of resources for the Solar Union, given the threat posed by the Thuldans. Such skills and views were absolutely vital for officers up to a point. Ibn Beighur hoped he'd taught Moreno something about the next step to diplomacy and national policy during the time Moreno had served under his command.

"Yes, sir?" the officer asked.

"We make starrise in thirty-three hours, correct?"

"Yes, Captain."

Ibn Beighur noted that Moreno didn't even need to check the engineering displays to come up with the answer. Of course, any engineer worth his salt would keep a constant eye on the performance of the stardrive and the process of the jump.

"Thank you, Mr. Moreno. How much of a lead does the *Blackguard* have on us?"

Moreno checked the navigation displays. "The *Blackguard* made starfall three hours and twenty-five minutes before we jumped, Captain. It took a long time to work out her jump coordinates from her departure signature." He paused, then added, "I informed Chief Gannon that I expected a more rapid solution next time."

"Understood." It was the best that could be done under the circumstances, ibn Beighur reminded himself. If he knew Moreno at all, the officer had already spoken to the chief astrogator about the situation at some length. The captain softened his tone. "Remember, Mr. Moreno, Chief Gannon just lost her best petty officer last week to reassignment. She's breaking in a new team. Besides, wherever Shanassin's going, he's only going to be a couple of hours ahead of us. We'll run him to ground before he recharges his drive."

"Anything else, Captain?"

"Make sure Chief Gannon is running more tracking drills with the new men on her team. We need to get them up to speed."

The executive officer smiled grimly. "I've been seeing to it personally, Captain. I have Chief Gannon running those drills on her team around the clock. Nasty stuff—damaged mass detector array, heavy mass cannon fire, several contacts sinking out at once. They'll do better next time."

"Good, Mr. Moreno. I'll be counting on it."

"Anything else, sir?"

The captain shook his head. "Not until starrise."

Moreno nodded and made his way down the steep stair leading back down to the *Sirocco*'s mess deck and crew lounge. Ibn Beighur swiveled away, returning his attention to the darkness outside the window. The silvery murk was gnawing at his mind, irritating him like some important fact that he'd forgotten. Sometimes he wondered if there was something out in the blackness, some psychoreactive ether that really did respond to human thought. He rubbed at his temples.

"Computer, close the blast shields," he said softly.

In silence, dark armored shutters dropped across the window, hiding him from the emptiness outside.

* * * * *

Chief Harmon let Sokolov out of his cell about half an hour before starrise. The security man didn't say a word; his broad back was hunched like a stressed trestle, and his jaw was clenched so hard Sokolov thought he might break some teeth. Harmon had taken it as a personal affront that Sokolov had managed to escape the brig, even if he'd been out for only twenty minutes. Sokolov guessed that Captain Mills must have been hard on Harmon for his lapse in vigilance, since he couldn't berate Karcen Borun for giving Sokolov the lighter he used to make his escape. Life wasn't fair sometimes.

"Come on, Sokolov," he grated. "Time to see if you get to stay onboard or continue this trip on the wrong side of the air lock."

Sokolov didn't bother to answer. Harmon and two other security specs shackled him with heavy plastic binders and escorted him to the *Adroit*'s bridge. The compartment was crowded with crewmen and technicians preparing for the return to normal space. Sensor systems and navigation boards that had been cold and dark for the last five days were reinitializing, starting up with clicks and whirs of activity as the technicians ran the start-up routines. Captain Mills sat in his chair, studying reports on his dataslate. Karcen Borun stood next to him, pacing impatiently as the last few minutes of the drivespace submergence ticked down.

Geille Monashi sat at the computer ops console, coordinating the *Adroit*'s information systems as the main computer collected status reports and comm checks from the dozens of smaller computers scattered around the bridge. She glanced up when Harmon and his men led him inside, holding his gaze for one long moment, her face impassive and neutral, then she returned to her work.

Better decide where you stand soon, Geille, he thought. Time's running out.

"Mr. Sokolov! Glad you could join us!" Karcen Borun stepped down from the raised step in the center of the bridge and ambled toward him, alive with excitement. He could hardly keep still, tapping his feet against the deck plates and rubbing his hands together. The executive grinned like a hungry shark. "How could you want to miss this?"

Sokolov didn't bother to answer. Borun's banter simply annoyed him. The exec's smile faded in the face of the bounty hunter's hostility.

Borun turned to Harmon and said, "Find a spare seat for Mr. Sokolov and encourage him to stay there. We don't want him to go wandering again."

Harmon pushed Sokolov into a seat and buckled the restraint straps in place, cinching them tight with a yank. With Sokolov's hands secured behind his back, he wasn't going anywhere.

He looked up at Harmon and asked, "How about a smoke, Chief?"

The security chief gave him a black look. "That's not funny, Sokolov. Shut up and be good."

Sokolov spent the remaining few minutes of the drivespace voyage watching the *Adroit*'s crew at work. The corvette's crew wore the gray jump suits of HelixTech's corporate fleet. Working calmly and quietly, they readied the ship for starrise. Borun's handpicked security specs and experts stood out in their black outfits, shadowing the bridge with suspicious looks as if they thought Captain Mills and his men might be up to something. The scientists and technicians of the contact team managed to get in the way of both the crewmen and the security team, absorbed in their own checklists for emergence.

"Ten seconds to starrise!" the *Adroit*'s computer announced.

Sokolov shifted to look out the nearest viewport. Black nothingness receded as star-speckled black rushed toward him, the eye-deceiving plummet back into reality that marked the end of every drivespace voyage. A ring of violent blue light, photons erased by their abrupt arrival, danced and streamed away from them.

"Starrise recorded at 1816 hours on May 21st, 2502," the computer stated.

There was no sign of the derelict. Even though he knew perfectly well that the most precise starrise would miss the target by millions of kilometers, Sokolov had half expected the hulking outline of the ship to greet them the instant they emerged. He tried to ignore the dark looks directed at him by the Helix-Tech people surrounding him. I keyed in the right coordinates, didn't I, he wondered, or did Geille load the wrong numbers into this file when she copied it into my nanocomputer?

He looked over at Geille; she returned his gaze with a vaguely puzzled look, as if to ask, "You didn't screw this up, did you?"

Karcen Borun leaned over the rail surrounding the command platform and stared hard at Sokolov. "Does anybody see any sign of a ship contact?" he called out. "Any sign at all?"

Mills responded for his crew. "Nothing out here, Mr. Borun. We're in interstellar space, within five million kilometers of the coordinates Sokolov punched into the nav system."

Borun's face darkened. "Mr. Sokolov, you have some explaining to do," he said. "We hit your coordinates within five million kilometers, but I don't see any titanic alien ship out here."

Sokolov glanced out the viewport, searching for anything familiar in the shape of the stars. He couldn't tell if everything looked right or not; the stars looked the same, but other than the brilliant dot of Lucullus, nothing jarred his memory. He shrugged, almost enjoying the moment. It would be the last laugh he'd ever have, of course, but it might be worth it.

"Give it time, Borun. If the ship's a couple of light-hours distant, you won't spot it for a while yet."

Captain Mills scratched at his chin. "What was the derelict's course and speed when you left it, Sokolov? Was it heading in any particular direction?"

"It was drifting at about one percent of light speed. Call it three thousand kilometers per second. Even if we're right on top of the coordinates, the derelict's had almost fourteen days to move away from here." He paused, allowing Nancy to do the math quickly. "Its momentum's carried it three and a half billion kilometers while we traveled to Lucullus and back. That's three and a half light-hours right there, even if we hit the coordinates dead on the mark."

"So we have to go catch this thing now?" Karcen Borun asked, annoyance in his voice.

"Let me have a look at your nav display," Sokolov said. "I'll show you which way it was heading. It shouldn't take us more than ten or fifteen hours to overhaul it."

"I'm running out of patience, Sokolov," Borun said. He nodded at Harmon. The security chief released Sokolov and stepped back, watching warily.

"Interstellar space is big, Borun. Don't blame me; I didn't make it that way." Freed of the chair, Sokolov stood and walked over to the astrogation station. He looked over the shoulder of the technician, studying the display. "Try setting a course of 045-030," he told the astrogator. "Take us back toward Lucullus. The derelict was heading that way."

The executive narrowed his eyes. "You'd better deliver, Sokolov. If you and Geille thought this whole thing up as a hoax to lure me out into the middle of nowhere . . ."

Monashi laughed in a low voice. "Your ego amazes me, Karcen. Do you really believe that I'd put myself in this situation just to make you look like a fool? I could have thought of less dangerous ways to do that."

The executive wheeled on her, his false geniality in his artificially colored eyes fading. "I don't know what I believe at the moment, Geille," he snapped. "As far as I know, you two have been in collaboration from the moment Sokolov brought you back."

"Think what you like, Borun," Sokolov said evenly. "Geille

bought her life with my derelict. I'm going to show you what you got in the deal."

"I'll give you six hours, Sokolov," Borun said. He motioned to Harmon. "Take him back down to the brig."

* * * * *

Sokolov spent the next three hours staring at the wall and wishing he had his smokes. He tried not to think about what would happen if *Adroit* failed to find the derelict. He'd given them the course and speed he had recorded in his nanocomputer, but the alien ship was a mystery. There was no rule that said that the derelict wasn't allowed to change course. He passed the time by imagining scenarios in which he broke into HelixTech and settled Karcen Borun's accounts in a permanent and dramatic fashion. Corporate security was good enough that it was actually a challenging mental exercise. It was more fun to think about what he might do if he were given his freedom than it was to contemplate the alternative.

Since Sokolov's escape, Security Chief Harmon had ordered a round-the-clock guard posted in the brig to keep an eye on him. The current guard now was a tall, barrel-shaped woman named Venters. He guessed that Venters weighed in at about a hundred kilos, all of it muscle. Unfortunately she was even more attentive to duty than Harmon was, and she spent her two-hour watch with her eyes glued to him. Sokolov was almost relieved to see the security chief when Harmon relieved her at the two-hour mark.

"Any sign of the derelict?" he asked the chief.

Harmon shrugged. "When I left the bridge, the sensor techs were looking at something they'd picked up on active radar. A long-range contact . . . no details of any kind."

"That's probably it. That's how I spotted it when I was out here a couple of weeks ago."

"Guess it's your lucky day, then."

Sokolov laughed sourly. "Could have fooled me. Has Borun told you when I'm supposed to go away?"

"He wants to see the derelict before he makes a decision. I

think it depends on whether or not you're going to be an asset or a liability," Harmon told him.

"Meaning as long as it looks like I have more to give him, I'm fine, but when he thinks he's got everything I know, then it's a matter of tidying up loose ends."

The chief might as well have been discussing a piece of equipment. "If it were up to me, I'd have shot you after you got out of the brig and tried for the guns. No sense taking chances." The door chimed. "Who is it?" the security officer called.

"Geille Monashi. I'm here to see Sokolov."

Harmon glanced at Sokolov, then set one hand on the butt of his pistol. "Come in."

The hatch slid open. Geille stepped inside, carrying a large black satchel. She set it down and opened it, pulling out a notebook computer and several datajacks. "I'm supposed to see if I can get into Sokolov's nanocomputer," she said, pulling up the small, wheeled stool by the desk. "Borun said to tell you that I needed privacy."

The security chief frowned. "I'm going to have to check this out."

Geille nodded at the intercom. "Go ahead. Mr. Borun is in his quarters."

Harmon drifted over to the intercom, keeping his eyes on both Geille and Sokolov. He punched in the number for the executive's quarters. "Mr. Borun? This is Harmon."

The display flickered. Karcen Borun appeared, looking up from the desk in his stateroom. "Geille's down there?" he asked.

"Yes, sir. She says she needs to work on Sokolov alone."

Borun nodded. "So what's the problem?"

Harmon jerked his head at the comptech. "You trust her alone with the prisoner?"

Borun paused, staring out of the screen at the security chief. After a long moment, he said, "Has it occurred to you, Harmon, that Sokolov may have information that I don't want very many people to know about? Geille's the only person on this ship who can crack his nanocomputer. I want to know what other dirty little secrets Sokolov's got rattling around inside his head. Stand guard outside the hatch if it makes you feel better, but I don't want you listening in."

The security chief scowled. "Mr. Borun, I don't think—"

"Keep it under your hat, Harmon. Understand?" The screen went dark.

"I understand, sir." Harmon glared at Geille and Sokolov. He scratched his head and picked up his flight jacket from the desktop. "Ms. Monashi, I'll be right outside. Yell if you need anything."

Geille gave him a pained look. "I can take care of myself, Chief." She wheeled the stool over to the cell door and looked at Sokolov. "Take off your coat and give me your arm," she said. Behind her, Harmon stomped out the door and sealed it behind him.

Sokolov shrugged off his duster, lifted his right arm into place, and thrust it through the bars of the cell. "What kind of line did you feed Borun to make him buy off on that?" he asked.

"I didn't feed him any lines at all," Geille said. She stripped the access panels from his arm and reeled out the datawire link from his forearm, plugging it into her computer. "Karcen doesn't know I'm down here. I faked the intercom conversation."

Sokolov glanced up, surprised. *That takes guts,* he thought, *and skill.* "What happens when Harmon says something about this to Borun? They'll figure it out real quick, Geille."

"Yeah, well, I'm kind of hoping that it doesn't occur to Harmon to ask Borun about it. I figured that if I gave Borun the right lines and had him step on Harmon a bit, Harmon wouldn't want to raise the question again." She started up the computer and began to run a series of interface programs.

Access Monashi-12, Nancy reported. *My directories and hardware configuration files are being scanned.*

Don't worry about it, Sokolov replied. He watched Geille work. "I can guess at how you borrowed an image of Borun and rigged the intercom to divert to your programmed response, but how in the world did you set up the conversation and cue the right answers?"

Geille looked up and gave him the first real smile he'd seen from her in two weeks. "I ran it from this computer with my psi-talent," she said. "It comes in handy for things like this. I bet you didn't even see my lips moving."

He laughed quietly. "Does this mean you're on my side?"

"Maybe. What it means is that you've managed to convince me that Karcen Borun won't hesitate to blow me out the air lock if he doesn't need me anymore." She rapped out a series of commands on her touch-interface pad. Nancy reported the software lockouts that had been installed to isolate him from his cybernetic enhancements were down. "You're not the only iron I have in the fire, Sokolov, but you might make for a good distraction when I need it."

Finished with the cybernetic software drivers, she unplugged her computer from the jack in Sokolov's arm and set it aside. From the satchel on the floor, she pulled out a small tool kit and a handful of spare parts.

"I couldn't find the exact models you wanted, but these are pretty close. We might have to readjust some power supply requirements, but they ought to work."

Nancy, retrieve the schematics on my arm, Sokolov told the nanocomp. "I'll walk you through it," he said.

Adroit wasn't big enough to boast a true cybernetics shop, but its general workshop included enough spare parts for the ship's various maintenance robots and probes for Geille to find power units matching the ones HelixTech had pulled out of his right arm. It took her about ten minutes to install them and run a basic systems check before replacing the molded pseudo-flesh that covered the limb.

"I think that does it," Geille said when she finished.

Sokolov stood and flexed his arm. *General system diagnostic, Nancy,* he ordered. *Check all reflex wiring and cybernetic systems.*

New units have been installed in systems 0100, 0225, 0348, and 0990. Interface secure. All systems green. The primary lanth cells have an estimated use-life of 1,495 hours before replacement will be necessary.

He tapped a pen against each of his fingertips, checking the sensitivity. "Good. I've been wanting to tie my own shoes all week."

Geille put away the tools and glanced at the door. "So what do we do now? Borun's going to run down the derelict in a couple of hours."

"Try to be useful, I guess. Don't give Borun a good reason to decide he's done with us. Stay on our toes and keep our eyes open for some kind of opportunity." Sokolov handed the pen back to Geille while she zipped up the satchel and double-checked for tools or components she'd left lying about. "Kill time until Borun's ready to leave the derelict, and then we see what happens."

Geille sighed. "That's the plan?"

"Let me know if you think of anything better," he replied.

Chapter Sixteen

THE HELIXTECH ship overtook the alien derelict four hours later. Once more Harmon and a pair of his security specialists brought Sokolov to the bridge. The bounty hunter was careful not to move his right arm. Harmon hadn't said a word to him about Geille's visit, but he didn't seem to have mentioned it to anyone else either. Karcen Borun's hatchet man wasn't in the habit of asking questions.

This time Mills greeted him, an absent expression on his face. "Mr. Sokolov, we've found your wreck. Would you be so kind as to join Chief Maris by the helm and let her know if you see anything that looks dangerous?"

His arms bound behind him, Sokolov shifted his weight and leaned back to gaze up through the broad viewports above the corvette's bridge. He could just barely make out a dark, looming shape illuminated by brilliant spotlights from the *Adroit*.

"It's a dead ship, Captain," he answered. He moved forward to take a position behind the master helmsman, anyway.

He found it oddly difficult to pull his eyes away from the derelict. Even as Borun and the rest of the *Adroit*'s crew hovered over their viewscreens, rapt with wonder, he was surprised to feel the same reverence, the same sense of focus, overtaking him as well. In the depths of interstellar space, the derelict was the only point of reference by which he could gauge the *Adroit*'s speed. As the rate of closure slowed, it seemed more and more as if Geille and he had led Karcen Borun to some sacred place.

"Anything different from the last time you were here?" Maris asked quietly. She was a lean, dark-haired woman with pronounced lines under her eyes and at the corners of her mouth.

"Looks the same," Sokolov answered. "Watch out for the

spires coming up. They jut out from the hull a couple of hundred meters."

Gaunt and gray, Captain Mills rose from his chair and moved down to stand behind Sokolov, caught up in the dawning awe that suffused the bridge. The old spacer ignored the flickering vidscreens; he gazed up through the corvette's generous viewports, studying the derelict with his own eyes. Meanwhile, Karcen Borun barked excited orders as he urged the men and women under his command to assay his prize. Despite Borun's manic intensity, the scientists and technicians worked smoothly in a dozen simultaneous tasks, recording every detail of the vessel's exterior, probing its depths with every sensor known to human technology.

"This is fantastic!" Borun crowed. "The bonus pool is getting bigger every minute, people. We're making history here!"

Sokolov glanced at Captain Mills and moved closer to follow the captain's gaze. Dark spires, glinting in the starlight, drifted slowly past, ringed by bladed buttresses and spined ridges.

"They sure didn't care about conserving material, did they?" he muttered. "Or structural integrity, for that matter. A simple cylinder or wedge would have been a lot stronger and a lot cheaper to build than a flying cathedral."

"The shipwrights built with different aesthetic values and different technology," Mills answered absently. "We've built structures every bit as complicated and as impractical: Angkor Wat, the Sphinx, Teotihuanaco. Mr. Borun would tell you that the builders of the derelict made it that way because that's the way they thought it should be."

"That seems like a good enough explanation to me," Sokolov said. "You think differently?"

Mills didn't take his eyes from the hulking vessel. "They put a vessel in deep space; they knew what they were doing. They made the ship this way for a purpose. If I had to guess, I'd say that this is a race that reveres the stars. To them, the act of voyaging into space wasn't a matter of simply getting from one place to another. It was a religious act." The captain finally looked away, meeting Sokolov's eyes. "What kind of creatures would build something like this, Mr. Sokolov?"

The bounty hunter shifted uncomfortably. His hands itched for a smoke. "I walked every corridor on that ship, Captain, and I have no idea. I know what they looked like—you saw the discs we shot of the pictures we found. I have an idea of what kind of technology they might have had, but as far as what kind of creatures they were, what kind of people?" Sokolov snorted. "The only thing I could tell you is that they couldn't stand to be near each other. I don't think more than thirty or forty of them crewed that entire ship."

"I understand that you and Monashi took to calling them dragons," Mills said.

"They have a vaguely reptilian appearance, and I think they were probably bigger than a full-grown weren," Sokolov said. "But even more than the physical resemblance, there's something about that ship that gives you chills. It says old and strong and wise but cruel. Don't ask me why I say that. It's just a feeling that I get when I look at that ship."

Adroit's captain fell silent, ruminating on Sokolov's words. He was a spacer, and he recognized the curious mix of superstition and intuition that permeated the otherwise perfectly physical phenomena of space travel. Travel between the stars taught many people to believe in something greater than they.

"Captain Mills!" Karcen Borun swaggered over to them, brimming with good cheer. The reverent hush that had fallen over the bridge seemed utterly lost on him. Sokolov wondered briefly if the man might be a manic-depressive. He decided that the exec was simply far too accustomed to winning. "Bring the *Adroit* alongside the alien ship. I want to begin the internal explorations immediately!"

The captain said slowly, "Our first contact protocols call for a period of observation."

"Screw the protocols, Mills. The ship's dead. I want to see Sokolov's zero-point power system with my own eyes." Borun grinned at Sokolov and clapped him on the shoulder like an old friend. "I can see why you wanted to keep this to yourself, Sokolov. The vid records Geille gave me were something, but this is incredible!"

I could stab him right now, Sokolov told himself. Deploy the fighting blade and jam it through his skull. They'd kill me, of course, but it would feel so good to see the asinine expression on Borun's face just before the steel sank into his head.

"So what are you going to do with it?" Sokolov rasped. "You're sure as hell not going to take it home and park it in your garage. It would take a fortress ship to drag that thing through drivespace."

Karcen Borun laughed loudly. "Oh, I'll bring it back to Lucullus, all right," he promised. "There's a chance we might figure out how to fly it there under its own power. We don't know if your derelict has an operable stardrive onboard. If we can't find any kind of FTL drive, then I'll get a fortress ship out here, if that's what it takes." He looked up through the viewport and whistled. "Harmon, take Sokolov down to the third deck air lock. I want him to suit up."

"What did you say?" Sokolov asked.

"Suit up, Sokolov. You and Monashi owe me a tour of this ship." Borun turned a predatory grin on him. "I'm not going to risk my survey team in there, not until I know that it's safe. If you know of any surprises on the wreck, I'm going to see to it that you've got a good reason to tell us about them."

"I don't work for you, Borun."

"You're going to if you want the money we talked about," Borun said. He looked across the command deck to where Geille Monashi stood idly watching the technical team at work. "Geille goes, too. That way, we've got her expertise with us if you try something stupid. Now are you going to help me, or do we have to renegotiate our deal?"

Sokolov snorted. Karcen Borun had no intention of letting him walk away with a million credits. Even if he sold Borun the salvage rights to the derelict, he still knew too much about the executive's sponsorship of Geille's sabotage for Borun to let him go, but if he cooperated, there was always the chance that he might live long enough to escape.

"Okay. I'll go," he growled. "Are you coming, or are you staying here?"

The exec smiled. "I'll let you show our advance team

around, Sokolov. They're the experts. Maybe I'll have a look for myself later on."

So much for the idea of a suit accident, Sokolov mused. Borun was smarter than he let on sometimes. Sokolov looked at Harmon and jerked his head down at the restraints.

"You want to take these off me, Chief?"

* * * * *

Lying patiently in a cold veil of dust and gas light-years beyond the reach of human space, the derelict's guardians began to wake from their deathlike sleep. They were smaller than the great ship they watched over, narrow and angular, although they shared the derelict's asymmetry. Power systems ignited, gathering energy from the very fabric of space. Quiescent engines shuddered and ramped through basic test cycles, shaking off the dust of years. Weapons and defenses were inventoried, tested, then left in readiness. Life-support systems carefully began to bring their frozen cargo to light and consciousness again.

The first signal, now several hundred hours old, had alerted the guardian fleet to the presence of intruders on the derelict, but something had gone wrong. Instead of the summons that should have brought the guardians to the derelict's side, only silence had followed. That, of course, was significant as well. The computing devices of the fleet conferred quietly while their masters slowly woke from their cryogenic sleep. Clearly the derelict had succeeded in luring a subject into its web of gravitational influence.

It was also clear that it had either been compromised in some way, or that it had failed to restrain the subject. The incomplete transfer of a few hundred hours ago seemed to indicate the former rather than the latter. If the subject had simply escaped after the transfer cycle had started, the derelict's computer would have completed the process, bringing the guardians to its side. The guardians knew every decision the derelict's computers were capable of making, and the failure to bring them to its location indicated a mechanical failure.

Now a new signal impinged upon the guardians in their place of waiting. A second ship approached the derelict, larger and more powerful than the fleeting contact they'd sensed days ago. Again they prepared for the transfer, and again it did not come.

The masters would not be pleased.

* * * * *

HelixTech didn't explore the derelict. They invaded it.

It took Sokolov hours to shake the impression that the derelict had somehow gotten smaller in the two weeks since he'd last been aboard. Surrounded by a dozen black e-suits emblazoned with the silver HelixTech logo, the cavernous chambers and winding passageways seemed less mysterious, less threatening, than they were when Geille and he had been the only humans within a trillion kilometers. The eerie silence of the wreck was gone, replaced by incessant radio chatter, the whine and stutter of power tools and generators. Even the darkness was dispelled by the glare of halogen floodlamps.

The scientists and technicians around him almost danced with glee as they absorbed detail after detail. Sokolov envied them their enthusiasm—all they saw was a technical challenge, the greatest mystery they might face in their respective careers. The chemist cursed joyously as she tried to determine exactly what the hull was made out of. The engineers argued vociferously about whether or not an anomalous reading in the deck beneath their magnetized feet could be a power conduit, a cable run, or simply an idiosyncracy of their equipment. The xenologist wanted to record every square meter of the ship's interior and flew into a rage when a pair of the *Adroit*'s veteran spacehands accidentally broke a tiny implement that looked like nothing more important than a rivet. Each of the specialists and experts on the boarding team felt he was making history.

Sokolov tried not to hate them for it. Most seemed like decent everyday people, professionals simply doing their jobs. They were the kind of people he never met in his line of work.

Karcen Borun had ordered Captain Mills to anchor the *Adroit* to the same air lock that Sokolov and Monashi had used during their previous visit. The corvette fixed its docking grapples into the derelict's hull. Under the command of Ms. Cartena, the *Adroit*'s second-in-command, the survey team established a base camp just inside the derelict's air lock, inflating a plastic dome to shelter their delicate equipment against the ship's numbing cold. From this base, they'd sent a number of teams out to explore the ship's passageways and map its interior. Sokolov considered giving them the maps he still held in Nancy's memory banks, then decided not to. He didn't feel like doing HelixTech any favors.

Sokolov and Monashi guided the first of the survey teams, leading Cartena, Harmon, and several of the technical specialists on a repeat of their earlier explorations. They carried their own lights, and in the absence of any artificial gravity, they clomped along slowly in magnetized boots, breathing canned air. Sokolov's suit gauges showed a temperature hovering at minus eighty degrees centigrade, almost exactly what it had been before.

While Sokolov and Monashi marched awkwardly, Harmon shadowed them constantly. The security chief made no effort to conceal his suspicion of the two ex-prisoners. He carried a wicked autolaser on a shoulder strap over his suit, and from time to time Sokolov caught Harmon checking the weapon, making sure it was charged and ready to fire. He was pretty sure he could get the drop on the security chief if he needed to . . . unless Harmon just decided to shoot him without provocation. *Nothing I can do about it if he does,* he reflected. *No sense worrying about it then.*

The others in their scouting party were gathered up ahead, examining one of the mazelike chambers he and Geille had explored. Sokolov moved up next to Geille. He lowered his helmet next to hers so that they could speak without being overheard.

"Have you heard anything about how long Borun's going to stay out here?" he asked.

Geille had found an e-suit closer to her size this time, a standard black HelixTech model. It was brand-new, made from a fabric so tough and light that it didn't conceal her figure the way an older, bulkier suit would have. She looked up, her face only a handspan from his.

"I've been talking with a couple of the techs. They're planning to stay about two weeks, maybe three, then it sounds like Borun will leave the survey team here while he takes the *Adroit* back to Lucullus for more personnel and supplies."

"He'll split the team?"

She shrugged. "He's got the provisions and the personnel, and there's nothing around here to indicate that there'd be any danger in leaving a technical team behind to examine the ship."

Sokolov wanted to scratch his chin, but his suit was in the way. He settled for a grimace. "We ought to try to stay together, keep a watch on each other. I wouldn't put it past Borun to tell Harmon to manufacture an excuse for shooting one or the other of us."

Geille looked past his shoulder. "In your case, Harmon might think of that himself. So what's next?"

"If Borun goes back with the ship, I think we want to stay here. If he stays here, we want to find a way to go back with the ship. No one will touch us without Borun's order. That might give us another couple of weeks to find some way out of this mess."

"Karcen is going to go back with the ship. Given the choice between staying here and overseeing a xenoarcheological dig or taking news of his discovery back to HelixTech, he's going to go with the news." Geille smiled and shook her head. "You know what's really funny? He feels he's got to go back, just to make sure that some other exec at HelixTech doesn't move in on his territory. If he's not there when the board learns about this find, they might put someone else in charge of the whole thing."

"So the ideal solution would be to figure out how to get Borun to stay here while sending us back with the *Adroit*."

"It won't happen. I know Karcen Borun. The only thing he's worrying about right now is whether or not someone is going to try to take this away from him."

"Well, I hope it's eating his guts out," Sokolov muttered. "It couldn't happen to a nicer guy."

He listened absently to the radio chatter. Cartena was trying to estimate the size of the dragons by the size of the passages connecting the low, dark chambers, while the others were guessing about the psychology of a sentient who'd live in such a room. He returned his attention to Geille. The faceplate conversation was strangely intimate after so many days of hostility, competition, and recrimination. He tried to focus on the matter at hand.

"We want to find a way to stay here when Borun leaves. When he comes back, he'll bring more people, more equipment, maybe even the media. It'll be harder to kill us without anyone noticing."

"All we have to do is stay alive," said Geille. She paused, then added, "Making ourselves useful could work in our favor. What have you told Borun about the stardrive effect?"

"Not a word." Sokolov laughed harshly. "That's the thing about interrogations. You only get answers for the questions you know to ask. They had me so drugged up I didn't even know who I was, but I don't think they ever asked me about the drive effects. I've been keeping that to myself. It's something I know and Borun doesn't. That could be useful."

"Maybe we should tell them. If we start volunteering information like the drive effect, Borun will have to wonder what else we might know."

Sokolov snorted. "That could backfire, you know. Let's keep the drive effect to ourselves for now. We'll use it when we need it."

Geille looked up, meeting his eyes. "All right. It's a plan for now."

Something of her fire, her spirit, still flickered in her gaze. She wasn't beaten yet, and she was devoting all of her intelligence to the question of how to stay alive. Sokolov realized two things in one abrupt insight. First of all, he was glad that she was on his side. Second, he'd tear his own heart out before he'd let Karcen Borun beat her. Geille might have made mistakes in the past, she might have played the wrong game against the wrong people, but she was better than he was. She deserved to walk away.

He broke the contact and examined the telltales of his suit so that she wouldn't see what was on his face. "Hey, Cartena," he said over the radio. "There's a lot more of the ship to see. Do you want to cover more ground or not?"

The officer tore herself away from her speculation with a vague nod. She paused and cocked her head, listening to a radio frequency Sokolov couldn't hear. The bounty hunter edged away and turned to keep Harmon in view, just in case the Helix-Tech team was receiving orders to dispose of him and Monashi. This is crazy, he thought angrily. Two or three weeks of this, and someone will shoot us by mistake. He tensed, but Cartena simply nodded her head back the way they'd come.

"Not right now, Sokolov. We're doubling back to the air lock. Mr. Borun is onboard, and he wants you to take him to the bridge."

Sokolov glanced over at Geille; their eyes met across the dark chamber. There was nothing to do but comply, so they followed the *Adroit*'s executive officer as she led the survey team out of the chamber and back toward the HelixTech base camp. Even in the hour they'd been gone, the dome tent had grown measurably. Glowing space heaters warmed its frosty interior, and a handful of techs in cold-weather jackets floated around, dispensing with the environment suits. A couple of folding tables and several high-powered computers had been brought over from the corvette and set up at the local station.

"They don't waste time, do they?" Sokolov remarked.

"The techs spent five days in drivespace planning out their moves," Geille answered. "So far everything's going by the numbers." She ignored Sokolov's pained look.

Standing outside the dome tent's air lock, Karcen Borun wore a tailored gray e-suit with a golden logo on the chest. Trust Borun to dress the part, Sokolov thought. Two more security men and a pair of techs stood next to him, waiting impatiently. The corporate exec clumped awkwardly in a half-circle, turning to meet their approach.

"There you are!" he called in a genial voice. "I understand you found something like a bridge when you were here before. I want to see it."

"Right this way," Sokolov growled.

He stomped into the right-hand passageway without bothering to see if Borun was ready to go or not. Just seeing the exec standing onboard his prize set Sokolov on edge.

It took the better part of an hour to reach the command stations. They paused a number of times to examine various features of the ship's architecture, the sloping ramps that joined the decks, the vast machinery rooms, the compressed slave quarters and spacious maze chambers. The metallic curtains absolutely stumped the technicians.

"You're saying that this corridor was walled off with a metal bulkhead?" one tech asked. "Are you certain you weren't seeing things?"

"I punched it and it hurt my hand," Sokolov said. "I'd say it was an awful tangible illusion."

"So they were able to cause matter to appear from energy," the second tech said. "That's incredible. It's outrageous."

"So? We've conducted experiments into the same technology," Borun observed. "We could do it if we wanted to."

"You don't get it, Karcen," Geille snapped. "Do you realize how much energy it takes to make just a little bit of matter? E equals MC squared; that means M equals E divided by C squared. That's the speed of light times the speed of light, Borun—a figure with one hell of a lot of zeroes behind it. It's not like turning on the refrigerator and freezing water into ice cubes. This takes real power."

"Well, the dragons had that kind of power with their zero-point technology, didn't they?" Borun replied with a sharklike grin. "Don't you wonder what we could do with a power generation system like that? How much we could sell that kind of tech for?"

"More to the point," Sokolov said, "I'd like to know what systems we tripped that caused the barriers to appear. It would be real easy to get trapped on this ship if we pushed the wrong button."

"You worry too much, Sokolov," Borun said. He stood and slapped his technicians on the back. "Come on, folks. There's more I want to see than empty doorways."

Borun kept up a constant radio chatter with the techs in their immediate party and with the leaders of several other teams, authorizing tests and procedures, demanding reports, sometimes just tuning in to see what everyone was finding. The man was driving Sokolov crazy, and Sokolov wasn't even working for him. Correction, he reminded himself: you are working for him. He says he's going to pay you a million credits for this find, and the moment he thinks you don't believe that anymore, he'll find a way to make you disappear.

The small party finally reached the ship's cavernous bridge. Niches and passageways spiraled off into shadows, hinting at depths uncharted. Even though it was his second trip to this room, Sokolov still found himself staring in wonder at the vaulted ceiling and the long, low consoles. The HelixTech people were awed into silence for a good sixty seconds, shining their lights into each corner of the room.

"Geille," Karcen Borun said slowly, "You didn't tell me the half of it when you described this ship. This might be the find of the century. I can't think of anything in the Verge that is so intact, so well preserved."

"Here's the really interesting part," Sokolov said. He moved over to the nav display and powered it up as he had before. Again the spinning brilliance of the Milky Way sprang into existence above the console. "They left a map onboard. Almost everything else has been stripped off this ship—every living creature, weapons, tools, everything except the most basic engineering systems and control panels. So why did they leave this behind?"

The HelixTech team gathered around, staring up at the display. Even Harmon's vigilance had faded, replaced by a blank-faced look of wonder. "If they didn't mean to leave it, it might be the biggest screw-up of all time," the security chief ventured. "It's like mailing a stranger the address to your house with a diagram of where you keep all your good stuff. It's nuts."

"If that's what really happened," Geille answered, "but when I look around this ship, I don't see anything else that was left behind. Well, nothing like this, anyway. It seems like a deliberate act."

"Spacefaring races generally aren't that stupid," Borun snorted. "The aliens who put this ship together obviously knew what they were doing. Maybe they're pacifists, and they think they'll find new friends out here."

Sokolov considered Borun's statement in silence. He thought of the sculpted relief picture they'd found in one of the maze rooms, the image of the dragonlike being. A creature with fangs and claws, fast and lean—a predator. A creature that couldn't even stand the company of its own kind, fortifying its personal quarters into a maze of twisting passageways at great expense in material and space.

They didn't strike him as naive pacifists, not in the least. The star map was there for a reason, but it wasn't an invitation to follow the derelict home.

Manipulating the display, he demonstrated the zooming-in feature that catapulted their view forward into the Orion Arm, and then forward again to a region that might or might not have been the Verge.

"I think they were from somewhere close by," he offered. Zooming in on a white-marked star, he showed them the images of planets drifting in space, girdled by cities and great structures.

"What star is that?" Borun demanded.

Sokolov shrugged. "Hard to say. I'd have to look at a good map of the Verge in order to see if it matched something. And we'd probably need a nav computer to apply known stellar drift to our own maps and run them backwards in time. We don't know if this is ten or ten thousand years old."

Borun moved closer to the map, using his hands to manipulate it as Sokolov had done. Sokolov moved back and leaned against a console, considering whether he wanted to risk frostbite by opening his faceplate for a quick smoke. His suit telltales indicated that the air in the bridge was fine, just damned cold.

Something shifted under his tailbone. He rocked off the console, surprised, and turned to see what he'd done. A new screen was illuminating behind him, small and faint. It echoed the planetary display that Borun was currently examining. A second panel showed a stylized representation of the derelict itself, alone in the darkness of space, but a smaller shiplike icon blinked on both screens. What the hell? he thought. He craned his head back to look over Borun's shoulder.

The small icon appeared to be another spacecraft of some kind, parked in a polar orbit around the planet in the display. Curious, Sokolov tinkered with various objects in his display. The planets didn't echo onto the second screen, the one showing the derelict, but anything resembling a spacecraft seemed to repeat easily and flash, as if awaiting some command.

He was startled by the abrupt touch of Geille's helmet to his. "I think I've found something major," she said in a low voice.

"You did this?" Sokolov asked. He leaned closer, studying the display. It flickered and danced, manipulated through her innate talent. What an advantage, he thought enviously. He understood computers better than most people could. Geille could actually *become* a computer by interfacing directly with her mind. Even the mechalus needed to touch the machines they bonded with. He watched her actions for a long moment.

"These icons seem to be moving from the main display over to the second screen."

"It's a navigational plot of some kind," she said. "If I knew more about astrogation, I could tell you exactly what was going on here, but I'm not sure what I'm looking at or what it's doing."

"You're not controlling it?"

"I seem to have cued up a standard program or default of some kind," she admitted. "What do you make of this? Could this be an astrogation solution of some kind?"

"Possibly," he conceded, "but if that's the case, why doesn't the derelict icon move over to the planetary display? Wouldn't that be the destination?"

"I thought so too, but the derelict seems to be telling me that it doesn't work that way." Geille looked back at the others and tapped his shoulder. "Better pay attention. Karcen Borun is going to demonstrate again his mastery of the derelict's navigational display."

Sokolov stared at the small display in front of him until

Geille cut it off again. It vanished into darkness. "If we're lucky, he'll be too entertained to remember to kill us."

Geille laughed softly. "I doubt—"

"Mr. Borun!" The emergency channel in their suit radios crackled with static, cutting off Geille in midsentence. "The *Adroit* is under attack!"

Chapter Seventeen

DEVRIELE SHANASSIN leaned forward in his command chair, simultaneously watching three different tactical displays. Beyond the *Blackguard*'s row of armored viewports, the black bulk of the derelict occluded the stars, reeling away as the corsair ship darted past.

"Bring us about!" the fraal barked anxiously. "I want to hit that ship again!"

Behind the streaking *Blackguard*, the *Adroit* rocked at her moorings to the derelict, her flanks glowing with the hellish light of molten metal and burning gas. Metal groaned and crumpled as the HelixTech corvette tried to disengage from the alien vessel in order to defend herself. Shanassin watched the weapon officer's tactical display, gripping the arms of his chair to conceal his excitement.

"Keep firing! Speed and surprise are our only advantages. We must cripple them now, before they raise their defenses!"

The corsair's helmsman threw the ex-freighter into a hard right turn, looping and spinning to bring the ship's particle cannon to bear again. The lights flickered and the deck thrummed with power as the dorsal turret pumped blast after blast of incandescent plasma at the *Adroit*, relentlessly pounding the larger vessel. Taking the *Blackguard* up against the *Adroit* was either an act of monumental stupidity or inspired genius, but with the *Adroit* clamped to the derelict's side and her sensors masked by the alien ship's bulk, Shanassin had ordered the attack. It was the best chance he'd get to wreck the heavier ship and take her prize.

The *Blackguard* completed her turn and drove hard at the HelixTech ship. The deck plates beneath Shanassin's feet shuddered with the power fluctuation as Yeiwei, his weapons officer, cut loose with the deadly particle beam again. This time the invisible lance of hard radiation glanced from its target without scoring a solid hit. The *Adroit* was moving, trailing the wreckage of her grapples and brilliant streams of condensation from breached compartments.

"They've activated their deflection inducer," reported his sensor op, a swarthy woman bedecked in gold jewelry. "Field strength at eighty G's and increasing. We're going to have a hard time driving our weapons through that."

"Not if we get closer," Shanassin snapped. "Helm! Dive and roll right! Get us below and behind them! Weapons—I want you to concentrate your fire on the *Adroit*'s main battery. If we can take out their heavy weapons, we'll win the day."

Around the fraal corsair, the *Blackguard*'s cagey veterans worked like a well-oiled machine, each hand an expert at his or her station. Under Shanassin, they'd survived dozens of space battles, and they knew their leader well enough to believe that he could carry them through any hazard on the force of his intelligence and daring. Sensor operators countered the target's automatic jammers, gracefully eluding the corvette's efforts to hide behind a wall of electronic noise. Gunners used experience and instinct to stay a split second ahead of the larger ship's defensive maneuvers, hammering blasts of energy through the *Adroit*'s fluxing grav shields. Engineers tripped well-known bypasses and overrides to squeeze every bit of performance out of the *Blackguard*'s engines. Stooping eaglelike against her prey, the corsair ship tore into the *Adroit*'s armored flanks with blinding speed and magnificent savagery.

It wasn't quite enough. Struggling to clear the derelict's awkward structure, compensating for a steady barrage of damage that knocked systems off line as soon as they were started up, the *Adroit* rumbled into clear space, staggering under the surprise attack. Scorched in a dozen spots, the HelixTech ship somehow found the means to survive the assault and then fight back. From two heavy turrets on her rear deck, she returned fire with two rapid-fire twin plasma cannons. Incandescent bolts of white-hot energy hammered back at the corsair in a brilliant salvo momentarily brighter than a sun. Damage control systems slowly mastered the most serious injuries the *Adroit* had suffered in the initial attack, and her defenses began to deflect more and more of the *Blackguard*'s attacks. Like a swordsman recovering from the shock of an unexpected wound, the *Adroit* slowly recovered her strength and skill.

"Missiles! Full salvo!" Shanassin screamed. He could sense opportunity slipping away. "Keep up the pressure! We almost have them!"

"Missiles away!" cried the weapon tech at the missile console.

He was thrown to the deck by a pair of powerful explosions, direct hits that rocked the *Blackguard* mercilessly. The bridge lights flickered and failed; sparks showered and hissed in the darkness over the screams and curses of the injured. Burning insulation wreathed the command deck in thin blue smoke.

"Depressurization in forward crew berthing and machinery room number three!" the bridge computer reported. "Power lost to the particle beam and number two induction engine."

"That's it, then," Shanassin whispered. Despite his peril, he bared his teeth in a feral grin. While his crew fought to right the ship and contain the damage, he hauled himself upright. *Adroit* would batter *Blackguard* to pieces. He'd failed to cripple the HelixTech ship in his first swift assault. "Keep the plasma cannons firing!" he called to his bridge crew. "I won't go to my death with my guns silent."

Across the bridge, Yeiwei Three-knives suddenly halted, turning his head up to a speaker set in the overhead of the compartment. He flared his damaged wings and hissed, calling for silence.

"The radio!" he said. "*Adroit* calls us!"

Shanassin frowned. *Blackguard* was crippled. Did Karcen Borun and his lackeys plan to offer him a chance to surrender? Had their positions been reversed, he would never have granted quarter.

"Put it on the general circuit," he told Yeiwei. He wanted his crewmen to know that he wouldn't give them up to the law.

"Unidentified vessel, this is the HelixTech corporate vessel

Adroit," the distant voice said. "We wish to negotiate an end to this fight. What do you want? Over."

The fraal coughed in the acrid blue haze. Why would the enemy seek to open communications now, at this moment? Unless . . . The fraal wheeled on the missile tech.

"Quickly. What happened with your last salvo of missiles?"

"I know I hit with two of them. Maybe a third, although I couldn't tell for sure. We took a big hit then."

"Warheads?"

The man checked his board. "Heavy anti-ship payloads. Three hundred kilos of Detonex."

Shanassin strode to the nearest sensor station and pushed a wounded man out of his way, searching for an exterior camera that worked. He found one and slaved it to the tac display, bringing the *Adroit* into view. She was only about a thousand kilometers away, slowly twisting away from the *Blackguard*'s frozen course.

Two ugly gouges pocked the corvette's flanks, like titanic shark bites in the *Adroit*'s hull. Fluids and gases vented freely into space, trailing a condensate fog.

"They're hurt," Shanassin whispered. "Of course they want to talk—they do not wish to continue the fight!"

Beside him, Yeiwei Three-knives motioned silently at the damage status display. The fraal corsair turned a fierce glare on the sesheyan, but the security chief held his ground and nodded at the blinking lights.

"Captain, we are grievously damaged, too," he said in a low voice. "Our spears are shattered: our arrows lost: and our arms grow too weak to continue the fray. I do not know if we can power a single weapon now."

Devriele Shanassin closed his eyes to hide his frustration. So close, he thought. "Give me a comm channel to the ship," he muttered. "They may not realize how badly we're hurt."

"You've got the speaker," the comm officer replied.

"*Adroit*, this is Devriele Shanassin of the *Blackguard*," the fraal said. "Cease your defensive maneuvers and de-power your weapon systems. If you cooperate, you will be spared. Resist, and you will be destroyed."

There was a long pause before the other ship answered. "*Blackguard*, this is Captain Mills of the HelixTech corporate vessel *Adroit*. You don't appear to be in any shape to enforce your demands, over."

"You are more seriously damaged than I am," Shanassin snapped.

"That may be the case," Mills drawled, "but I have superior weapons, engines, and sensors. If you think you can take us, feel free to resume the attack. Before you do, though, I'd like to know who the hell you think you are and why you attacked us without warning."

The fraal gestured at the comm officer, cutting out the bridge speaker. He looked at Yeiwei. "I think Mills is stalling for time to make repairs," he said quietly. "We must make our own repairs before the *Adroit* completes hers. Leave the helm, sensor, and comm operators at their stations. Everyone else is assigned to damage control. Give me back my guns, Yeiwei."

The sesheyan nodded. "It shall be as you say." At once he turned his attention to the damage status board and began issuing orders to the *Blackguard*'s engineering team.

Shanassin returned his attention to the speaker. "*Adroit*, this is Shanassin. You are currently in possession of two things I desire. Your alien vessel seems like it may be quite a find. I will leave and allow you to continue your explorations for the reasonable compensation of ten million Concord dollars. Second, you are carrying a prisoner named Peter Sokolov. I want him turned over to me at once."

Mills's voice crackled in the acrid air. "You want Sokolov? Why?"

"He has wronged me. That is enough for you to know."

"How do we know that you'll leave once we pay your ransom and deliver Sokolov to you, *Blackguard?*"

"You have my word of honor," Shanassin replied with a smile. "My information suggests that Karcen Borun is the leader of your expedition. Put Borun on the radio so I can negotiate with him."

There was a long pause. Shanassin studied the bridge absently, cataloging the indicators and alarms that flashed on every console. Finally Mills returned to the radio.

"You'll have to wait a couple of minutes, *Blackguard*. We're rigging communications to Borun's quarters. You damaged our internal comms."

Shanassin folded his arms with a smile. He wondered what he would do if HelixTech caved in to his threat and actually delivered Sokolov to him, wrapped up in a ten-million-dollar bow. He'd come out here for the bounty hunter, after all, but the dark spires of the derelict gleamed in his viewport, turning slowly against the majestic field of stars.

*   *   *   *   *

On the derelict's bridge, Sokolov listened in on the progress of the space battle. Their suit radios were keyed to a general radio circuit that gave them comms inside the derelict's hull. Since radio signals didn't penetrate the ship's hull, the Helix-Tech exploration team had brought a mass transceiver—a gravity radio—aboard in order to stay in touch with the *Adroit* outside. Everyone in their immediate party—Sokolov, Monashi, Borun, Harmon, the two technicians and the two security men—paused to listen to the desperate reports.

"Number Three Mass Reactor is gone! Direct hit!" An engineer onboard *Adroit*.

"Breakaway, breakaway!" Captain Mills, shouting over the general circuit. "Release all docking clamps! Sever the umbilicals! We need to get under way now!"

Karcen Borun pivoted away from the starchart, raising one hand to his helmet as if he could key his suit mike louder. "Countermand that order!" he shouted. "Mills, you will not break contact with the derelict. Is that understood!"

"Carry out the breakaway," Mills responded at once. "Mr. Borun, we cannot remain alongside the derelict. We'll be destroyed if we do. We must find cover and wait it out. We'll be back as soon as we can."

"Mills! Don't even think—"

"Read your corporate charter, Mr. Borun," Mills snapped. "I'm responsible for my ship. Now get off this channel and stop giving me orders! I have a major fight on my hands here."

"We lost the B turret. The power lines are cut." The *Adroit*'s weapon officer.

"Decompression in Compartments Two-dash-Five through Two-dash-Nine. Multiple casualties!"

"Missiles! We have missiles in—" Abruptly the radio contact stopped, replaced by the quiet hiss of a dead channel.

"Mills?" said Borun into his mike. He was facing Sokolov. The bounty hunter could see concern in the exec's face. "Mills! Are you there?"

"Maybe he just cut the channel," Harmon said quietly. The security chief shrugged. "Captain Mills wouldn't want to advertise the fact that we have personnel onboard by talking over an open channel."

Sokolov edged slowly toward a nearby console, carefully watching everyone. *Nancy, stack Speed Five and Deadeye,* he instructed his nanocomputer. He couldn't imagine who might have attacked the *Adroit*, but as far as he knew, he didn't have a friend in the galaxy. Any shift in circumstances might cause Borun to rethink their current understanding. Carefully he signaled Monashi and shot her a warning look with his eyes.

She nodded imperceptibly inside her helmet then turned to watch the HelixTech men as well.

An anxious two, then three minutes passed in the silence of the derelict's bridge. Sokolov heard nothing but the sound of his own breathing. Abruptly Mills returned to the radio.

"Unidentified vessel, this is the HelixTech corporate vessel *Adroit,*" he said. "We wish to negotiate an end to this fight. What do you want? Over."

"What the hell?" snarled Borun. He started to adjust his comm settings. "I didn't give him permission to negotiate!"

"Hold on, Karcen," Geille said. "He's not talking to you; he's talking to the other ship. Radio signals can't penetrate the derelict's outer hull. That means Mills is forwarding his transmissions to you with the mass transceiver relay." She leaned against the console behind her. "He wants you to be able to hear this."

Standing in the floodlit darkness, they heard every word of the conversation between Mills and Shanassin. Sokolov tensed, astounded, when the fraal corsair identified himself. *He wants me that bad?* he thought. *He must have been waiting for weeks to learn my whereabouts!* When the corsair stated his demand, everyone in the small party turned to look at Sokolov, Geille with concern, Borun with simple measurement.

"You're a popular man, Mr. Sokolov," the executive observed.

"He ought to be mad at you," Sokolov replied. "You hired me and sent me there. In a court of law, that makes you an accessory, at the very least."

"Well, we're not in a court of law, are we?" Borun said. He raised his hand to silence the others, listening to the end of the relayed conversation between the ships.

"You'll have to wait a couple of minutes, *Blackguard,*" Mills said. "We're rigging communications to Borun's quarters. You damaged our internal comms."

"He'll never believe it," Borun muttered. The exec craned his head upward, as if he might somehow see through a hundred meters of metal and darkness between the bridge and the exterior of the ship. "Come on, Mills. Vaporize that criminal."

"He might not be able to," Harmon observed. "Captain Mills wouldn't have opened communications with Shanassin unless he felt the ship was threatened."

"You know Shanassin," Borun said to Sokolov. "Can he take the *Adroit?*"

Sokolov shook his head. "Under normal circumstances, no. Your corvette's a much tougher ship than the *Blackguard,* but a surprise attack while you're tethered to this derelict . . . He might have inflicted real damage to the *Adroit* before Mills got clear. Shanassin's not afraid to take chances, that's for sure."

"So what are you going to do?" Geille asked.

"It depends on how badly the *Adroit* is damaged," Borun said. "I'm not about to give in to Devriele Shanassin's bluster." Suddenly he looked away, raising his hand to his helmet again. He turned away, pacing a little distance from the group.

Mills is talking to him on another frequency, Sokolov realized.

He toggled his own suit radio and set it to scan the other channels; he didn't want to be surprised by the executive's information. It only took a moment for his radio to lock in on the HelixTech conversation.

"What do I tell him?" Mills asked Borun.

"Tell him it will take about an hour to get Sokolov to the air lock," Borun replied. "Is that enough time?"

"I'll be able to take the *Blackguard* in about forty minutes," Mills replied. "If we stall him that long, we can tell him to go to hell. He caught us sleeping the first time, but that won't happen again."

Borun paused, thinking. "Don't make a move against the *Blackguard* until I say so, Captain. I don't see any reason why I can't accommodate Mr. Shanassin's request, or part of it anyway. We'll see if Sokolov and a more reasonable sum of money might buy him off."

The captain stayed silent for a long time. "We can't trust him, Mr. Borun. If we give him Sokolov, he might resume his attack anyway."

"So? As long as that's thirty or forty minutes from now, I don't care what he does. If Shanassin takes Sokolov and leaves, fine. If he takes him and then forces us to blow him out of space, well, that's fine, too." The exec laughed heartily. "We're just buying time, Captain Mills."

The captain sighed. "Understood."

Sokolov couldn't see Borun's face from where he was standing, but he could imagine the exec nodding with a broad smile on his face, delighted with his own cleverness.

"I don't know how you made captain in the corporate fleet, Mills. You don't have the right mind-set for this job. Call Shanassin back and tell him he can get Sokolov at the air lock in an hour."

Sokolov switched off the second channel, thinking hard. If there was anything worse than the situation he was in now, falling into Devriele Shanassin's hands might be it. Casually he moved closer to Geille and touched his helmet to hers.

"Do you recognize the panel you're leaning against?" he asked her.

She looked down, puzzled. "Yes. It's the environmental controls for the ship."

"Can you bring it on line for me?"

"I think so," she said. She met his eyes. "What are you going to do?"

"If Karcen Borun is going to hand me over to Shanassin, I'll do my best to make him wish he hadn't tried it. When I give you the signal, you power up this console and turn on the lights. That should give me a good head start."

"Wait," Geille said quickly. "If you run, I'm in trouble. Borun can make me vanish any time he likes. At least he's got to think about it if you're around. Besides, where are you going to go?"

"I don't know, but the longer I wait, the more likely it is that someone besides Karcen Borun and Devriele Shanassin will get involved. If I double back to the staging area, I can probably pick up enough rations to last for a long time."

Geille winced. "What happens when they find you, Sokolov?"

"That's a problem for another day. Are you going to help me or not?"

Monashi sighed and nodded. "We'll both make a break for it. I don't like my odds without you."

Sokolov offered her a spartan smile. "If you come with me, they won't have anyone around who knows the derelict like we do. We might be able to stay ahead of them for a long time."

"Are you certain that Borun's going to turn you over to Shanassin? They've been talking a long time. Maybe they're working out another deal."

The bounty hunter laughed. "You have to be kidding."

He broke contact and moved away, studying the scene carefully. Harmon was watching him closely, the autolaser pointed at some spot in the deck about a meter in front of Sokolov's feet. That's the first problem, Sokolov decided. Behind the master-at-arms, the other two security men stared at the chamber around them. Borun himself wore a sidearm, a laser pistol that seemed more decorative than useful. Do I wait until Borun tells me what's going to happen, or do I act now? Sokolov thought.

Do I really think that Karcen Borun isn't going to buy off Shanassin with my life?

No, Sokolov decided. That's not very likely. He darkened his visor and gestured at Geille.

She casually manipulated the controls on the console. Before anyone even noticed what she was doing, brilliant light flooded the chamber and gravity returned with startling force. Borun flailed for balance and shouted in consternation.

"What the hell?" he cried.

Nancy, execute Speed Five, Blade Three. Sokolov flexed his knees, adjusting to the shift in gravity. He launched himself into motion, deploying the gleaming blade from his right arm with a simple flick of his wrist. Several of the HelixTech men and women sprawled to the ground, unbalanced as their magnetic boots failed in the sudden return of weight. They flailed in midair, frozen in the instant of time caught by Sokolov's nanocomputer.

Slam. Borun sagged to his knees but managed to draw his laser pistol. Blinded by the bright light, the HelixTech security specs groped for their weapons in alarm. Harmon, balanced precariously, raised his heavy laser toward Sokolov. It was too late.

Slam. Sokolov reached Harmon and batted the laser aside with the heel of his left hand. Harmon staggered under the impact. Sokolov drove the deadly point of his cyber-blade through the middle of the security chief's faceplate. Transplas shattered. Harmon screamed horribly, loud enough for Sokolov to hear him even through his helmet. Sokolov yanked his arm back, trailing blood and ice from the blade. Harmon crumpled like a broken toy, firing his laser across the deck. The brilliant green beam sliced off half a technician's foot before it burned out in the alien metal deck plates.

Slam. Sokolov caught Harmon by the arm and spun it around behind him, ripping the autolaser from the security chief's twitching fingers. *Nancy, halt Blade Three. Load Deadeye. Execute!* As Harmon hit the deck with a crunch of broken glass and scarlet ice, Sokolov raised the autolaser, zeroing the weapon on the first of the two security specs. Borun was preparing to shoot, but the autolasers the guards carried were too dangerous to ignore. Emerald death flashed from Sokolov's weapon, scorching a long, dark seam across the man's torso. A scream rang in Sokolov's ears, carried by the linked suit radios. He ignored it.

Slam. Borun fired, burning a hole in the bulkhead a meter to Sokolov's right. The bounty hunter began to move. Venters, the second guard, had rolled with the return of gravity. From the deck, she raised her weapon at Sokolov, but Geille kicked the autolaser out of her hands. Geille followed with a vicious snap kick to the side of the woman's head, slamming her back down to the deck plates. She stooped and recovered Venters' weapon from the deck.

"Time to go, Pete!" she yelled.

Aches and twinges began to gather in Sokolov's joints, announcing the price of his enhanced reflexes. No one beside Borun, Geille, and he were standing. With a grim smile, Sokolov set the pain aside and deliberately aimed his laser at the golden gleam of Karcen Borun's faceplate.

"Dosvedanya, Borun," he said as he fired.

The air around the kneeling exec seemed to shimmer in a heat mirage, rippling away from the iridescent beam like a splash of water. The green laser blast bent away from Borun, hissing like a wildfire as it burned into a console behind the executive. Deflection inducer, Sokolov realized. *I should have known that Borun wouldn't be an easy target.* The grav shielding wouldn't last long, but it bought Karcen Borun another shot.

Slam. The exec's deflection device interfered with his next shot, imparting a visible curve to the laser's arrow-straight lance of light. It burned a small hole in Sokolov's left calf, an injury countered by the electric precision driving his body under the nanocomputer's control. Sokolov ignored Borun, seizing Geille in his free hand and dragging her to the nearest exit. They dodged behind a heavy stanchion as Borun fired again, then they were clear, stretching out in a long-legged run down the bright passageway.

Nancy, terminate Speed Five and Deadeye, Sokolov ordered. His calf stung but seemed to function. His leg held his weight, and he didn't feel like he was losing blood. A laser burn that didn't strike a vital organ rarely caused any serious damage, but he'd tend to it when he could.

"Come on," he gasped to Geille. "We have to get out of sight before Borun calls for help."

"I thought you shot him," she replied. "I saw you fire!"

"Deflection belt," he answered. "I'm afraid I didn't get him." The neural burn of his reflex wiring hit him, a whip of fire that flayed him mercilessly. Sokolov staggered and howled, crashing against the bulkhead before finding his footing again.

"Pete! Are you okay?" Geille slowed, catching his arm. "What is it?"

"Cyberware," he panted. "Keep going. I'll be okay."

"No chance," Geille said. She braced her shoulder against his torso and supported some of his weight. "We're together in this thing now. I'm staying with you."

Together they fled down the labyrinthine corridors of the ship.

* * * * *

Marius Grayes studied the sensor display without really understanding what he was looking at. He wasn't a spacer and had no shipboard experience whatsoever; his expertise was in dealing with people face-to-face. Low and massive, he crossed his thick arms in front of his torso and looked up at the woman who captained the *Fair Chance*.

"Explain this to me again, Ikai. At least two other ships are already here—" he stabbed one blunt finger at the tac display, where two red lights flickered and dodged—"and they're fighting around a third ship, here, that looks big enough and dead enough to be the mysterious derelict we're out here to find. Is that more or less the picture?"

Ikai inclined her head in a slight bow. "As you have stated it," she sang.

The captain of *Fair Chance* was a middle-aged woman of bountiful proportions, round as an oil drum; she had permanently dyed her skin jade green, and her coiffed hair was a glittering forest of emerald spikes. Her voice had been surgically altered at some point in the past, possibly her speech centers as well. Every word she spoke was musically modulated.

"The smaller ship we might defeat, but not the larger one, and certainly not both of them together," she continued.

Grayes scowled. He didn't like that assessment of the situation, although he would trust the captain's opinion. Despite Ikai's extreme appearance, she was a competent spacer with decades of experience, and the *Fair Chance* was one of the best-run ships in the Syndicate's fleet pool. As with any technical service in Syndicate territory, captains owned and operated their vessels, leasing them out to their superiors in the organization under exclusive agreements. That meant that Ikai had won the *Fair Chance* through competence, treachery, and a carefully built alliance of her fellow crewmen. She was smarter than she looked—and sounded. As far as Grayes was concerned, Ikai could have had herself rooted in a planter like some kind of earth mother, as long as the *Fair Chance* was run efficiently.

"Can you identify either of those ships?"

The captain checked a second sensor station, warbling questions at the ship's computer. She returned a moment later.

"The larger of the two is the corvette *Adroit*, a ship of the HelixTech fleet," she sang. "The other ship carries no identity . . . a pirate vessel, I believe."

On his other side, Nona leaned against the bulkhead, her guns in easy reach even though Ikai and her crew posed no threat to Grayes. She took in the scene with an air of affected disinterest. "So more than one person received that mysterious message from HelixTech," she observed. "Looks like we're third in line for the feeding frenzy, Marius."

"So I see," he answered. "I don't like being third, Nona." He studied the display a long moment, then blinked in surprise when several indicator lights changed around both vessels. "Ikai, what's that?" he asked.

The captain examined the display and sang a single note in surprise. "They cease their battle," she said. "Look! The corsair relents; his weapons are silent. And the larger ship is damaged, too."

"That's our break," Marius said, his dark face splitting in an impossibly wide smile. "If they blow each other to hell, well, we're not third in line anymore, are we?"

"Unless they're discussing what to do about the *Fair Chance*," Nona observed. "Maybe they're thinking about calling a truce until they deal with us."

"Mr. Grayes, shall we remain at a distance and observe, or should we venture closer?" Ikai asked. "Caught up in their battle, neither ship may have noted our approach."

The Syndicate man smiled dangerously, considering. Three sides in a fight usually meant that two of the players would set aside their differences until the third had been dealt with, then they'd turn on each other. The first step was clear—make sure that the *Fair Chance* wasn't the odd man out.

"Bring us in slowly," he told the captain. "I want a better look at what's going on, but I don't want to make them think we're a threat to both of them." He relaxed his powerful shoulders and rolled his head. "It's more important for us to look like an opportunity."

* * * * *

Anxious minutes passed on the bridge of the *Blackguard* as Devriele Shanassin waited for the *Adroit* to bring Karcen Borun to the radio. He was beginning to suspect that the executive had been incapacitated or killed in his initial assault—if he'd even been onboard. The HelixTech ship had been docked with the looming derelict. Now it seemed likely that Borun might have been on the other ship when the Blackguard appeared. Absently the fraal performed a set of calming and focusing exercises while he waited, stretching his muscles and distracting himself with the old rituals of hand-to-hand combat. The skeleton crew left on the corsair's bridge fell silent, attending to their duties and leaving him to concentrate.

Gliding and spinning, he launched deadly attacks against imaginary foes. In motion, his gaunt gray form transformed into a graceful, spidery thing, elegant and deceptive. While he focused on his movements, one compartment of his mind considered his next move, watching the clock.

"Yeiwei? Report on the status of repairs," he said softly, without breaking his routine.

"I will make the particle beam operational in just a moment more," the sesheyan replied from his station, "and we have restored power to the plasma cannon for now. The induction drive is more seriously harmed, but we may be able to operate the engine at reduced capacity. I have ordered the others to return to their stations."

"Good. I think HelixTech is simply stalling for time." Shanassin looked over at his sensor operator. "What's the range to the *Adroit?* I want the tac display updated."

"Three thousand five hundred kilometers, sir," the man replied. "We're about a thousand kilometers away from the derelict." He quickly repeated his information to the tac display, which updated with a flicker. "It's on the board—wait, I've got something else. Captain Shanassin! There's another ship approaching!"

The fraal corsair dropped his guard and straightened in astonishment. "What? That can't be! No one would pass this way by chance!"

"Incoming comms," the communication officer reported. "We're being signaled."

"On the speaker!" Shanassin barked.

"Unidentified vessel, this is the *Fair Chance*, out of Port Royal. Marius Grayes speaking. It seems to me that you're in over your head against the HelixTech ship out there. What do you say to joining forces to take those corporate bastards down? We'll split the prize. Over."

The fraal smiled coldly. He reached down to the console and keyed the transmitter. "*Fair Chance*, this is Devriele Shanassin of the *Blackguard*. Your proposal strikes me as eminently reasonable, but how do you propose to share the derelict? Over."

Quietly the gunners and techs of his bridge crew were returning from their work below, strapping in to their stations and checking over their systems. Yeiwei caught Shanassin's eye and offered a deliberate nod, his tiny red eyes gleaming in the half-light of the command deck.

"We can work out the details after we've dealt with the *Adroit*," Grayes replied. "I'd advise you to think fast, Shanassin. I'm currently making the same offer to the *Adroit*, but I'd rather have you on my side."

"He thinks he can turn against us once the *Adroit* is destroyed," Yeiwei said in a low voice. "If he cooperates with HelixTech, he may be left with a partner too strong to betray."

Shanassin pressed his hands together, his long fingers steepled in front of his face. "So it would seem. Yeiwei, give me the *Adroit*. Marius Grayes may be too smart for his own good."

* * * * *

Captain Mills tried to find a comfortable position for his arm but failed. From his knuckles to his shoulders, the limb was locked in a plastic gel-cast, deadening the pain of shattered bones and shredded flesh. The last missile hit had sent white-hot shrapnel spraying through the *Adroit*'s bridge, killing or maiming half the command crew. He was lucky to have survived. Somehow his good fortune did little to lighten his dour mood.

"So let me get this straight, Shanassin," he said to the comm station's video screen. "You're suggesting that we both turn on the *Fair Chance* and take Marius Grayes out of the picture before he plays kingmaker between us?"

The fraal's expressionless visage peered out of the screen, dead and alien. "I want Sokolov and compensation for the damage he caused to Icewalk. You've already agreed to settle in principle. The only detail left to negotiate is the size of the payment. I now extend to you the opportunity to retain my services for an additional fee, in exchange for which I will help you to destroy the *Fair Chance*. You will keep your new discovery secret, and I will be compensated fairly."

Mills glowered at the screen. "Grayes is offering to help me blast you into radioactive particles, Shanassin, and he's not asking for five million credits to join the fight."

"You cannot be that naive, Captain Mills," Shanassin said. "What will he do as soon as I am defeated? He will turn on you, of course. He wants your prize. I do not. I can deal in good faith.

Marius Grayes cannot." The fraal paused then added, "The derelict is clearly an extremely valuable find. I suspect that my offer to help you secure it for only five million credits may be overly generous."

"I've been checking up on the *Fair Chance*. I'm pretty sure we can keep her at arm's length after we've dealt with you, Shanassin."

The fraal leaned forward. "Possibly, Captain Mills, but I promise you this: if you and Grayes join forces against me, I won't bother to return fire against the *Fair Chance*. I will concentrate all of my attacks on the *Adroit* for as long as I last. You might survive my remaining missiles, Captain, but are you so certain that you will be able to defeat the *Fair Chance* if you bear the brunt of my assault?"

"That's a hollow threat," Mills snapped. "Grayes might say the same thing to me."

"Decide quickly, Captain Mills, otherwise I may take Marius Grayes's offer instead."

Mills swore. "He's talking to you, too?"

"Of course. Marius Grayes suggests that I should help him to destroy your vessel." Shanassin raised one hand to his chin in thought. "Perhaps I should see if he is willing to pay me for my help. The Syndicate has deep coffers, after all."

"Grayes wants you to help him because he knows he'll be able to handle you after you defeat the *Adroit*," Mills said angrily. "If you cooperate with him, you'll be digging your own grave."

"Then perhaps we should both consider the question of how much my help is worth," Shanassin retorted. He turned his head aside and muted his transmitter, distracted by another conversation with a speaker who didn't appear in the image on the *Adroit*'s bridge. After a moment, the fraal returned his attention to Mills, with a cold gray smile on his face. "Excuse me, Captain Mills," he said amiably. "Marius Grayes wishes to speak with me." The screen went dark.

Mills slammed his good fist on the console in frustration. The abrupt movement jarred his damaged arm, sending fierce claws of pain through it.

"Damn him!" he growled. "Comms, get me Borun. Now!"

Chapter Eighteen

IGNORING THE ACHE in the back of his left leg, Sokolov trotted through the cyclopean corridors of the derelict in his heavy e-suit. Monashi followed a step behind him, keeping a wary eye over her shoulder for any signs of pursuit. Condensation fogged the faceplates of their suits; the heavy soles of their boots rang on the metallic deck.

Sokolov thought as he moved, examining scenarios while he listened to the rasp of his breath inside his suit. Borun meant to give him to Shanassin, but he couldn't imagine that the Helix-Tech exec would allow the corsair to board the derelict in order to track him down in person. Borun wouldn't want Shanassin to see with his own eyes what the derelict might or might not be worth. That meant Karcen Borun had to assemble a team from those currently onboard the alien vessel to recover Sokolov.

The longer Sokolov delayed his capture, the more likely it was that Shanassin would tire of waiting and resume the space battle. That might not be all bad, especially if the *Adroit* blew the *Blackguard* out of the sky.

On the other hand, if the *Blackguard* defeated the *Adroit* . . . Sokolov grimaced. Whoever wins, I'm screwed, he thought. Karcen Borun won't be taking me home if he comes out on top, and Shanassin would be even worse. The best I can hope for is to delay long enough for Shanassin and Borun to come to blows again. Then the *Blackguard*'s got to be destroyed or driven off. After that, I need the *Adroit* so weak or crippled that I can sneak onboard or take her by force to get myself out of here. Maybe she'll be so damaged that Borun has to take her back soon, and then I'm left to hope that the next expedition isn't under Borun's control and shows up out here before I starve to death. I don't have a chance in hell.

The two fugitives came to one of the black metal barriers sealing the corridor and halted, panting inside their own suits. Sokolov leaned forward, his hands on his knees, and touched his helmet to Geille's.

"Try not to use the suit radios," he told her. "I don't think Borun could trace emissions inside this hull, but there's no reason we should let him listen in on what we're saying. Just get my attention, and we'll talk glass-to-glass."

"Okay," Geille said. A faint sheen of sweat glistened on her face. She licked her lips and sipped at the water nozzle in her helmet. "I've been thinking," she said. "You're going to have a tough time doubling back to the air locks. As long as the ship has power, these black doors are going to prevent us from moving toward the surface."

"Damn. I'd forgotten about that. Can't you open them with your psi-interface?"

"Sorry. It's not that easy. All I figured out before was how to turn the security program on and off. I don't have enough control to set specific parameters of operation."

He looked into her eyes. "You know, I've been meaning to ask you, what do you *see* when you do that? How can you figure out the first thing about a completely alien computer system? After all, we don't even know if these guys are counting in base ten."

"Base eight. They do their math in base eight." Geille shrugged. "I don't know if I can explain it, Sokolov. I've just always had a knack with computers. It's like I can feel where the data is going, what the computer wants to know from me next. If you can imagine being able to see your bloodstream, your heart, your lungs, and understand what's happening in each organ of your body and why . . . what I get from my psionic talent is something like that, only for computers."

"Amazing," Sokolov said quietly. He grinned fiercely. "It's a shame you can't tell this ship to squash Karcen Borun like a bug and then hail us an aircab home."

Geille furrowed her brow. "Nothing that dramatic, I'm afraid, but that's an interesting thought. So what do we do now?"

Sokolov grunted. "Sooner or later, we'll need food, water, and lanth cells. I'd rather make a try for them now, while the *Adroit* is standing away from the derelict. If we wait too long, the ship might come back and send more men into this wreck."

Geille winced. "I guess it's a gamble no matter what we do. How are we going to get out of this alive, Pete?"

He met her eyes with a forced smile. "I have no idea, but I'd give a hundred dollars for a good smoke now." He took a few minutes to explain his reasoning about Shanassin and Borun, and then continued, "I think I talked you into something you shouldn't have done, Geille. I don't have any way out of this, but there's no reason for you to get yourself killed, too. If Shanassin wins, you ought to be fine. He has nothing against you, and he might even feel he owes you some kind of compensation for failing to protect you on Icewalk. If Borun wins, think of something you can offer him. The man won't turn down a good bargain."

"Forget Borun," she replied. "I'm not going to put myself in his power again."

She paused, her face tightened into a pensive frown as she examined the possibilities. Sokolov watched the play of thought on her features as she wrestled with several ideas and discarded them. Finally she spoke again.

"Pete, about the only thing I can think of is for the two of us to get into Shanassin's hands. If we can keep him from killing you for a little while, maybe I can break you out. Shanassin shouldn't have any reason to suspect I might be on your side."

He looked up at her when she said that, hope as keen and cold as a razor piercing his chest. Geille didn't notice his sharp glance. She was absorbed in the possibilities, thinking hard, but Sokolov felt as if she'd opened his veins when she said she might be on his side. He'd done nothing to win her loyalty, but she'd decided to give it to him anyway, or it was just another sophisticated ploy in her campaign to win her freedom.

She couldn't survive for long in Karcen Borun's power; she was too much of a threat to the exec. He'd find a way to make her disappear soon if he caught the two of them again. Maybe it would be a suit accident, or perhaps a tragic mishap while exploring the derelict. Whatever it was, Borun would return with a commendation and she'd go home in a box. Under those circumstances, she had to consider placing herself under Shanassin's protection. Talking him into giving himself to the fraal corsair lord might be her ticket out.

He hated himself for thinking that she might be deceiving him again, but he'd do it for her if he had to. He'd let Devriele Shanassin flay him alive if that meant Geille could walk away from the whole mess. The realization staggered him like a punch to the solar plexus.

Quickly he looked away before she could see how much she'd unsettled him. Closing his eyes against the faint sting of sweat, he forced himself to come up with another excuse.

"Too risky. He's a fraal. Who knows what he might be able to pick out of your mind with his mindwalking? All it takes is just the least suspicion, and then he'll be peeling your brain like an onion."

"It's a better chance than playing cat and mouse on this ship until our food and water run out," Geille countered. "Come on, Sokolov. I'm just trying to think of better answers."

"Maybe there aren't any." Sokolov took a long glance down the corridor behind them; nothing was in sight, but that didn't reassure him. Borun probably had reinforcements on the way already. "This is just one of those scenarios you're not supposed to win. We need a ride on one of those two ships, and we can't board either one without getting killed. It's a shame this damned derelict doesn't have a stardrive of its own that we could work. I'd love to punch in a starfall and just leave Borun and Shanassin sitting here in the middle of nowhere."

"Borun would still be with us," Geille pointed out.

"Sure, but it would be like hijacking his private yacht and taking him along for the ride."

Sokolov laughed quietly, taking vicarious pleasure in the imaginary scene. He'd sit up on the dragons' bridge with his feet on the console, watching the darkness of drivespace on the screen while Borun . . .

The black of drivespace. He straightened slowly, trying to sort out the thought. He almost forgot to touch his helmet to

Geille's before he spoke again.

"Geille, what do we know about the dragons?"

"What?" She looked at him, confused by the non sequitur. "They were long and powerful, probably carnivorous, bigger than us. They carried slaves. They—"

"No, no. I mean, what do we know about their ships and how they work? What do we know about this derelict?"

"You're a better judge of that than I am, Sokolov." Geille studied his face for a long moment, guessing at his train of thought. "I don't know. It's a large ship with a mammoth power source, the zero-point plant. It might have held a crew of forty or fifty dragons, plus hundreds of servants, slaves, whatever. Not much armament, as far as we know, but it's well built and heavily armored. Looks more like a flying city than a ship."

"It's in the middle of interstellar space, travelling at a fraction of the speed you'd want to reach another star in any reasonable time," Sokolov said, "but it's loaded with a navigational database of incredible detail and extent. It pulled us out of drivespace, Geille. It pulled us out early. Somehow this ship exerts an influence on drivespace that interferes with normal travel, or it sensed our impending arrival and altered it somehow."

Geille stared hard at him. "What are you getting at?"

"I'm beginning to wonder if this is a starship at all, Geille. What if it's some kind of base or station?"

She shrugged. "What's the difference?"

"A starship is something that you fly to another star. A base or station is something that supports starships or launches them." Sokolov tapped his fingers against his helmet. "What if this derelict is built around an inside-out stardrive? A gate device, something that establishes a link to a place where a ship is waiting and pulls it through to its current location? It has to creep along at sublight speeds, taking years to reach the destination, but once the advance ship was in position, it would be as good as having a stardrive on the trailing vessel. All you'd have to do is call up and say, 'Okay, we're ready to fly.' Then they launch you through the gate to the other side—this ship, this derelict."

Geille weighed that for a long time. "A stardrive would be much more efficient. On a ship with a stardrive, you don't need any base station on the receiving end. You can go anywhere you want. If that's the way the dragons do FTL, the initial investment is tremendous. It works great once you set it up, but it takes you years to go someplace you've never been before."

"Who ever said the stardrive was the only way to beat Einstein?" Sokolov asked. "The dragons clearly have their own metallurgical and power system technologies. Maybe the gate is simply the best way they've found to do interstellar flight." He gestured back in the direction of the bridge. "Think about that navigational database. It's got to be there for a reason."

"All right," Geille admitted. "Your suggestion makes sense, considering the information and the control systems I interfaced with back at the nav board. I didn't see any systems that seemed to do anything in the way of FTL activation or astrogation, but there was a major system linked to navigation that I didn't understand. That might be your gate device."

"Do you think you could activate it?" he asked her.

"I guess so, Pete, but what would be the point? We have more immediate concerns."

"We have to find some way to change this scenario, Geille. There's no way we're going to come out of this alive if we can't give everyone something else to worry about besides us." Sokolov massaged the hot needle in his leg, trying to keep the muscle from locking up. "We know this alien wreck better than anyone else. If we can figure out some way to use it to our advantage, maybe we'll have the edge we need to get out of this mess."

"Wishful thinking, Sokolov."

"Yeah, I know." He stood and raised her by her arm. "Come on. We'd better move again. I think I want to double back to the bridge."

"You're serious about this?"

Sokolov offered a wicked smile. "I'm going to see what happens if you turn on this ship and push the 'go' button. If I'm right, we might have the distraction we need to get out of this alive."

* * * * *

A million kilometers away, Ramil ibn Beighur paced across the bridge of the *Sirocco*, examining his tactical display. A dashing figure in the black and gold of the Solar Navy, he exuded confidence, readiness, hoping to instill the same qualities in his crew. Ibn Beighur expected a fight in the near future, and he wanted to make sure his crew was ready for it.

In the ten hours since starrise, the converted freighter had trailed the *Blackguard* far enough behind the pirate vessel that Shanassin had not yet noted their presence. In open space, the *Sirocco* might not ever overtake the corsair before the smaller vessel recharged her stardrive and jumped again, but now *Blackguard* had slowed to a virtual halt. Ibn Beighur instantly ordered the *Sirocco* to go cold and dark, drifting quietly through the endless night of space as she neared the other ship. If he could get into weapon range before the corsair detected his presence, ibn Beighur stood an excellent chance of crippling the pirate vessel before they fled the scene, but things weren't that simple.

His tac display showed a colossal derelict, a vessel two or three times the size of ibn Beighur's *Birmingham* back on Lucullus. A HelixTech warship, the *Adroit*, circled the wreck, standing off Shanassin in the *Blackguard* and a third ship, the Syndicate warship *Fair Chance*. Ibn Beighur grinned fiercely as he wrestled with the implications. This was the kind of challenge he lived for.

First, the *Blackguard*. He should be able to go in after Shanassin with no interference from the other two ships. Neither the Syndicate nor HelixTech would have any reason to protect the corsair or interfere with the Solars' pursuit of justice in open space. A pirate of Devriele Shanassin's stature had no friends outside of his native system, and even in the familiar ground of Lucullus, neither the Syndicate nor HelixTech would have hesitated a moment before turning the fraal over to the Solars.

But there is more going on here than meets the eye, ibn Beighur reminded himself. The Lucullans would gladly tear out each others' throats left to their own devices, but on occasion they would fight to the death to preserve their right to kill and plunder each other as they pleased. The return of the Solar Union to its former colony meant the fall of many powerful individuals, and on any given day, some of them might be willing to bar Solar authority with armed resistance. The captain couldn't count on the acquiescence of the *Fair Chance* and the *Adroit*, and that made him hesitate.

If all three ships unite against me, he reasoned, the *Sirocco* doesn't stand a chance. Even an experienced crew and top-notch equipment couldn't overcome that kind of disadvantage. If he'd had the *Birmingham* out here, ibn Beighur would instantly rule the scene. The largest of the Lucullan ships, the *Adroit*, wasn't more than a quarter the size of the heavy cruiser.

But he didn't have the *Birmingham*; he had the *Sirocco,* and that meant that ibn Beighur was going to have to rely on the advantages of speed, training, and information. He knew that the enemy ships were there, while no one had yet spotted him. The *Sirocco* was therefore the deciding factor in whatever conflict was playing out around the alien wreck. Captain Ramil ibn Beighur would write the history of the action. It only remained for him to determine how he should proceed.

As for the wreck itself, one glance told him all he needed to know. It was an intact ship from a completely unknown species, and that made it absolutely mandatory for the Solar Union to have it. First-contact situations with spacefaring races didn't happen every day. Several other nations had profited immensely through proprietary contact with new civilizations. The Rigunmor Consortium's alliance with the mechalus race was perhaps the best example of what trade and technology exchanges between species could add to a nation's wealth, stature, and military power.

Ibn Beighur had been in Lucullus long enough to know that no Lucullans had the authority, experience, or moral certitude to conduct a first contact. If the Solar Union didn't step in, some other nation—perhaps VoidCorp, the Thuldans, the Rigunmors, or even the Galactic Concord—would quickly deprive the Syndicate or HelixTech of their prize. He couldn't allow that to happen.

"Ms. Gannon! Set a course for the alien vessel. Bring us alongside at a distance of one hundred kilometers. Ms. Wright! Ready primary batteries! I want firing solutions on all three ships out there."

He strode over to the comm pit and motioned at the crewmen there. "Give me standard contact frequency and a vid uplink." He waited while the crewmen hurriedly keyed their equipment, and then he spoke into the lens. "Attention, all vessels present. This is Captain Ramil ibn Beighur of the Solar ship *Sirocco*. I am declaring this region of space to be a first-contact exclusion zone under Article Thirty-Three of the Treaty of Concord. *Adroit* and *Fair Chance*, you will remove yourselves to a distance of no less than one million kilometers from the alien vessel. *Blackguard*, you will stand by for boarding. Ibn Beighur, out."

He looked over at the helmsman. "Full thrust, Ms. Gannon. Take us in."

* * * * *

Sokolov and Monashi crouched in the shadows of one of the great open corridors of the alien vessel. Fifty or so meters down the passageway, a team of HelixTech gunmen moved cautiously away from them, slowly investigating each branching corridor. Bursts of garbled static in Sokolov's ears marked their radio transmissions; Borun had finally realized that he needed to encrypt his communications, and the HelixTech security teams were now using a code that Sokolov's suit couldn't break.

"Where to now?" Geille asked quietly, whispering through her faceplate.

"We'll wait a few minutes for them to go on by, and then we'll slip past behind them," Sokolov replied.

He couldn't be certain, but it looked as if the HelixTech gunmen were using hand-held IR scanners to track the heat of their footprints on the icy deck. If the two fugitives had tried to return to the bridge the same way they'd fled, they would have run right into Borun's soldiers. Their e-suits would have lit up like torches in any kind of thermal scanner. By circling around, they'd managed to get behind the HelixTech search. Eventually, however, the security team would follow their footsteps right back to the bridge.

"They're going to find us sooner or later, Sokolov," Geille said. "We won't be able to stay ahead of them forever."

"I know," he muttered. Ahead of them, the HelixTech team padded softly out of sight, intent on their scanners. "Looks like we're clear. Come on."

Moving as quietly as he could in the bulky suit, he led Geille into the intersection where the HelixTech security specs had been moments before and then turned back the way the corporates had come. He anticipated a bullet in his back at any moment, but the trackers were heading the other way, and their floodlights blinded them to anything but the corridor directly ahead. Ten meters put the two fugitives safely around a bend in the passageway and out of sight.

They traveled silently down two more corridors before they discovered one of the entrances to the sprawling command center. Harsh yellow light, the natural glare of the ship's own illumination, flooded the dark passageway outside. Sokolov checked Harmon's autolaser and nodded to Monashi; she readied the weapon she'd taken from Venters. Carefully he crept up to the doorway and quickly peeked inside.

The room was empty. Harmon and the other dead guard sprawled on the floor where Sokolov had left them, but there was no sign of Borun or the other technicians.

"Good. Maybe our luck's changing," Sokolov said through his helmet. "Let's see what we can find."

"I hope you understand that I have no real idea what will happen if I trigger this program," Geille said.

She padded over to the nav console and set down her gun. Quickly she activated the main display and then the secondary display she'd shown him before. It illuminated at once, showing nothing but darkness. She concentrated on the alien systems as she reached out with her psi-link. Abruptly the console came to life, holographic images of strange worlds and mysterious structures glimmering in the darkness.

Sokolov kept watch, occasionally glancing back over his

shoulder to see what she was doing. "Any luck?" he asked.

Geille's voice was distant. All of her attention was absorbed in her task. "When I manipulated this before, I found some indicators that moved from this screen over to the other one—a kind of graphic interface, I'd guess, a little reminiscent of the old click-and-drag computers, if you've ever seen one of them."

"Huh?"

"Never mind. Real old graphic interface techniques, that's all. You run across them in ancient systems every now and then."

"How often do you work on stuff like that?" Sokolov asked.

"Parts of Santiago date back as far as 2350 or so. A lot of the sanitation and circulation mechanicals are still run by the original computers. I guess some of them are close to two hundred years old now." Geille flipped through display after display, trying to gauge the boundaries of the navigation system. "One of the first things I learned to do was take systems like those apart and jury-rig them for the Picts. They didn't know how to keep them running."

The screen in front of Geille suddenly flashed and clicked through several images, finally settling on a dark, dusty nebula where a dozen arrowhead icons began to flash. "What the hell?" she muttered. "I didn't do that. I want to go back to the planets."

Sokolov turned to look. "Try deactivating the board and starting it again. That works on our systems when you reach a dead end."

"Something's happening, Pete. This console's now under remote operation from a much larger and more powerful computer," Geille said. She took a half-step back as the displays flickered and then settled into place. "I think I'm in contact with the ship's main computer. "

"Are you in any danger, Geille? Is it reacting to your presence?"

She frowned. "It knows I'm here, but it's not interfering."

"Great. Get the planets back on the screen."

"I can't. It's locked on this setting now. I can't seem to retrace my steps."

Something whirred softly under Geille's hands; she jumped

back with a startled curse. The console slowly opened, sliding aside to present a single hand panel like the other controls they'd seen elsewhere in the derelict. The panel glowed a soft blue.

"What did you do?" Sokolov demanded.

Despite his intention to keep a watch out for the HelixTech gunmen, he was riveted to the display—the dark nebula with its flotilla of sleek, sharklike shapes on one side, the derelict itself on the other, with the slender vessels blinking, ghostlike, on the display.

"I think the console defaulted to some kind of program," Geille answered. "I think the hand panel is the trigger for this thing." She took another step back as she studied the display. She flinched. "I don't know about this, Sokolov. All of a sudden, I don't think this is a good idea anymore."

The bounty hunter studied the display, trying to make sense of it. Who knew what the dragons had really used the console for? He might be making a phone call, playing a game, firing a weapon, performing a religious obeisance, or setting off a self-destruct device.

"I'm sure it's not a good idea," he said, "but I think that we're dealing with a gate or drive device of some kind here. I also think that it's armed."

"What now?"

He reached out and set her hands over the panel. "I can't see that we have anything to lose. Time to spin the wheel." Deliberately he helped her push the control pad down.

The icons vanished from the nebula, but nothing else happened. Sokolov waited a minute, then pushed the control again. Nothing else changed.

"Damn. I was hoping something would happen," he said angrily. "A shudder in the ship, a power spike, acceleration, something."

"Something did happen," Geille said. "There are major new datastreams tying this console to every part of the ship." Geille turned away from the alien machine and crossed her arms, leaning against the console. "It's engaged in some major operations, Sokolov."

He thumped his fist down on the controls one last time, then faced her. "Maybe the machinery this device controlled isn't functional anymore. Who knows? I'm grasping at straws here."

Lights flickered in the darkness behind Geille's back, the steady bob and dance of suit lights approaching down the passageway. Sokolov hissed a warning and reached out to pull her down out of sight.

Geille sprawled to the deck. "What?" she demanded.

"HelixTech is back," he said. "Come on. It's time to go."

* * * * *

"Captain Shanassin! There's a Solar gunboat approaching!"

The fraal pirate staggered as if he'd been physically punched. "What?" he gasped in surprised. He surged to his feet from the comm station, ignoring the flickering image of the HelixTech captain in the station's video display. "That's impossible! How could they have found this place?"

From the navigator's station, Eh'tel shrugged. "Either they followed us, they followed someone else, or they were advised of where the other ships were going. Does it matter?"

"Do not point out the obvious to me, old woman," Shanassin barked in his own language. Eh'tel and he were the only fraal onboard. "I am in no mood to debate such puerile statements."

The old navigator bowed her head in silence. For a moment, the bridge of the *Blackguard* fell silent. Shanassin took three deep breaths to calm himself. "Yeiwei, update the tactical display. I want to see how the *Adroit* and the *Fair Chance* are reacting to this development."

Leaping into action, the *Blackguard*'s crewmen fed the sensor readouts into the ship's tactical computers. Shanassin gripped the edge of the console until his knuckles turned white. The *Sirocco* dived toward them, a lethal white icon flashing a few hundred thousand kilometers from the dark shape representing the derelict and the green dots that marked the position of the corsair ship, the *Adroit*, and the *Fair Chance*. "This is madness," he growled. "How many more

ships are going to starrise here today? Did Karcen Borun send
out written invitations before he left Penates?"

No one dared reply. Shanassin grimaced, studying the tactical data. "What is our weapons status?" he asked softly.

"The particle beam is operational, my lord. We can't traverse
the plasma gun turret, but we can fire it straight ahead," the
senior weapon tech replied. "I have seven missiles left—four
high-explosive, two submunitions, and one EM pulse bird."

"If I had two more missiles, I would dance with the *Sirocco*,"
Shanassin snarled. "Their arrogance deserves punishment." He
looked over to the engineering station. "Can we outrun the
Solars?"

Cringing, the chief engineer, a gaunt woman with two artificial arms, shook her head. "No, Captain. We took too much
damage to the induction drives during our exchange with the
Adroit. We're down to about sixty percent of normal acceleration. The *Sirocco* would run us down within twenty or thirty
minutes."

Shanassin fell silent, weighing the information. Behind him,
Yeiwei softly scratched the deck plates with his talons. Among
his people, it was something like clearing one's throat to attract
attention. "I beg your pardon, but the *Sirocco* is transmitting. I
have put it on the bridge speakers."

The fraal listened without taking his attention from the display: " . . . First Contact exclusion zone under Article Thirty-
Three of the Treaty of Concord. *Adroit* and *Fair Chance*, you
will remove yourselves to a distance of no less than one million
kilometers from the alien vessel. *Blackguard*, you will stand by
for boarding. I will open fire on any vessel that does not comply
with my instructions."

"Indeed," he said dryly. "How long until the *Sirocco* is in
range, Yeiwei?"

"Less than five minutes, my lord," the sesheyan replied.

"Helm! Turn us to heading 025-000 and give me maximum
acceleration!" Shanassin wrenched himself away from the display and mounted the ship's command chair, strapping himself
in. "All stations, prepare for action!"

Lowering his voice, Yeiwei moved closer. "We are fleeing?

They will surely overtake us, Shanassin."

The fraal ignored his lieutenant's temerity. "It would seem so. Get me a secure channel to the *Adroit* and the *Fair Chance*." He offered a cold smile. "The *Sirocco* has few friends out here today."

Limping from its damage, the *Blackguard* swung away from the other ships and began to climb toward the dim and distant stars.

*   *   *   *   *

"*Blackguard* is making a run for it, Captain," said the chief sensor operator. "The other two ships are moving away slowly. Looks like they're getting out of our way."

Ramil ibn Beighur pulled absently at one end of his flaring mustache. "Follow *Blackguard*. I don't want Shanassin to get away again. We can come back and secure the alien vessel later, but keep an eye on the Syndicate ship and the HelixTech vessel. They won't be happy about our appearance."

"Both vessels are hailing us, Captain," the comms officer said.

"Tell them to wait a few minutes and move away from the derelict. I'll deal with them after we've run *Blackguard* to ground."

"Neither vessel is complying, sir. They're just keeping station," the sensor operator reported.

"So be it. Drive right by them if you have to, helm." Ibn Beighur glanced over at Moreno, manning the main weapon station. "Check the *Blackguard*. I want to know how damaged she is, Mr. Moreno."

The Solar captain sat back, studying the situation. Around him, the veteran crew worked quietly and competently. It had taken him most of a year, but he'd turned the untried officers and young enlisted men of the *Birmingham* into a crack team of nearly five hundred seasoned hands with a year's experience in the Lucullus system. *Sirocco* was manned by twelve of the best of those. When ibn Beighur returned from his pirate hunting, he'd have to start the process all over again. The naval bureaucracy intended to rotate almost fifteen percent of his crew back to Old Space at the end of the duty cycle. Ibn Beighur had protested vigorously but to no avail. He'd trained his people so well that Fleet Command felt he could bring a lot of recruits up to speed. Serves me right for doing my job, he grumbled silently. Next year I'll find a way to hide some of these people and keep them around a bit longer.

"Range to the *Blackguard?*" he asked.

"Ninety thousand kilometers and closing, sir," the sensor operator reported.

"Good. Make ready to open fire." The captain leaned forward on his chair, studying the scene. Both *Adroit* and *Fair Chance* stood well out to the flanks now; the derelict was about four thousand kilometers to one side. Ahead of *Sirocco,* the display showed a small scattering of yellow pinpoints, a trail behind *Blackguard* as the pirate vessel accelerated away.

"What's that ahead of us?" the captain asked.

"Debris, Captain. It looks like *Blackguard* took a real beating out here."

"Maneuver to avoid it, but stay on Shanassin's tail," ibn Beighur said automatically.

He kept a wary eye on the icons representing the Syndicate and HelixTech vessels as they slid back toward his flanks. *Sirocco* was driving right between them, chasing after the corsair ship.

Fair Chance drifted quietly, watching him pass, while the *Adroit* turned slowly toward open space, moving away from the derelict at a leisurely pace. Ibn Beighur checked the range to the two ships; both were only fifteen thousand kilometers away, and only about twenty from the alien ship.

"What part of one million kilometers didn't they understand?" he asked the bridge around him. "Mr. Moreno, fire on *Blackguard* as soon as we come within range. Mr. Piper, obtain a set of firing solutions on the *Adroit*. Let's send the message to HelixTech first."

Suddenly the lights failed on the bridge. Radar displays flickered and died; warning klaxons sounded from all stations. A moment later the *Sirocco* rocked from the force of a nearby

explosion, jarring ibn Beighur so hard that he bit through his lip.
Blood streaming down his chin, he stood dizzily, trying to make
sense out of the flicker of static-filled screens and the startled
cries of his bridge crew.

"Sensors! What happened?"

"EMP, captain!" Piper, the sensor tech, replied. "A big one,
real close by! We've lost the primary sensor circuits."

"Comms?"

"I've got nothing but static now, Captain."

Red emergency lights flickered on, illuminating a scene of
darkness and panic. Ibn Beighur leaned forward, gripping the
rail surrounding the command platform. "Engineering, how bad
are we hurt?"

From the darkness on one side of the bridge, the chief engineer answered. "No hull breaches, Captain, but we lost some of
the computer control systems for the engines. Looks like we'll
have to change some boards."

Ibn Beighur swore in Turkish. "The debris. Shanassin must
have dropped a bomb in the middle of it, and then he fled to lead
us right through it. It's the oldest trick in the book, and I fell for
it. Sensors and fire control have priority, Mr. Kile. I want to see
what's going on."

"Captain! We're under fire!" At the opposite side of the
bridge, Ensign Piper's voice was strident with alarm. "The
HelixTech ship is moving in to attack!"

"Helm! Turn hard to port! All weapon stations, fire in local
control mode! Repeat, fire at whatever targets you can see from
your stations!"

Ibn Beighur slammed one fist against the arm of his seat,
fuming. The *Blackguard* had fled simply to lure him into the
middle of all three Lucullan vessels. In open space, the
Sirocco's speed and firepower could probably have bested any
one of the three ships, especially considering the *Adroit*'s
damage. Shanassin's ploy had thrust the Solar gunboat into the
middle of a Lucullan brawl. The *Sirocco* rocked and shuddered
with the distant impact of missiles and mass weapons.

The deck plates thrummed with the mighty jolts of the
Sirocco's mass cannon, hammering back at their unseen

assailants. Ibn Beighur looked around at the panic and disarray ruling his bridge.

"Calm down, people," he said in a stern voice. "Steady! We'll get some sensors working again, and then we'll show the Lucullans a thing or two about shooting."

We'd better get the sensors back fast, he added to himself.

Chapter Nineteen

I'D GIVE MY left arm for a box of grenades," Sokolov muttered to himself.

Leading Geille by one hand, he loped down a secondary passage leading away from the derelict's bridge, hunched over to reduce the chance of catching a bullet in the back. Behind him, the HelixTech security team crackled and hissed to each other in their coded transmissions, leapfrogging down the passageway behind the two fugitives. Laser fire scorched brilliant green lines over Sokolov's head.

At the first intersection they came to, Sokolov turned abruptly and ducked behind the corner, pulling Geille out of the way. *Deadeye, Nancy,* he thought at his nanocomputer. He counted to three and then spun in toward the wall, peering back into the passageway he'd just vacated. Thirty meters behind him, two men in black HelixTech e-suits froze in surprise, caught in the middle of their sprint for cover.

Guided by his computer, Sokolov deliberately shot one of them through the thigh, crumpling the man to the deck. A nasty leg wound would slow the HelixTech thugs down more than a clean kill. They'd have to look after their comrade instead of leaving him on the deck and coming back later. The bounty hunter fired two more shots at the other guard, but a storm of laser beams drove him back around the corner.

"That ought to slow 'em down. They won't be so quick to chase after us."

Geille shook her head. "We can't keep this up forever, Pete."

"I know, I know. Come on. Let's keep moving."

He started down the passageway, but Geille halted, holding

him back. "Is this the right passageway? This place is like a damned maze."

"Trust me, I don't forget a place I've been. This connects back to the main corridor circling the power plant." Sokolov tapped the side of his helmet. "Besides, I've still got the maps we made the first time we explored this ship locked up in my nanocomp."

"Okay, I guess you've convinced me. Take the lead. I'll cover our trail."

Sokolov nodded and set off at a fast pace, leading Geille through a series of small chambers and equipment rooms. They clambered through a section of compartments devoted to the smaller bipedal race, passing vast dark rows of empty cubicles, and then emerged again near the central corridor ring. Geille stayed an arm's length behind him; with their radios silenced, cut off from direct contact, they might have been the only two people in the universe.

In the silence of his suit, Sokolov thought about the absent dragons. Are you coming back? Why did you leave this gigantic mausoleum drifting out here, anyway? Where did the crew go? Why didn't they leave something behind?

Is this all some kind of crazy game? A test of some kind? Sokolov didn't believe in coincidence. He knew that everything happened for a reason, and if someone didn't like the way things were turning out, then he had only to look at what he'd been doing a day ago, a week ago, to find out how he'd arranged for his failures. Sometimes he was forced to apply the same cold logic to his own life.

First he'd underestimated Devriele Shanassin, then he'd underestimated Geille Monashi. When he'd been faced with the choice of trying to be someone better than he was, someone who could turn away from a comfortable amorality and take sides, make decisions, he'd found it easy to fail. Geille Monashi had offered him a chance to challenge everything he was, to defy common sense, to deny what he perceived as his duty, to stop making excuses for the things he did. He'd crumpled under the challenge, retreating to the familiar comfort of his cold and friendless existence.

In some perverse way, betraying Geille had earned him Karcen Borun's betrayal. Sokolov laughed out loud at that thought. Here he was, probably minutes or at best hours from a bullet in the back of his head, and he'd put himself here by doing exactly what he was expected to do.

Geille, how can you stand the sight of me? What kind of life did you have that could make you desperate enough to trust me—to think that I might be able to get you out of this alive?

Ahead of them, the passageway opened out into the great circular corridor ringing the heart of the ship. Sokolov halted, looking left and right. He turned back to Geille, a tight frown stretching his face. Geille met his eyes, panting for breath. A single dark strand of hair crossed her face, plastered by perspiration. She leaned close and touched faceplates.

"I think we lost them for now. Which way?"

"Back to the engineering control room. We'll have to cut things off again so we can open up the damned disappearing barriers. Otherwise we'll never get back to the air lock."

"You're still thinking of doubling back for HelixTech's supplies?"

He gave her a helpless look. "I don't know what else to do, Geille. The longer we stay free, the more likely it is that something else will happen."

"That's not much of a plan," Geille observed. "We're in the middle of nowhere, Sokolov. There won't be any knights in white armor riding by to rescue us. Not out here."

"I'd settle for a villain in black, but I get your point," he replied. "Still—"

He was interrupted by the sudden squeal of his suit radio. A cold, melodious voice spoke into his ear. "Sokolov, are you listening? I'm here now. Time to finish our game."

"Shanassin," the bounty hunter stated flatly. "Great." He keyed his mike and replied. "I hear you, Shanassin."

"I am here, Sokolov. Run and hide wherever you want in this dusty shrine. I will find you. Consider well how you would like to meet your end, human. It will not be long in coming."

Sokolov started to reply, but Geille suddenly raised her hand

and stopped him with a cautious look. Carefully she keyed her own mike and spoke.

"You know, you're standing on the find of the century," she said. "Think about it, Shanassin. Station raids and piracy are small change, but this derelict is the real thing. It has a power system that might be worth billions to the right buyer. It would be a shame to let Karcen Borun have it for nothing."

"Geille Monashi. I am surprised to hear that you are still keeping Sokolov's company." The fraal seemed coldly amused.

"There aren't many alternatives at the moment, Shanassin." Geille paused, then added, "If you can get us out of here, we'll give you the ship. We explored every meter of this wreck. We can show you everything about it. What would you say to that?"

The fraal laughed, a bitter sound that reminded Sokolov of frost on glass. "I'd say that Marius Grayes and Captain ibn Beighur might not be willing to let me claim the prize you offer, Geille Monashi, not to mention Karcen Borun. The Solars seem determined to claim the derelict for themselves. I don't see how you can possibly give me this ship when the Syndicate, Helix-Tech, and the Solar Union are already fighting for it."

Syndicate? Solars? Sokolov killed his transmitter and whispered to Geille, "Something else is going on here. The Solars must be out there somewhere. It sounds like the *Adroit* is in some kind of struggle for control of this ship."

To his surprise, Geille smiled. "Not only the Solars. Shanassin mentioned Marius Grayes of the Syndicate, too. I had Peri send him the coordinates of the derelict when I found out that you were going to take me back to HelixTech." She shook her head. "I don't believe he actually came out here himself."

Sokolov grimaced. "So you framed me with that message. I knew it."

"Do you really want to discuss who did what to whom, Sokolov? Does it really matter at this point? Karcen Borun would have thought up some reason to question you after I told him about this ship. I figured there was a small chance that the Syndicate might be willing to bail me out."

"Think they'd be willing to now?"

"We could always call and ask. . . ."

"Not until we get to the skin of the ship, Geille. Suit radios won't penetrate the derelict's hull." Sokolov growled in frustration and clambered to his feet. "Damn! We've still got to go kill the power plant if we want to get outside."

Shanassin interrupted with another transmission. "Under normal circumstances, Sokolov, I might offer you a sporting chance to earn your freedom. I'm afraid I may not have the time to engage in such games now. Make your peace with whatever god you worship. I am coming for you." The radio clicked as the fraal killed his transmission.

"I don't know what century that fraal thinks he's living in, but it's pretty damned medieval," Sokolov muttered. He reached down to help Geille to her feet. "We'd better get to the control chamber fast. I don't want to stay on this godforsaken alien wreck any longer than I have to."

*   *   *   *   *

Karcen Borun studied the indicator in his gauntleted hand and grinned. Two red blips blinked a hundred meters away.

"I think we've got them," he said quietly. "They're moving again."

"Kill the lights," Lieutenant Cartena ordered the other men on the detail.

One by one their lights blinked out, leaving the small party standing in the eerie darkness of the derelict's cavernous passageways. Around Borun, two more security specs and three technicians who'd been pressed into service checked their weapons nervously, looking down the corridor.

"Everybody switch to thermal sights. Let's not advertise that we're in the neighborhood."

"Remember, Lieutenant, I want Monashi alive. She may still prove useful." Borun set off down the corridor, following the tracking devices he'd had installed in Sokolov's and Monashi's suits. He would have run the two fugitives to ground an hour or more ago, but Harmon had been carrying the tracking device, and Sokolov had hacked it to pieces in the process of killing the leader of the security detail. Borun had had to double back to the HelixTech base camp and pick up another receiver as well as reinforcements before taking up the chase himself.

Somewhere thousands upon thousand of kilometers away, the *Adroit* ruthlessly pressed its attack home against the Solar gunboat. Shanassin had sparred briefly with the Solars, too, before withdrawing from the fight and allowing the *Adroit* to carry on alone. Marius Grayes, aboard the *Fair Chance,* simply sat and watched, allowing his rivals to weaken themselves before making his own move. Borun didn't give Mills a chance in hell of driving the Solars, the Syndicate, and Shanassin away from his find, but if the *Adroit* could distract the *Sirocco* long enough, he'd have time to run Sokolov and Monashi to ground and cut a deal with Grayes to finish off Shanassin and then clear out.

The Solars weren't going to take his prize away. Neither were Devriele Shanassin or Marius Grayes. They weren't going to find out anything about the derelict that he didn't tell them.

"Pick up the pace, Lieutenant," Borun said. "I don't want to leave this loose end dangling any longer."

* * * * *

Something brilliant and terrible was occurring in the great central chamber of the derelict. The massive hollow was alive with energy; a dance of pinprick sparkles too bright to look at flickered around the globe in the center of the room, crackling and popping in Sokolov's suit radio. He kept his eyes on the featureless catwalk beneath his feet, refusing to let the horrible vertigo caused by his precarious perch overwhelm him. Deliberately he placed one foot in front of the other.

"What's happening, Geille?" he called. The energy discharges masked his radio transmission with static. "It wasn't doing anything like this before!"

"I think it's the drive!" she replied. "This is what we started up on the bridge!"

"What's it doing?"

"Your guess is as good as mine, Sokolov," she said.

Despite his resolve, Sokolov looked up at the device that

hovered in the exact center of the ship. It revolved slowly, shining with a strange luminescence. Hundreds, maybe thousands, of tiny motes flashed each second with the brightness of a tiny sun, then vanished.

"I'd love to know what the light show is all about," he muttered.

"Quantum fluctuation," Geille replied. "Each point of light is a pair of opposing virtual particles, annihilating each other in the instant of their creation."

"So if each particle's destroying its opposite number, how can it be creating energy? Wouldn't that be a zero-sum process?"

Monashi shook her head. "I'd guess that the central device is harnessing the energy bursts of each collision. It's really creating energy, Sokolov. That's the miracle of the zero-point power generation system. It's harnessing energy that wasn't there before."

"The laws of thermodynamics say there's no such thing as a free lunch," he said. "There has to be a catch somewhere."

Geille steadied herself with one hand and glanced down at the orb spinning under their feet. She and Sokolov stood on the inside surface of the black metal track that ran over the inside of the spherical room. There was an imperceptible tug of gravity toward the center of the chamber, so that it felt as if they clung to a catwalk suspended from the ceiling of a monstrous dome with nothing but vast open space beneath them.

"Maybe," she admitted, "but the dragons didn't build this ship just to make pretty lights sparkle, Sokolov. Looks to me like they've found a way to defer the energy debt."

"It can't be healthy for us to stay in here for long." Sokolov had looked at his suit's radiation gauges, and he knew he didn't want to drag his feet. "Come on. We'd better keep moving."

They reached the small domed station that stood directly over the central sphere. Geille started to work the door mechanism; Sokolov checked their rear, making sure they were still alone. That basic precaution probably saved his life.

Forty meters behind them, clinging to the black catwalk crisscrossing the interior of the sphere, six black-suited Helix-

Tech gunmen emerged from the vertical lock leading into the vacuum chamber. Momentarily astonished by the vastness of the room and the spinning sphere of light in its center, they paused in confusion, trying to gain their bearings. Sokolov ducked behind one of the walk supports, trying to get out of sight, and elbowed Geille.

"Hurry up with the door! Borun's right behind us!"

She snapped a look over her shoulder and replied in a strained voice, "Pete, the door won't open."

"What? Are you sure you're doing it right? It opened last time!"

"I'm doing it right! I'm telling you, the door won't open!"

"Use your psi-talent. Get the computer to do it!"

"It's not computerized, Pete. It's a dumb lock. I can't do anything about it." Geille swore viciously.

A burst of computer-coded static filled Sokolov's suit speakers as the HelixTech gunmen wheeled to face them. Upside down on the catwalk from Sokolov's perspective, they dropped awkwardly toward the wide metal rail, moving to right themselves. They've spotted us, he realized. No cover, no way out, but I'll be damned if I'm going down without a fight. "Get out of here, Geille. I'll try to hold them off." *Nancy, stack Speed Five and Deadeye. Execute!*

Time ground to a halt, lurching through picture-frame instants as the nanocomputer divided his consciousness into a brilliant strobe of action and sensation. The autolaser hummed soundlessly in his hands as he fired at the first of the gunmen, but his shots went wide. The curvature of the room and the strange reversal of position threw off his aim. Automatically the nanocomputer corrected his bearing. He fired again, blasting the HelixTech guard from the catwalk. Limbs flailing, the guard began a long, slow drop toward the spinning maelstrom of energy in the center of the room.

Coded bursts flew like electric birdsong in his ears as the HelixTech men shouted for help or issued orders to each other. At the rear of the band, a man in a bronze-colored suit took cover behind the catwalk support and gesticulated wildly. Karcen Borun, Sokolov noted. He turned his weapon on the next gunman, but this man had taken cover, too, and the laser beam gouged the walkway with a shower of sparks.

"Forget it, Pete!" Geille yelled. Distantly he realized that she was trying to pull him away. "You can't take them all!"

Hot needles of pain appeared in his arms, his legs, his head as the cyber-burn began to sear his muscles and nerves. Laser blasts charred bright pits in the black metal of the ramp and its supports, scattering tiny beads of molten metal like droplets of fire. Sokolov dodged like a man moving through molasses. Abandoning his position, he caught Geille by the arm and scrambled over the edge of the catwalk, climbing around to the structure's inner face.

"Come on," he grated. "Your boots are strong enough to hold you against the microgravity!"

Gasping in terror, Geille followed him, stooping to swing her body out over the gaping abyss. Flailing clumsily, she managed to plant the sole of one magnetic boot against the black metal of the catwalk's underside and then the other. She reeled against the tug of gravity; Sokolov lunged to catch her. He nearly lost the autolaser, catching it with his other hand at the last instant.

"Pete! Something's happening!" she cried.

Burning alive with the feedback from his cyber systems, Sokolov hardly noticed when the walls vanished. He fought to breathe against the white pain in his chest, in his whole body. Overhead, the spherical device in the center of the chamber now glowed as brilliantly as a sun, throwing stark shadows across the entire room.

At the poles of the great chamber, two vast openings appeared. Each was more than a hundred meters in diameter, a straight-sided shaft that sliced through the hull of the derelict to open space outside. Dark and distant, Sokolov could make out the stars beyond the alien vessel's hull.

"*Bolzhe moi,*" he murmured. "What did we do?"

Geille's features were hidden behind the polarization of her helmet, but he could hear the open wonder in her voice. "I—I don't know," she whispered.

The great central chamber of the derelict was now a gaping hole that sliced through the middle of the ship. The zero-point chamber was a bulbous hollow in the center.

The device in the center of it all sank into nothingness. Sokolov looked straight up at where it had hung over his head only a moment ago. It was like looking into the naked face of eternity. Red-tinted clouds flickered with lightning; hot young stars blazed with the glory of a sunrise in the tenuous wisps of gas. Imperfectly, Sokolov grasped the fact that he was looking through space at some other place, maybe even some other time, a discontinuity in the fabric of reality.

"It's a gate," he said quietly. "Damn! I was right. We've opened some kind of dimensional gate."

Geille clutched at his arm, frozen by the scene. Karcen Borun and the rest of the HelixTech gunmen peered over the edge of the railless catwalk, distracted by the spectacle unfolding before them. Sokolov's radio, his suit telltales, and the cybernetic machinery inside his head all thrummed and crackled as strange energies impinged on the mechanical devices.

"Something's coming through," Geille said.

He saw it now, too, a dark needle of whorled metal. It seemed to sail right at him, as if it intended to impale him on its bitter spire, yet in a strange shift of perception, he realized abruptly that it was sliding past him, gracefully moving over him like a wall of metal. Slender and spartan compared to the derelict itself, the new arrival was nevertheless obviously the handiwork of the same builders, its hull marked by the same kind of convoluted and complex structures. Perhaps one hundred meters in length, it was easily twenty meters in diameter, fitted with stubby winglike structures and razor-sharp spars. Brilliant white lights glared from its hull, revealing the tiny humans clinging to the inside of the gate chamber. Small devices swiveled and tracked on Sokolov and Monashi as the great dark hull slid past. A warship, Sokolov thought, a live warship. That's what we've summoned. Suddenly he began to wonder whether activating the derelict's drive mechanisms had been a good idea after all.

Accelerating, the slender vessel drove for open space, clearing the gateway and climbing clear of the derelict's hull like some kind of deadly phoenix rising from the wreckage of the

ancient ship. No sooner had it cleared the massive corridor leading to open space when a second needle ship, its twin in every
respect, began to slide through the dimensional portal. In the
storm-wracked clouds of gas visible through the open portal,
more of the needle ships waited their turn to pass.

Geille interrupted his blank stare with a hard elbow in the
ribs. "I think we'd better get out of here, Sokolov," she said
quietly. "There's another air lock on the other side of the control station. Let's see if we can reach it before Borun wakes up
and realizes we're gone."

"And before the dragons realize we're here," he added under
his breath.

Shrinking from the alien vessels passing by overhead, he followed Geille toward the next air lock around the perimeter of
the gate chamber. He'd thrown his dice; now they'd have to see
what numbers came up when they stopped rolling.

                    *   *   *   *   *

Ramil ibn Beighur surged out of his seat, astonished. "What,
by the stars, is that?" he demanded.

Around him, the crewmen on the *Sirocco*'s bridge paused in
their duties, caught by the video image displayed across the
main screen. A huge opening had appeared in the side of the
alien vessel a few thousand kilometers behind them. From the
vast portal, dark, needle-shaped vessels were emerging. The
Solar captain gripped the narrow railing in front of the command station, staring at the apparition before him.

"Is it some kind of carrier?" he asked aloud. "A transport for
the smaller ships?"

"Impossible, Captain," the chief sensor tech replied. "Those
vessels couldn't possibly have all fit inside the derelict's hull.
They're coming from somewhere else."

"They seem to be making starrise inside the ship then
coming out," ibn Beighur snapped in disbelief. "That's insane!"

"My mass detector readings are all over the chart, Captain.
It's nothing like a normal starrise. I think we're seeing some
other kind of mass-based technology at work here."

"The *Adroit*'s firing missiles, Captain!" Moreno cried. "She's turning back toward us!"

"Evasive maneuvers!" ibn Beighur barked. "Divert the aft mount to anti-missile fire! Comms, activate the ECM suite!"

Despite his reputation for calm, considered action, ibn Beighur was livid with anger. Like a fighter blinded by a handful of sand in his eyes, the *Sirocco* had suffered an insulting barrage of blows while she'd struggled to restore her sensors and fire control systems. Outnumbered, blinded, and surprised, the ship had managed to stay in one piece only by a series of radical and desperate evasive tactics.

Now that *Sirocco* was starting to get her eyes back, ibn Beighur didn't like what he saw. Thank Allah the *Fair Chance* is waiting this one out, the Solar captain thought. If all three Lucullan ships had elected to attack at the same time, he and his crew would be nothing more than molten debris drifting in the interstellar void.

As it was, the *Sirocco*'s damage control boards glowed with lights indicating breached compartments, fires, equipment failures, and casualty reports. Ibn Beighur saw each one as a glaring indictment of his carelessness. He'd taken the bait Shanassin had offered. Now the corsair had fled the scene, doubling back to the alien vessel and leaving the *Sirocco* half-crippled and engaged with a determined and tenacious opponent.

When ibn Beighur got around to writing his post-action report to his superiors, he decided that he'd entitle it "Why You Should Never Turn Your Back on a Lucullan."

Now the derelict was disgorging warships of its own. The captain fumed. First contact scenarios took priority over everything. That was the standing order to all military commanders in the service of any stellar nation.

"Break off the action," he instructed Moreno. "Get us clear of the *Adroit* and the *Fair Chance*. Comms, I want you to start signaling the alien ships. Use the standard unknown race hail programs."

He studied the tac display. Seven of the needle-shaped vessels now, arrowing out away from the derelict, speeding toward them with a silent celerity that brought cold dread to his heart.

"Comms? Any answer to our signals?" he asked quietly.

"Nothing yet, Captain," the young comm operator answered. "I'm repeating the cycle."

Ibn Beighur lifted his eyes from the tach display to the dim starlight and flickering shadows outside, as if his own eyes could glean more insight across thousands of kilometers. At one side of the bridge, a video pickup at high magnification showed the scene as he would see it if he were close enough. In the video image, the vessels were narrow knives of shadow, deadly predators schooling for a swift, silent attack.

The Solar captain realized two things at once. First, his fight with the Lucullans was over. They were insignificant in the face of this new development. No human on the scene was going to take possession of the alien wreck, and the capture of Devriele Shanassin was nothing more than an incidental goal.

The second thing he understood as the alien vessels bore down on the human ships was that his real fight was about to begin.

* * * * *

"This one's sealed, too," Geille said. She straightened from the air lock hatch and slapped her hand against the bulkhead in frustration. "We're running out of time, Sokolov."

"Yeah, I know," he replied. He looked up and across the gate chamber at one squad of black-suited gunmen, gauging their course, and then back over his shoulder at Borun's team, which followed in their tracks. This was the third hatch they'd tried to open since the black ships had started coming through. "The air locks must be secured with some kind of safety interlock while the gate's open."

"I guess no one's supposed to be in the central channel when vessels are going through the gate," Geille said. "Didn't the dragons think that someone might get trapped in here by mistake?"

"Maybe their engineers couldn't see why any reasonable sentient wouldn't have the common sense to stay clear of the inside of a quantum reactor, or whatever you call this thing,"

Sokolov answered. "I guess we're stuck here until the gate closes."

He looked up at the terrible spectacle overhead. Tenuous streamers of gas shrieked through the awful portal. Great sheets of scarlet lightning washed across the chamber, matter annihilation barely contained by the drive's shielding or control fields. The displaced gases and powerful detonations were violent enough to hammer Sokolov and Monashi with faint concussions despite the partial vacuum in the room. Had there been anything like a fully pressurized atmosphere in the central chamber, the blasts would have hammered the humans into paste. Another black needle shape was emerging.

"That's five now," he observed.

How many of these things are lined up on the other side? he wondered. Ten? Twenty? A hundred? He took Geille by the elbow and steered her on a course away from the dark figures that slowly pursued them. Scuttling from one hatchway to the next, the two fugitives clung to the railless catwalk and slowly circumnavigated the great spherical chamber.

Behind them, Borun's men toiled in pursuit, carefully moving to surround them. One paused to try a shot across the open space of the curving chamber, a laser blast that was deflected by the potent fields of unseen force containing the gate. Sokolov didn't even bother to shoot back. Anytime he tried to shoot across the core of the quantum reactor, his laser beam simply vanished in a burst of light. Still, sooner or later Borun's men would get close enough that they'd be able to fire straight at the two fugitives without shooting across the maelstrom of energy. When that happened, he'd have to surrender or go down fighting.

Neither option appealed to him. "The next air lock's just ahead," he said to Geille.

"You really think one's going to open?" she asked acerbically.

He shrugged. "Can't stay here."

They approached the opening, reversing themselves so that their feet pointed toward the outer surface of the spherical room and started to push their way down from the three-meter high

catwalk that ringed the chamber. Karcen Borun watched them
maneuver toward the air lock, then directed his men to move to
intercept them. They're going to be on top of us in two, maybe
three minutes, Sokolov decided. Time to start thinking of a new
plan.

He turned back to the hatch in front of them just in time to
see it explode. Blasted open from the other side, the two-meter
disk spun from its mount and slammed into the suspended
walkway with astonishing violence, only four or five meters
from where Sokolov and Monashi stood. The impact knocked
both of them free of the catwalk with a jolt that snapped
Sokolov's teeth together and knocked the breath out of his
lungs. A blast of air and vapor roared into the vacuum-filled
gate chamber through the shattered doorway.

"Sokolov!" Geille cried in alarm.

Flailing in the microgravity, she started to drift past the
twisted mass of metal that had been the walkway, drifting
inevitably toward the swirling maelstrom of energy and annihilation above them. He tumbled crazily a meter away, trying to
regain his bearings.

When his head stopped spinning, the wreckage of the catwalk was drifting past his faceplate. Nothing but empty space
and inconceivable energies waited beneath his feet. Lunging
desperately, Sokolov managed to hook one arm around a piece
of the walkway, arresting his fall.

Geille floated past him, heading down. She reached out
toward him, but her fingers fell short. Without hesitation, he
dropped the autolaser in his free hand and caught her by the
wrist. Swinging in a grand, slow arc, she dangled beneath him
as he clung to the walkway. In full gravity, he probably couldn't
have done it, but the negligible gravity of the ship's central
chamber gave each of them the weight of a small child.

"What happened?" he gasped.

Geille didn't answer immediately. She was looking past him
at the hatchway that had just blown. Sokolov followed her
eyes. Four suited men clambered through the wrecked air lock,
guns leveled at the incredible scene before their eyes. None of
them looked the same. Their suits showed a variety of styles and

decorations, some plain, others festooned with menacing paintings and markings.

Corsairs. Shanassin's men. The figure in the lead was dressed in a narrow-waisted e-suit of scarlet and gold. The helmeted head swiveled toward Sokolov and Monashi, clinging to the walkway a few meters away, then looked down to lock gazes with the bounty hunter. Devriele Shanassin grinned a predatory grin, ignoring the fantastic scene in front of him.

"I have anticipated this moment for weeks, Sokolov," the fraal hissed, "but I did not expect to catch you so easily."

Shanassin drew a short cleaverlike knife from a sheath at his belt and leaped down to the walkway Sokolov clung to, turning head over heels to land cleanly on the twisted metal. The knife gleamed as he squatted over Sokolov's head.

"Haul Monashi up here, if you please," the pirate said. "I don't have any quarrel with her, and you're going to be too busy to hold on to her for much longer." He laughed wickedly.

This isn't good, Sokolov decided. Even if he wasn't holding on to Geille, his gun was gone now, lost in the vortex at the center of the derelict. He looked up at the fraal.

"Okay, Shanassin. You've got me, but don't let Karcen Borun get his hands on Geille. Get her out of here while you can."

"I don't see why Mr. Shanassin should do that."

It was Karcen Borun's voice, crackling in Sokolov's ear. He looked over his shoulder; the exec and his gunmen were closing in. Corsairs and security guards eyed each other uneasily, guns at the ready. Brilliant lightning and howling wind built to a crescendo that shook the ancient derelict from its bow to its stern.

Raising his voice over the radio interference, Borun shouted, "Sokolov is yours, Shanassin! That was our deal. But I want Monashi!"

The fraal offered a feral grin. "I'm willing to entertain offers, Borun. Make it a good one. I don't think our hosts will let us remain here forever."

The executive licked his lips. "A million credits," he said. "As soon as we get out of here."

"Don't believe him, Shanassin!" Sokolov interrupted. "Borun will never pay you. He's lost the derelict; he's ruined. He'll be looking for a job next week. Take Geille under your protection. She can help you."

"Sokolov, you don't have to speak for me," Geille snapped. "Shanassin, I can give you a fortune in research data if you'll spare Sokolov and get the two of us out of here. However Sokolov wronged you, remember that it was Karcen Borun who sent him to Icewalk. He's the one who is responsible."

The corsairs and the corporate agents muttered uneasily and slowly maneuvered for position against each other. Shanassin rocked back on his heels, considering.

"That may be true, Monashi, but Sokolov is the instrument of my embarrassment. I greatly desire the opportunity to claim restitution from him." The heavy knife whirled in the fraal's hand. "You haven't offered me anything I couldn't obtain myself in time."

Sokolov shifted slowly, trying to find a surer hold on the cat-walk. He glanced down at Monashi; her eyes, wide and dark, locked on his. He felt an electric jolt, a sudden sympathy or understanding, pass between them. Somehow they'd both recognized in the same instant that they each had nothing left to lose. All that was left was simply a matter of details, some more unpleasant than others.

Speaking to her, even though the others would hear it on their radios, he said simply, "I didn't expect it to turn out like this. I'm sorry."

She smiled but didn't reply.

Beyond Monashi, the gate abruptly collapsed. One moment the chamber was filled with brilliant flashes of light, a raging torment of energy and gas, and then it was dark and silent. The last vessel moved out of the portal, its baroque flanks gliding past, a wall of impassive metal, blind and deaf to the human drama transpiring at the edge of the chamber. It struck Sokolov as almost contemptuous, as if the dragons had determined that they posed no threat.

Why were the aliens ignoring them? Sokolov answered himself a moment later: either they didn't know the humans were in the chamber, or they didn't care. Suddenly he conceived a desperate idea, an insane gamble.

He looked back at Geille and said quietly, "Do you trust me?"

She fixed her eyes on his. "Why?" she asked in a guarded voice. "What are you—"

Before she could finish her answer, Sokolov curled his feet up under the catwalk, released his grip on the walkway, and then kicked both Geille and himself into the abyss. Tumbling together, they fell toward the dark hull gliding by underneath while Shanassin and Borun gaped in surprise. Mere moments ago, the flickering storm of energy and debris in the center of the chamber would have destroyed them instantly, but it was gone now, the memory of a thunderclap, fading in the darkness of the derelict's heart. The gate had closed. The quantum reactor, no longer needed, had flickered out like a snuffed candle.

Geille screamed in terror; he managed to turn her so that her feet were pointed downward. The dark, moving hull, a remote and wondrous thing from the vantage of the walkway, now loomed in front of them, a wall of metal thirty meters high and five or six times that length, smoothly accelerating out toward the open stars. They hit, slamming into the hull with bone-jarring force after a free fall of twenty or twenty-five meters, potentially lethal under full gravity, but the equivalent of a four- or five-meter fall in the heart of the derelict.

Sokolov landed badly in an effort to steady Geille, wrenching his knee. He grunted and sprawled to the black metal surface of the alien ship. Geille flailed for balance and caught herself on a protruding fin or structure. Hot green lasers sizzled against the alien's hull. Charge-rifle fire sparked and ricocheted all around them. One slug creased Geille's shoulder, and another one punched a hole through Sokolov's artificial arm, but then the slow, stately roll of the ship carried them out of the line of fire.

"Damn it, Sokolov, you could have warned me!" Geille cried. "What the hell were you thinking about? What are we going to do now?"

She cradled her injured arm. A thin puff of vapor leaking

from her suit streamed away into the darkness before the self-sealing liner covered the puncture.

"The vessel's heading out," he replied, climbing to his feet. The internal partitioning of his e-suit limited the loss of atmosphere to his lower right arm, which wouldn't be damaged by a lack of air. "We're going to jump clear before we exit the derelict, then make our way to the outer hull. Maybe we can signal the Solars or the Syndicate from there and arrange a pickup."

She glared at him, but then her expression softened. "All right. I guess anywhere is better than where we just were."

Behind her, Devriele Shanassin suddenly alighted on the hull of the alien ship, knife held ready. Two of his corsairs sailed past in the darkness, mistiming their jumps and falling short. They vanished into the blackness at the heart of the vessel, their suit lights spinning bright beams across the open chamber. The fraal landed with the grace of a cat, rolling easily, and then sprinted across the ship's hull, bounding across the irregular surface with reckless leaps and jumps.

"You won't escape me so easily, Sokolov!" he hissed.

Geille wheeled and crouched, striking at the fraal as he dashed by, but Shanassin slashed her once across her arm and sent her reeling away. Sokolov barely had time to set himself for the fraal's charge before Shanassin was upon him, slashing and cutting with the broad-bladed knife. Hard slashes cut him across the left forearm, the quadriceps, then a light scrape across his abdomen that might have eviscerated Sokolov if he hadn't thrown himself to the deck to evade the blow. Suddenly the fraal was past him, wheeling and preparing for another attack.

The alien vessel entered the short channel that led to the exterior of the derelict's hull. Sokolov could see the ribbed ceiling of the passageway descending toward him as the spherical zero-point chamber gave way to the smaller egress. He rolled to his hands and knees and stood, studying his opponent. I have to finish this fast, or we'll be carried away from the derelict when this ship clears the hull.

Shanassin whirled his knife from hand to hand, gloating. "I could shoot you down like a dog," he snarled, patting a pistol at

his side, "but I find that killing with a knife is much more satis-
fying. You will be the seventeenth man to die under my blade.
This is the price you pay for daring to challenge me!"

"I know a thing or two about knife fighting, too," Sokolov
growled.

With a single thought, he caused a hidden blade to spring
from his damaged arm, a glittering spike twenty centimeters
long emerging between the knuckles of his right hand. The
blade punched through the glove of his suit, but seals at the
elbow and shoulder prevented him from losing any more air.
Stack Speed Five, Blade Three, Nancy, Sokolov thought at his
nanocomputer. *Execute.*

The fraal pirate darted in with the speed of a striking snake,
blade flashing. Sokolov met each attack with the cyber-blade of
his right arm, a deadly and beautiful pattern of strike and riposte
that slowed down to a dance of light in the timeless acceleration
of his reflex programming. The fraal was faster than any man
Sokolov had ever fought, leaping into the attack with a feral
glee that almost overwhelmed Sokolov's combination of
instinct and mechanical response.

Shanassin slashed at his face. Sokolov deflected the blow
and hammered a low thrust at the fraal's midsection, but
Shanassin danced away and returned a slash that Sokolov parried with a hard block of his left hand. He wheeled and kicked;
Shanassin leaped over him, using the microgravity to get above
Sokolov and hacking furiously as he passed. The bounty hunter
threw himself flat, the rasping of his own breath heavy in his
ears.

Shanassin bled freely from a deep cut high on his arm, and
puffs of air streamed from cuts on his left leg and torso. The
fraal howled in rage and leapt at Sokolov. The bounty hunter
gave unexpectedly, rolling back to kick Shanassin hard and send
him spinning toward Geille. The fraal's knife drifted away from
his hand.

Poised for a strike, Monashi hammered the ball of her heavy
boot into Shanassin's sternum, crushing him against one of the
alien ship's black fins. Deftly she plucked the spinning knife
from the air as it drifted past her, then she drove it through

Shanassin's collarbone, pinning the fraal to the needle ship's sharklike fin.

Shanassin screamed and arched his back, trying to wrench himself away from the impaling knife. Air streamed from the puncture in his suit, high on the left side of his chest.

"I had no quarrel with you!" he gasped.

"You had a quarrel with Sokolov," she retorted. "That's good enough for me."

Clamping one hand over the cut across her arm, she reached down and yanked the fraal's mass pistol from his suit belt. She staggered back toward the bounty hunter, leaving Shanassin writhing on the alien hull.

Sokolov caught her and turned her to face him. The end of the passageway was approaching fast; the distant stars glimmered just past the black edge of the hull.

"Hold on to me tight!" he rasped at her. "It's now or never!"

Geille wrapped her arms around Sokolov's torso, then with all the strength he could muster, he leaped away from the needle ship's hull.

Shanassin's scream faded into the night as the alien vessel emerged into space.

Chapter Twenty

TWO NEEDLE SHAPES drove hard at the *Adroit*, maneuvering with silent power. Captain Mills studied the tactical display; the *Sirocco* was ignoring him, turning away from its fight against HelixTech in order to fend off the assault of two more of the lethal black arrows.

"Captain, the alien ships are closing fast!" called the tac officer. "Should I pursue the *Sirocco* or turn to meet them? Should we withdraw?"

The officer looked up at the captain, an unspoken question in his eyes: should we abandon Borun and the rest of the recovery team currently trapped onboard the alien vessel?

Mills looked at the display again. Seven of the needle ships had emerged from the derelict. Whatever had happened onboard the ancient vessel, it had been drastic and significant. Karcen Borun and the others might still be alive, but in order to get to them, he'd have to fight his way past the alien warships. Somehow Mills didn't believe he was likely to succeed in any such attempt. Leaving crewmen behind made him ache with guilt; leaving Karcen Borun wherever he was didn't bother him much at all.

"Withdraw," he ordered. "Helm, turn us to a heading clear of any vessels and get us the hell out of here. Engineering, I want every ounce of acceleration we've got left."

Banking hard, the *Adroit* turned away from the fight and climbed toward the distant stars. Two slender needles climbed after her, driving faster, slowly overtaking their quarry. Mills studied the sensor readouts for several more minutes as the derelict receded in the distance behind them and their pursuers inched closer and closer despite the corvette's speed.

"Captain! The alien ships are firing on us!" the tac officer reported.

Something hammered the *Adroit*'s hull like a sledgehammer, slewing the ship off course and setting off dozens of alarms and monitors. Mills steadied himself on a stanchion and closed his eyes in despair.

"They're not going to let us get away," he muttered. "Mr. Singh! Get ready to turn and fight. All other stations, begin emergency destruction of all sensitive materials and equipment. If they take us, they're not going to find anything but wrecked computers and useless files."

* * * * *

Twelve thousand kilometers away, the *Sirocco* fought for her life. With all of her cannon blazing furiously at her unknown assailants, the gunboat shuddered and rocked under the assault of massive energy torpedoes and scalpel-like beams. Huge wounds had been gouged out of the *Sirocco*'s flanks by the torpedoes and beams of the alien ships, marks of death narrowly avoided by the gunboat's skill and agility. Half of her guns were silent, wrecked by enemy fire or deprived of power by damage to the ship's engineering systems.

"Damage control! I need power restored to the after mount immediately!" ibn Beighur shouted above the din on his bridge. "Helm! Roll us left, quickly! We're losing the deflection inducers on the starboard side! Fire control, concentrate your fire on the lead enemy ship. We need to even the odds!"

"Incoming torpedoes, Captain!" Moreno called. "Stacking the inducers to compensate!"

"Careful!" the captain snapped. "Don't overload the damaged sectors!"

He fixed his eyes on the video displays, watching three coruscating green missiles streaking toward his ship. So far they hadn't identified any of the alien weapons for certain. The torpedoes appeared to be some kind of unguided plasma device, but that was only a guess. The evasive maneuver and Moreno's desperate defense caused two of the missiles to miss wide, streaking off to burst in the cold vacuum behind them, but the third slammed into the rear quarter of the gunboat. The explosive vaporization of a piece of the *Sirocco*'s hull kicked the ship sideways and up, sending half the bridge crew to the deck with the force of the blow and ripping heavy consoles loose from their mountings.

A vidscreen crashed to the deck in a shower of sparks, nearly crushing a sensor operator. Ibn Beighur picked himself up off the deck with a savage curse in his native tongue.

"Weapons, I want that ship dead!"

Lights flickered and deck plates thrummed as the gunboat fired her remaining mass cannons in a single devastating salvo. Four thousand kilometers away, the nose of the first vessel crumpled like a piece of foil smashed by a ball peen hammer. A moment later, a secondary explosion blasted the front half of the ship to molten wreckage in a spectacular bloom of light. The needle ship tumbled out of control, metal fires flaring from some source of oxidation in the wrecked ship's hull. Forgetting his normal reserve, ibn Beighur whooped in triumph.

"Good shooting, Weps! Shift your fire to the next one. We'll teach them to respect our guns!"

One of the sinister ships still pursued the wounded *Sirocco*, but at a more circumspect distance, jinking and dodging to spoil the gunboat's aim. Ibn Beighur used the respite to survey the damage boards and blinked in disbelief. Between the Lucullans' ambush and the fierce fighting against the alien ships, the *Sirocco* had sustained the beating of her career. It would take months of repair work to put her back in working order . . . *if* they got the opportunity to repair her. He looked over at the tactical officer.

"What's going on with the Lucullans?" he asked.

"The *Adroit* is running for her life, but she has two of them on her tail. I don't think she's going to get away," Moreno replied. "The *Fair Chance* ceased fire a few minutes ago. One of the enemy vessels is alongside her. They might be boarding the Syndicate ship."

"Damn. We ought to go back to destroy the *Fair Chance*. I don't like the idea of allowing a human ship to be captured intact by whomever it is we're fighting. There's just too much they can learn from that."

"I'd advise against it, Captain. We'll be taking on at least four of the alien ships, and if the two following the *Adroit* double back, we could be facing six of them. I don't think we could fight our way out of that, not on the best day of our lives."

Ibn Beighur dismissed the advice. "So noted. What about Shanassin?"

"No sign of the *Blackguard*, sir. The last I saw, he was heading toward the large vessel, before the attack craft appeared." Moreno looked up from his display. "What are your orders, Captain? Do we go back in?"

Ramil ibn Beighur rarely ran from a fight. If he saw any chance to carry the day, he was willing to gamble, but not against these odds, he decided.

"We're going to withdraw," he said slowly. "First contact protocols demand that we report the encounter regardless of the circumstances. It's clear that we've met a well-organized, technologically advanced, and warlike species. We need to make sure that humankind doesn't have to wait months or years to find out that they're out here." He looked over at the engineering officer. "Chief, how long until the tachyon accumulators are charged?"

"Estimated time of recharge is thirty-seven hours, Captain," the officer replied.

"A day and a half until we can make starfall and get out of here," ibn Beighur said softly. "Helm, turn us away from the derelict and the enemy contacts, maximum acceleration. We need to make sure that they can't catch us before we enter drive-space."

Pulling away from the scene of the battle, the gunboat streamed molten metal and leaking gases like a comet's tail. Despite her damage, she accelerated steadily to get away from the scene, firing a few parting salvos to discourage the needle ships from pursuit.

Captain Ramil ibn Beighur later counted it as one of the luckiest days of his life.

* * * * *

Clinging to the derelict's vast hull, Sokolov and Monashi watched the distant space battle in awed silence. Bursts of light and dim streaks of energy marked the spot of the fiercest fighting, now thousands of kilometers from the derelict. At that distance, they could see nothing of the ships involved, but they could see the spectacular explosions and glowing vapors left behind when one of them died.

"Try it again," Geille said quietly.

"It's no use. They're not responding to our distress calls." Sokolov shook his head. "They're too busy getting their asses kicked by the dragons. No one's coming back here to pick us up."

"Try it one more time anyway," Geille insisted. "I'll see what I can do about your suit."

Working awkwardly in her heavy gloves, she applied a small patch to the last of the slashes and punctures across Sokolov's environment suit. He's already done the same for her, stapling the gash on her arm closed with a suit repair kit.

He shrugged with a fierce scowl. "Sure. We have nothing else to do." He keyed the suit's long-range transmitter and looked up at the distant lights and glimmering shapes, visible now only at the visor's highest magnification. "Mayday, mayday! We're trapped on the hull of the alien derelict. Request retrieval by any human vessel in the vicinity. Come on, you lazy bastards, we need help! Mayday, mayday!"

Static roared and crackled in his ears, the electronic debris of sensors, jamming devices, and electromagnetic weapons. A suit radio was nothing but a candle flickering beside a bonfire in comparison. Sokolov growled in disgust and triggered the distress code transponder, hoping that the automated signal might attract attention where the voice comms failed.

A few dozen kilometers away, the last needle ship soared majestically away from the alien derelict, climbing slowly toward the battle overhead. Sokolov watched it maneuvering toward the fray. Out in the open, it was easier to put the vessel in perspective. It was about the size of the *Adroit*, the size of a small human destroyer or escort ship.

He wondered whether the dragons would get around to removing Shanassin from their hull, or if the fraal would be left there as some kind of macabre ornament, a trophy of their victory. For that matter, what happens to us when the dragons come back and find us? he wondered.

Geille fumbled with the repair kit, a small set of emergency patches included with all spacesuits. She shook her head in disbelief.

"How are you still alive? Shanassin cut your suit to ribbons, Pete."

"Suits are tougher than you think," he answered absently. "Self-sealing liners cover most punctures pretty quick." He glanced down at the time display on the suit's control unit. "Of course, you still need air and power. We can enjoy the view for about another forty-five minutes, and then we're out of oxygen."

"So what do we do? Do we try to work our way back inside the hull? At least there's air inside, and we might be able to get to HelixTech's heated shelter."

"I guess it's the next step," he said. "Let's start—"

His suit radio crackled with a faint, static-warped signal. ". . . humans in distress on the alien ship, this is . . . .vessel *Sirocco* . . . Beighur speaking. We can't recover you . . . enemy vessels in between. We'd never get there. Over."

"*Sirocco*, this is Sokolov. Come on, send us an automated launch or something! Give us a chance to get the hell off this ship, or tell one of the other ships out there to come back for us!"

" . . . problems of their own, Sokolov . . . not getting away, either. I suggest you . . . aliens for help, but they're not real friendly. Over."

"Beighur, don't leave us here!" Geille called angrily.

" . . . nassin's ship might be near your position. He might take you aboard. Good luck." Static broke up the transmission, silencing the distant voice.

A bright burst of light flared in the distance. Sokolov closed his eyes and pounded his fist against the hull. "It's all my fault," he said. "The Solars were out here, the Syndicate was out here, and I led the dragons right to them! Hell, I made you fire up the gate device for them. They ought to give me a medal."

"How could you have known?" Geille replied. "Borun was going to hand you over to Shanassin. Everything you did, you did in response to his treachery." She reached up to touch his helmet with her hand and offered a wry smile. "Besides, it seemed like a good idea at the time. I don't see Shanassin or Borun standing here."

"Shanassin . . ." Sokolov climbed to his feet and wheeled, searching the hull of the derelict. "That's it, Geille! Shanassin's ship must be here somewhere. He boarded the derelict. The *Blackguard* will wait for him to come back as long as they can. We might have a chance after all."

She drew in her breath. "They'll never let you onboard."

"I wasn't planning on asking," he replied. "Any idea of where he might have left his ship?"

Geille studied the jagged spires and gaping rifts of the derelict. "We're pretty close to the center of the ship. The *Adroit* was docked over that way. Would Shanassin use the same air lock after chasing the *Adroit* away?"

"There's a good chance of it. He wouldn't have known how to get inside, so why would he waste time looking for his own entrance?" Sokolov followed Geille's gesture. It seemed as good a guess as any. "Let's go."

Steadying her with his hand, they set off across the alien landscape of the derelict's hull. Now that the gate chamber had shut down, the ship seemed powerless again. No artificial gravity held them to the hull, only the faintest attraction of the massive ship itself. Black spires towered over them; buttresses and minarets soared crazily a hundred meters or more from the main hull, a cathedral of darkness beneath the distant stars. They had to leap two canyonlike openings that crisscrossed the hull, drifting dozens of meters across yawning chasms.

They drifted up along a great black ridge running along the derelict's length, rounding the top like rock climbers topping a cliff. There on the hull, a sleek vessel crouched over the derelict's air lock, surrounded by glaring floodlights.

"What do you know?" Sokolov breathed. "There she is."

He crouched low and scuttled forward, using the contorted surface of the hull for cover until he reached a low dome about fifty meters short of the corsair vessel.

"Are you still armed?" he asked Monashi.

"I lost my laser back in the zero-point chamber, but I have Shanassin's pistol. What about you?"

"I lost my gun back there, too," he said. "How many of Shanassin's men did you see?"

"Maybe half a dozen," she answered. "It was hard to tell, with everything going on."

"I'm guessing that the *Blackguard* would have a crew of ten or twelve. We'd better figure on at least four to six people onboard the ship." He paused to consider, studying the ship in front of them. His arm and belly throbbed in pain from the slashes Shanassin had given him. Nancy advised him of damage to his cybernetic arm from the deep puncture. Sweat trickled down his face, stinging his eyes. "How are we going to do this?"

"We'd better not waste time," Geille said. "Sooner or later the dragons are going to come back and clean up anything left onboard this ship. I don't want to be here then."

"Good point. We don't have time for subtlety."

Sokolov clambered over the hull structure and dashed toward the *Blackguard*, bounding and clattering across the derelict's surface. Geille sprinted a few steps behind him, flailing clumsily to keep her balance. They reached the ship unchallenged, but that didn't surprise Sokolov—anyone left on watch would probably be keeping an eye on the space battle, not the hull around the ship. They crossed into the shadows under the corsair's hull. The *Blackguard*'s belly hatch rested about two meters from the derelict's air lock. Sokolov looked around and found a vid lens trained on the area in front of the ship's air lock. He covered it with an adhesive patch from the suit repair kit. With a cautioning glance at Geille, he pressed the cycle button.

Nothing happened. A moment later their suit radios crackled. "Who is out there?" hissed a nonhuman voice. "Identify yourselves at once!"

I know that voice, Sokolov realized. He keyed his mike. "Yeiwei, Shanassin has been hurt! He needs medical attention right now!"

"What did you say? Shanassin is injured?" The sesheyan paused.

He's looking for the video of the hatch, Sokolov guessed. That will make him suspicious. "Hurry up," he growled over the radio. "He's bleeding badly!"

"Don't overdo it," Geille whispered. "He might view this as an opportunity to replace Shanassin."

Sokolov nodded. He held his tongue, waiting.

After a long moment, the corsair lieutenant came back over the radio. "Enter," he said. The air lock door rotated open. Sokolov and Monashi climbed inside; the outer door slid shut behind him. The chamber began to fill with air. "Hand me the gun," he muttered to her.

Geille passed the pistol to him. *Stack Speed Five and Dead-eye, Nancy*, he told the nanocomputer. "I think Yeiwei's going to meet us at the lock, probably with a couple of men. We're going to have to move fast," he said quietly. "Stay out of the line of sight from the porthole. Sooner or later they'll open up." He pushed back against one wall, moving away from the tiny view-port set in the interior door of the air lock.

"Wait," Geille said. "I have a better idea. Find something to hold on to."

She knelt in front of the lock's control panel. Working quickly, she stripped the cover off the panel and reached in to rip out a handful of leads. With a shower of sparks, she short-circuited the door controls and opened both the interior and the exterior doors of the lock at the same time.

A blast of air screamed through the air lock chamber, sucked out into the vacuum of interstellar space. A surprised corsair flew past, kicking and screaming, carried by the force of the ship's decompression, followed by a second man, who managed to catch hold of the hatchway. Anchored against the blast, Sokolov punched the man hard in the gut; he crumpled and was whisked away, joining his comrade on the desolate surface of the alien ship.

Sokolov peered around the corner, struggling to maintain his hold. In the center of the passageway, Yeiwei Three-knives clung with hands and feet to a hatchway three meters down. Screaming wordlessly in the rush of air, the sesheyan struggled to raise a flechette gun at Sokolov . . . and then his grip failed. In a rush of wings and limbs, the corsair tumbled out into the vacuum.

"Not *agaaain!*" he wailed.

Geille crossed another pair of wire leads and rotated the outer air lock door shut. The screaming blast of wind and debris came to a stop. Then she jammed a small tool from the suit's belt into the control mechanism.

"There. No one will open the outer door with that in place."

"When did you learn that much about entry systems?" he asked her.

"When you grow up on the streets of Santiago, you learn all kinds of things," she said. "Come on. Let's secure the ship."

They darted down the passageway and turned right at the first intersection, just in time to encounter two more corsairs stumbling back toward the air lock, emergency masks on their faces. Sokolov bludgeoned one to the ground with the heavy barrel of the pistol. Geille seized the other and slammed her elbow into the woman's face, knocking her senseless. She secured the two with a roll of tape from her suit's tool belt while Sokolov covered the passageway. When she finished, he passed her the gun and knelt beside the first one, knotting his hand in the crewman's collar.

"How many people are onboard?" he asked.

"Go to hell," the pirate mumbled. Blood trickled down the side of his face.

Sokolov rolled his eyes. He reached up and took the gun out of Geille's hand, menacing both corsairs at the same time. "Fine. Let's try this again. The first one to tell me what I want to know doesn't get his or her head blown off. *Comprende?*"

The woman looked over at the other corsair and then back to Sokolov. "Six."

"I saw Yeiwei and two gunmen at the air lock. You two are right in front of me. Where's the last one?"

"Engineering watch," the woman said. "All the others are with Shanassin."

"Not anymore they're not," Sokolov remarked. He looked at the first corsair, who flinched away, and offered a vicious smile. "It's good to work with people you can trust, isn't it?"

He gagged both corsairs with duct tape and left them lying in the passage, tied back to back. Geille armed herself with the woman's zero-g pistol; Sokolov tucked the man's weapon into his belt.

"Geille, go find the computer room and start killing Shanassin's lockouts or security programs. I'll take care of the one in engineering."

She nodded once and moved forward, gun at the ready. "Got it. Be careful. She might have lied to us."

Sokolov looked down at the two prisoners. "For your sake, I hope you didn't," he said casually. "Right now, you've got a ride out of here, but if you forgot to tell us anything, you'll be out the door without a suit."

They simply glared at him over their gags. Sokolov turned aft and hurried back along the *Blackguard*'s spine passageway until he reached a heavy blast door at the back of the ship. Whoever's in there knows I'm coming. Yeiwei would have told everyone to expect trouble, and the pressure drop inside the ship probably triggered every alarm they've got. He slapped the door's switch plate and stepped to one side of the passageway, waiting while the heavy piece of steel rumbled aside. *Get ready, Nancy,* he thought.

The door hissed open, and there was a blast of air as the engineering compartment vented to the half-depressurized passageway. Dark machinery and a tangle of pipes and conduits filled the room beyond. Sokolov glimpsed a figure behind a heavy console just before a burst of gunfire sent him diving to the deck for cover. Flechette needles hummed and sparked in the doorway over his head.

"You'll never take me alive!" the man inside yelled.

"Stupid bastard," Sokolov muttered. "I don't have time for this."

Lying on his belly, he couldn't hit the man behind the console.

If he tried to move, the corsair would cut him down. He peered through the open doorway to study the layout of the compartment. A second burst of flechettes drove him back to cover. One needle tugged on the side of his helmet, missing a dead-center shot through his faceplate by no more than ten centimeters.

Sokolov yelped a curse in Narislavic and yanked his head back, but he'd seen what he needed to see. A heavy ventilation unit was suspended over the control console the pirate was using for cover. *Deadeye, Nancy,* he thought at the nanocomputer.

His arm steadied by the cybernetic device, Sokolov rolled into the doorway, squinted, and aimed Shanassin's mass pistol at the bulky housing. He squeezed the trigger; the weapon hummed and hurled its deadly point mass at the vent unit. With the force of a pile driver, it hammered into the housing and blasted it from its mount. Metal creaked and groaned. Then the unit swung down from its ceiling mount, smashing into the console underneath it.

Sokolov scrambled to his feet and bolted across the compartment. He hurled the console aside, only to find the corsair behind it pinned, unmoving, under the ventilation unit. He pushed the fan off the pirate and secured him, even though he wasn't sure if the corsair was breathing or not.

"Serves you right," he muttered at the unconscious man. He keyed his radio. "Geille? How are you doing?"

"I have the computer off line, Sokolov, but you should be able to fly the ship manually." She hesitated a second, then added, "You'd better get up here quick. Two of those needle ships are coming back this way now."

"We need more time," Sokolov growled. He climbed back out of the engineering room and sprinted forward toward the two corsairs bound in the passageway. He took one quick glance at them; they still seemed secure. "Stay put," he told them. "You're coming with us whether you like it or not."

The two corsairs watched him silently, struggling against their bonds. He left them behind and scrambled up onto the *Blackguard*'s command deck, where Geille worked furiously at the computer station. She looked over her shoulder at him.

"I'm trying to bring up weapons and defenses, but I don't have anything yet. All I have is the induction engines."

"That's good enough," he replied.

He hurled himself into the pilot's chair and quickly sized up the ship's controls. He punched switch after switch, cutting unnecessary systems and activating the ship's engines.

A shadow fell over the nose of the ship. Sokolov looked up. One of the dragon ships was moving over them, cutting off their retreat.

"Oh, no, you don't," he rasped. "Hang on, Geille!"

He rammed the throttle as far forward as it would go and wrenched the control yoke hard left, slewing out from under the ship. *Blackguard*'s port side dipped low enough to smash structures on the hull of the derelict and send a shower of sparks cascading across its black hull. Sokolov slammed the ship back the other way to avoid a towering spire, driving underneath a soaring buttress as he flew across the surface of the derelict.

"They're coming after us!" Geille cried, watching the sensor displays.

Sokolov ignored her. *Dogfight, Nancy. Execute!*

In his head, vectors and windows opened, an intuitive display that evaluated the information at hand and began to plot his course to escape. The green flight path in front of him narrowed second by second as the needle ship followed his reckless maneuvers, then disappeared entirely as a second vessel cut in front of him, trying to head him off.

"Come on, Shanassin," he muttered. "Tell me that this ship can fly."

Incoming fire, Nancy advised him. *Evade right!*

Sokolov wrenched the control yoke right and then plunged it downward, darting past the hull of the derelict and out into open space. He twisted away from a green flash of plasma, and then a gap between two of the dark ships began to open. He rushed it like a drowning man floundering for a boat.

"Where are they?" he asked Monashi. "Where are the dragons?"

"Behind us," she answered. "Two by the *Adroit*, another by a ship I don't recognize. Looks like two more are near another human ship, but one of them isn't maneuvering at all."

"Good," he replied. "Time to see how much power Shanassin's ship really has." He turned the Blackguard's nose to the distant stars and locked down the throttles at maximum acceleration. "God help us if it isn't enough."

* * * * *

Clanking along the passageway one awkward step at a time in the negligible gravity of the powerless derelict, Karcen Borun led the half-dozen employees in his charge back toward the base camp by the air lock. With the departure of the last of the needle ships, the derelict had killed its power plant again. The massive channel in the heart of the ship had closed, returning the zero-point chamber to its spherical form. All across the ship, the lights failed and the black partitions vanished, leaving its vast corridors empty and open again.

Behind him, the HelixTech contingent muttered darkly among themselves. Cartena, the second officer of the *Adroit*, brought up the rear, keeping a wary eye over her shoulder for anyone approaching from behind. Shanassin had abandoned half his crew in his foolhardy leap of faith. The corsairs were still trying to decide what to do when Borun pulled his team out.

Temporary setback, he told himself. Okay, so the scenario's getting tricky. I can figure out what to do next. That's why I make the big bucks.

Did Monashi set this whole thing up? The derelict, Shanassin, Sokolov, the whole thing? Could she have done that?

He told himself that was a crazy idea, but in the vast stillness of the derelict's passageways, he wasn't so sure. The place felt like a tomb, his tomb.

"Mr. Borun, what's our plan of action?" It was Cartena, contacting him on the private command channel. "Are we heading back to the base camp? Do you have contact with the *Adroit?*"

He didn't bother to turn to face her. "We'll regroup at the base camp," he said. "The *Adroit*'s having some difficulties, so it might take a while to arrange a pickup."

Borun's suit was the only one equipped with a mass transceiver, a gravity radio that could penetrate the derelict's hull. Right now he didn't feel like telling Cartena or anyone else that the *Adroit* had gone off line almost thirty minutes ago. The mass transceiver had a range of dozens of light-hours; Borun wasn't a spacer, but he knew enough to guess that the HelixTech ship hadn't suddenly removed itself beyond the range of his comm gear. Mills wasn't answering his calls because he wasn't there anymore. *Adroit* wasn't coming back.

Okay, the Syndicate's out there and the Solars, too. Shanassin's ship is back this way. I can cut a deal with him. Karcen Borun allowed himself a smile inside his tailored suit. The situation was still recoverable. Buoyed by his bravado, the exec turned a corner and found himself staring up at a monstrous creature.

It towered over him, easily two and half meters in height, a powerful being of serpentine muscle and short, powerful limbs. Its dark coils gleamed behind its body, ending in a long whiplike tail that danced and curled behind its wide, needle-fanged snout. Its limbs were bare to the intense cold, but a weblike harness crossed its upper torso, supporting a breastplate of metal bands and flexible mail.

He could feel the heat of the creature through his suit. It steamed in the bitterly cold air, wisps of breath curling away from its maw like smoke. It cocked its head to one side, fixing a single golden eye on him to study him. In one taloned claw, it held something that was clearly a weapon, a heavy short-barreled device that looked as big as a cannon. Two more of the creatures weaved languorously in the passageway behind the first.

"God in heaven," Karcen Borun said numbly. "There really are dragons."

Epilogue

DRIVESPACE again.

Black and empty, the featureless waste pressed in on the viewports of *Blackguard*'s bridge like a thick sea fog. Sokolov brooded absently, staring at the blankness as he nursed a cup of strong black coffee. He felt as if he ought to be doing something, anything, but he could hardly bring himself to blink his eyes. His capacity for physical action had been exhausted. If he never came out of drivespace, he didn't think he would care.

"Mind if I join you?"

He turned at the interruption. Geille stood in the hatchway, dressed in a tight-fitting body suit and a bulky flight jacket. One or two of the women in Shanassin's crew had been close to her size, and she'd rooted through footlockers until she found something appropriate. She'd spaced her HelixTech clothing, as if throwing it away couldn't distance her enough from Karcen Borun.

Geille had also cropped her hair short, another severance from her past. It made her look tougher, more confrontational. She moved up behind him and set her hands on his shoulders.

"Just checked on our stowaways. They're tired of watching Jack Everstar holos, and they're starting to get real worried about what happens next."

He shrugged. "Beats me. As long as they don't try anything stupid, I'll let them go at the first place I can."

"That's an answer," she pointed out. She waited in silence for a long time, staring out into the darkness with him, and then moved around to slump into the seat opposite him. Her quiet gaze pulled his attention from the viewports. "You know, I'm wondering what happens next, too," she said. "Where do you go from here, Sokolov?"

"Not Lucullus," he said. "I think I've worn out my welcome in that system, and *Blackguard*'s too well known there."

"You're keeping the ship?"

"Shanassin doesn't need it anymore, and I can't see how I'd ever get Peri out of HelixTech in one piece." He laughed sourly. "Borun only paid me half of what he promised me for tracing you. He confiscated my ship, and I had the find of a lifetime in my hands and blew it. You're damned right I'm keeping the ship."

"Oh."

He shook his head and stared into his coffee. In a carefully neutral voice, he asked, "What about you, Geille? What are you going to do next?"

"I guess that depends on you." She shifted in her seat, keeping her eyes on him. "Are you ready for a partner?"

He looked up sharply. Geille flashed a spartan smile. "I think we'd make a hell of a team, Sokolov. I don't have anything else to do. My research data is just as lost as your ship. I don't know anyone outside of HelixTech or Santiago, and I'm not going back there. Not ever."

"Geille, how could you—"

"Trust you? Stay with you? I have some conditions, Pete. I think you need a new line of work, for one thing. I don't care what we do with this ship as long as we're not working for people like Karcen Borun. We could take survey contracts, hire out as couriers, run cargo and passengers. I don't care as long as it's legal and moral.

"And as far as you and me being together—" she hesitated and frowned—"well, I want a fresh start, a clean slate, nothing carried over from what we just went through. That's the only way it could work. Do you understand?"

He stared at her for a long moment. "Yeah, I understand."

She nodded and stood up, tugging at her jacket. "Okay. Think it over, then." With an awkward smile, she wrapped her arms around her and moved back toward the hatch.

He watched her for about ten heartbeats before he managed to stand and find his voice. "Geille, wait!"

She turned back toward him, leaning against the hatch. "What?"

Sokolov stood and rubbed at his jaw, shifting his weight nervously. "I'm done thinking."

Geille blushed and looked down at the deck before raising her eyes to his with a surprisingly shy smile. "Good," she said.

On the Verge
Roland J. Green

Danger and intrigue explode in the Verge as Arist, a frozen world on the borders of known space, erupts into a war between weren and human colonists. When Concord Marines charge in to prevent the conflict from escalating off-world, but they soon discover that even darker forces are at work on Arist.

Starfall
Edited by Martin H. Greenberg

Contributors include Diane Duane, Kristine Kathryn Rusch, Robert Silverberg and Karen Haber, Dean Wesley Smith, and Michael A. Stackpole. A collection of short stories detailing the adventure, the mystery, and the unending wonder in the Verge!

Zero Point
Richard Baker

Peter Sokolov, a bounty hunter and cybernetic killer for hire, is caught up in a deadly struggle for power and supremacy in the black abyss between the stars.

First in the past.
First in the future.

STAR✶DRIVE.

Diane Duane's Harbinger Trilogy

"Duane is tops in the high adventure business..."
—Publishers Weekly

STARRISE AT CORRIVALE
VOLUME ONE

Gabriel Connor is up against it. Expelled from the Concord Marines and exiled in disgrace, the Concord offers him one last chance to redeem himself. All it involves is gambling his life in a vicious game of death.

STORM AT ELDALA
VOLUME TWO

Gabriel and Enda stumble onto dark forces that may destroy a newfound civilization before moving into the worlds of the Verge. Only their deaths seem likely to avert the disaster about to flood into civilized space—until an astonishing revelation from out of the depths of time makes the prospect of survival even more terrible than a clean death.

NIGHTFALL AT ALGEMRON
VOLUME THREE

The stunning conclusion to the Harbinger Trilogy brings Gabriel and Enda to a war-ravaged world whose only hope for salvation may be a discovery out of the depths of time.

Available April 2000